K
Tl

KAVANAGH Q.C.
The Ties That Bind

Wendy Holden

CORONET BOOKS
Hodder and Stoughton

First published in Great Britain in 1998
by Hodder and Stoughton
A division of Hodder Headline PLC

10 9 8 7 6 5 4 3 2 1

British Library Cataloguing in Publication data

ISBN 0 340 70760 7

Typeset by Hewer Text Composition Services, Edinburgh
Printed and bound in Great Britain by
Mackays of Chatham PLC

Hodder and Stoughton
A division of Hodder Headline PLC
338 Euston Road
London NW1 3BH

PART ONE

Diplomatic Baggage

1

The Austrian ambassador rose to his feet, carefully placing his crumpled napkin on to the white damask tablecloth in front of him. Tall, silver-haired and impeccably dressed, Baron Gunter Schroder was the epitome of diplomacy and elegance; a leading figure in Anglo-Austrian relations over the previous two decades, fluent in six languages and an excellent host. He cleared his throat to speak while the polite chatter among his lunch-time guests gradually subsided.

'Ladies and gentlemen,' he began in his distinctive Tyrolean accent, as his audience set down their wine goblets and turned in their chairs to listen. 'It gives me great pleasure to introduce the man who is to be my opposite number in Vienna, returning to the city where his diplomatic career began.' He glanced from the assembled gathering of diplomats and dignitaries seated at the sumptuously laid table before him to the balding, slender man immediately to his right.

'I give you Her Majesty's Ambassador Designate to Austria, Sir Alan Jackson.' The ornate galleried dining hall in London's Austrian embassy, the illustrious venue of generations of balls and galas held in honour of kings and noblemen, echoed with the sound of applause.

Sir Alan was quickly on his feet, his double-breasted pin-stripe suit done up neatly across his crisp white shirt and red checked tie. He smiled winningly at those selected to attend the welcoming luncheon, celebrating the announcement of his new position, but reserved a special smile for the dark-haired young woman at his side.

'Your Excellency, ladies and gentlemen,' he began, his cut-glass accent knifing through the expectant hush as all eyes fell upon him. 'First let me apologise for my wife's absence today. Alas, she has fallen victim to Norwegian flu . . .' He paused for the predictable murmur of sympathy from around the table, before adding: '. . . demonstrating that after more than a thousand years the Vikings can still lay us low.'

The murmur quickly changed to laughter as the guests turned to each other and marvelled at the easy charm of the recently knighted diplomat. Most of them were well acquainted with Sir Alan's impeccable background, from his earliest days as an Oxford graduate at the Foreign Office, through to his first posting as the youngest vice-consul in Vienna nearly thirty years ago, and finally his brilliantly orchestrated marriage to Margaret Smith-Johnson, the only daughter of Lord Harnden, the man who was largely responsible for brokering the peace treaties with Germany and Austria after World War II. Now Sir Alan had been knighted in the New Year's Honours List and was to be Britain's new ambassador to Austria, a well-deserved post that would almost certainly last until his retirement in twelve years' time.

Sir Alan continued to address the assembled guests, many of whom were already known to him, with renewed confidence now that he had broken the ice. Well aware of the diplomatic *faux pas* of arriving at such an important luncheon without his wife, he added: 'However, I am

4

happy to say – indeed I am proud to say – that her place has been taken by my daughter Natasha.' He turned again to the stunning young woman next to him and flashed her a beam of such warm affection that she could only bask in it self-consciously while the lunch guests looked on with approval.

At St James' Court, Sir Alan's imposing Edwardian home in St John's Wood, west London, a young woman pulled insistently on the ornate wrought-iron gates that barred unwelcome visitors. She peered through them at the turreted red-brick mansion set in several acres of neatly trimmed gardens and smiled to herself. Checking the address on the brass nameplate with a piece of crumpled paper she held in her hand, the blond-haired visitor released her grip on the railings and looked around for another way in.

Lady Margaret Jackson, thin, pale of face and wrapped in a pale blue silk dressing gown, was not accustomed to intrusions into her private world. Peering out from under a mop of tousled grey hair, she watched, frowning, from the hallway window as the stranger found a way around the gates, through the straggly privet hedge that bordered the garden and up the drive. Barely glancing at the gleaming red Alfa Romeo Spider parked by the large urns that marked the start of the sweeping stone steps to the house, the plump young woman in a bright yellow patent-leather jacket did not falter as she made her way up them and round to the tradesman's entrance, before knocking forcefully on the glass-panelled kitchen door.

Lady Margaret hesitated for a moment, then drew her dressing gown more tightly across her chest and opened the door tentatively, a quizzical look across her heavily lined face. How irritating that it was the maid's day off. There would be no chance now to claim that she was socially indisposed.

'I'm sorry to disturb you, Lady Jackson,' the stranger said, half smiling. Lady Margaret tried to place her accent. 'Is your husband at home?' She looked past her as if she wouldn't believe her answer in any event, before pushing her way inside, uninvited.

Lady Jackson's face registered alarm and indignation as she followed the woman through the kitchen and into the grand entrance hall with its heavily carved wooden staircase. The visitor paced the Persian rugs with great deliberation, as if she were somehow taking stock. Lady Jackson watched her suspiciously. Apart from her rather tacky clothes, she wore cheap perfume that now pervaded the room. Overweight, square-jawed and quite unattractive, she exuded Teutonic arrogance.

'He's out. You'll have to phone the office on Monday,' Lady Jackson said through thin lips, as her unwanted guest stood admiring a huge bronze sculpture on a polished centre table. Her Ladyship greatly resented this intrusion into her home, especially from someone who evidently had no manners. It was surely obvious that she was unwell and was hardly dressed to entertain. The woman must have seen that, Lady Jackson brooded, and she let her feelings show.

But the stranger ignored her expression. 'No,' she said suddenly, turning to her with a smile, her large earrings dangling on her shoulders. 'I will talk to you instead.' She paused and her mouth twisted slightly at the corner. 'Not that you will like what I have to say.'

Lady Jackson stared at the unknown and unwelcome face before her and wondered what on earth she could mean.

*   *   *

It was two hours before Sir Alan's sleek black limousine deposited him and Natasha on the gravel drive leading to their home. Laughing, they emerged from the Rover Vitesse hand in hand and made their way up the steps and into the hall. They had each drunk a little too much wine at the reception and were feeling giggly. The flush on Natasha's cheeks – the combined product of the excitement of the day and the wine – made her even more attractive, her father thought.

'You all right, darling?' Sir Alan asked his daughter.

'Mmm.' She smiled and turned to face him, her glossy, dark brown hair bouncing on her shoulder as she did so. Her eyes were like deep pools of liquid chocolate.

'Actually I was rather jealous of them when they started chatting you up,' he said, still clasping her hand. Pulling her towards him, he leaned forward and tenderly kissed her cheek, narrowly missing her mouth. She looked up at him affectionately, her pupils even more luminous and dark.

'Coffee?' she asked quietly, squeezing his hand in hers.

'Mmm,' he responded, almost in a whisper.

Their reverie was broken by the sharp voice of Lady Jackson, sitting watching them in silence from a sofa in the drawing room, her pet boxer Trudy sitting panting at her feet.

'I've had a visitor,' Lady Jackson said frostily, her hand to her head. The pair jumped slightly and stared at her. They hadn't known she was there, let alone watching them.

'Oh?' Sir Alan asked, stepping away from his daughter self-consciously and thrusting his hands into his trouser pockets. 'Who was that?'

'Lise Auerbach,' Lady Jackson answered, getting to her feet. She carefully pronounced the first name 'Lisa' – her visitor had made that quite clear – and she repeated it now, allowing her words to find their mark, before adding simply: 'Austrian.' Shuffling towards her husband in her slippers, she stared deep into his eyes for several seconds, holding his unblinking gaze with a silent but telling look. The high cheekbones, that arrogant stance of his which had so attracted her all those years before and which had allowed her to forget that he was only marrying her for her money and status, were still there, only now they repulsed her. She brushed past him and climbed the stairs, the faithful Trudy – her only bed companion for many years – ever at her heels.

Natasha witnessed the exchange between her parents with curiosity. There was something even icier than usual in the atmosphere between them. With no explanation forthcoming from her father, who stood stock still in the middle of the room like a statue, she went into the kitchen to put the kettle on.

James Kavanagh pulled his diesel Citroën estate car into Nottinghill Street and negotiated his way between the skips, dustbins and parked cars that cluttered the roadside. Almost every front railing of the white Georgian townhouses that lined the street had a 'For Sale' sign tied to it, and rows of bicycles were chained to the peeling black rails. Leaning forward over the steering wheel, he looked in vain for a street sign.

'This'll do, Dad, drop us off here,' his teenage son Matt called from the back seat as he grabbed his rucksack and other belongings and made as if for the door handle.

'But Hatchley Street's round the back somewhere,' Kavanagh said, glancing at his wife Lizzie in the front seat. She had hardly said a word all morning and he thought she looked rather strained.

'I said I'd meet the other two here,' said Matt, indicating a spot where his father could pull over between rubbish bags.

Kavanagh did as he was told and stopped the car. Stepping out, he lifted the tailgate and helped his son with several more canvas bags and overfilled dustbin liners, all of which had been haphazardly thrown into the car by Matt an hour before. Lizzie got out and looked around, nervously fingering her wedding ring. She didn't dare open her mouth for fear of what she might say.

'So where are they, then?' Kavanagh asked his son, expecting to see a group of school chums waiting on the doorstep of one of the houses. Matt had certainly led his parents to believe that there would be some sort of reception committee for him at the new flat he was moving into, but there was no one about.

'Don't worry, they'll turn up. Thanks for the lift,' said Matt, a little too breezily, as he hoisted his backpack on to his shoulder and grabbed the remaining bags from his father. He started to wander off up the street as if this was nothing more unusual than being dropped off at the school gates on a normal day.

Lizzie grabbed her son's arm rather too hastily. She released her hold slightly and tried to look more nonchalant. 'But I was looking forward to meeting them,' she said. Her face and voice registered her disappointment.

Matt, thin, scruffy-haired and spotty in rugby shirt and jeans, grimaced. She could hardly believe that this tall young man before her was the baby boy she had held in her arms all those years ago; the same boy whom she had nursed through childhood illnesses and accidents, even the young teenager who had been so rebellious at home. 'You will, later,' Matt reassured her. Seeing the look in his mother's eyes he added, softly: 'I'll phone you. 'Bye.' Before she knew it he was gone, laden with bags of clothes and belongings. She watched him suspiciously as he disappeared around a corner.

9

'I smell a rat,' Lizzie said, crossing and uncrossing her cardigan across her chest, the way she always did when something was bothering her. Her face taut, she felt as if she could scream. How dare Matt just abandon her like that, walk out of her life in such a flippant way?' At least with her daughter Kate, there had been the tearful farewells at the university campus, the packing and the preparation months in advance, and the chance for a good weep in the car all the way home from Cambridge. 'Do you smell a rat?' she asked her husband, a catch in her voice.

'A small one, maybe,' said Kavanagh, his Lancashire accent making one of its periodic appearances in his speech. 'He was anxious to get rid of us, certainly.' While his wife stared after her son in disbelief, Kavanagh watched as two teenage girls carrying similar loads to Matt crossed the street behind them and walked their way. Both wore faded jeans and extremely tight T-shirts which left little or nothing to the imagination.

Lizzie was exasperated. 'James,' she said with some urgency. 'We haven't seen the flat, met the landlord, or the people he's sharing with.' She tried her hardest not to sound hysterical. Her husband was still watching the pretty young girls approaching.

'I think we're about to,' he told her, as he stepped up to greet them. 'Excuse me, are you looking for Matt Kavanagh?'

The girls giggled. 'Yeah,' said the one wearing a bright fluorescent T-shirt which read 'No Fear'. Kavanagh noticed that her tongue was pierced along with her nose and every surface of her earlobes.

'Who are you?' asked the other, her hair plaited into beaded braids, wearing little more than a bra top. She stood uncomfortably under Lizzie's sullen stare.

'We're his parents,' said Kavanagh with a placatory smile.

10

There was an awkward silence. If Kavanagh didn't know better, he'd have said the girls looked somehow guilty, but then that was probably just his suspicious legal mind. 'Tell him we met, would you?' he said finally, releasing them from their embarrassment.

The girls nodded in relief and bid the couple goodbye. They set off after Matt as Kavanagh and his wife watched in appreciation and amazement respectively. This was not what they had expected at all.

A few hours later, sitting out in the back garden of their white-painted Victorian home in Wimbledon, Kavanagh handed his wife a cut crystal tumbler full of Pimm's and tried to reassure her. 'It's hardly the end of the world,' he reminded her. 'He *is* eighteen.' No matter how many times he said that out loud, the fact still astonished him as much as it did his wife. He too found it hard to equate the young man they had just deposited at his new flat in London with the child he still visualised in his head when he thought of Matt. And, against all his expectations, he also felt none of the anticipated relief and joy at having finally got Lizzie and his home back to himself.

Lizzie sighed and stared dejectedly into her glass. 'Yes, but why wouldn't he let us see the place?' she whined. She felt as if she could burst into tears. As clinical as she was trying to be about the departure of her youngest bird from the nest, she couldn't help but feel premenstrual and emotional.

Kavanagh studied his wife of twenty-five years with the usual warm glow he felt whenever he saw her. Dressed in slacks and a T-shirt, she was still so very slim and beautiful with her finely sculpted features. She had hardly changed from the moment he had seen her across a crowded courtroom all those years ago. Then, as one of the clients

11

he was defending in an anti-abortion case, arrested for disturbing the peace after taking part in a violent rally in Hyde Park – two days after being similarly arrested for disorder at an anti-Vietnam War demonstration – her blazing eyes and fiery temperament had excited him like no other woman before or since. Getting her off quickly became more than a professional obsession.

The only daughter of Lord and Lady Probyn, Lizzie's anti-Establishment views had been so unexpected from one with such an aristocratic background, but her strong, left-wing ideals had never left her. Now a fund-raiser for a new hospital project, she had carved herself a brilliant career as a vociferous campaigner, and had simultaneously supported Kavanagh as he rose through the ranks from his earliest days as a radical solicitor to become one of the chosen few – a Queen's Counsel and one of the country's foremost criminal barristers.

They had certainly had their share of problems – he had very nearly lost her to one of his colleagues, Miles Petersham, two years earlier – but he knew the brief affair was largely caused by his long absences and his obsession with work. Once they'd both realised that, Lizzie had come home for good. As well as saving their marriage, she had successfully juggled bringing up their two children, Matt and Kate, with her busy career, and still seemed to have time for all his problems.

So they had ridden the storm, and had even survived her six months in Strasbourg as chief executive of a leading European aid programme – until she quit, that is, out of frustration at not getting the funding she needed, and at only seeing her husband at weekends. Now they were closer than ever, he realised as he too faced the truth that their children had finally left them alone. Those penetrating blue eyes and that beguiling mouth could still melt his heart, and there

12

was only a hint of grey in Lizzie's shoulder-length chestnut hair. He couldn't imagine life without her.

He knew that she had been under considerable strain recently, what with Kate taking her English Lit finals at university and now Matt leaving home, after eighteen months of being in trouble at school and too difficult by half at home. Then there had been problems at her new job for the hospital trust, sorting out its status under new laws, coupled with the unexpected departure of a key colleague. Catching her face now in the evening sun, he could see the stress lines etched across it for the first time. He proceeded as gently as he could.

Pulling a slice of cucumber from his glass, he shrugged his shoulders. 'I dunno why Matt didn't want us to see the place,' he replied. 'Rites of passage, maybe. Anyway, why should he tell us everything?' He could see from her expression that he wasn't winning, so he added: 'Either that or he thought I'd be envious.'

Lizzie looked askance at her husband in genuine surprise. 'What of?'

'Him sharing a flat with two beautiful women . . . But you're right, I couldn't stand it.' He feigned a deeply hurt look.

Lizzie's face broke into a grin at last and she leaned across and kissed Kavanagh's cheek. God, she loved him.

2

Natasha Jackson tiptoed down the stairs of her parents' house and into the dimly lit entrance hall. Wearing jeans, a T-shirt and a denim jacket, she stopped in the darkness outside the closed door to her father's study and listened to her parents arguing, as she had done for years.

'. . . for a bit of instant passion,' her mother was saying, her words thick with emotion. How many times had Natasha heard that slightly hysterical tone to her mother's voice? she wondered.

'Look, we'll talk about this later.' Her father sounded worn out. As usual, he was trying to avoid confrontation and all that went with it. The true diplomat.

But her mother wasn't going to let it go that easily. 'Just when things were going so well, the ghosts begin to walk,' she sobbed. The heavy panelled door was suddenly pulled open and Natasha found herself face to face with her parents. Lady Jackson, dishevelled in her dressing gown, was red-eyed and clutching a handkerchief. Her father, his jacket half across his shoulders, looked visibly upset.

'Where are *you* going?' Lady Jackson asked Natasha as her husband pulled on his jacket behind her. As usual, they both appeared to be abandoning her.

Natasha stared at her mother coldly. 'I need a change of scenery. I'm going to see some friends,' she said tersely. Softening as she turned to her father, she asked: 'Are you okay?'

He stepped forward to reassure her. 'We're fine,' he said, but the sadness in his eyes belied his response. Natasha stopped herself from kissing him and headed for the front door. Pushing past his wife, Sir Alan watched his daughter stride across the hall. 'Drive carefully,' he called after her, before walking away purposefully from his tearful wife.

Natasha found a parking space right outside the Verona Hotel just off London's Queensway and switched off the lights of her red Alfa Romeo. Stepping out, she glanced at a piece of paper in her hand and checked the name above the hotel doorway before walking in.

The small wooden reception desk appeared unmanned, but as Natasha approached, she could see the young porter reflected in a mirror suspended above him in a small back room. Feet up on a table, the brown-haired young man was transfixed by the picture on a television screen immediately in front of him. A football match was well under way and the noise from the crowd was drowned only by the porter's cries of 'Come on, get moving, get moving' as he swigged from a can of lager and urged the players on. Natasha's hand hovered momentarily over the little brass bell on the front desk as she thought of ringing for his attention, but she decided against it and slipped past reception and up the stairs to the first floor.

Through a fire door and into an upper lobby, she quickly scanned the corridor before her eyes settled on a door. Checking her piece of paper again before consigning it to her back pocket, she crossed the carpeted floor silently and knocked on the door of Room 6.

Downstairs the football match was coming to a climax. The commentator's voice was at fever pitch. 'And now it's Newcastle going forward. That's a lovely ball to Gillespie . . .' The porter was sitting upright in his chair, his thin face just a few inches from the screen, an anguished expression in his pale eyes, his beer can held midway between the table and his lips.

'Go on. That's it, my son. Tackle him!' he yelled, his lank hair flopping forward over his eyes. As he watched, open-mouthed, the goalkeeper made a stunning save only to see the ball headed back into the net by another player. The porter slammed his fist on the table in rage and screamed aloud, as if in physical pain. Hearing the commentator announce the half-time whistle, he turned the sound down in disgust, picked up his beer and walked away from the television, groaning. Flicking angrily through a newspaper on the reception desk, he had just started to read the small ads when he heard a sudden loud thud from above which made him look up.

Straining to listen, he thought the hotel sounded unusually quiet. Then he heard an upper fire door creak and the sound of someone running down the stairs. Stepping out from behind the desk, he stopped at the foot of the steps to see Natasha hurtling down towards him, panting, her face shiny with perspiration, glancing repeatedly back over her shoulder.

' 'Ere!' he shouted, and held up his arm instinctively to bar her way. He'd never seen her before but he thought she looked up to no good. And what had made that thud upstairs? He wanted a word with her and no mistake. 'What the . . .' he began to say, as she stalled on the bottom step and tried to sidestep him.

Looking down at her left sleeve, he saw that her jacket was heavily bloodstained, with fresh blood dripping down her hand. Their eyes met for a second, Natasha's on fire, and then she shoved him violently aside with her elbow, almost knocking him off his feet before running past him and out into the street.

Moaning and clutching his deadened arm, the porter called out after her and followed her outside. He watched from the doorway as she jumped into her sports car and sped off, cutting the corner of an adjacent street and almost colliding with a parked car. His lips mouthed the letters of the distinctive number plate before he turned and made his way upstairs.

Peering along the landing on the first floor, he worked out that Room 6 was the one directly above reception. The corridor was in semi-darkness and there wasn't a sound to be heard. With an uneasy feeling in the pit of his stomach, he wiped his sweaty palm on his jeans then knocked gently on the door before turning the handle and stepping inside. Switching on the light, he walked gingerly past the bathroom and into the bedroom. The sight that met him made him gasp aloud.

There, on the floor at the foot of the bed, lay a young woman – the person he knew only as Miss Auerbach, a foreigner who had checked in the day before. She was still wearing the leopard-print top and skirt he had seen her in earlier that day but her clothes were slightly ruffled as if she had been involved in some sort of struggle. Her long blond hair covered her face, but at the back of her head her hair was caked with blood. A heavily bloodstained lampshade and its gilt and onyx base lay on the floor next to her.

Leaning over her to check for signs of life, all the porter could see was blood and brain tissue seeping through fragments of shattered skull. Recoiling in horror, he fled backwards and out of the room to call the police. He had watched television often enough to know that the woman in Room 6 was well and truly dead.

Kavanagh had just rounded the corner into River Court, the cobbled courtyard leading to his comfortable chambers in Lincoln's Inn, when he bumped into Jeremy Aldermarten, an old adversary and recently appointed Queen's Counsel at his chambers. There had always been an element of half-hearted rivalry between them, and as they bade each other good morning Kavanagh thought he noticed an especially sardonic expression on Aldermarten's simpering face.

'I hear you've taken the Jackson brief,' he said, his head bobbing to one side, as it always did. Kavanagh wondered if he noticed a hint of envy in his colleague's voice.

'I have indeed,' he replied. 'It's right up your street, Jeremy. Wealth, privilege, influence.' Aldermarten was too preoccupied to notice the tongue in Kavanagh's cheek. They both nodded a greeting at two mounted policemen who passed by on their horses.

'There's certainly enough money there to bail the daughter,' Aldermarten commented knowingly. A roaring snob who liked to use his position to keep in with the great and the good, Aldermarten prided himself on his inside knowledge of those whose names fill *Who's Who*. Kavanagh sometimes wondered if he took the book to bed with him. Afflicted by an unfortunate manner, balding pate and chinless looks, his bedfellow was rarely a woman.

'Lady J's people own half of Devonshire, I'm told,' Aldermarten added, looking askance at his infamous colleague. With his distinctive collar-length white hair and down-to-earth manner, Kavanagh had a working-class Bolton background that was a million miles from his own private education at Eton, yet Aldermarten wished he could command an iota of the respect that Kavanagh did.

One of the most sought-after criminal barristers in Lincoln's Inn, despite being such a 'rough diamond', he had a formidable reputation as a defence counsel, and, irritatingly, a growing one as a prosecution brief as well. Tenacious in his cross-examination, direct in his questioning, unflinching in his principles, he had a knack of getting things out of people that they often didn't even know they had in them. Wryly, Aldermarten added: 'Lady J'll love the spit-and-sawdust approach.'

Kavanagh allowed his accent free rein. 'She can like it or lump it – it's Natasha I'm defending.' Not for the first time, he found Aldermarten's rather high-handed attitude tiresome. There had been many like him, those with the plummy accents and the right parentage whose legal careers were mapped out long before they were born, and who strongly disapproved of the likes of Kavanagh joining their hallowed chambers. He had crossed swords with them before, and not always won. They were the type of men his father, Alf – once a leading light in the Bolton trade union movement – would have called 'southern jessies' – the same men who secretly deplored the advent of women in the legal profession, but who were only too happy to flirt, fawn and maul the prettiest of the female juniors in their midst.

As the two men entered their offices at River Court Chambers in silent contemplation of each other, Charles Beaufort, Kavanagh's able young junior and very much a new man whose modern approach Kavanagh embraced, stepped out of a side office. Ignoring Aldermarten as he usually did, Beaufort addressed his senior counsel. 'The Jackson Three are here, James, with solicitor,' he said. 'I've put them in your room.'

Kavanagh liked Beaufort. Only thirty, a former navy man, he had come to the Bar when he realised that the path to promotion was fast receding under defence cuts. After a taste of command, he sometimes found it difficult to adjust to the chambers' pecking order and was consequently rather impetuous with a lot to learn; but his devilish good looks and natural charm counterbalanced Kavanagh's own social shortcomings, and he would make a bloody good Q.C. one day, he thought.

Aldermarten took his leave of them and headed for his own office just along the corridor. Jealous of Beaufort and his easy manner with women, envious of the younger man's professional relationship with Kavanagh, he wished for the umpteenth time in his life that someone would let him in on the secret of being naturally popular. Unable to resist a parting shot, however, he turned and called out: 'Any advice on protocol, James, don't hesitate.' Kavanagh scowled and turned back to talk to Beaufort.

The Jackson case should have been right up his street – it had all the elements of high drama in the courtroom that pumped the adrenalin around his veins and had become his life's blood ever since he had first been entranced by the profession during a visit to Manchester Crown Court on his sixteenth birthday. He was looking forward to seeing Natasha Jackson in person, to peering into her eyes, into her very soul, and to seeking the truth there. But there was already something niggling at the back of his mind about the case, something he couldn't put his finger on as he had read through the solicitor's notes and police interviews in bed the previous night, something that had prevented him from getting a good night's sleep.

Making for his office as they were discussing the case, he and Beaufort were ambushed by Helen Ames, the latest recruit to the chambers and the replacement for Julia Piper, the first woman junior ever taken on by the chambers, after Kavanagh's direct intervention. Julia had stayed for five years before leaving for Nairobi and marriage to the man she loved. When Helen Ames had first been suggested as her successor, Kavanagh had not been at all happy. They were old foes from court and he found her overbearing attitude difficult to stomach from one so junior. But she had already made her mark at River Court and his opinion of her was changing. It had taken Lizzie to point out that Helen was probably no less overbearing than he had been at her age.

'Can I borrow Charlie for a moment, James?' asked the new junior, smiling, her blond hair glinting in the light. Before he could reply, she had grabbed Beaufort's arm and was leading him away down the corridor. 'Spot of bother,' she told him, hands clasped to her chest. 'I said I'd give a talk on Tuesday lunch-time for my charity. Problem is, I'll be in Manchester and they'll be in a room over a pub in south London.' She looked pleadingly at the tall, handsome Beaufort.

Rubbing his chin and appearing to be thinking hard, Beaufort nodded sagely. 'Yes, I see your problem,' he said, arms folded across his chest.

Helen realised she was going to have to spell it out for him. 'I really don't want to let them down,' she added, pulling herself up to her full five feet six inches. 'So I thought you could stand in for me.' She flashed him what she hoped was her most winning smile. Kavanagh stood a few paces away and wondered how on earth Charlie was going to get out of that one; but he needn't have worried.

Beaufort looked a picture of disappointment as he said: 'Stand? Oh, 'fraid not. The old war wound.' He pointed to his leg and walked off, without a trace of a limp. Helen's shoulders, elegantly clad in an expensive black jacket, drooped. Kavanagh shook his head in admiration of Beaufort's audacity. Not only was he far too young to have served in any war, but he had never visibly suffered from anything in his life. Almost at his office door, he heard Helen's husky voice calling after him.

'James, I don't suppose you could . . .' But Kavanagh's salvation was at hand. Just as Helen reached him, Peter Foxcott, Q.C., the senior partner and Head of Chambers, passed them and nodded a cheery hello. He was wearing a particularly colourful bow tie, what was left of his greying hair was newly clipped around the edges of his head, and he appeared to be in the best of humour. Kavanagh interrupted Helen and lowered his voice.

'Why don't you try Peter?' he suggested, his grey eyebrows arched. 'I happen to know his case has just settled.' Helen's face lit up as Foxcott eyed the pair suspiciously from his door.

'Excellent,' she beamed, squeezing Kavanagh's arm, then quickly followed Foxcott into his office, calling out his name. Kavanagh grinned briefly and then steeled himself for the meeting ahead.

Turning the handle of his office door, he came face to face with the Jackson family – Natasha, slim, dark and elegant in a fashionably smart linen suit in duck-egg blue, the skirt just high enough above the knee to reveal a pair of shapely legs. Lady Jackson, gaunt and strained, wearing a pleated beige skirt and matching jacket, a cream and brown Hermès scarf thrown across a shoulder. Sir Alan, in a dark three-piece suit, reminded Kavanagh somehow of a fox. He had sharp features, a large nose, high cheekbones and deep-set eyes, and although he stood ramrod straight, hands clasped behind his back, there were telltale lines of tension across his forehead. Kavanagh acknowledged the family with a slight bow of his head.

'Ah, Kavanagh,' said Richard Dynevor, the Jacksons'

portly solicitor, before introducing his clients. Kavanagh knew Dynevor well and liked him enormously. Despite his rather rough-and-ready appearance, he had a quick wit and a good brain. Physically, he was unattractive – overweight, ungainly and with a pronounced squint – a complete contrast to Charles Beaufort, who stood dashing and needle-thin at Kavanagh's side, a bundle of files under his arm, his blue eyes locked on to the beautiful Natasha.

Kavanagh addressed Natasha's father directly. 'I always see my clients alone, Sir Alan.' He attempted a smile.

The ambassador designate bristled and stepped forward. He was not accustomed to being so summarily dismissed. He had long regarded his wife's presence at the meeting as an irrelevance, but could not countenance the idea of his beloved Natasha facing this surly barrister without him by her side. 'But surely it's possible for me to . . .' he began.

Natasha interrupted him and smiled. 'Daddy, please. I can handle it,' she said softly. Sir Alan and Lady Jackson studied her in silent thought.

Kavanagh interjected. 'There is also a legal reason. I may decide to call you or your wife as a witness. You'd agree to that, would you?' He watched a vein in Sir Alan's temple twitch.

Sir Alan glowered at his wife, who stood unmoved between her husband and her daughter. 'Of course,' he replied.

'In that case,' continued Kavanagh, 'I am not permitted to discuss your daughter's defence with you.' He uttered the statement in such a way that it simply did not require a response.

Sir Alan considered the leading counsel's words for a moment and then turned reluctantly to his daughter, placing a hand on each of her shoulders. He smiled encouragingly.

'Chin up, Tash.' She sighed as he added, quietly: 'Remember what we agreed?' Lady Jackson shot her daughter a look before her husband led her out the door, adding: 'We'll be just outside.'

Natasha turned to Kavanagh and sighed heavily once more. He looked at this striking young woman who was no older than his teenage son and wondered what was going on inside her head.

'What did you agree?' he asked her suspiciously, not making any moves to sit down or put his client at ease in his comfortable book-lined office.

'That if I tell the truth nothing awful will happen to me,' Natasha said, her large brown eyes looking up at the stuccoed ceiling as if reciting a prepared speech.

Kavanagh smiled. 'Good. Our judge is very impressed by people who tell the truth.' His mind conjured up the face of Judge Griffin, a severe-looking but scrupulously fair man.

'You mean there are those who aren't?' Natasha countered, her eyes flashing a warning. They were already getting the measure of each other.

Kavanagh moved round to the other side of his large walnut desk and delved into his briefcase for his spectacles. Beaufort gestured gallantly for Natasha to sit down and he and Dynevor sat on either side. The four of them settled into their seats and examined their surroundings. Kavanagh's office was painted blood red, the walls lined with shelf after shelf of legal tomes. Natasha was surprised to see the odd political biography interspersed between the issues of the lawyer's bible, Archbold – several of them about radical, mould-breaking statesmen and philosophers on whose principles the new Labour Party was founded. She was impressed. Photographs of a beautiful, middle-aged woman Natasha assumed to be Kavanagh's wife, and those of a handsome teenage boy and sporty-looking girl – she assumed his children – adorned a mahogany-and-brass tallboy in one corner. A large wooden model of a black-and-white sailing boat, complete with cream linen sails and full working parts, took pride of place on an ebony chest. Natasha leaned forward to examine the brass plate underneath the boat. It read only 'Nicholson's Sloop'.

'Miss Jackson,' Kavanagh said, his face a picture of paternal concern as he tried to drag her attention back to the matter in hand. 'You've been charged with a very serious crime. The circumstantial evidence against you is . . .' He paused for effect. '. . . impressive.' He reached into his pocket for his Parker pen – a fiftieth birthday present from Kate – and clicked it twice to punctuate his sentence.

Natasha appeared unfazed and crossed her willowy legs as Beaufort swallowed hard. 'What about the man in Room Four?' she asked, rather too confidently, Kavanagh thought.

Her solicitor pulled a police statement from his briefcase and held it up triumphantly. 'Markovic,' he reminded the senior counsel. 'He said he saw a male figure leave the hotel by a fire escape.'

It was Kavanagh's turn to look unimpressed. 'Unfortunately, the police found his statement rather vague,' he told Dynevor, reflecting on the police inspector's handwritten comment that Markovic was 'an unreliable witness'. Turning to Natasha, he added: 'You, on the other hand, were clearly identified by another witness, a . . .' He glanced at his notes about the hotel porter. '. . . a Mr Pike.' Natasha winced visibly. Maintaining direct eye contact with his client, Kavanagh added: 'Now the prosecution will try to establish a motive for you to have killed Lise Auerbach . . . Is there one?'

Natasha raised her eyes to the heavens once more. 'Of course not,' she answered, her eyes settling almost immediately back on his. She knew the question would be asked but she had expected Kavanagh to be less blunt about it, to toy with her a bit first. He was clearly someone who liked to get to the point.

'So you had never met before the night of the murder?' Kavanagh studied his client's face closely. In order to weigh up how she would appear to the jury, he needed to gauge her reactions carefully now.

'I didn't meet her then. Not to speak to, anyway . . . She was dead.' Natasha deftly fended off the trick question and continued to stare him out.

Nodding and twirling his pen slowly in his hand, he decided to digress for a while, to see if he could catch her off her guard later. Taking her step by step through her statement, he asked: 'She told your mother she was a journalist wanting to interview you?' Natasha nodded. 'What about?'

'I'm not really sure.' Natasha shrugged her shoulders. 'Daughter of new British ambassador moving to Austria, how does it feel, that kind of thing.'

Kavanagh frowned slightly and made a quick note. 'So Lise and your mother agreed a time for you to go round to the hotel?' He knew she had gone through all this a dozen times with the police and again with her solicitor, but he needed to hear it from her own lips.

Natasha glanced at her solicitor ruefully. 'Half past eight,' she confirmed. She looked as if she genuinely wished she had never kept the appointment, Kavanagh thought.

Putting on his spectacles, he read from her statement. 'And you went up to the room, you knocked on the door.'

'Twice, I think, no answer.' Natasha finished his sentence

as Beaufort and Dynevor both took notes. Beaufort took his eyes off Natasha just long enough to notice that Kavanagh had a pained expression on his face. The junior counsel had seen it many times before. It appeared whenever his senior counsel thought someone might be lying to him.

'So you tried the handle. Why?' Kavanagh asked Natasha, unable to mask his disbelief. It was something that had stuck in his gullet when he first read the statement; why on earth would she walk into a stranger's hotel room uninvited? It just wasn't something he thought someone like Natasha would do.

Natasha rolled her eyes once again. 'I don't know. I . . . I had . . . a weird feeling, I can't explain it. Like I knew something was wrong.'

Kavanagh groaned inwardly but then stopped himself. Lizzie was a great believer in women's intuition, he reminded himself sharply. She would argue that it was not something to be lightly dismissed.

He watched Natasha carefully and said nothing for several seconds as he mentally weighed up the strength of her last words. Then, finally, he asked softly: 'Why did you pick up the table lamp?' The fingerprints on it had also bothered him. Why didn't she just recoil in horror like any normal human being?

The young woman looked down at her hands. Her nails were beautifully manicured and she fingered a large square-cut diamond ring her father had bought for her eighteenth birthday. 'It was over her head. I wanted to see if she was still alive,' she replied. Then, lifting her face, she flinched. 'It was a mess . . . absolutely horrible.' For the first time since she had walked into his office that morning she looked as if she might cry.

Kavanagh removed his spectacles to study her more closely. 'So you dropped the table lamp, turned and ran?

Why didn't you call the police? There was a phone in the room.' He recalled seeing the official police photographs of Room 6, the telephone on the bedside table, the television in one corner, a double bed and an armchair.

'I was afraid,' Natasha said simply, her eyes enormous. Beaufort was mesmerised and stopped taking notes.

Kavanagh clasped his hands together in a gesture of infinite patience. 'But why? You hadn't done anything.' Or had she? That was the crucial question, he pondered, but as with all barristers it was not his place to ask her whether she was guilty or innocent, simply to enquire which way she was pleading.

'No, um, my father. I didn't want to involve him,' Natasha stammered. 'New ambassador, just knighted. Surely you can understand that?' Beaufort saw the pained expression return to Kavanagh's face, followed by one of open incredulity.

'Come on, Miss Jackson,' he countered, the Lancashire brogue creeping in. 'There's a dead body in front of you – the first you've ever seen – brains all over the carpet and the first thing you think about is your father?' He couldn't conceive that she expected him to believe her, let alone a jury. And he could just imagine what Mike Faraday, prosecution counsel, would try to make of this in court. A formidable opponent, Faraday would chew her up and spit her out for breakfast.

But the look of utter indignation on Natasha's face at the question soon wiped the expression off his. 'And what's wrong with that?' she asked, innocently, her composure regained. Eyeball to eyeball, she added: 'I didn't kill her, Mr Kavanagh. If you don't believe that, what chance have I got?'

What chance indeed, thought Kavanagh, as he sat facing her in silence.

*   *   *

A few hours later in the Benjamin Stillingfleet wine bar off the Strand, Kavanagh was still mulling Natasha's words over and over in his mind, mentally assessing the arguments for and against what she had told him. Something certainly wasn't quite right, but he was damned if he could put his finger on it.

Beaufort brought a round of drinks over to their table, an impish grin on his face. 'Good-looking woman, our Natasha,' he smirked. 'Always helps.' He handed a glass of wine to Kavanagh and a bottle of lager to Dynevor.

Kavanagh picked up his glass and turned it distractedly in his large hand. 'She needs something, Charlie. All she's got at the moment is a witness who thinks he saw a man leaving the hotel by a fire escape.'

'And heard voices in the room next door, don't forget,' chipped in Dynevor, trying to be helpful. Like Kavanagh, he had also been unsettled about Natasha's story for some time. But from the moment he had arrived at St John's Wood police station and met her wide-eyed in the cells, he sensed that – whatever she was lying about – she was not a murderer.

'It's not enough,' Kavanagh reminded him, 'but we'll have to play it for all it's worth.' Dynevor walked up to the food counter and collected a ploughman's lunch. Kavanagh turned to Beaufort. 'Let's just hope her father doesn't try and coach her through it. You heard what he said on the way out: "Remember what we agreed."' He sipped thoughtfully from his glass.

Beaufort tried to offer an explanation. 'Keep your pecker up? Think positive, it'll be all right on the night?' He desperately wanted to believe Natasha, to fall into the pools of her eyes and swim there gullibly, but he feared that Kavanagh was probably right; that there was more to the story than they knew. The senior counsel's scepticism was catching and neither man felt like lunch – less so when Dynevor returned with his plate piled high with bread and cheese.

Kavanagh was still uneasy. Thinking aloud, he said: 'A journalist comes all the way from Austria, turns up on the doorstep, no introduction, no phone call first, no letter?' He had worked with journalists all his life and he knew that wasn't how they operated. Even taking into account the fact that Lise Auerbach was foreign did not account for her strange behaviour. What editor worth his salt would sanction the expense of flying a hack off on some wild-goose chase with not even a promise of an interview in the bag?

Dynevor swallowed a mouthful of bread and tried to offer an explanation for Lise's behaviour. 'Bad manners, that's all,' he suggested, the crumbs spilling from his mouth.

Kavanagh continued with his line of thought while he watched Dynevor feeding. 'And wants to interview the daughter? Who's not even going to Vienna, she's going to Keele University. Well, why not the mother? Why not the father?'

Beaufort thought the answer obvious. 'You did notice, James, that Natasha has certain charms that her parents do not possess.' Like any good barrister Beaufort knew that half the battle in winning a case was in convincing the jury; at the end of the day, despite the strengths or weaknesses of the evidence, it was largely a matter of which side put on a better show. If the jury favoured one barrister over another, or one defendant or witness, that could be enough to sway their decision. Having met Natasha's charmless parents, Beaufort knew who he would prefer to write a news feature on. And when faced with the lovely Natasha, alone and vulnerable in the dock, he felt sure any red-blooded male on the jury would acquit her.

Kavanagh watched Beaufort daydreaming and smiled knowingly at Dynevor. 'Well, her charms certainly worked on you,' he told Beaufort. The junior counsel, young, single and unashamedly soft when it came to women, blushed.

Dynevor hardly noticed. Something was troubling him enough to rest his fork on his plate for a moment and ponder. 'Her charms even work on her father,' he commented. 'They're close. Too close . . . Always touching.' He said the last two words with a shudder. It was almost enough to put him off his food.

Kavanagh frowned and thought for a moment. Yes, he had also noticed their special intimacy – the kind that made the hairs on the back of his neck prickle. It was more than just fatherly pride – God knows, Kavanagh knew all about that with Kate – it was something else. What was it about Sir Alan Jackson that he instinctively disliked? Trying to drag his mind away from the father/daughter relationship, he asked Dynevor: 'What do we know about the victim?'

'Lise Auerbach? Very little, I'm afraid. Twenty-nine years old, Austrian, parents dead, worked on a German paper called . . .' He searched his memory banks for the name as he crunched on a huge pickled onion.

'*Der Sonntagsermittler.*' Beaufort furnished the answer and took a sip of his Chardonnay. He had read European Languages at Cambridge and knew enough about the German media to have recognised the name of the popular down-market Sunday tabloid whose name translated to the *Sunday Enquirer*.

Kavanagh still wasn't happy. 'I want to know why someone might have a reason to kill her,' he said. Nothing in the prosecution papers had yet supplied him with a single believable motive for the killing, either by Natasha or anyone else. There was no suggestion of a random, sexual motive. Her clothes were dishevelled but she had not

32

been touched. He had checked into the porter's background just in case and he was as clean as a whistle. According to the police investigation, Lise had arrived at London's Heathrow airport the day before she visited Lady Jackson and was due to fly home two days later. The police had found nothing unusual in her luggage or personal effects, no one seemed to be expecting her, and no calls had been made to or from her room.

Why had she come to London? Was it really for an interview with Natasha? Could Natasha have got upset by something she said to her in that room and flipped? He knew of cases where that had happened – where perfectly sane, reasonable people had suffered some sort of brainstorm and lost control – but Natasha didn't somehow seem to fit the bill. And what if it was as Natasha and Markovic said, that she simply happened to be in the wrong place at the wrong time? That she wandered into a room a few minutes after a seemingly motiveless attack by the man seen leaving via a fire escape? Why, then, did he have the niggling feeling that something wasn't right? That her reaction was somehow too . . . controlled? Whatever happened in Room 6, he needed to know. Draining his glass, he turned to Dynevor and said: 'See what you can dig up.'

3

Peter Foxcott was just starting his speech when the ginger-haired woman in a red suit slipped into the back of the high-ceilinged function room. A large, avuncular man, looking every part the kindly counsel, he was just beginning to explain the reason why he, and not Helen Ames, as they expected, was standing in an upstairs room at the Fox & Goose pub addressing them.

'When Helen found herself so suddenly unavailable, she persuaded me – not that I needed a great deal of persuading – to talk to you for a few minutes on a subject of great relevance to your foundation.' There were polite mumbles of approval from the thirty or so foundation members who were sitting in neat rows of chairs, many of them taking notes. His hand across his heart, Foxcott looked down briefly at the cue cards Helen had kindly prepared for him and continued: 'Epilepsy, however, seems to me to present a particular problem, namely the law as it applies to discrimination in the workplace.' An acknowledged expert on corporate law and unfair dismissal cases, he had nonetheless had to bone up on the subject of discrimination against epilepsy and had been genuinely surprised by what he had found.

Glancing up, his eyes met those of the late arrival, and, removing his spectacles, he faltered for a moment as he recognised her and smiled. As she returned a happy look of recognition, he heard a cough and was suddenly aware that he had abandoned his audience mid-sentence, so he carried on.

'Er . . . I can't promise you a barrel of laughs, I'm afraid. Quite the opposite for, sadly, there is still much prejudice against epilepsy, as there is against a whole range of medical conditions.' He gazed at his watch and counted the seconds ticking by.

Less than two hours later Peter Foxcott was sitting on the terrace of the Trafalgar pub in Greenwich, overlooking the River Thames, with Teresa Ashburn, the widow of Donald Ashburn, former circuit judge and a man he went to law school with. It had been ten years since they had met. They simply lost contact after Donald died, but Peter had always had a weakness for Teresa and she was often in his thoughts.

'To be honest,' she was saying in a lilting voice, 'I nearly didn't show up today. We're gearing up for next season. The buyers are over.' He couldn't take his eyes off her – that mass of flaming hair against the scarlet jacket, those emerald-green eyes, her delicate mouth. She looked just the same as he remembered her; in fact, he thought she looked even more attractive.

'Well, I'm glad you did, Teresa,' he said, with feeling. 'And may they buy everything you wish to sell them.' He hesitated awkwardly. 'Which is . . . what?'

Teresa giggled, that girlish laugh he thought he had long forgotten. 'I'm sorry, I'm talking as if you know. I run a small company now – ski-wear.' She reached into her gold-chain handbag and fished out a business card, offering it to him between elegant scarlet fingertips.

Everything suddenly clicked into place. 'Oh, ski-wear. Skiing became quite an obsession with Donald, didn't it?' Peter remembered envying the winter holidays Donald always raved about in the fashionable mountain resorts of Europe, how he and Teresa mingled with the royals and film stars, while Peter and Eleanor religiously packed their bags every year for Bournemouth. 'You can't beat a British seaside holiday,' Eleanor would always say before asking him if he'd like another ice-cream cone.

'He liked it because it took him away from courts and villains. He could stop being a judge for a while,' Teresa said.

Peter nodded knowingly as they made their way to a table. Donald was certainly the type of man to take his work very seriously. Peter remembered him sending some IRA terrorists down for life and then spurning Special Branch offers to protect him and his family. 'Goes with the territory,' he told his colleagues bravely.

'I hope I never let it show,' Peter confided to Teresa, 'but do you know, I rather envied Donald? Brilliant in court, charming and witty outside it. If you ever caught him outside it.' He remembered the long hours Donald used to work, and how much he loved the camaraderie that went with a judge's life. The life and soul, Donald Ashburn was, until his tragic and untimely death – a massive heart attack on the eleventh hole at St Andrews, halfway through an inter-chambers tournament.

Teresa Ashburn looked distant. 'Do you remember that jazz concert the four of us were meant to go to?' Foxcott nodded and smiled. Mention of a foursome suddenly reminded Teresa of something. Turning to him, an inquisitive look on her face, she asked gently: 'How is Eleanor?'

Peter Foxcott reddened. 'Oh, she's well, yes. Busy . . .

Happy . . . Same as ever, I suppose.' He hadn't meant that to come out quite as it did; he might as well have been talking about his mother as his wife. Images of both women flashed across his eyes and then merged into one. He shuddered and tried to recover lost ground. 'The Reuben MacAvoy Quintet,' he said, deftly changing the subject. 'You and Donald didn't show up. Why was that?'

'Unavoidably detained at a chambers party. Oh, you know what he was like with an audience.' Teresa looked almost rueful. Had he noticed a hint of bitterness in her voice?

Foxcott dismissed the idea and chuckled. 'Oh, I do indeed. He is greatly missed.' Particularly at the inter-chambers golf tournament, he thought privately. He peered into those green eyes again and sighed. 'Isn't it marvellous when you meet someone again after so many years and carry on as though it were yesterday?' Teresa smiled affectionately at her husband's old friend as he added: 'That's how it was with Donald, and that's how it is with you.'

She reached across the table and squeezed his hand.

Natasha Jackson stood in front of her father in the ornate marble lobby of the Central Criminal Court, the Old Bailey, and looked up at the Italianate frescoes on the ceiling. Immediately above the pastel pictures of nymphs and cherubs stood the statue of Justice, more than two hundred feet above the ground, a marker to all who entered within that justice would be done here. She closed her eyes and offered a quiet prayer to the famous bronze lady with the scales.

Light and airy, with windows set into the dome above, the first-floor lobby was buzzing with people – reporters, clerks, ushers, police officers and witnesses, all waiting for their various cases to begin – but none was more nervous than Natasha.

Part of her still couldn't believe she was here, in this hallowed place, about to stand trial in the same building as Crippen, Christie and the Yorkshire Ripper, to name but an infamous few. It had been months since she first met Kavanagh to discuss her case, almost a year since Lise Auerbach had first booked into the Verona Hotel, and a seeming eternity to her and her family in between as their legal 'team' had poked and prodded, picked and scratched at the evidence, written report after report and interviewed more people than she ever thought possible.

Despite all their hard work, at her last meeting with Kavanagh a week earlier, he had seemed no more optimistic about her chances of acquittal than when he first met her. He had kept asking her if there was anything else she wanted to tell him, and she had kept telling him no. It was like some horrible giant game of chess – and she felt little more than a pawn, being moved from square to square by unseen hands as the knights and bishops closed in.

Her life and that of her family had effectively been frozen in time until the trial. Her father's new job had been put on hold for 'tactical' reasons and an ingratiating deputy had been sent to Vienna to cover for him until the trial was over. Natasha's university place had been kindly 'held open' pending the outcome, although her heart no longer felt so committed to her planned degree in economics and politics. Her mother – instead of packing up their belongings for the long-awaited move to Vienna – had spent much of the past few months confined to her room, migraine after migraine debilitating her.

She had emerged just once – to take Natasha to Harvey Nichols to buy her an appropriate 'trousseau' for her forthcoming trial. Sober designer outfits had been carefully chosen for each day of the expected two-week ordeal; deliberately picked to intermingle without looking as if they had. Jackets and blouses, skirts and scarves, shoes and handbags to match. Lady Jackson was born to it, her natural good taste and elegance coming to the fore effortlessly. She had expected to do this for Natasha one day, but not for this, a murder trial. She had hoped to do it on the occasion of her daughter's wedding, preferably to someone with a double-barrelled surname whose estates adjoined those of her ancestors.

On her mother's precise instructions, Natasha had dressed for the first day of the trial in a black linen bolero jacket by Giorgio Armani and a blue and black striped silk dress by Paul Costelloe. The shoes were Manolo Blahnik, the handbag Gucci, the understated earrings Butler & Wilson. She looked for all the world like a grown woman, her father thought sadly, as he leaned forward in his seat and held both her hands.

'I'll be all right, Dad. The point is, will you?' Natasha had heard him pacing his room the last few nights, had watched as he poured himself one too many Scotches and had heard his blazing rows with her mother. Looking down at him now, she thought she had never seen him looking so utterly defeated, and it frightened the life out of her.

He stood up unsteadily and tried to reassure her. 'I'll do my best,' he replied with a placatory smile, but his eyes could not hide his anxiety. Natasha couldn't bear to see it and she walked away, the black patent handbag which cost more than a court clerk's weekly wage clasped to her stomach in a comforting gesture. Sir Alan followed her as Kavanagh watched from across the lobby.

'Remember, just answer questions briefly,' Sir Alan told his daughter, his hands pinning her arms to her side, his face inches from hers. He had gone over everything with her a hundred times and yet he was still afraid she might crack under pressure.

'Okay, don't worry,' she whispered. She wished he would calm down and allow her some breathing space. She was suddenly very hot and her mouth felt dry.

'Only that's how they trip you up, getting you to talk,' he continued, urgently trying to drum home the importance of her responses under cross-examination. His hands gripped her even more firmly. If only they had had more time to prepare, he thought now – even though the waiting had been interminable for him as well.

Natasha pulled away and stepped several paces from him, gasping for breath. The ambassador designate saw the look of panic in her eyes and followed, hard on her heels. Reaching for her hand, he raised it to his lips and kissed it tenderly. He hoped in that one gesture to convey to her how much she meant to him. Natasha softened – as she always did when her father was like this – and even managed a smile. Lady Jackson, flanked by a grey-haired man in a dark grey suit, who her father said was an observer from the Foreign Office, watched them both with expressionless eyes.

Kavanagh, unable to witness any more, walked towards them to escort Natasha into court. Sir Alan conceded reluctantly, telling his daughter: 'I'll be with you, Tash, every step of the way.'

Pulling away from him for the final time, Natasha Jackson stepped towards the courtroom door and, turning for a moment, saw her parents and the grey-suited man talking and watching her. The trial was about to begin and she had never felt so alone in her life.

'Sergeant Cobbold,' Michael Faraday, Q.C., for the prosecution, was saying, 'we've heard Dr Graham say that Lise Auerbach was killed by a single blow to the back of the skull some time during the evening of May the third.'

41

Natasha looked distractedly around the austere, oak-panelled courtroom from her seat in the dock in the centre of the court. The press benches immediately to her right and the public gallery above and slightly behind her were packed to the gunwales. She felt uncomfortably hot as the dozens of pairs of eyes bored into her, the journalists taking note of her every item of clothing and facial expression, the ghouls in the gallery just wanting to see her break down and cry. This was good theatre, after all, an ambassador's daughter up for murder. It would make good copy in the morning papers, she thought dryly. They'd probably have to issue tickets to sightseers tomorrow. Why didn't they just bring their knitting along and have done with it?

Directly in front of her was a sea of black robes and grey wigs – worn by the various barristers representing her and the Crown, the court clerk and finally by the grey-haired judge, who sat imperious on a wooden dais facing her, dressed, by contrast, in a red gown with a black sash and white tie. His face was thin and heavily lined, his eyes the colour of steel. She caught him watching her on more than one occasion, and each time he looked away when her eyes met his. Both he and the other court officials were surrounded by rows of leather-bound books, volumes of which they constantly referred to, as matters of law were discussed. This was the third day of the trial and she was already growing accustomed to the archaic methods, costumes and routines of the court.

The seven men and five women on the jury sat to her left, and often looked as bored as she felt. She noticed that one elderly gentleman in the front row was having trouble keeping awake. A fat white woman in the back row appeared to be permanently fidgeting. The only ones showing any interest in the proceedings were a middle-aged white man and a young black woman with an impressive collection of rings.

Immediately to the left of the judge, in the witness box, Detective Sergeant Tom Cobbold, fresh-faced and looking younger than his years, was being taken through his evidence by Faraday, a thin weasel of a man, she thought, with a pinched face, large nose and beady dark eyes. The prosecution counsel had a habit of jutting out his angular lower jaw when making a point of some relevance; a gesture that made him look like a Punch and Judy character in profile. There was a slight stir in the courtroom as he asked for Exhibit 4, the green onyx lamp base found on the floor next to the victim, to be shown to the detective and then to the jury.

'A series of DNA tests were also conducted on blood found on the table lamp, and it's accepted that it matched that of Lise Auerbach. Did you examine the lamp for fingerprints?' asked Faraday, his jaw fully extended.

DS Cobbold, a red-haired Scot with freckles, nodded. 'Yes, sir, I did.' The shorthand writer sitting in front of him dutifully tapped his response into her machine. Faraday asked him to tell the court what he had found.

'Two clear sets. One was Lise Auerbach's, another belonged to the defendant, Natasha Jackson.' DS Cobbold's lilting Scottish accent resounded around the courtroom walls. All eyes turned to the dock as Natasha tried not to blush.

It seemed an age to her before it was Kavanagh's turn to cross-examine the forensics officer. When he eventually rose to his feet and asked DS Cobbold a question, she wasn't sure that the reply was nearly convincing enough.

'In your view, had other people, apart from the victim and the defendant, handled the table lamp recently?' Kavanagh asked rather wearily.

'Probably,' came the answer, and she straightened her back to better examine the jury. Catching her father's eye in the public gallery above the court, her demeanour softened slightly. Sitting next to him, as always, was the grey-suited man she now knew as Merridew, an unfathomable expression on his face. Her mother, it seemed, had gone home, presumably with one of her headaches.

After DS Cobbold stepped down from the witness box, it was Detective Inspector Paul Benyon's turn. A tall, dapper man in a double-breasted navy blue suit with a mop of well-groomed brown hair, he had been the investigating officer in the case and the one who had first interviewed Natasha at the police station after her arrest on that dreadful night. He had been kind to her then, offering her a cup of tea and trying to put her at her ease. She had genuinely felt that he believed her story. He didn't seem nearly so benevolent now, telling the court in flat tones everything that had passed between them.

Fenella Shepherd, junior prosecution counsel and Faraday's deputy, was asking him about the denim jacket the defendant had been wearing on the night of the murder. DI Benyon had specifically asked Natasha for it.

'What did she say?' asked Miss Shepherd, a dark-featured woman with large almond-shaped eyes and a long nose.

DI Benyon glanced at Natasha in the dock. 'She told me she couldn't find it. I said I'd get a WPC to help her go through her wardrobe.' He recalled that this incident had been the first time he had started to have his doubts about her story.

'And was the jacket then found?' Miss Shepherd enquired, her eyes wide in anticipation. She was almost salivating, Natasha thought.

'Easily.'

Miss Shepherd asked the detective why he had wanted the jacket in the first place. He reminded the court that Mr Pike, the porter, had claimed to have seen blood on the defendant's sleeve when she was running from the hotel.

'And the jacket you found. What state was that in?' asked Miss Shepherd.

'Clean,' said the detective, decisively.

Miss Shepherd shot the jury a meaningful look. 'Worn? Creased? Stained?'

'None of those things,' came the reply.

Natasha studied her fingernails.

When it was his turn to cross-examine the inspector, Kavanagh wasn't going to let him off so lightly. 'Wouldn't you have expected my client to have thrown away the jacket if there had been blood on it?' he asked, his expression one of fatherly impatience to a child.

'People don't always,' DI Benyon replied stiffly. He knew what the barrister was trying to make him say and he wasn't having any of it. Kavanagh had caught him out in court once before, and this time he was on his guard.

'Was there any blood found on it?' Kavanagh tried a different tack.

'No trace.' DI Benyon stared at the woman in the dock.

'Was it a new jacket, as my learned friend appears to be insinuating?' Kavanagh glanced over at Miss Shepherd and wondered absently if she knew that behind closed chamber doors she was known as 'The Doberman'. Looking up at the public gallery, his eyes met those of the grey-suited man sitting next to Sir Alan Jackson, who nodded at him almost imperceptibly. Kavanagh felt suddenly uneasy.

'Impossible to tell,' DI Benyon answered carefully.

Kavanagh moved on. He asked the inspector if Natasha had ever departed from her explanation to police that she had gone to the Verona Hotel to be interviewed by the victim. The inspector confirmed that in six hours of police interviews she had not. Convinced that there was nothing more to gain from the inspector's testimony this time, Kavanagh sat down. DI Benyon left the witness box with a sigh of relief.

During the two-hour luncheon adjournment, Kavanagh hoped for nothing more than a quiet drink and some time for reflection, but his plans were interrupted by a note handed to him by Dynevor.

'From the pin-stripe up in the gallery. Said his name was Merridew,' the solicitor said, adding with a twinkle in his eye: 'I think I'd have had that changed, myself.'

Kavanagh opened the neatly folded piece of paper and frowned. Giving nothing away to either Dynevor or Beaufort standing by his side, he put it in his top pocket and stalked off. So much for it being his round, thought Dynevor.

Peter Foxcott closed his office door behind him and furtively pulled a folded magazine out from inside his jacket. Taking a deep breath, he moved to his leather-topped desk and spread open the copy of *Time Out*, the London entertainment listings magazine. Flicking to a page in the music section with its corner already carefully turned down, he studied the advertisement for the Reuben MacAvoy Quintet before reaching into his wallet and pulling out Teresa Ashburn's business card. Minutes later, he found himself dialling her number, and before he could change his mind, she had answered.

'Teresa, it's Peter Foxcott,' he said in his best telephone voice.

'Who?' Her reply shattered his already frazzled nerves.

'Peter Foxcott,' he repeated, slowly, willing her to

remember as he twisted the telephone cord round and round his hand.

'Oh, Peter, I'm sorry,' she replied, laughingly. 'Hello.'

Relieved that she had finally recognised his voice, he chuckled and asked as casually as he could: 'Guess who's playing at La Chouette on Thursday night?'

She smiled. 'Well, it can only be the dreaded Reuben MacAvoy Quintet. They were ancient then. This must be their grandchildren.'

The two of them laughed in unison and Peter felt more at ease. Getting into his stride, he asked suddenly: 'Why don't we go and find out? They do an adequate supper there, I'm told.'

Teresa stopped smiling and paused. 'Would Eleanor come?'

Peter hesitated. 'Er . . . no, no. She's not one for live music these days . . . So, what do you say?' He clenched and unclenched his jaw.

Teresa thought for a moment before answering. Sitting at her desk in her smart Chelsea office, she accepted a glass of Scotch from a young man at her side. 'I'd love to,' she said into the receiver, smiling up at her companion.

Kavanagh stepped out of a black cab and through the revolving doors of Runagates in Crispian Street, W1, one of the most exclusive gentleman's clubs in London. A doorman took his bag as he crossed the cool marble lobby, and he looked up admiringly at the classic architecture of the spiral stone staircase and the high glass atrium above it. Standing at the top of the staircase, the man he had seen in court all week waved his acknowledgment and called out his name.

Three flights later and Kavanagh was at his side, unable to disguise the inquisitive look on his face. 'I'm so glad you could join me,' Merridew told him, leading his guest into the clubby atmosphere of the wood-panelled bar.

'I was intrigued,' replied Kavanagh.

Merridew gestured at the room around them – with its dark wood, polished floors and large mirrors reflecting elegant lighting, it looked for all the world like a colonial enclave. 'I love this place,' he said with feeling. 'It's like a desert island without the flies.' Turning to the barrister, he added: 'Your bolthole's in *Nicholson's Sloop*, I gather.'

'You've been looking into me,' Kavanagh commented, unable to hide a slight frostiness in his tone. He considered the elderly but much-loved sailing boat he kept moored down on the Hampshire estuary as nobody else's business.

'No, Mr Kavanagh, gazing, crystal ball fashion. See what the future holds.' Merridew appeared to smirk.

Kavanagh pointed towards the bar. 'You didn't see a gin and tonic there, by any chance?' Merridew ordered them both a drink and ushered his guest into a leather armchair in the comfortable lounge.

'A desert island but handy for the office, I imagine,' remarked Kavanagh, fishing now. 'Whitehall?' He had already guessed that Merridew worked for one of the government agencies, he just didn't know which one.

There was that smirk again. 'Mmm,' Merridew answered. 'Approximately.' True to his profession, he was not one to give anything away.

Seated and waiting for their drinks, Kavanagh and his companion could not have been more in contrast. Smooth and slippery in both appearance and manner, Merridew was slight of build and bland of feature. Balding, with a watery complexion and thin nose, he spoke softly and with a slight lisp. His grey suits exactly matched the colour of his eyes, and he gave the overall impression of being almost ghost-like.

Kavanagh, sitting a few feet away, was at the other end of the spectrum. Well built, verging on the portly, his heavy jowls and large nose punctuated a face full of character and strength. His piercing blue eyes contrasted perfectly with his shock of white hair, which was several inches longer than convention dictated. His hair was further offset by the dark pin-stripe suit he wore, in which the stripes looked like bold chalk lines set a good inch apart. It was the garb of a man who was not afraid of anything.

Waiting to be told why he had been summoned, Kavanagh looked around the room and examined the sombre oil paintings of former illustrious club members, all of which hung on heavy gilt chains from a lofty picture rail. The ceiling cornicing was some of the best he had ever seen, with its stucco acorns and plaster oak leaves, and the walls were thick with years of brick-red distemper.

Spotting a fleshy figure across the room, who nodded and smiled at him, Kavanagh acknowledged the greeting but looked momentarily perplexed.

'A friend?' asked Merridew.

'Acquaintance. MP for somewhere or other.' Kavanagh rubbed his chin, trying to remember which constituency.

Merridew provided the answer. 'Ah, yes. I seem to recall you defended him a few years back on a somewhat exotic charge. Got him off, if memory serves.'

Kavanagh nodded ruefully, his memory returning. 'Unfortunately. Since when he's gone from strength to strength.' He remembered reading somewhere that the Tory politician whom he had defended in a rape claim brought by a high-class call-girl had recently been elected to the new Commons Select Committee on Law and Order.

Merridew leaned back in his chair and swung his arm

over a wing. Nodding in agreement, he commented: 'No doubt deluding himself that he has a part to play in ruling the world. You'd think they'd have learned by now, wouldn't you, that somewhere between Parliament and God there are the real Keepers of the Keys.' His lips were moist.

Kavanagh was rapidly going off Merridew. 'Guardian angels?' he asked, sarcastically. He had met his type before and he hadn't liked what he had seen.

'Mmm, it's rather more Greek than that. It's a pity they didn't do Greek at Bolton Grammar School.' Merridew sneered again, waiting for his words to sink in. 'Still, "*chre hemas kath'hemeran hodon biou poreusethai*".'

Kavanagh was fast losing patience. 'Meaning?' His lips were tight.

'One must travel life's path each and every day.' Merridew smiled patronisingly.

The waiter brought their drinks and set them down on the low table before them. 'What's the Greek for "when in doubt, state the obvious"?' Kavanagh asked, picking up his gin and tonic. 'Cheers.'

Merridew ignored his sarcasm. 'Question for you, Mr Kavanagh. When did the world ever stop turning because of a war here, a famine there?'

'All those emotive things that get in the way,' Kavanagh interjected. He was beginning to wish he had gone to the pub.

Merridew nodded. 'Precisely. These crises don't rock the boat because we play out our battles in miniature – on a chessboard – with ambassadors as pieces – well, pawns really.' He paused to take a sip from his vodka and orange and studied his guest's pained expression. Trying a different approach, he added: 'Distressing language, German, don't you think? A perpetual state of hawk and spit.'

'But we both know a man who speaks it like an

Austrian.' Kavanagh was beginning to get his companion's drift.

Merridew looked suddenly serious and leaned towards Kavanagh threateningly. 'An ambassador with a daughter in the dock is not good, Mr Kavanagh.' He paused. 'But I like the way you're handling her defence. Blindingly obvious that she didn't do it, of course. Some yob just walked in off the street, smashed the poor girl's skull and ran away.'

How very convenient, thought Kavanagh. Pity there wasn't a shred of evidence to support the theory. Still, with Merridew around, anything was possible.

Merridew leaned back in his chair and fixed his eyes on Kavanagh, before adding, right on cue: 'Your witness – the man who saw him. I feel sure he won't let you down.'

The barrister's eyes narrowed further as he downed his drink in one.

4

Kavanagh stood at the counter of the Chinese takeaway, his severe legal robes swapped for a casual shirt, jacket and trousers. He rattled the loose change in his trouser pocket restlessly as Lizzie, perched on a stool next to him, flicked impatiently through a menu.

'It was like wrestling treacle,' Kavanagh complained. 'Grab it and it moves.' He was still highly agitated by his meeting with Merridew.

His wife nodded knowingly. 'Health service is full of men like that. And women too, I have to say.' She shivered at the thought of a formidable spinster she had just crossed swords with over a question of funding. Then, distractedly, she added: 'Jim, should I have brought some flowers or something?'

Her husband, on the other side of the room now, a Chinese daily newspaper in his hand, looked incredulous. 'What? For Matt?'

Lizzie laughed. 'No – for the girls. Peace offering.' She was beginning to wish that she had made more of an effort for her son's unofficial house-warming. It had been weeks since they had dropped him off at his new home, and although he had called round several times – always with a huge pile of washing and to raid the fridge – she had been waiting for the invitation back with bated breath.

'Never at war, were we? Only in your head,' responded Kavanagh, scathingly. No matter how hard he tried, he sometimes found it very hard to understand women.

Lizzie couldn't help but look worried. 'Well, it's taken such a long time for them to invite us round.' She dared not let on how many nights she had lain awake worrying about it while her husband slept soundly.

The waiter returned and Kavanagh reached over the counter and picked up the brown paper bags full of food. 'Well, they have now – "Come and see how we live," they're saying. "No secrets."' He paid the bill and fondly ruffled his wife's hair. She was an old fuss-pot sometimes.

Pacing the stripped floorboards of Matt's new living room a few minutes later, Kavanagh poured his son's flatmates a glass of red wine each and studied the recently decorated walls. Everything was stark white – walls, ceilings, doors, even the shutters on the windows – but it looked fresh and relatively clean. The high ceilings and long windows gave the place a light and airy feel, and the rooms were much larger than Kavanagh had imagined they would be.

Lizzie, Matt and the girls were all seated around a wallpaper pasting table balanced precariously between two ladders in the middle of the room. What little furniture they had scattered elsewhere was protected by paint-covered dustsheets. Strips of material hung in the windows as makeshift curtains.

'You've made a very nice job of this place,' said Kavanagh. 'I'm impressed.' He was secretly very glad that Matt had finally invited them over. He felt relieved now that he was here and had seen the place for himself. It was really quite classy – much more up-market than he had expected it to be – and he was proud of Matt for having made such a find. Lizzie, sitting on a tea chest between the two girls, looked happier than she had in weeks.

George, the prettier of the two flatmates, gulped down a prawn ball and asked cheekily: 'Any good at plumbing, Jim? That's the next job.' She pointed at the pile of rusty copper pipes she and Matt had pulled out of a skip as Kavanagh scoffed aloud, indicating his refusal to get involved.

Lizzie was confused. 'Shouldn't the landlord be doing that?' she asked, scooping some noodles and bean sprouts on to a paper plate. Come to think of it, she thought, shouldn't the landlord have decorated the place too?

George suddenly took a closer interest in her meal, while Harry, the other girl, piped up: 'That's the good thing about our landlord – he said if we did it then he'd pay us the going rate.' Matt relaxed visibly.

Kavanagh poured himself a glass of wine and settled down to his crispy fried duck. 'Quite right, too,' he said, happy that his son finally appeared to be standing on his own two feet. There was a time the previous year when he had nearly kicked him out of the house because of his attitude. He was relieved not only that the boy had left home of his own volition but that he still considered his parents part of his life.

Matt, gulping wine from a half-pint beer glass while he watched his parents eat, quickly changed the subject by asking for the sweet-and-sour sauce.

At the gates to a central London park, Merridew, accompanied by a borrowed Golden Labrador on a leash, paid off his black cab and walked towards a large man sitting alone on a bench. A green Barbour over his dark grey suit, he strolled casually up to the bench and past it, as the taller man got to his feet and fell quickly into step.

They walked in silence for a while, the older man in a

thick black leather jacket and casual shirt and trousers, his shoulders bowed, a heavy expression on his unshaven face. Finally, in an accent thick with foreign vowels, he spoke.

'Do you know how my father would speak of the British?' The slight Merridew made no answer so he continued: 'As men come out of the sky on the end of parachutes. To set people free.' He looked to the heavens briefly, his hands plaintive.

Merridew kept the dog on a tight rein. 'Still holds good, I hope. At least as a metaphor,' he said. His slightly effeminate Harrow School accent contrasted sharply with that of his burly companion.

The dark-haired man snorted derisively. 'Oh, no. I know now, after my time here, those days are gone.' He thought back to the months of waiting, of the loneliness and sense of confinement and fear he had been forced to endure since his arrival in Britain as a political refugee.

'But still you want your wife and son to join you?' Merridew appeared confused.

The man nodded emphatically. 'Of course,' he said, his eyes wide with anger. 'You know this!' At least with his beloved Irina and his little Alexei at his side he hoped that he could start to live again after the terrible events of the previous five years.

Merridew reassured him. 'It's all in hand.'

The man was not convinced. 'It takes so long.' He shook his head in disbelief at how many months had passed since he had last seen his family. He closed his eyes briefly and tried to conjure up their image. The longer he went without seeing them, the more the picture faded, like an old photograph incorrectly fixed. He hoped to God they were still safe, he hoped they would forgive him, and most of all he prayed his young son would not blame him for their hardship and enforced separation.

Merridew stiffened and pulled himself up to his full five feet eight inches. 'This is England, Mr Markovic. If I give you my word that your wife and son will join you here, they will.' He stopped walking and turned to face him. Looking up into the heavily lidded eyes of the foreigner, Merridew added poisonously: 'And if I say they won't, they won't.'

Markovic blinked and swallowed hard as his duodenal ulcer spluttered into life.

Walking into Court 10 at the Old Bailey, Kavanagh made for his customary bench with a large bundle of legal papers under his arm. After so many years in law, he was no longer impressed by a courtroom's forbidding grandeur. It was almost his second home, the place where he had fought and won many a battle in the past, but where he now felt as if things were running beyond his control. Turning to Dynevor, standing behind him, he asked impatiently: 'Anything on Lise Auerbach yet?'

Dynevor was not hopeful. 'I've had a private investigator on it for weeks in Vienna.' Secretly, he wondered if he were being taken for a ride by the man he had employed through the auspices of the Austrian embassy. Every time he telephoned, the investigator offered no new information. He had already decided to put a new man on the case.

'Well, couldn't the Austrian embassy help?' Kavanagh was increasingly frustrated at the lack of information his team had been able to come up with on the victim. No matter how many times they went over the events of 3 May, he still didn't fully understand what Lise Auerbach was doing in the country. He could smell something fishy, and if only they could find out more about her, he felt sure everything would suddenly fall into place.

Dynevor frowned at the memory of the dozens of fruitless telephone conversations he had had with the friendly but utterly useless staff in the embassy's foreign affairs department. 'They mean well but they've not come up with anything,' he said.

Kavanagh looked up into the public gallery to see Sir Alan Jackson taking his seat, the ever-present Merridew at his side. Leaning in towards Dynevor and Beaufort, the barrister adjusted his worn and tattered wig and whispered: 'Listen, it sounds daft but don't ring me at home about anything to do with this case.' The two men eyed Kavanagh and then each other.

'Problem?' Dynevor enquired as the usher called for silence and asked the court to rise for the morning session.

'Precaution,' Kavanagh whispered, and turned to face the judge.

Christopher Pike felt quite overwhelmed when he first stepped into the witness box to give evidence. The thin-faced hotel porter from east London had never been inside a courtroom before, although he had seen them many times on television, and he was struck now by the draconian nature of the place.

Dressed in a navy blue suit on the recommendation of the prosecution brief, he tried to control the trembling in his right hand as he held the Bible and repeated the oath after the usher. The truth, the whole truth and nothing but the truth, so help him God.

Faraday got to his feet and gently led him through the statement he had made to the police; how he had arrived for work that evening, how he had seen Miss Auerbach return to the hotel shortly afterwards and what he had been doing at the time of the murder.

Mr Pike, his freshly washed hair groomed neatly into a side parting, his troublesome nasal hairs specially plucked, gradually increased in confidence as his nerves subsided. Brushing the dandruff nervously from his shoulders, he allowed his Cockney accent to slip more and more into his speech and even managed the occasional smile at Faraday as he answered the questions in a loud, clear voice. In response to the prosecution counsel as to what he did when he heard the thud upstairs, he answered simply: 'I thought I'd better investigate. And just as I put one foot on the stairs, this young woman comes hurtling down 'em.' The memory of it still surprised him.

Faraday, spectacles clasped in his hand, knew he was getting to the important part, the most damning evidence against the defendant. 'What time would this be?' he asked, his jaw jutting well out.

'Eight forty-five, sir,' Pike answered without hesitating. Kavanagh leaned forward and scribbled something on his notepad.

'Can you describe her?' Faraday asked the witness.

Pike nodded. 'Dark hair, blue denim jacket, jeans.' He smoothed his side parting over a forehead shiny with perspiration.

'And do you see her in court?'

The witness nodded again. Raising his left arm and extending a finger, he pointed at the defendant sitting in the dock. 'Natasha Jackson,' he said simply. Natasha once again felt the eyes of the courtroom upon her, but she held the witness's gaze.

'What happened next, Mr Pike?' The jury turned back to face the witness box, quite riveted now.

'We both kinda stopped,' Mr Pike explained. 'Then I saw blood on her left sleeve. She saw me see it, kind of thing, then she shoved me in the chest and ran out of the building.' He gestured with his elbow to indicate the manner in which he had been unceremoniously deflected.

59

'Did you go after her?' Faraday did his best to prompt the witness without giving him too much of a leading question, something that was not allowed under the complicated legal rules governing court procedures.

'Well, as best I could, sir. But she was too quick for me,' Pike said, painfully aware that – shocked and winded as he had been when Natasha elbowed him in the chest – he hadn't really tried. 'I got her registration number though,' he added, as helpfully as he could.

The jury looked at each other knowingly and then at Natasha.

When Kavanagh got to his feet to cross-examine Pike, the hotel porter was ready for him. He straightened his neck, folded his spindly arms across his narrow chest and planted his large feet firmly on the ground, as if preparing for a physical assault of some kind. The junior prosecution counsel had warned him time and again to watch himself, not to be swayed from his statement under cross-examination. Facing Kavanagh now, he faltered slightly. The defence counsel looked so unthreatening – almost genial in his manner and stance – that Pike was beginning to wonder what the woman had been on about.

He led him gently through his evidence again, point by point, and Pike saw no reason to remain on his guard. Then the tone began to change. 'The blood on the sleeve, Mr Pike. You say it was there, the police couldn't find it. Are you saying they've got it wrong?' Kavanagh asked, well into his cross-examination.

Watch yourself, thought Pike. This could be the trick question. Don't want to be accused of landing the cops in it. Just answer the question straight. Ignore the smile on the slippery bastard's face. 'I know what I saw,' he replied, head held high.

'And what time did you start work that evening?'

Pike wondered why he was being asked that again. Surely, he'd already covered that one. He was beginning to feel nervous again. 'Eight p.m., sir.'

Faraday removed his spectacles and studied Kavanagh closely. He guessed what was coming.

'And you heard the thud upstairs at . . .' Kavanagh glanced down at his notes. '. . . eight forty-five.' He paused and smiled; like the spider to the fly. 'How can you pinpoint the time so accurately?'

That was an easy one, thought Pike. 'There was a football match on telly, sir. Newcastle versus Arsenal. Ref had just blown for half-time.' He grinned broadly.

Kavanagh smiled and led him gently on. 'So, you'd been watching this match? . . . Where?'

Pike nodded, hands behind his back. 'In the porter's room, just off reception.'

Kavanagh started to circle his prey, smilingly. 'When you're in that room, how do you keep an eye on reception?'

Pike beamed back. 'Sounds a bit Heath Robinson, I know, but we have a mirror rigged up – you can see the desk.' He was proud of that mirror – it had been his idea four years earlier, despite the protestations of Sam Smyth, the day porter, who said it would never work and that the management would never allow it. They did and it did and he had won a five-pound bet.

More grins from Kavanagh. 'Foolproof, is it? Works every time?'

'Yes, sir.' Pike sounded quite sure of himself. He had single-handedly persuaded the hotel manager that it was an infallible system and he wasn't going to let himself be wrong-footed now.

'So during the match, no one came to reception . . . to

the best of your knowledge?' Kavanagh inclined his head slightly, waiting for the answer.

'No one came, full stop, sir.' Pike looked quite certain.

'Except Miss Jackson, of course,' Kavanagh interjected.

Pike frowned and shook his head. 'Not even Miss Jackson.'

Kavanagh feigned a look of puzzlement. 'Then how do you account for her presence in the hotel?'

Pike had already figured out the answer to that one. 'She must already have been there when I came on duty, sir.' It seemed obvious to him.

Kavanagh frowned. 'That's quite an assumption, Mr Pike.' He paused to let the jury digest his words before retracing his steps. 'Now, this football match. Good game, was it?'

'Very.' Pike grinned again. He was on home turf now.

'Who won?' Kavanagh looked as if he didn't know the answer.

Pike radiated pride. 'We did . . . I mean, the Gunners did, three–one.' He used his north London team's nickname with genuine affection.

'It sounds like you're a big fan.' Kavanagh glanced knowingly at the jury.

'Since I was a kid,' Pike said, adding: 'It's like a life sentence.' He shrugged his shoulders in resignation as several in the courtroom, including the judge, chuckled aloud. Pike smiled along with them.

Kavanagh, beaming at him now, asked: 'Wasn't there a goal just before half-time?' He made it sound as if they were just two blokes having a regular Saturday afternoon chat about soccer.

'Yes.' Pike winced, remembered the nail-biting moment as if it were yesterday.

Kavanagh went in for the kill. 'How do you know?'

Caught off his guard, Pike began: 'What do you mean, how do I know? I was watching the . . .' Almost in time, he realised the consequences of his admission and tried to stop himself mid-sentence. But it was too late. The jury and the entire courtroom were left in no doubt whatsoever where Mr Pike's full attention had been focused at the time of Natasha Jackson's arrival at the Verona Hotel.

Faraday did all that he could to retrieve the situation. Rising suddenly to his feet, he addressed the judge. 'M'lud. Touching though the mutual enthusiasm of my learned friend and the witness for the Gunners may be, I fail to see how it helps the jury.'

But Kavanagh wasn't finished. 'I think my learned friend knows only too well, my Lord,' he said, as Faraday resumed his seat in defeat. Turning now to face Pike, who looked more and more like a frightened rabbit caught in the headlights, Kavanagh no longer looked like the jovial fellow football fan as he bore down on the witness with a frown. Going for the jugular, he thundered: 'I put it to you, Mr Pike, that you were so engrossed in the match that anyone, from the *real* murderer of Lise Auerbach to the band of the Coldstream Guards, could have walked in, past reception, without you noticing.'

His face flushed crimson, Christopher Pike rued the day he had ever set eyes on Natasha Jackson or James Kavanagh. 'No!' he shouted in indignation, but he knew the damage had already been done.

Lunch that day was on Kavanagh. He and Beaufort sat out in the sunshine on the roof terrace of the trendy Blueprint Café, overlooking Tower Bridge, discussing the morning's progress. Kavanagh had good reason to celebrate. Pike had been the prosecution's linchpin and he had just weakened it considerably. Now all he had to do was get Natasha to come up trumps in the box and he might even stand a chance of getting her off – something he had not thought possible until now.

Shortly after they'd ordered their meal and were just starting to do some damage to a half-decent bottle of Montrachet, Merridew appeared before them, as if by sorcery. Kavanagh put his glass down with a thump and looked up with a sigh at the one person who could give him indigestion sufficient to put him off his food.

'Excellent, Mr Kavanagh,' Merridew simpered, by way of a greeting. 'Thoroughly enjoyed your performance.' He stood waiting to be invited to take a seat.

Kavanagh grimaced. 'It's not meant to be a cabaret.' He hated Merridew's twisted turn of phrase. Glancing at his lunch-time companion, he added, with sarcasm: 'Presumably you know Charles Beaufort – parentage, schooling, size of his bank balance, that kind of thing.' Beaufort nodded.

Not waiting any longer for an invitation to sit down, Merridew pulled up a chair. 'I also know the Jacksons' solicitor, Richard Dynevor,' he said, speaking directly for a change. 'He's been badgering the Austrian embassy for information.' He paused before adding: 'He should have come to me – I'd have been happy to help.'

Kavanagh looked suddenly serious. 'Then tell me about the German newspaper Lise Auerbach worked for – *Der Sonntagsermittler*.'

Merridew gave a dismissive wave. 'Oh, absolute rag, no doubt about it. Scandal sheet.' He paused and narrowed his eyes. 'Anything else I can help you with, Mr Kavanagh?' There was a new and sinister emphasis to his voice.

Kavanagh stared back. 'Like what?' He felt the hairs bristle on the back of his neck.

Beaufort watched in silence as the two men circled each

other mentally. Merridew half smiled. 'Information, of course,' he said quietly. 'What did you think I meant?' His pale grey eyes seemed to be piercing Kavanagh's soul.

The barrister stiffened visibly. 'Tell me, how far would you go to keep Sir Alan Jackson squeaky clean? I mean, if his daughter is found guilty of murder.'

Merridew scoffed. 'You speak as if I care about the individuals in this case. I don't. My only concern is to keep madmen in their asylums, nuclear weapons in their silos, armies in their barracks.'

Beaufort could hold back no longer. 'You mean that if she's found guilty, World War Three would break out?' He spoke with undisguised hostility.

Merridew maintained direct eye contact with Kavanagh while replying, curtly: 'I'll attribute your flippancy to youth, Mr Beaufort. I'm talking about our international standing which, to some, still matters a great deal.'

Kavanagh flinched. 'And God forbid that a trivial murder should get in the way.' He thought of Lise Auerbach sprawled on the bedroom floor, her head caved in, her life's blood spilled on to the carpet.

Merridew lowered his voice menacingly. 'Before you expand on that, Mr Kavanagh, do remember that you and I are in the same camp.'

Beaufort couldn't help but defend his senior counsel. 'Except that he's still his own man and you're clearly someone else's,' he spat.

Merridew almost laughed. 'Oh yes, I was forgetting his millstone-grit principles,' he said. Still looking directly at Kavanagh, he added: 'After all, look who you married, look how much money you earn. A *real* man of the people if ever I saw one.' His top lip curled at the corner.

Beaufort thought Kavanagh might punch Merridew, but

before he could, the small man got to his feet, adding: 'Still, "*avgolemono kai karpoi*".'

'More Greek wisdom?' Kavanagh said, his face twisted with anger.

'No,' Merridew grinned. 'It's on the menu . . . Rather fancy the look of it.' With that, he was gone, leaving Kavanagh seething.

'James?' Beaufort wondered if he should pour his red-faced companion a glass of water. He had never seen him look this way before.

Kavanagh could barely open his mouth to speak for rage. Eventually, he growled: 'A week ago I'd never met that man – now I can't move without falling over him.'

Lunch seemed somehow wholly indigestible after that encounter, so Kavanagh cut it short, leaving half his meal and even some wine in the bottle, Beaufort noticed. Back in chambers and still fuming, the two men were intercepted as they walked into the office. Peter Foxcott, a look of paternal indulgence on his face, accompanied by the meddling Aldermarten, headed them off as they stepped through the door. Bustling them both inside, Aldermarten closed the door as Peter Foxcott took up position behind a chair opposite his friend and colleague.

'James, a friend of mine in Whitehall has been in touch.' Foxcott's tone was inquisitive but admonishing, as he stood the other side of Kavanagh's desk.

Kavanagh prickled. 'And?'

'Puzzled as to why Charlie's been delving into one of their people – a Ralph Merridew?' Kavanagh shot Beaufort a look, registered his guilty blush and sighed aloud in exasperation.

Beaufort, still scarlet under his mop of dark curls, looked contrite. 'All I did was ask a few mates at the MoD if they'd heard of him,' he told Kavanagh defensively. Many of the young men he'd been in the navy with had ended up quite well placed in government departments and he had decided to made a few discreet enquiries. Or so he thought.

Kavanagh was not happy. 'What did you hope to find that isn't blindingly obvious, Charlie?' he asked with impatience.

Foxcott interrupted. 'Not to me, I'm afraid,' he said, sitting down. 'Never met the man.' It was clear he was expecting a full explanation.

Beaufort felt obliged to give his Head of Chambers an answer. 'He looks after Sir Alan Jackson. I think he must be MI5, 6, 7, one of that lot.' He was distressed to see that Kavanagh still looked cross. 'Look, I'm sorry, James, it's just that at times he seems to be running the case.'

Kavanagh didn't like that suggestion one little bit, least of all in front of Peter Foxcott and Jeremy Aldermarten. 'Well, if you let him get under your skin, he will be,' he snapped.

Beaufort, still smarting, came back at him as quick as a flash. 'He's not under yours?'

Peter Foxcott raised an eyebrow at the unusual public spat as Kavanagh held his head in his hands. Looking up at his old friend, Kavanagh knew it was his turn to explain. 'He's a constant presence. When he speaks it's in a kind of shorthand, translatable in several ways.' His fingertips formed an unstable pyramid in front of his face.

Foxcott needed to know more. 'For example?'

'Well, he asks you if he can help. Fixes you with a stare. You say: "What do you mean?" and he says: "What do you *think* I mean?" And then the moment's gone.'

Foxcott wasn't sure he understood. He had never met Merridew, it was difficult to know what Kavanagh meant, and anyway he didn't understand the motive. 'Why would he put pressure on you, not on Mike Faraday?' he asked.

To Kavanagh the answer was simple. Sitting upright in his chair, he replied: 'Because Faraday's as straight as a die, and it's my job to get her off anyway. Merridew's gonna be there to see that happens.'

Peter Foxcott was beginning to understand. 'Which puts you on the same side, only playing different games,' he mused. 'Does he have any useful suggestions?'

'Not really. He's conjured up some random yob who walked in off the street and killed her.' Kavanagh wished once again that he knew more about what happened that night in the Verona Hotel.

'Isn't that roughly the defence line anyway?' Foxcott asked. He was trying to be helpful, but it didn't sound that way.

'Yes, an intruder was seen,' Kavanagh said resentfully. 'But you can't help wondering if a few strings were being pulled.'

Peter Foxcott had a point to make. 'Regardless of your qualms,' he said, in his best schoolmasterly tone, 'you won't be treading on too many toes, will you? I mean, it is a question of their business being none of ours.'

Kavanagh knew exactly what the man in charge of the chambers budgets was getting at. 'And it would help if I remembered that several colleagues here make a very good living out of government inquiries and Royal Commissions?' He glanced up at Aldermarten, who was standing like a sentry behind the Head of Chambers.

Peter Foxcott nodded and admitted: 'Well, now you mention it, yes, that is a consideration,' as Kavanagh shook his head in disbelief at how he had ever allowed himself to stray this far from the original principles of his youth. This shouldn't be about money or stepping on high-placed toes.

This was a murder trial and all he was trying to do was to get some answers to the question of how an innocent woman might have ended up in the dock. Foxcott saw his angst and offered a salve. 'More to the point, James,' he said, with feeling, 'if Merridew's people murdered Lise Auerbach, then your client did not, and all you're looking for is a reasonable doubt.' Kavanagh's face softened. He knew Foxcott was right. 'Still,' Foxcott added, 'if it were my case, I'd find another yob.'

Looking at his watch and standing suddenly, the Head of Chambers apologised. 'You really must excuse me,' he said, and quickly left the room. It was only as he closed the door behind him that Kavanagh noticed he was wearing a corduroy jacket and a rather loud yellow shirt. Most unlike Peter, he thought absent-mindedly.

By the time that corduroy jacket had walked into the north London jazz club La Chouette half an hour later, with Peter Foxcott still inside it, it was 7.30 p.m. The place was almost deserted, which made rather a mockery of the approach of a waiter who asked him if he had booked.

'Well, er, anywhere you like, sir,' the waiter faltered, pointing at the dozens of empty tables around the large low-ceilinged room, each one with a small blue table lamp on it. Foxcott picked one, sat down and watched the Reuben MacAvoy Quintet tuning up. 'Can I get you a drink?' the waiter asked.

'No, I'll wait if I may,' said Foxcott, still looking around. 'I'm expecting a friend.' He saw the knowing look in the waiter's eye and blushed.

Two hours later, he was still alone at his table and the ageing quintet, with their receding hairlines and pot bellies, were in full flow. Still jolly good though, he thought, as he tapped his fingers against his thigh. The room was full of diners and drinkers, of happy couples laughing together. Foxcott could only watch them miserably over his glass of beer. As the waiter passed, he gestured for him to come over. Raising his voice above the music, he shouted: 'There have been no messages for me, have there?'

'Your name, sir?'

For the sixth time that evening, the Q.C. reminded him. 'Foxcott. The message would be from Ashburn, Mrs Teresa Ashburn.' He almost willed the man to answer in the affirmative.

Seeing the desperation in his eyes, the waiter smiled kindly. 'I'll check again for you, sir,' he said, and wandered off as Foxcott sighed dejectedly and checked his watch once more. It was too late. He knew she wasn't coming and he couldn't imagine now why he had ever believed she would.

5

Natasha was feeling increasingly detached from the court proceedings. Nothing in the daily routine made her any more comfortable with the incredible fact that here she was, on trial for murder, instead of packing to go off to university, a golden life of privilege and indolence awaiting her. Each morning she dutifully arrived with her father, took her place in the dock and watched in helpless confusion as the bewildering theatrical showcase continued before her. It was all like some terrible dream.

She had long ago stopped wondering if Kavanagh was winning or losing. It was pointless trying to gauge the reaction on the faces of the jury – faces she now knew intimately, from the sour-faced woman in the back row, past the dozing grandfather, to the impudent young man at the front who kept eyeing her lasciviously.

These were the men and women who were to decide her fate, and yet many of them looked as if they couldn't make a decision about what topping they wanted on their pizzas. What did they know? What did anyone in this courtroom know about what really happened the night Lise Auerbach died? She wished to God she had never heard the name, never gone to the Verona Hotel, never did what she did. The longer the case went on, the more depressed and despondent she became about the outcome.

Charles Beaufort, ever the gentleman, recognised the signs. He had seen enough defendants struggling mentally with the possibility of imprisonment to know that Natasha Jackson was suffering, and that furthermore her dejected demeanour could have an adverse effect on the jurors' decision. His special interest in the young woman who aroused feelings in him that were not entirely professional led him to have a quiet word with Kavanagh on the morning the defence was about to start its evidence – the day on which Natasha was to take the witness stand for the first time.

'Shouldn't one of us have a few words with Natasha? Humanise her for the sake of the jury?' Beaufort asked, leaning forward and speaking over Kavanagh's left shoulder. The elder counsel listened to his young friend's advice and nodded his head.

'Or even give her some encouragement,' he agreed. 'Good idea.' As Beaufort rose to speak to their client, Kavanagh wagged his finger at him. 'No, no, I'll do it.' Beaufort sat down hard, unable to hide his disappointment.

Walking to the back of the court, Kavanagh stepped up to the dock, as Natasha leaned forward in her seat towards him. The two women prison officers guarding her kept a watchful eye. Their young charge might have been a free woman on bail until now, but that didn't mean she might not make a run for it in the face of the ordeal she was about to face.

Kavanagh put his arm on the edge of the wooden box and smiled. 'You're doing very well, Miss Jackson,' he told her. He had been genuinely impressed by her lack of tears, and her continued concern for her father's reputation despite her own dire situation. Every time he had looked at her in the dock, she had appeared serene, righteous almost –

as if she simply expected that she would be believed and set free.

Studying her face closely now, he realised that she had not been quite as unaffected by the trial as he had first thought. Through supreme effort, she had managed to mask her true feelings from almost everyone, especially her father, and Kavanagh saw that now. His words could not soothe the stress in her voice or remove the fear in her eyes, but she attempted a smile and thanked him all the same. Kavanagh knew there was no point in trying to hide the truth from her, so he added: 'Things could get tougher from now on. Faraday knows his stuff.' Seeing her flinch slightly, he asked her, for the last time: 'There's nothing you'd like to tell me, is there, before I call you? Nothing in your story you'd like to change?'

Natasha tightened her lips and held his gaze. Tears welled in her eyes and she clenched her fists. 'I've told you the truth, Mr Kavanagh,' she said quietly, but somehow he still didn't believe her.

When Josef Markovic took the witness stand, dressed in an ill-fitting double-breasted grey suit, white shirt and black tie, his hands were trembling. Everything about his posture and countenance told Kavanagh that he was a reluctant witness. This was the man Merridew had spoken of and, although he was the defence's best means of introducing an element of doubt into the jury's mind, Kavanagh knew that if he could sense Markovic's unease, then so could the jury. He needed to dig deeper.

'Would you tell the court how you came to be in London?' Kavanagh asked, as the jury watched the proceedings closely.

Markovic, his hands on the edge of the witness box

to steady himself, answered simply: 'I came here to be . . . safe.'

Even the judge looked up at this answer as Kavanagh asked him to explain. 'Safe from what, Mr Markovic?'

'I came here for asylum after the Bosnian war.' The large man's heavily accented voice boomed across the hushed courtroom. He added, more hesitantly: 'I was an informer to the United Nations. Many Serbs will never forgive me.' All eyes were upon him now.

'And where were you staying on the night of May the third?' Kavanagh enquired.

'Verona Hotel, Queensway,' came the reply.

'Tell the court what you heard around eight o'clock.' Kavanagh glanced down at the statement Markovic had volunteered to the police immediately after Lise Auerbach's body was discovered. Merridew watched from the public gallery.

Markovic gripped the witness box even more firmly as he gave his answer. Several people in the room noticed his unusually long fingernails. 'From the room next door I heard two voices – a man and a woman – arguing.' Struggling with his English, he added: 'Very quickly they went from peace to anger . . . and then a gasp and nothing.' His large hands opened and closed in imitation of the sounds he had heard. The courtroom was hushed with rapt attention.

'Did you hear what was said?' Kavanagh asked.

'Not clearly.' Markovic shook his head in a helpless gesture. 'Er . . . I didn't understand and, er, it was not my business anyway.' He said the final part of his sentence hurriedly, as if he were keen to dismiss accusations of nosiness.

Kavanagh put his hands behind his back and leaned back on his bench. 'Go on,' he encouraged. He wished the witness would relax a little, make his testimony more convincing.

Markovic continued. 'Um, then I heard a door slam, footsteps down the landing, the fire escape. And from my window I saw a man run down the, er, the iron stairs.' Sir Alan Jackson, sitting next to Merridew in the public gallery, sat upright in his seat and watched the witness carefully.

'He was in a hurry?' Kavanagh asked.

'Oh yes, yes, yes,' Markovic emphasised. 'Yes, he moved to bottom and, er, ran across the yard, opened the gate and . . .' He shrugged. '. . . disappeared.'

'And from your window you had a clear view of this – in daylight?' Kavanagh wanted to make the evidence patently obvious to the jury.

Markovic nodded. 'His back . . . yes, yes.'

Kavanagh saw, to his relief, that the jury were transfixed. He didn't want to lose the momentum. 'Were you disturbed again that evening, Mr Markovic?' he asked.

Markovic looked up at the judge as he answered. 'Yes. Um, a little later I heard someone at Miss Auerbach's door. There was a sound of something being dropped perhaps, and then silent.'

Natasha watched hopefully from the dock as he spoke, willing the jury to believe his testimony. She knew now that he was probably her last chance – or, indeed, her only chance.

As Michael Faraday, Q.C., rose to his feet to cross-examine the witness, it was no mistake that he had a look of open disbelief on his face. An eminent counsel, well experienced in the ways of the court, he knew that he had to destroy the credibility of this witness completely or all would be lost. Kavanagh might have reduced Mr Pike's testimony to that of a distracted football fanatic, but Faraday wasn't finished yet.

'This man you saw, how old was he?' he asked briskly, the first hint of suspicion in his voice.

Markovic was uncomfortable under his gaze. 'I . . . er, couldn't say.'

Faraday looked knowingly across at the jury. 'An old man? A teenager?'

'In between.' Markovic could feel the pain in his stomach starting.

'Well, a young man, would you say? A middle-aged man?'

'Young.' The Serb reached into his pocket for a large white handkerchief and mopped his sweating brow.

'How was he dressed?' The questions were coming even faster.

'Dark clothes,' Markovic answered, wishing he could have a glass of water.

'Smart? Casual? Working clothes? Leather jacket? Anorak?' The questions came quick-fire.

Markovic lowered his head as if in thought. 'I do not remember,' he said, blinking constantly.

'You don't recall his clothes and yet you feel perfectly able to guess at his age?' Faraday allowed even more incredulity into his tone and looked again at the jury.

'He must be young, he . . . he moved quickly,' Markovic answered falteringly, the pitch in his own voice rising.

'Well, that's quite an assumption.' Faraday looked indignant. 'You are sure this was a man?'

Markovic didn't understand, so Faraday repeated the question until he did. It was Markovic's turn to look indignant. 'Of course, I can tell man from woman!' he said.

'Yes?'

'Ya.'

Merridew allowed himself a small smile in the gallery.

'The argument you heard, a man's voice and a woman's voice. Perhaps you can distinguish just one or two words?' Faraday folded his arms across his chest in a gesture of impatience.

'I couldn't hear clearly. It wasn't clear,' Markovic answered, reddening. All these questions, always questions, questions. First in Bosnia, then when he first arrived in this country and now here, in this courtroom. He was fast losing patience.

'Clear enough to distinguish a man and a woman?' Faraday wouldn't let the matter rest.

Markovic shook his head repeatedly, his ulcer burning. 'Even so, my English is not good.'

Faraday straightened his back. 'Oh, I think your English is perfectly splendid,' he said, fixing Markovic with a steely stare.

'Maybe now. Then it was not.' His face purple with frustration, Markovic suddenly exploded: 'You ask me what I saw,' he shouted. 'I saw a man run from the hotel, from the room next door where the girl was murdered!' He pointed as if towards a room, and glared at Faraday in anger and resentment.

The prosecution counsel waited a moment, allowing the silent courtroom to reverberate to the sudden outburst, to watch Markovic's chest rise and fall with his heavy breathing, to let the jury see the thunderous look on the witness's face. 'Thank you,' he said quietly, and sat down, turning to his junior counsel with a satisfied smile.

By the time Natasha Jackson stepped down from the dock and took the first few paces across the room towards the witness box, her knees had turned to jelly. It was all she could do to complete the short journey without collapsing. Dressed in a crisp black suit, the skirt cut

77

high above the knee, with a pale blue blouse and simple, understated jewellery, she looked every bit the ambassador's daughter.

Kavanagh watched the expressions on the faces of the jury as their eyes followed the defendant across the room. Without exception there was a look of appreciation; indeed, in the face of one young man in the front row, there was indecent interest, he noticed. But there was also a hint of suspicion, a feeling – just as he had had – that something was not quite right. His heart sank.

Her hand clammy as she picked up the Bible and held it in her right hand, Natasha looked to the public gallery for reassurance and found it in the eyes of her father. He was willing her through this. His whole demeanour, sitting on the edge of his seat, leaning over towards her, his hands tightly clasped together, was one of total love and support. Sitting next to him, her mother, her gaze steely, said nothing. Natasha closed her eyes briefly, inhaled deeply and recited the oath, her voice tremulous.

Kavanagh let her acclimatise to her situation gradually as her coaxed her gently through the first few questions. He asked her a little about herself, her early life travelling the world with her parents and about her plans to go to university. As she answered in a soft, quiet voice, he couldn't help but compare her to his own daughter Kate, in her last year at university, her whole life ahead of her too. He wondered how he would feel as a father if Kate were on trial for murder.

As Natasha relaxed into the routine of questions and answers, she gained her confidence bit by bit and the tension in her shoulders lessened. Moving her on to the evening of 3 May, her barrister did everything he could by his casual pose and unhurried questioning to keep her calm and composed. To win the jury's hearts and minds, he had to let them see the genteel side of her, the natural grace and charm of the ambassador's daughter, the well-mannered, even-tempered young woman who could no sooner bash a stranger's skull in with a table lamp than fly in the air.

'What time did you arrive at the Verona Hotel?' he asked her gently.

'I'm not sure exactly,' came the reply. Natasha's heart was pounding so hard in her chest she felt sure the jury could hear it.

'Well, was it light outside or dark?' He needed her to be more specific but she seemed to have forgotten all her preparation for this moment.

'Getting dark.' She took a few deep breaths and remembered what she had been groomed to say. 'I remember turning my headlights off when I parked.'

Peering at the judge over his spectacles, Kavanagh told the court: 'Lighting-up time, my Lord, on May the third, was eight thirty-two p.m.' The judge nodded and Faraday made a note. Kavanagh turned again to Natasha. 'What was the first thing you saw in the victim's bedroom?'

Natasha blanched at the memory. 'Her body,' she said, softly. 'Beside the bed. The lampshade covering her face.' How many times had she seen that image since, in her nightmares and in her waking hours too? No matter how many of her mother's sleeping pills she took, the vision of Lise Auerbach's blood-soaked room woke her night after night.

The court was completely silent as Kavanagh commented: 'Exhibit Five, my Lord.' He asked the usher to show it to Natasha, and she paled once more as the heavily bloodstained shade, wrapped in protective cellophane for forensic purposes, was lifted up in front of her. Her father's expression was pained.

'Yes,' she whispered, 'that's the one. I moved it to look

79

at her face – to see if she was still alive.' Glancing at the jury momentarily, she added: 'She wasn't.'

'But there was no light on in the room. How could you see her?' Kavanagh asked. It was his job to try to put all the questions Faraday might ask, to fend off any attack on the credibility of her story. In so doing, he had read and reread the police and forensic reports, questioned Natasha and Dynevor over and over, asked the solicitor to practise cross-examining her to see if there were any pitfalls.

'Well, it was still dusk and there was a streetlight shining in,' said Natasha, the image of that room flashing vividly before her eyes like a strobe.

'So the curtains were open?'

'Yes,' Natasha remembered. 'Half open.'

'When you left the room and ran down the stairs, what was in your mind?' Kavanagh asked the question he knew Faraday and every member of the jury would want to know the answer to. Everyone in the courtroom appeared to be holding their breath.

Natasha nodded in understanding. 'I must get away from here. How will this look to police? Sir Alan Jackson's daughter found in hotel with murdered girl.' Her eyes met her father's and then those of Merridew. She forced herself to look back at her counsel.

Kavanagh asked: 'Then you saw Mr Pike blocking your way and you shoved him. Why?'

All eyes were upon her as she answered: 'I'd just seen a dead woman with her head smashed in.' Her voice cracked with emotion for the first time as she added: 'For all I know he might have done it.' The court artist, making chalk etchings of each of the characters in the case for the evening news bulletins, coloured in her dark hair.

* * *

When Faraday rose to his feet to start his cross-examination, Natasha suddenly felt incredibly tired. She asked the usher for a glass of water and drank from it thirstily, her mouth dry. She hoped this would all be over very soon.

'Miss Jackson, my learned friend has been suggesting that Miss Auerbach was murdered in the hours of daylight. What time did you leave home that night?' He knew very well but he needed to talk her through it.

'Half past seven.' Natasha remembered the evening and her parents' row vividly. She even remembered the grandfather clock striking the half-hour as she fled from the house.

'You say in your statement that your appointment with Miss Auerbach was at eight thirty.' Faraday flicked through Natasha's police statement and then glanced at the map of the area the jury had already been shown. 'Ten-minute drive to the hotel, that leaves three-quarters of an hour unaccounted for.' Putting down the statement and removing his spectacles, he addressed her directly. 'Can you help us with that?'

Natasha looked exasperated. 'I've told the police. My mother had just bought me a new car and I wanted to drive around in it.' She remembered receiving the gift with the same detachment that she accepted all the other gifts her mother had bought her over the years. There was no warm embrace, no sense of surprise or wonderment to go with it. It had been a practical present – a car to get her to and from university in the chic designer style to which she had grown accustomed under her mother's auspices. She had simply been handed the keys and been told to be careful not to crash it.

'What sort of car?' Faraday was asking.

Natasha frowned slightly. 'An Alfa Spider.' Bright red with a personalised number plate, if you must know, she thought.

Judge Griffin peered disapprovingly at the prosecution counsel and interjected. 'I'm not sure that the make of car has any relevance, Mr Faraday, in which case you needn't trouble the jury with it.'

Faraday accepted the reprimand. 'Quite so, m'lud.' Turning to Natasha, he added: 'No matter what the make of car, Miss Jackson. You either drove around west London for three-quarters of an hour, unwitnessed, or you murdered Lise Auerbach. Which was it?'

Natasha was taken aback by the directness of his question. Gripping the witness box, she replied: 'I drove.'

'But you did go to the Verona?' Faraday increased the pace.

'Eventually, yes.' Her heart started pounding again.

'And why did you go into Miss Auerbach's room uninvited?' Faraday had the same look on his face as Kavanagh when he had asked her the identical question all those months before.

Natasha wondered how many times she was going to have to go through this. 'I just knew something was wrong,' she said for the umpteenth time, sighing, her eyes rolling.

Faraday leaned back on his bench and folded his arms. 'Ah, yes. A premonition, is that it?' He squinted at the jury, his jaw like a boomerang.

Natasha shrugged. 'If you like, yes.'

Faraday paused a moment to let the jury register her response. Picking up a folder from his desk, he asked Natasha if she had ever seen a copy of the Sunday tabloid newspaper Miss Auerbach worked for. She hadn't.

Turning to the judge, he added: 'I've had one or two articles from a typical edition translated, m'lud. Appropriately enough, the *blue* folder in Your Lordship's bundle.' The judge smiled coyly and reached for the relevant file as Faraday continued: 'Its staple diet is lurid speculation about the private lives of the great and the good throughout Europe. The paper's been sued countless times, but circulation continues to rise.'

Judge Griffin shook his head. 'Inevitably, Mr Faraday,' he remarked sadly, and put on his reading glasses to better view the lurid material.

Peering at Natasha over his spectacles, Faraday moved in for the kill. 'I put it to you, Miss Jackson, that Miss Auerbach wanted such a story about your parents.'

Natasha shook her head in surprise. 'There isn't one.'

'These journalists can be very inventive. What if they'd threatened to concoct such a story about your family – your father, even? You'd try to prevent that, wouldn't you?' He had a strange new look on his face that worried her.

Natasha's voice rose in anger. 'I've told you, there is no story.'

Faraday heard the pitch in her voice increase and kept up the pressure. 'Maybe not,' he countered. 'But isn't this the truth of it, Miss Jackson? For some reason you confronted Lise Auerbach, and in the course of that confrontation, you picked up the nearest object and struck her with it – a fatal blow.' Faraday almost shouted the accusation, his face animated as he delivered his finale.

'No!' Natasha shouted back, close to tears, her nostrils flaring. 'No!'

6

Kavanagh was in desperate need of some good news as he walked into River Court that evening. He had just spent the last half-hour with a distraught Natasha Jackson, trying to reassure her that she had been fine in the witness box, that she had kept Faraday at bay, when he knew in his heart of hearts that she had not. Without her testimony convincing the jury, he feared he had lost the case, and it was no longer a matter of professional pride. He felt instinctively that Natasha was innocent of murder, yet he also suspected her of lying. Time and again he had tried to persuade her that unless he knew the whole story, there was nothing he could do to help her. Constantly reminded of Kate, he felt strangely paternal towards his client and wished he could get her to trust him.

Deep in thought, his head bowed, he hadn't even had time to take off his raincoat before Beaufort and Dynevor appeared before him in the corridor, smiling like Cheshire cats.

'James, the Austrian private eye has come up trumps,' Beaufort announced triumphantly. He knew Dynevor had been right to put a new man on the job. That last detective had been a complete waste of time and money.

'Mmm?' It took Kavanagh a couple of seconds to take in what he was being told. His mind had been on other matters.

Dynevor explained. 'I've had a phone call from a Viennese lawyer, been looking for Lise Auerbach himself – holding money from her mother's estate.'

They had his interest now. Her mother's estate? That meant this lawyer knew something about the victim's past; something that could explain her presence in London. It was the best lead they'd had so far and, God knew, he needed a lucky break now. Considerably brighter, Kavanagh barked at Dynevor: 'Get a statement,' and headed for his office. He had work to do.

At the Jackson house, Sir Alan and his wife had spent that evening avoiding each other, each in contemplative thought. Dressed casually in a cardigan and open-necked shirt, Sir Alan paced the hall and kitchen, hands in his pockets, forehead furrowed. His wife sat in the drawing room, trying to read the newspaper, her beloved Trudy at her feet, watching her husband out of the corner of her eye.

The trial was still getting extensive coverage in the *Daily Telegraph*. Page three had been full of it for weeks. Lady Jackson digested every word and then carefully clipped the story from the paper, placing the cutting into a large buff-coloured file she kept with her tapestry. Once that task had been done, she carried on reading every word in the paper, paying special attention to the social diary and the obituaries.

Natasha had come home with her parents from court and run upstairs in tears. Locking herself in her room, she had jumped straight into a hot, deep bath in her own private bathroom adjacent to her bedroom. Refusing all offers of supper, she had lain half submerged under the steaming water, listening to Mozart on CD, going over the events of the day in her mind. If only she had remained calm, and not yelled her rejection of Faraday's suggestion across the courtroom. 'The lady doth protest too much, methinks?' The words of Hamlet echoed accusingly in her ears and she sank under the water in despair.

Stepping from the bath and into a soft towel, she patted herself dry and wondered absently whether they had baths or just showers in prison. Pulling on her short cotton broderie anglaise nightdress and dressing gown, she padded downstairs barefoot to bid her parents goodnight.

Sir Alan Jackson watched his daughter descend the grand staircase into the hall. Her shapely legs revealed to the thigh, her hair still damp from the bath, she stepped forward on to the bottom step and allowed him to embrace her. She smelled delicious, he thought. A combination of scented soap and wet skin. He closed his eyes and let his memories flow.

'Early night,' she said simply as she let him clasp her to him.

'Goodnight, darling.' He held her in his arms and kissed her tenderly on the cheek as Lady Jackson watched from the drawing room.

Catching her mother's eye, Natasha said nothing as she turned and made her way back up the stairs. Lady Jackson stepped into the hall and stood awkwardly beside her husband. 'Night-night, Tash,' she called after her only child, as Natasha faltered briefly on the stairs. She hadn't heard her mother call her that in years, and the fact that she did so now only served to further unsettle her. Hurrying up the last few steps, she ran to her room and shut the door. Lady Jackson turned to her husband and added, matter-of-factly: 'You can't do any more to help her.'

'No,' Sir Alan said, his eyes moist, and he wandered into the kitchen, his head bowed.

Beaufort turned the wheel of his harvest-gold MGB GT sports car into Kavanagh's gravel drive and pulled up behind the barrister's dew-covered Citroën estate. The dawn chorus was in its final phase as he rang on the doorbell.

It took two rings before Beaufort heard footsteps shuffling on the other side of the large wooden and stained-glass door, and the bolts being drawn across. A pale, bleary face peered out at him through the crack in the doorway afforded by the heavy-duty security chain.

'James, I'm sorry . . .' Beaufort began, '. . . but you said don't phone.'

'I should have said don't come round either,' Kavanagh said hoarsely, sliding the security chain across and opening the door to reveal himself in plain cotton pyjamas and a red silk paisley dressing gown. 'Not in the middle of the night.' Looking up at the purple sky, he frowned and asked: 'What time is it?'

'Five thirty.' Beaufort looked genuinely contrite as the older man stepped aside to let him in. He hadn't been looking forward to making the early morning visit and had been waiting round the corner for half an hour before he felt he could call.

Kavanagh knew Beaufort wouldn't have troubled him unless it was important, but he was still annoyed at having been woken so early. Lizzie had dragged him along to some charity film premiere the previous night and they hadn't got to bed until past 1 a.m. Now, four and a half hours later, he was about to be asked to consider some important legal matter, on a day that could turn out to be the most crucial of the trial. Releasing the catch on the window blind in the

88

kitchen to allow in the morning sun, Kavanagh squinted at his junior counsel and wiped the sleep from his eyes.

Immaculately dressed in a suit, tie and overcoat, the perky young man clicked open his briefcase and pulled out a file. He must have been up all night, but he certainly didn't look as if he had. The advantage of youth, Kavanagh mused. 'It's the Austrian lawyer's statement – Dr Weit Wyler. If you're calling Jackson today, you need to read it,' Beaufort said. Kavanagh still looked half asleep, so his junior added for effect: 'It seems that Lise Auerbach was rather more than a journalist.' The senior counsel grabbed the statement from the smiling young man and held it out in front of him as he tried desperately to focus without his spectacles.

More appropriately dressed in wig and gown a few hours later, James Kavanagh looked in no mood for interruptions as he strode across the marble lobby of the Old Bailey with Charles Beaufort at his side. His long gown flapping in his wake, he looked like a large black bird about to swoop on its prey. Undeterred, Sir Alan Jackson scurried over to greet him, his hands gripped firmly behind his back.

'You wanted to talk to us, Mr Kavanagh?' The ambassador looked more than a little worried. He had been this anxious ever since Charles Beaufort had telephoned him at 8 a.m. requesting an urgent pre-hearing meeting.

'Not you. Natasha,' Kavanagh replied curtly, not slowing his pace.

Almost running alongside him, Sir Alan adopted an insistent tone. 'I need to know what you intend to do,' he said. He turned and stood in front of the man whose job it was to defend his daughter, blocking his path and wringing his hands

Kavanagh faced the man he had taken an instant dislike to, and now understood why. 'I intend to discuss the defence with my client,' he said. 'I have no intention of covering up your indiscretions in a court of law.' His teeth were clenched as he spoke.

Sir Alan looked as if he had suffered a body blow. 'I . . . I see. You anticipate problems?' He tried to keep his voice level but his face gave everything away.

Kavanagh started to walk away. 'I have been forced to defend your daughter with half the truth,' he told the diplomat, with unconcealed hostility.

Sir Alan was close on his heels, his expression a picture of paternal concern. 'I understand your feelings, Mr Kavanagh, but the point is, surely, where do we go from here?'

Kavanagh spun round and faced him again. 'When exactly did you discover that Lise Auerbach was your illegitimate daughter?' he said, with all the invective he could muster. He glared at the man who had made his career out of smoothing the waters over difficult and tense situations and wondered how he thought he was going to wriggle out of this one.

Jackson raised his hand to his head defensively and steadied himself. 'How did you get on to this?' The charm offensive was over and his eyes had narrowed to slits.

'A Viennese lawyer who not only represented Lise's mother but became a trusted friend.' Kavanagh emphasised the last two words and allowed them to find their target.

Sir Alan glanced beyond Kavanagh at his wife and daughter, standing stock still a few paces behind, and knew he had to do something. Mr Kavanagh was not someone to be diced with. 'L-Lise came to see my wife the day of the m-murder,' he stammered. 'That's the first I knew of her, I swear it.'

'Why keep her a secret since then?' Kavanagh was finally getting some answers but he needed to know more. Sir Alan was foundering on the rocks and he knew it.

Lady Jackson, standing silent and stiff as a board as she watched her husband squirming, intervened. 'I advised it, Mr Kavanagh,' she said, stepping forward. 'At least until we'd talked it over with someone at the Foreign Office.' The glance she gave her husband told him to pull himself together. Turning to Kavanagh, she added: 'They put us on to Ralph Merridew.'

It was Kavanagh's turn to look to the heavens. Everything was suddenly falling into place. 'I see,' he said, his eyes flashing anger at all of them for having so deluded him. Addressing Natasha, motionless at her mother's side, he said: 'Miss Jackson, follow me,' before turning and walking away.

Natasha took a step towards the ambassador and grabbed his forearm. 'I want my father to come,' she said, defensively. She was afraid of Kavanagh, afraid of what he might do, and she wanted some moral support.

Kavanagh spun round and scowled at her. 'What for? So far he's done you nothing but harm.' Natasha sighed wearily and followed her counsel alone.

In the confines of a private consulting room, Kavanagh handed Natasha Dr Wyler's statement. She barely glanced at it before putting it down on the table in front of her. 'Well, what difference will it make? . . . I don't understand all of this.' She was tired of all the games.

Kavanagh spelled it out for her. 'It means,' he said, 'that Lise was your half-sister. It also means that three other people, besides yourself, had reason to wish she hadn't turned up – your father, your mother and Ralph Merridew.'

Natasha exhaled at the mention of Merridew. 'He was the one who told us to keep quiet about her,' she said. 'He took over – things like the denim jacket – he made me give it to him.'

'And bought you a new one?' Beaufort asked, scribbling notes.

Kavanagh walked round to the other side of the table. His face was like thunder. 'So you lied about that,' he said through gritted teeth. 'Juries don't like people changing their stories – they tend to disbelieve both versions.'

Natasha flashed him a venomous look. 'Then stick with the first,' she said. To her, it all seemed so simple. There was no point changing tactics now.

Kavanagh sat opposite her and fixed her with a stare. 'Miss Jackson,' he hissed, 'this isn't some sort of guessing game. This is a serious attempt to reach the truth and use it in your favour. Now if you're not happy with that, I suggest you find yourself another counsel.' He was angry, very angry. He didn't like losing cases, least of all one as highly publicised as this, and so far he had been forced into the role of a puppet by people who were playing with life and death as if it were some kind of commodity. If he was going to carry on with this case, then he had to take back control.

Before Natasha could open her mouth to answer, Dynevor interrupted. 'She wants you,' he said, glaring defiantly at his client. Natasha glanced up at him and brought her hand to her mouth guiltily. Dynevor was a good lawyer, she knew that, and he had made it quite clear from the outset that Kavanagh was the best money could buy. She had lied to him and to Kavanagh and now she had the two of them bearing down on her.

'Then she'd better tell me what *really* happened and make me believe it,' Kavanagh seethed. He opened his notebook and clicked his pen and sat expectantly for the truth.

Two hours later, Kavanagh and Beaufort took their leave of an exhausted Natasha and her lawyer and marched across the lobby, their notebooks full of new information. Kavanagh's head was spinning. He needed some time to think, to assess the chances and decide how best to proceed with the case. Lizzie would help, he was sure. Her input at times like these was invaluable. He couldn't wait to get home and talk it all through with her. It was going to be a long night.

Beaufort was fired up. 'The one person who could clear this whole thing up for us is Merridew. Why don't you call him, James?' he asked. He'd thought of it from the moment Lady Jackson admitted that Merridew was involved and he had been forced to wait until now to suggest it to Kavanagh. He truly believed there was some legal sense in putting Merridew on the stand, and tried to persuade himself that it wasn't just that he would have really enjoyed seeing the jumped-up civil servant squirming in the witness box under Kavanagh's relentless questioning.

The thought appealed to Kavanagh too, but he was much more experienced than his young colleague. 'And have him deny everything – in Greek?' he asked.

'Oh, come on.' Beaufort stopped Kavanagh mid-stride. 'You could have him for breakfast! He's sat there in court, day in, day out, watching you, me, Mike Faraday, his people, play out his scenario. Put him on the stand, James, and have his guts.'

Kavanagh wondered about Beaufort sometimes. When would he ever learn? 'Get this into your head once and for all, Charlie,' he told his junior. 'Merridew lies for a living.' He softened a little as he saw Beaufort's face fall. Leaning over the railings that looked down on to the storeys below, Kavanagh added: 'Look, much as I appreciate your faith in me, it is not our job to put Merridew behind bars. It is our job to get Natasha Jackson off. All we can do is explain to the jury why she lied. We may even make them understand why she left the scene.'

Beaufort tried to reason with his friend. 'But we . . .' he started.

'And that's it!' Kavanagh stressed. Sighing, he explained: 'If I even mention Merridew's name we don't just risk losing, we risk being laughed out of court. All we can do is rely on what Markovic saw.'

As he and Beaufort contemplated that thought silently together, their faces registered their private doubts as to what the outcome might be.

Teresa Ashburn recognised James Kavanagh the minute she saw him approaching the steps to River Court. Those rakish good looks, the intense blue eyes, that unkempt hair – now much whiter than she remembered. She had secretly nurtured a bit of a soft spot for the man who never quite fitted in with the Lincoln's Inn set, the only barrister she had ever heard her husband describe sniffily as 'not really one of us'.

Seeing him now, approaching the building with Beaufort, her heart warmed a little. She had not been looking forward to dropping her apology note into Peter Foxcott and now she hoped Kavanagh might do her dirty work for her.

Almost bumping into her as she stood by the chambers door, Kavanagh could be forgiven for not recognising the wife of one of the judges he had liked the least in his career. Judge Ashburn had been a cantankerous so-and-so in the courtroom and a malevolent jester outside it, he had always thought. Kavanagh had not been one of his coterie and had had little to do with his wife.

'Can I help you?' he asked politely, seeing the red-haired woman in a smart white raincoat standing hesitantly before him, reading from the list of names on the wall.

Teresa smiled. 'Thank you, no. It's Peter Foxcott I'm after.' She paused. 'You don't remember me, do you, Mr Kavanagh? I'm Donald Ashburn's wife, Teresa.'

Kavanagh quickly searched his memory banks and flashed up an image of the elegant young beauty who had often accompanied her husband to chambers parties. Now that he had her name, he remembered her instantly, and also that he had always felt somehow rather sorry for her. 'But of course you are,' he grinned. To Beaufort standing waiting at the door, he said: 'Charlie, just give us a second, will you?' Beaufort knew when he was surplus to requirements and disappeared. Kavanagh turned once again to Teresa. 'Would you like to wait inside?' he asked, taking her arm.

Teresa shook her head. 'No, no, I can't stop. I'd be grateful if you'd give Peter this.' Reaching into the pocket of her coat, she pulled out a small white envelope. Kavanagh was intrigued.

Half an hour later, when Peter Foxcott popped his head around Kavanagh's door, he had a quizzical look on his face. 'Charlie tells me you've been burning the midnight oil, James,' he said, fishing for more information on how the Jackson case was going.

Kavanagh liked Foxcott and normally welcomed his interest in his work, but with Foxcott's warning about Merridew still ringing in his ears, coupled with his own fears about how the case was progressing, he was not in the mood to share information. Reaching into his briefcase for the small white envelope, he deftly changed the subject. 'How was the live jazz?' he asked, a mischievous spark in his eyes.

It was Foxcott's turn to be reluctant. 'Splendid,' he said, walking into his own office, wondering how Kavanagh knew. The latter was hard on his heels.

'Pity Teresa Ashburn couldn't make it,' Kavanagh remarked casually. Foxcott spun round, his mouth open.

'How in God's name did you? . . .' He looked like the cat caught with all four paws in the cream.

Kavanagh smiled and put him out of his misery. 'She called here earlier, she left a note. Some sort of family crisis, she said. She'll phone you.' He handed him the envelope.

Foxcott took it and held it delicately in both hands. 'Do you remember him, James? Donald Ashburn?' He looked contrite.

'Yeah.' Kavanagh nodded. 'I didn't find him an easy man.'

Foxcott was surprised. He was beginning to wonder if he had been naïve about the man he had so admired. 'Eleanor didn't take to him, either. Said there was an unpleasant streak there somewhere. I thought he was the life and soul.'

Kavanagh walked to the window. 'That was the problem. He was the life and soul twenty-four hours a day, seven days a week. Made me wonder what he was trying to hide.' Turning back to his old friend, he added, softly: 'I liked her, though.'

Peter Foxcott knew it was time for an explanation. 'James, it's now how it looks, you know,' he said, hesitantly. Kavanagh was not a man to spread gossip in the chambers, thankfully, but he nonetheless felt honour-bound to reassure him that he was not being unfaithful to Eleanor.

Kavanagh raised an eyebrow. 'How does it look, Peter?'

Foxcott was nonplussed. 'Er, well . . . broadly speaking . . . that she and I . . . you know . . .' His face reddened still further.

Kavanagh smiled and adopted his most paternal tone as he said: 'Peter, if there was any of the "you know" to it, she'd hardly turn up on our doorstep, would she?'

He couldn't help but notice a look of disappointment on Foxcott's face when he conceded. 'I suppose not,' he said. Looking into the distance, he added: 'It's a mistake to relight old fires, isn't it?'

Kavanagh smiled. 'Perhaps,' he said mysteriously, leaving his friend alone with his thoughts and the small white envelope.

Minutes later, dialling Teresa Ashburn's number, Peter Foxcott wondered if he was flogging a dead horse. The telephone was answered almost immediately and just as he was about to speak to the woman who had not after all, it seemed, stood him up deliberately, he heard a man's voice answer.

'Hello?' the voice said. 'Hello?'

A frown creased Foxcott's forehead. Unable to speak, he replaced the receiver with a sigh and sat, arms folded, on the edge of his desk.

7

Lady Margaret Jackson chose a severe black dress by Jean Muir as the appropriate outfit to wear in the witness box. Without a trace of make-up, jewellery or perfume, she still somehow managed to ooze poise and wealth as she stood rigidly to attention facing the court while Kavanagh took her through her evidence.

After much soul-searching and with advice from Lizzie, Beaufort and Dynevor, Kavanagh had decided that the best policy was to tell the court the truth – that Lise Auerbach was Sir Alan Jackson's illegitimate daughter. He didn't have to by law, but it would have put him in an impossible situation at the closing speeches. How could he truly persuade the jury that Natasha's first version of events was true when he had now received direct information that it was not? It was a risky tactical decision, but he thought the jury probably didn't believe Natasha's first version either, and he hoped they would now be impressed by her telling them the truth. If he didn't come clean about Lise Auerbach, the prosecution might – there was no telling if the same Viennese lawyer had contacted them – and it would look far worse for Natasha if the trial was halted and it went to a second trial with that new information presented by the prosecution.

After a lengthy legal submission on the matter to the judge in chambers, the jury had been summoned and told that some important new evidence had come to light which the defence wished to share with them. Kavanagh had chosen Lady Jackson to break the news. That way the jury would see that, despite the shocking revelation, Sir Alan's loyal wife had stuck by her husband and was now speaking on his behalf. He hoped the jury would sympathise with a woman who had recently discovered her husband's murky past and whose only daughter was on trial for a murder she did not commit.

Halfway into her evidence, however, Kavanagh was beginning to wonder if he had done the right thing. Lady Jackson was so utterly devoid of emotion, so impassive in the giving of her answers, that he could that see the jury had not warmed to her at all.

'Lady Margaret, Lise was twenty-nine years old,' he prompted. She nodded, almost imperceptibly. 'It's a bit late in the day to go searching for your natural father. Did she say why she'd left it so long?'

'Yes,' Lady Jackson answered, her vowels tightly clipped. 'Her mother only told her about Alan a week before she died.'

Faraday looked incredulously at his junior and whispered to her urgently. She, in turn, whispered to DI Benyon behind her and the three of them watched the witness closely.

'So she came to your house to meet your husband but he was out. Why didn't you ask her to wait?' Kavanagh asked.

Lady Jackson studied her daughter as she answered. 'I thought it best if I broke the news to him and Natasha.' She hesitated slightly before adding: 'I wasn't sure how they'd take it.' It was her first sign of uncertainty.

'And how did they take it?' Kavanagh enquired, mentally

urging her to show more emotion, to let the women jurors at least sympathise with her dreadful predicament – the dutiful wife who learns of the existence of her husband's other daughter just as she is preparing to stand at his side in Vienna.

Lady Margaret thought for a moment before responding. 'Shock – which turned to curiosity,' she said flatly as Kavanagh groaned inwardly. 'They wanted to see her.' In the public gallery, her husband closed his eyes at the memory.

'Both of them?' Kavanagh asked.

'Yes.' Lady Margaret stood stock still and stared unblinkingly at her questioner.

'So why did you advise them to get in touch with the Foreign Office?' Kavanagh asked, once again hoping for some wifely words of wisdom.

But instead, Lady Margaret snorted. 'I didn't want my husband's career wrecked by a sudden scandal,' she said. She was a woman who had grown up in a house where duty and national honour mattered above all else. 'Besides,' she added tartly, 'I thought someone should check Lise's story.' Her face was as acid as if she had just swallowed a pear-drop whole.

Kavanagh gave up trying to wring any drops of sympathy out of her and decided to address the question of government interference in the case. He turned to the jury with emphasis as he asked his next question. 'So you received advice from the Foreign Office . . . which was?'

'They told us to keep calm – it would be dealt with. But then Natasha came back in a terrible state. She'd been to the hotel – to see Lise. Just to see her.' The jury eyed Lady Jackson suspiciously as she concluded her evidence as coldly as she had begun it.

*　　*　　*

101

There was a general murmuring in court as Kavanagh turned to the judge and announced: 'With your permission, my Lord, I now recall Natasha Jackson.'

If Natasha had felt every pair of eyes boring into her before, this time it was far worse. As she rose to her feet from the dock and made her way steadily across the courtroom to the witness box she had hoped never to stand in again, she felt naked, exposed and utterly vulnerable. She could hear the coughs and whispers, feel the palpable tension in the air, and believed she could almost smell the hostility towards her for lying to the court the last time.

Taking her place on the stand, she glanced at the judge, who looked disapprovingly at her over his gold-rimmed spectacles. 'You are still under oath, Miss Jackson. Do you understand that?' His face was like thunder. It was patently obvious that he didn't care for those who lied on oath in his courtroom.

'I do, my Lord,' Natasha answered, before turning to face her counsel with a heavy sigh. She hoped he knew what he was doing.

'Miss Jackson,' Kavanagh asked, his expression one of infinite patience, 'why didn't you tell the court earlier who Lise Auerbach really was?'

Faraday and his team were not the only ones on the edge of their seats.

'I was protecting my father,' Natasha replied, simply.

'From what, exactly?' Kavanagh knew he had to be tough on her, because Faraday certainly would be. His colleague was virtually salivating next to him.

'If the press had found out he'd had an illegitimate daughter, they'd have made life hell for him. Probably wrecked his career.' Natasha's unquestioning devotion to her father was all she had left to her now and her defence team wondered if it would be enough.

Kavanagh tried to explain her actions to the jury. 'So you made a conscious decision not so much to lie about as to keep quiet about the family connection. Is that right?' It sounded so much better that way, he hoped.

Natasha nodded. 'That was the advice we were given,' she replied carefully. She was disturbed to find every member of the jury glaring at her with malevolence, even the young man who had so patently fancied her before.

Kavanagh moved her quickly on. 'At the Verona Hotel, Mr Pike says he saw you coming down the stairs with blood on the sleeve of your denim jacket. Was there blood on it?'

'Yes.' Natasha hung her head.

'And did you later buy a new one?'

'I didn't. A new one was bought for me.' Natasha's parents watched anxiously from the gallery. Merridew, sitting behind them, didn't even flinch.

'You were happy with that?' Kavanagh enquired.

Natasha was quite firm. 'Yes,' she said. 'It was only an accident that I was there.' Her eyes were blazing now. She was hating every minute of this and wished her counsel would hurry up.

'I see.' Kavanagh paused. 'Miss Jackson, who would you say was more anxious to keep Miss Auerbach's identity a secret – you or your father's advisers?'

Natasha knew the answer. 'Them. I was worried about Lise being dead. They were more worried about who she was.'

Kavanagh straightened his back and prepared himself for what he considered to be the most crucial question of the trial. 'In your view,' he said, 'would these advisers have preferred Lise never to have had the chance to speak?'

Before Faraday could jump to his feet and protest, Natasha had given her answer and the jury had heard it. 'I'm certain of it,' she replied above the hubbub, as the jurors looked askance at each other. The seed had been sown.

Faraday was incandescent with rage. 'M'lud,' he began, but Kavanagh wasn't quite finished. The judge waved a hand at the prosecution counsel, who sat down with a thud.

'So, having been charged with murder,' Kavanagh continued, 'you kept quiet about the true identity of Lise Auerbach for the sake of your father's career. Am I right?'

'Yes. I was told I'd get bail and, on the evidence, the court would never find me guilty,' Natasha answered. Her father turned in his seat and fixed Merridew with a stare.

'And you believed this?' Kavanagh still found her naïvety impossible to credit.

'Well, my father did. . . . My mother did. Why shouldn't I? I hadn't done it.' To Natasha it all seemed so simple and she was fed up with the suggestion that it was not.

When it was Michael Faraday's turn to cross-examine the defendant after the revelations that had shocked both him and the court, he was in fighting mood. Through thin lips and in clipped tones, he asked Natasha briskly: 'On the night of the murder, you told your parents you were meeting friends. Was that the truth or a lie?' He leaned forward for her answer.

Natasha tried not to get riled. 'It wasn't the truth,' she said.

Faraday's eyes narrowed. 'Why the evasiveness, Miss Jackson? Do you suppose it makes a lie more palatable?' The weasel-like face sneered contemptuously at her.

Natasha looked at the ceiling. 'Very well, then, yes,

104

it was a lie.' Her slim fingers gripped the side of the witness box.

'You said there'd been no blood on the sleeve of the denim jacket. Truth or a lie?' Faraday's jaw moved in and out like a nutcracker.

Natasha could see the way the questioning was going, but could do nothing to avoid it. 'A lie,' she answered.

'You said you hadn't replaced the denim jacket. Truth or a lie?'

Natasha was indignant. 'I didn't. Mr Merridew did.'

Kavanagh stiffened at the mention of the name. He had told her to try not to bring Merridew into it; names would only cloud the issue further. He didn't want a senior government official claiming that everything Natasha said was a pack of lies and he thought it best to keep him nameless.

The judge was confused. 'Who?' he asked, leaning forward.

Natasha addressed him directly. 'One of my father's advisers.'

Kavanagh winced as the judge turned to him for clarification. 'Mr Kavanagh, are we going to hear from this Mr Merridew in the fullness of time?' The judge looked as if he had chronic indigestion.

Kavanagh stood wearily. 'I have no plans to call him, my Lord,' he said, before resuming his seat without offering further explanation.

Judge Griffin looked even more uncomfortable. 'It's just that he and his shadowy colleagues have been alluded to so often, I'm beginning to think of them as old friends,' he commented. It was Kavanagh's turn to look uncomfortable.

Faraday did not welcome the interruption and was keen to keep on at Natasha. Jumping to his feet as soon as the judge had finished talking, he continued: 'How would you describe the relationship between you and your father?' His face had that curious contorted look.

Natasha was immediately on the defensive. 'How do you mean?' she asked.

'Close? Distant? Easy-going? Intense?' Faraday listed her options.

'Close.'

'And how do you address him?'

She almost laughed. 'What?'

'Father, Dad, Daddy?'

'All those. Sometimes by his Christian name.'

Faraday leaned even closer. 'How often do you stand in for your mother at official engagements?' He was staring her out now.

Natasha glanced up at her father and then back at Faraday. 'Whenever I'm asked.' She recalled the luncheon at the Austrian embassy on that fateful day.

'Have you ever been mistaken for her at one of these engagements? For your father's wife, I mean?' Faraday lowered his voice.

'Once or twice, yes,' Natasha answered. She didn't like the way the questioning was going and it showed.

'Does that bother you?' Faraday was trying to wrong-foot her.

'Not at all.' Natasha shook her head to emphasise the point.

Faraday's lip curled. 'What about at home? Do you stand in for your mother there sometimes?'

Natasha felt herself blush. 'Doesn't every daughter?'

Faraday didn't like being answered with a question. 'That may or may not be the case,' he commented. 'It's you I want to know about.'

Natasha grimaced. 'You're making too much of this.

My father and I get on very well. Is that a crime?' Her voice cracked slightly with emotion.

'Just answer the question, Miss Jackson,' the judge snarled.

Natasha's eyes filled with tears. 'Yes, I take my mother's place at home sometimes – when she is ill, which she often seems to be . . . He confides in me, we talk over problems.'

Faraday closed in. 'And you give him advice, comfort, encouragement, whatever's needed?'

'Yes.' Natasha shrugged her shoulders.

'It's a rather special relationship, then?' Faraday leaned back and looked at the jury as if he had said something of great significance.

'My father's a special man.' Natasha looked up at the ambassador once again. His face was pale and his eyes filled with tears.

'And a rival for his attentions might not be welcome?' Faraday almost spat the words out.

Natasha frowned. 'What are you trying to say? . . .' Her voice rose to a falsetto. 'That I've been having an incestuous relationship with my father?'

Faraday and Kavanagh shot each other a look as the jury shifted uncomfortably in their seats. A murmur rippled around the courtroom like a Mexican wave. Kavanagh held his head in his hands and wished he were somewhere else.

Now he had got Natasha to voice what he had dared not but which he always hoped she might, Faraday softened his tone. 'I merely suggested that you enjoyed having your father all to yourself. And then a half-sister turns up.'

Natasha was still flushed and thoroughly confused. 'Are you saying I was jealous of her?'

'Were you?' The question came back at her like a ricochet.

She closed her eyes and shook her head emphatically. 'No.' Opening her eyes again, she stared at Faraday. 'You're saying I killed her.' Suddenly her expression changed. Her lip curling, her eyes flashing anger, she cried out: 'I've had enough. You all do it . . . you . . . Kavanagh . . . my parents.' She looked around the court in desperation.

Faraday interjected. 'Perhaps, like me, all they want to hear is the truth.'

Natasha blinked back the tears. 'I just wanted to see her. Everything I did, all the lies I told, wasn't for me, it was for other people.' Addressing the jury directly, she told them: 'All I wanted was to see her.'

The four hours it took the jury to deliberate nearly brought Natasha's nerves to breaking point. Nothing in the trial beforehand compared to this – not even being cross-examined by Faraday. Waiting with her parents in an anteroom just off the main lobby, she couldn't settle to anything. She felt alternately hot and cold, sick to the stomach and then hungry. If she ate anything, she got indigestion; if she drank anything, she needed the lavatory.

Led from the witness box in tears, she had almost fainted in the privacy of her room. Kavanagh couldn't face her, Dynevor had looked as if he had just found out that a close relative had died, and even Charles Beaufort had to force a smile.

Her parents sat with her in stony silence, unable to offer any further consolation or advice. Her father was a beaten man; he knew his diplomatic career was in tatters, but that didn't matter now. Nothing he could say or do could help the situation any more. He knew it was all his fault and he could hardly bear the guilt. His wife remained stoic, as her background and breeding dictated, but inside she felt as tight as a corkscrew and one of her migraines was coming on.

When Charles Beaufort popped his head around the door and announced, as breezily as he could, that the jury were back, he might as well have fired a shotgun into the room, the occupants jumped so much. Natasha grabbed her jacket and fled to the ladies' lavatory to compose herself, her mother followed, and Sir Alan Jackson sank back into his chair, his head in his hands, unable to move.

'Members of the jury, have you reached a verdict on which you are all agreed?' The court clerk stood in her long black robe and addressed the jury foreman, a smartly dressed young woman in the front row, sitting next to the white-haired old man who had found it so difficult to keep awake during much of the proceedings.

Wide-eyed now, he watched as the foreman answered stiffly: 'We have.'

Natasha dug her fingernails deep into her flesh.

'Do you find the defendant, Natasha Elizabeth Jackson, guilty or not guilty of the charge of murder?' There was a collective intake of breath as the response was awaited.

'Guilty.' The words rang out, resounded off the walls and reverberated again and again inside Natasha's head. Gripping the rail of the dock for support, she stumbled forward and fought for breath. White-faced, she looked up pleadingly at her parents, on their feet in the public gallery and clutching each other in shock. Lady Jackson looked close to collapse, her husband was ashen as he attempted to take in what he had just heard. Trying to open his mouth to shout his daughter's name, he found that he was incapable of speech.

Kavanagh watched them all and sighed heavily. He had suspected it was coming, but the verdict had still winded him physically. He wished there were something he could do, something he could say, but he knew there was not. God, he hated this feeling. He didn't have it very often – Kavanagh was a man who generally won his cases – but there was more than professional disappointment now, there was a profound sense of sadness that an innocent woman had been wrongly convicted and that he had been the only person between her and injustice. Leaning forward over his papers, he ran his hands through his hair and wondered again how he would feel if it was Kate in the dock, Kate found guilty of murder. It didn't bear thinking about. Unable even to acknowledge the 'victory' of Michael Faraday, someone he had known for years, he gathered up his papers and staggered from the courtroom in silence.

Natasha threw her head back and closed her eyes. Where was Lady Justice now, she wondered. She felt a hand on each arm and turned to see the women prison officers ready to escort her down to the cells. A door behind her opened, and she stumbled down the stone steps to what felt like Hades. This was her first sight of the clinical bowels of the court and every clank of a key, every bang of a door, jangled her nerves to fraying point. Finally left alone in a cell, she stood silently staring up at the small window, its iron bars casting long shadows across her face and the floor.

She remained quite numb, motionless in that position for over an hour before the door finally clanked open and her parents and Kavanagh stepped in. Sir Alan Jackson, his face knotted in pain, approached his daughter warily and stood a few paces behind her. 'I'm so sorry,' was all he could whisper.

Natasha did not, could not face him. 'Don't be,' she said,

coldly, sounding remarkably like her mother for the first time. Walking a few paces further into the shadows, she swallowed hard and addressed a question to Kavanagh. 'How long will I get?' The catch in her voice was almost too painful to hear.

Kavanagh tried to be as gentle as he could. 'It's very hard to say . . . the sentence has to be life.' He watched her spin towards him as he added: 'You could serve fifteen years.'

Natasha turned now to face her parents for the first time, every drop of blood drained from her features, her eyes glazed over. Lady Jackson, as stoic as ever, tried to control the quivering of her bottom lip and said nothing. Sir Alan met his beloved daughter's gaze and could only look away at her pain, as his own eyes spilled over with tears.

8

Whitehall was choked with traffic as Merridew and Sir Alan Jackson strode together along its tree-lined walkway. Both men had their hands stuffed deep in their mackintoshes; both were stony-faced and silent until the former diplomat could no longer contain his anger. 'But you said it couldn't happen,' he reminded Merridew insistently.

Merridew kept walking. 'Kavanagh wasted too much time pointing the finger at me,' he replied. He hadn't wanted this meeting, in fact he had actively avoided it, but Sir Alan had been waiting for him at the Foreign Office steps and so he had suggested they take a stroll.

'He was after the truth and he damn nearly got there,' Sir Alan countered, before adding, wistfully: 'Part of me wishes he had.'

Merridew stopped and turned to face the would-be ambassador, his face venomous. 'Don't tell me all of a sudden you're devoted to the truth. That's a luxury you can't afford.' His face inches from Sir Alan's, he added: 'And if you jump ship now, I shall personally see to it that you drown.'

'What about Natasha?' Sir Alan's eyes were blazing, his voice breaking.

'It's too late,' Merridew answered simply.

Sir Alan shook his head vehemently. 'No it bloody isn't,' he said. 'There'll be an appeal. And this time Mr Markovic can tell the whole story.' Sir Alan stared at Merridew for several seconds, wondering what he was thinking. Without a word, the civil servant turned on his heel and walked away, an urgency in his step.

Peter Foxcott sipped his Scotch and soda and studied Teresa Ashburn over the rim of his glass. He had finally got through, she had agreed to meet that night and here they were, sitting in the American Bar of the Savoy, romantic piano music playing in the background. He felt almost serene.

'Thank you for the note,' he said. 'And yes, I did phone – yesterday afternoon.' He waited for his words to drop.

Teresa looked up from the silver dish of nuts she had been picking at. 'At the flat?' She was surprised she hadn't received any message.

'A man answered.' Foxcott looked almost sorry.

Teresa stifled a smile and said, guiltily: 'His name is John. He's twenty-two.'

Foxcott raised his eyebrows. 'Ahhh. How long have you known him?' Then, suddenly contrite, he added: 'Oh, I'm sorry, I'm being a lawyer. It's none of my business.'

Teresa didn't flinch. 'I've know him, oh, twenty-two years, it must be.' Foxcott looked perplexed. 'He's my son,' she added, finally allowing herself a smile.

A wave of relief swept over Peter Foxcott and he sighed as Teresa went on to explain that John was the 'family crisis'. He asked her to expand.

'John's an epileptic, hence my involvement with the foundation. He had a bad fit and fell. We thought he'd broken his wrist, but he went to casualty and it was only a sprain.'

Foxcott looked suddenly sympathetic and chastised himself for thinking that she had another man in her life. 'What's the cause of his epilepsy, do they know?'

Teresa nodded. 'A blow to the head. Unlike your Helen, who inherited it from her father, I believe.'

The Head of Chambers was shocked. 'Helen? Helen Ames? I had no idea.' He thought of the competent young junior and her ebullient manner and could hardly equate the two.

Teresa Ashburn stared into her wineglass, pensively. Quietly, she said: 'You all thought Donald was such an impressive man, didn't you?'

Foxcott nodded and smiled. 'The lawyer's lawyer.'

Teresa raised her eyebrows. 'Yes, well he also had a rather frightening side ... A violent temper. The most trivial thing could spark it.' She paused. 'He was working at home one day. John was five. He came up to him, asked for some silly thing, you know, whining, moaning, as kids do. Donald slapped him hard across the back of his head.' Peter Foxcott winced as if he could feel the slap himself. Teresa went on: 'Three months later, the fits began.' She paused again and looked deep into Peter's eyes, her own eyes glistening. 'You're the first person I've ever told.'

Foxcott sighed and took her hand in his, squeezing it gently. He was so glad she had confided in him like that. What a wonderful woman she was.

Back in his office the next morning, he was roused from his faraway thoughts by a knock at the door. Helen Ames walked in, dressed with her customary panache in a smart black dress, her long blond hair piled up on the back of her head in a French plait.

Beaming at him, she said: 'I never thanked you properly for standing in for me the other day, so ... thank you.' She placed a bottle of his favourite claret on his desk.

Peter Foxcott took off his glasses and smiled back. Getting to his feet, he said, rather awkwardly: 'Helen, about the epilepsy thing . . .'

She turned and faced him: 'Yes, Peter?' She guessed he might have found out at the foundation meeting.

'I understand that you, er, yourself, er, suffer from it.' This was not coming out as well as he had hoped, he thought.

Helen Ames giggled. 'Peter, I never suffer from or about anything,' she said, patting his arm reassuringly.

'Of course not, no. I mean that, er, you have turns.' Oh, how he wished he had Kavanagh's way with words.

Helen looked more serious now. 'Fits,' she corrected him. 'Yes, I do, occasionally.' He was taking this more seriously than she had expected and she didn't quite know what was coming next.

'Might have been wise to tell us. Safety and all that,' Foxcott scolded mildly, his head tilted to one side in what he hoped was his most endearing look. As Head of Chambers he knew only too well about health and safety and the need to admit to all medical problems among staff on the relevant insurance forms.

'I really think of it as no one else's business but my own,' Helen answered, rather curtly, making as if to leave the office. She had guessed that the truth would come out sooner or later and she wasn't naïve enough to think that her boss wouldn't find out at the foundation meeting, but she had hoped he might simply overlook it, as she had.

Peter Foxcott hadn't quite finished. 'Teresa Ashburn wondered if you'd mind speaking to her son about coping with it.' He smiled hopefully.

Helen nodded, relieved. 'Well, I can only tell him what

116

my father told me: "Julius Caesar had it, Alexander the Great had it, Dostoevsky had it. And now you've got it."' She smiled triumphantly. It was obviously a speech she had used to great effect before.

'Yes, I see.' Foxcott was impressed. 'That would explain your . . .'

'Arrogance?' Helen interjected with an impish look.

Peter Foxcott stepped forward hurriedly. 'No, no. Confidence, Helen. Confidence.' He smiled at her warmly and she returned his smile with a knowing grin.

In the next office, Kavanagh was poring over the papers in the Jackson case for the hundredth time, making notes and trying to prepare himself for the appeal that Natasha's father had insisted upon. Pulling rank on some well-placed associates at the High Court, Sir Alan had managed to get an emergency hearing in a few days on the grounds that he had important new evidence and his daughter should not stay a day longer in custody than she had to.

Kavanagh, who had not yet been let in on the 'new evidence', had serious doubts that it would succeed in any event, but after his failure to get Natasha off he was going to give it his very best shot, even if there was hardly any time to prepare. Jacket off, in shirtsleeves and waistcoat, he was deeply engrossed in his mound of paperwork when there was an intrusive knock on the half-open door.

Jeremy Aldermarten's face peered sheepishly into the room, a room he coveted himself – it was by far the best in the chambers. 'I have an odd question, James,' he said.

Kavanagh thought he could detect the slightest trace of a sneer. Probably he had come to gloat – 'spit-and-sawdust approach doesn't always work with the great and the good' – that sort of thing. Kavanagh was not in the mood. Carrying

117

on writing, he said impatiently: 'Can't it wait? It's not been the best of days.'

Ignoring the rebuff, Aldemarten opened the door wider and stepped in. 'No, I'm afraid it can't,' he said. Kavanagh looked up to see his colleague holding a legal-looking document in his hands. 'How well do you know your son, James?' he suddenly blurted out.

Kavanagh was puzzled. 'I don't know. As well as he wants me to,' he said. What on earth had Matt got to do with anything, he wondered, and took off his spectacles to better examine Aldermarten.

'Well, you know I'm defending a man who owes the Inland Revenue two million pounds?' Aldermarten began, waving the document in the air. 'The deal I'm trying to arrange involves the sale of several London properties and many of them, unfortunately, are occupied by squatters.' The frowning look on Kavanagh's face indicated that he still didn't get it, so Aldermarten spelled it out for him. Handing him the document he was holding, he said: 'I think you should look at the names of those squatting in number twenty-seven Hatchley Street.'

Kavanagh, open-mouthed, took the document and put on his spectacles. There on the piece of paper in front of him was the name Matthew James Kavanagh.

'Out!' Kavanagh stood confronting his son and his two flatmates, his face purple with rage. He repeated the command and waited for a response. It had been a dreadful few weeks and now this, the discovery that his only son was a common squatter, no less. He should have guessed when the devious little rat wouldn't let him and Lizzie meet the landlord. Oh, how gullible he had been.

Matt shook his head. 'No way!' He even had the nerve to smile at his father as he said the words. Lizzie, hands across her chest, folding and unfolding her cardigan, stood uncomfortably to one side, wishing her husband would calm down. He'd been like this ever since he arrived home from work unexpectedly and ordered her into the car.

Kavanagh was fuming. 'You heard me!' he commanded Matt. 'This is someone else's property. He wants it back.' Lizzie looked at the thick rope of veins throbbing in her husband's neck and wondered if he was about to have an aneurism.

Their only son and his two friends stood facing him defiantly in the lounge of 27 Hatchley Street, legs apart, arms folded, as if they were manning a human barricade. Harry, the ungainly one of the two women, with all the facial piercings, didn't understand what all the fuss was about. 'He's been happy letting us live here until now,' she shrugged, referring to the landlord.

'Under licence,' George added helpfully, picking at her hair braids uncertainly.

Kavanagh put his hand to his head and glared at them. 'I gather from that that you know your rights. Do you also know his?' He paused for effect. 'What will you do when the bailiffs arrive? Barricade yourselves in? Sit on the roof?'

Matt's face was a picture of Lancashire determination. He looked just like Kavanagh's father, Alf, in some of the old photographs he had seen of him as a young man. 'If necessary, yes,' Matt said. 'This whole row has been empty for two years. Do you know why? He thought they were gonna widen the road and he stood to make a fortune.' Kavanagh was not impressed.

Lizzie stepped forward, a worried look on her face. Her social conscience pricked, she was beginning to understand her son's motives. 'Are there squatters living in the other houses?' she asked.

Matt grinned. 'They're the reason we can't just go.'

Kavanagh didn't understand. 'Well, what do you owe them?'

Matt sighed as if having to explain something to a child. 'We're the ones who set 'em up here – advertising in the *Big Issue*, interviewing them.' The girls nodded and looked at Matt proudly. It was all his idea and they both thought he was wonderful.

Kavanagh could hardly believe his ears. He turned to his wife in exasperation. 'My God! They're running an estate agency – for squatters!' Lizzie blushed at her son's audacity and didn't know what to say.

'That's right.' Matt held his father's angry stare. 'And we're staying.'

Kavanagh was still tight-lipped by the time his wife handed him a glass of red wine on the patio of their home an hour later. Still in his suit and tie, he was sitting staring down the garden and wondering where he had gone wrong. It had been mortifying, finding out that way, and he hated the idea of being had over by Matt. There had been problems in the past, but he had hoped that they were over. Now this.

'Come on, Jim, you know you secretly admire him for it.' Lizzie had adopted her most reasoned tone. Her eyes were on fire; she had found her son's sudden anti-Establishment fervour quite exhilarating. It reminded her of her own rebellious youth.

'So what?' Kavanagh was in no mood for reason.

Lizzie sighed heavily. 'But they're right. It's immoral, a whole row of empty houses.' The look she had seen on her son's face that afternoon had also reminded her of the zeal she had first seen in the eyes of a handsome young lawyer all those years ago. She was secretly terribly proud of Matt – she honestly never knew he had it in him.

'They're not empty now, are they, thanks to your son.' Kavanagh emphasised the 'your' – he wanted nothing to do with him. It had been humiliating having Aldermarten tell him what his own child was up to.

'Thank God the kids are doing something about it,' Lizzie remarked. 'I mean, who else gives a damn?' There was a fire in her eyes he hadn't seen for years.

'I have a daughter who's heading for a first at Cambridge and a son who hasn't the faintest idea what to do with the rest of his life – except live in a squat,' said Kavanagh, refusing to budge an inch. He was as entrenched as a tortoise in his shell.

Lizzie sighed and gulped from her glass. She knew there was no point in arguing when he was like this. She might as well go and put the supper on.

9

Charles Beaufort knocked gently on Kavanagh's door the following morning and listened for the call to come in. He had heard the news about Matt – everyone in the chambers had, thanks to Aldermarten – and he knew what his boss could be like when riled. Opening the door, he found Kavanagh quietly working at some papers on his desk. There was none of the bear-with-a-sore-head routine he had expected, just an air of quiet resignation. Beaufort actually felt quite sorry for him.

'Sir Alan Jackson is here, with Dynevor, about the appeal.'

Kavanagh took off his spectacles and laid them on his desk. 'Wheel 'em in,' he said. They were the last people he wanted to see right now, but he knew that he had to get it over with sooner rather than later. And anyway, he wanted to know what Merridew and Jackson would come up with next. It had better be good.

Half an hour later, after listening carefully to what the two men had to say about the extraordinary speed with which they had managed to get an appeal hearing, Kavanagh made his views known.

'Your reservations are understandable, Mr Kavanagh,'

Sir Alan responded. 'You see it as another Merridew ploy, no doubt.' One leg crossed over the other, his hand tapping his foot, he had the air of a man who was about to reveal vital information and believed it to be the complete answer.

Kavanagh was not in the mood for puzzles. 'Well, isn't it?' he said. 'We've had two versions of "the truth" so far.'

Sir Alan half smiled. 'You may be pleased to hear that I've parted company with Mr Merridew.' He reached out his hand towards Dynevor, who handed him a piece of paper. 'Markovic's statement,' he added. 'Take another look. Markovic was at the hotel all right, and he did see a man. Not a young man, though. Merridew told him to say that.' He fixed Kavanagh with a knowing stare.

'An older man, then . . . You?' Kavanagh spoke with quiet deliberation.

'Yes.' Sir Alan held his head high as he answered.

'Why?' Kavanagh studied the man in front of him with renewed interest.

'When I knew Lise had arrived, I had to confront her.' Sir Alan's face was twisted. It was all Beaufort could do to drag his eyes away from him and take notes.

'Confront her? She was your daughter.' Kavanagh was incredulous.

Sir Alan swallowed hard and looked down. His expression was one of shame. 'She was . . . but she . . . her birth was . . .'

'Inauspicious?' Kavanagh completed the sentence. Seeing Sir Alan's difficulty in explaining himself, he put on his spectacles and studied the statement in front of him. Reading aloud, he recited: 'Lise Auerbach. Born Vienna 1967.' He paused. 'Mother, Frieda, born . . .' He stopped and stared at Her Majesty's ambassador designate to Austria. 'So that's it.' His face was one of utter condemnation.

Sir Alan spelled it out for Dynevor and Beaufort, who

had yet to fully understand the implications of what was being said. 'Frieda was only fourteen when I . . .' he began. Dynevor hung his head.

Kavanagh nodded, knowingly. 'And Lise threatened to reveal it.' For the first time since he had taken this case on, the pieces of the jigsaw were finally coming together.

Sir Alan looked distant. 'That night I had to see her,' he said, breathlessly. 'After Natasha left I went to the hotel. The first thing she said to me was: "You owe me a lot. Let's start with thirty thousand pounds."' He grimaced. 'I refused. She called me a child molester, a rapist. That . . .' He gulped and looked Kavanagh directly in the eye with what little pride he had left. '. . . I was not.'

Kavanagh did not wish to know the sordid details of Sir Alan's past but he did want to know what had really happened on the night Lise Auerbach was killed. As Beaufort and Dynevor sat in stunned silence, the senior counsel indicated for Sir Alan to go on.

'I . . . I'm not absolutely sure what happened next,' Sir Alan continued, his eyes misting over. 'I . . . I took the nearest thing to hand and . . .' He stopped. '. . . I killed her.' He spoke the last three words with great emphasis and leaned forward in his seat.

There was no pained expression on Kavanagh's face this time, Beaufort noticed. He held his breath as Kavanagh asked quietly: 'Who knows this?'

'Just you, me and Merridew.' Sir Alan's response was almost whispered, but then he composed himself and sat up. 'I want you to use it,' he told Kavanagh. 'I want Natasha out of there.' A frown flickered across Kavanagh's forehead.

In the same London park where they had met several times before, Merridew and Markovic were walking the government dog. Markovic, jacket in hand, an immediacy in his gait, was flushed of face as Merridew marched, expressionless, beside him.

'You said that after the trial my wife and son would join me,' Markovic reminded his companion. He was at his wits' end. He had done exactly as he had been told and yet there had been no news. Merridew had failed to return any of his calls, and then had suddenly demanded a meeting. Markovic intended to use this opportunity to make his anger felt.

Merridew chuckled. 'I think that's gained a little in the translation, Mr Markovic,' he said, patronisingly.

Markovic grabbed his arm and frowned. 'I'm sorry . . . what . . . what do you mean?'

Merridew kept walking. 'Bad news, I'm afraid. Problems with Immigration.' He shrugged. 'Even I have my limitations.'

Markovic's heart was thumping in his chest and his stomach felt suddenly sore. 'Speak plainly!' he shouted, stopping mid-stride and grabbing Merridew's arm once more.

Merridew hardly slowed down. 'Your wife and son are not the issue,' he said, as casually as if he were discussing the weather. 'The difficulty stems from your own status here.' Markovic's jaw dropped open in shock as he stood watching Merridew carry on strolling through the park with his dog.

Natasha looked like a different woman as she sat in the dock at the Appeal Court hearing into her case. It may only have been a few weeks since she had been incarcerated at Holloway women's prison in north London, but it had been long enough to remove the light from her eyes. Each morning when she had awoken, she had hoped that it was all a bad dream, that when she opened her eyes she would be back in her comfortable bed in her room in her parents'

126

house in St John's Wood. And each morning, she had been bitterly disappointed to find herself lying under a stiff blanket in little more than a camp-bed, with two hardened shoplifters for cell-mates, the stench and the sounds overwhelming her.

She had switched herself off mentally; she no longer cared. All she wanted to do was sleep. She could hardly raise her eyes long enough to look at her father as he stood giving his extraordinary evidence over two days in the witness box, and when she did, she failed to return the conciliatory smile he attempted to give her several times across the crowded courtroom.

The three senior Appeal Court judges, dressed sombrely in their wigs and red-and-black gowns, seated high on a dais in front of her, also eyed the witness with suspicion throughout his evidence, no more so than when he was being cross-examined by Michael Faraday.

'Sir Alan, you ask us to believe that you went to Lise's hotel with every chance that, as a public figure, you'd be recognised?' he asked.

'Yes.' Sir Alan stood erect and defiant in a black pin-stripe suit, looking every inch the well-groomed diplomat.

'And then you let your other daughter stand trial for the crime she did not commit, but you did?' Faraday raised an eyebrow at the learned judges who, in turn, glanced across at the sad figure of the defendant, hunched over herself in the dock.

'Yes.' Sir Alan tried not to look as uncomfortable as he felt.

Faraday wasn't finished. 'But you can't give us one piece of evidence that you were ever there,' he argued. 'Did Mr Pike see you? No. Did you leave fingerprints on the lamp? No. Perhaps you can show us the clothes you were wearing that evening, or have they been replaced?'

'No.' Sir Alan's bottom lip was trembling. Merridew had disposed of the lot and he knew that to introduce his name now wouldn't help matters.

'So we have to take your word for it, do we, that you killed a young woman who merely *said* she was your daughter?' Faraday's jaw was working overtime.

'Yes,' said Sir Alan stiffly, willing his answer to have some effect.

Faraday glanced at the judges with a look of impatience and incredulity, before adding 'Nothing further, m'lud,' and sitting down.

The senior judge leaned forward and addressed Natasha's counsel. 'I think we'll leave it there, Mr Kavanagh. This afternoon, we shall hear from . . . ?'

Kavanagh stood up. 'Mr Markovic, my Lord.' He tried to ignore the look of contempt on the judges' faces as they rose for lunch. The look had been there from the start and it was getting worse.

Long after the judges had left the court, Sir Alan Jackson remained fixed to the spot in the witness box as he stared anxiously at his daughter across the room. Nothing in her expression indicated her feelings towards him as he had hoped. Instead, she too rose to be escorted down to the cells, without even giving him a second glance.

Kavanagh watched the exchange between the two with sadness. 'Come on, Charlie,' he told his junior. 'I need a drink.'

Crossing the exquisite mosaic floor of the High Court on their way to lunch a few minutes later, the pair were intercepted by a recognisable, but unwelcome, figure.

'Er, Mr Kavanagh, did I hear correctly?' Merridew enquired, his smooth manner even smoother. 'Mr Markovic takes the stand this afternoon?'

Kavanagh could not hide his contempt. 'Yes,' he said

acidly. 'We think, after all, that he may have recognised the man on the fire escape.'

Merridew shook his head as if in sympathy. 'Bad luck seems to dog you in this case, doesn't it?' Kavanagh looked confused. 'Markovic went back to Sarajevo this morning . . . Anxious to rejoin his wife and son.' He walked away, leaving Kavanagh's top lip curled, as if he had just encountered a deeply unpleasant smell.

The senior Appeal Court judge was winding up his labyrinthine speech as his audience sat in tense anticipation. The atmosphere was electric. Every member of the press and public, court staff and legal counsel was straining to listen to each unfathomable word, to try to be the first to extract some commonsense meaning from the long-winded and problematic wording so commonly used in the highest court in the land. Sir Alan and his wife sat stiffly together at the back of the court, like mannequins in both posture and pallor. Natasha was still hunched over herself, rocking gently in a semi-trance in the dock, and Kavanagh sat stony-faced and restless on his bench.

Having outlined the main arguments of the appeal, Mr Justice Leonard finally reached the conclusion. Peering over his pince-nez spectacles at Sir Alan Jackson, he said forcefully: 'Whilst we sympathise with the desire of any father to spare his daughter the agony of a life sentence, we find the fresh evidence wholly incredible. Accordingly, this appeal is dismissed.'

Lady Margaret closed her eyes and caught her breath. After all she had been through, all the years of unhappiness, now she was being asked to endure this. Her daughter was lost to her, in every sense of the word. Natasha looked over at her parents from the dock with a distant, glazed expression, unable either to accept or acknowledge the court's decision. It was all a bad dream, wasn't it? She'd wake up tomorrow at her university digs and this would all have been a terrible dream. Sir Alan registered his daughter's insensibility and matched it win his own. Trembling with shock, he tried to comprehend the enormity of what he had done, and the tears coursed down his cheeks.

Kavanagh walked along the galleried mezzanine of the High Court, alone with his thoughts. He couldn't remember the last time he had felt so defeated, so helpless in the face of needless tragedy. The logical part of him told him that it wasn't his fault, that he couldn't have done any more than he did to help Natasha, with his hands tied the way they had been. His heart told him otherwise, especially when he peered through the defendant's dulled eyes and into her soul that very morning. Now she was being taken back to prison for at least the next ten years of her life, and there was nothing anyone could do to help her. James Kavanagh, the great Q.C., the barrister who was going to show the world a thing or two, had apparently lost his magic.

The demented voice of Sir Alan Jackson in the lobby below stopped him in his tracks. 'You bastard!' Natasha's father was screaming. Kavanagh's heart stopped at the accusation, and he peered guiltily over the balustrade to see the diplomat being restrained by his wife and Charles Beaufort. But Sir Alan was shouting abuse not up at him, as he had first thought, but at Merridew, standing on the landing a few paces behind him.

Realising that Merridew was totally impervious to his outburst, Sir Alan started shouting to anyone who would listen. 'Why won't you believe me?' he screamed. 'I murdered Lise Auerbach.' His wife urged her husband to be quiet, but he shoved her aside. 'Out of my way! I'm guilty, I killed her!' he shouted, as two burly security guards ran towards him, batons in hand. 'I murdered Lise Auerbach and nobody wants to know. My own daughter . . .' Sir Alan was still shouting as he was dragged forcibly away and unceremoniously evicted from the court and into the street.

Kavanagh's heart was chilled by the sight, and he felt quite shaken as he watched a man he had only ever seen in total control of himself go to pieces so publicly. Suddenly, quite close behind him, he heard a familiar voice. 'What drives a man to do that, I wonder?' It was Merridew.

Kavanagh turned to confront the man who had been the cause of so much grief. 'Tell the truth, you mean?' he snapped. He felt like punching his sneering face.

Merridew folded his arms nonchalantly and leaned against the balustrade. 'You sound as if you believed him . . . Their Lordships didn't.' His eyebrow arched patronisingly.

Kavanagh wasn't in the mood for his games. 'We both know he's guilty,' he said, angrily. Thinking of it now, he knew he had suspected it all along but had been put off the scent by all the red herrings.

'What price truth, eh?' Merridew pondered, going off on one of his tangents. 'Fascinating commodity. You see it as an end in itself, I see it as a tool of the trade.' He paused and, responding to Kavanagh's look of open hostility, added: 'If you hadn't been so curious about Lise Auerbach, you and I might have got Natasha off.'

Kavanagh no longer tried to hide his loathing of Merridew. 'If you hadn't despatched my witness, I could have got her off here.' His teeth were clenched.

Merridew smiled. 'Forgive me,' he interrupted, 'but you're missing the implications. Impregnating a child prostitute is one thing, killing the bastard offspring is quite another.'

Kavanagh looked at him with utter scorn. 'Not British, you mean?' He almost spat the words out. Merridew and his like represented all that Kavanagh detested about the Establishment. Maybe Matt was right, maybe the only way forward was to make a stand for what you believed in, against those who believe they have a God-given right to do as they please.

Merridew shrugged. 'Ah, well, spilt milk and all that.'

Kavanagh was incandescent. 'Spilt milk! The man's lost both his daughters, for God's sake!'

Merridew, as ever, was unrepentant. 'He let the side down. He was selected to bat for Britain, not drag us into the gutter.'

Kavanagh could hardly contain himself. 'If people like you are running the show, we're there already.' Moving his face inches from Merridew's, he added: 'Up to your neck in it. You can't even smell it any more.'

Merridew smiled and offered his hand. 'Nice working with you, Mr Kavanagh.'

Kavanagh looked at the proffered hand with contempt. 'Get out of my sight,' he said as Merridew shrugged again and stalked off.

At Holloway prison for women, prisoner number 654 was informed that she had a visitor. Dressed in navy blue sweater and jeans, devoid of all make-up or jewellery, her hair scraped back, she swung her legs down from the top bunk in her stifling cell and allowed herself to be led the half-mile to the visiting block, through one locked door after another, each one carefully locked again behind her.

Sir Alan Jackson sat alone on the other side of a glass partition, his eyes red-rimmed, his posture one of total defeat. He watched Natasha listlessly shuffle into the room and sit down opposite him, too far away to touch, even if the security glass hadn't been between them. Hand to her chin, the sleeve of her regulation-issue jumper in her mouth, she avoided his gaze for several seconds before looking up. His eyes were pleading and moist. Hers had acquired a hard look, something he had never seen in them before, in all the years that he had gazed into them tenderly. Now he saw something else, something he hoped never to see. Disgust. And worse. Hate.

There were a hundred things he wanted to tell her and he had rehearsed them in his mind a dozen ways. He wanted to try to explain about Frieda, about Lise, the child he never knew, and about how he had come to betray Natasha so despicably. But facing her now, with that look in her eyes, he found himself rendered speechless for fear of what he might not say. Instead, he sat in silence, the tears flooding down his face.

Natasha watched and waited for several minutes. There were things she wanted to say to him, and much more that she wanted to hear. But now, in this place, at this time, it all seemed utterly pointless. She had to learn to come to terms with the life sentence her father had handed her, to deal with her own grief about the terrible events that had devastated her life, and to make it clear to her parents that she never wanted to see either of them again. Watching him unflinchingly now, she knew that nothing needed to be said. They both knew what the other one was planning to say and it was understood. Placing her hands on the table in front of her, she used them to lever herself up, before turning and walking away.

The former British ambassador designate to Austria, now an unemployed civilian, with the one true love of his life locked away from him for ever, remained motionless in his seat, a broken man.

*　　*　　*

James Kavanagh couldn't face going back to his office after such an awful day in court; the last people he wanted to see were Peter Foxcott and Jeremy Aldermarten with their words of consolation. There was only one person who could console him now and that was Lizzie. She would make sense of it all, she always did. He never felt more in need of a hug, of seeing the face that always made his heart beat a little faster.

He drove home in silence, not even the radio on for company, his thoughts miles away from the grinding traffic as it crawled through south-west London. He'd telephone Kate at university tonight, he decided, and suggest he and Lizzie drove up to see her at the weekend, to take her out to dinner. And, perhaps more importantly, he'd try to make his peace with Matt. His children were very precious to him, much more than he had appreciated recently, and he never wanted to forget that again.

The house looked welcoming and familiar as he pulled into the drive and switched off the engine. He turned the key in the lock, entered the hallway and dumped his briefcase and raincoat on a chair. All he wanted was Lizzie and a large Scotch and soda and everything would start to feel good again. But to his surprise, as he walked into the kitchen, he found that his wife was not alone. A rather dishevelled-looking Matt, Harry and George were all sitting at the kitchen table, eating ravenously as Lizzie served them from a hot dish of lasagne fresh out of the oven. They stopped mid-mouthful as Kavanagh walked in and stared at them all, his expression unfathomable.

Lizzie stopped too and waited for her husband to speak, a serving spoon poised in mid-air. Kavanagh looked at her quizzically and frowned. Clearing his throat, he asked: 'What's wrong?' He knew they wouldn't be there unless something dramatic had happened.

The teenagers looked contrite and hung their heads. No one offered an answer so Lizzie answered for them. 'They've been kicked out,' she said, putting down the spoon. 'Bailiffs, boarding up, belongings all over the street . . . the works.' Her face was disapproving. How dare they treat her son like that, she was thinking. Wiping her hands on her apron, she sauntered over to her husband, peering up into his face with a hopeful smile. 'Still, the good news,' she added, her eyes shining brightly, 'is that they'll be staying with us for a little while . . . just till they get back on their feet.'

Kavanagh looked into Lizzie's bright blue eyes and loved her even more than he had ever thought possible. His wife, his son and the two girls all appeared to be holding their breath while they waited for his response.

Finally, unable to pretend to be cross any more, he smiled. 'Good,' he said, as Matt and the girls all sighed with relief. Pulling Lizzie towards him, he grinned broadly and repeated his verdict. 'Good . . . Now how about some of that lasagne?'

PART TWO

The Ties That Bind

10

When Paddy Spence walked down the red-carpeted corridor towards James Kavanagh's office three months later, little did he know how perfect his timing would be. Still reeling from the aftermath of the Jackson case, and with niggling questions about his own social conscience after his reaction to Matt's unlawful activities troubling him, the senior counsel was ripe for the plucking.

His 'In' tray may have been full of lucrative cases shunted his way by Tom Buckley, the senior clerk at River Court Chambers – all high-profile, high-paying, combative stuff, right up Kavanagh's street – but he wanted something more; something to get his teeth into, something to remind him why he 'took Silk' in the first place. Something to assuage his guilt over Natasha Jackson.

Buckley, a well-built Cockney with a cropped haircut and rounded face, was not someone to be trifled with. A bit of a 'wide boy', as Kavanagh liked to call him, he had been at River Court for twenty years and had learned long ago how to keep his barristers happy at the same time as making them pay their way. Like all senior clerks at chambers, it was his job to assign cases to individuals – he could make or break careers

– and to keep the money rolling in to the chambers coffers.

As was the case in most chambers, each of the thirty-three barristers at River Court was self-employed, but they paid a percentage of their earnings to the clerks and towards their rent and administrative costs. Gone were the days when the clerks earned a fixed-rate percentage of ten per cent per case. With a current average annual income of £4–5 million coming into the chambers, that would have been a ridiculous sum of money to have paid out to someone who was basically untrained and who acted as a conduit for the work that came in through the solicitors. Nowadays, people like Tom Buckley were on a fixed income, with a bonus scheme topping up their salaries, capped at one to two per cent. Even taking into account the capping system, a good senior clerk could earn around £70–80,000 with bonuses, so it was worth his while keeping the work coming in.

Kavanagh, with his unrivalled reputation for success (the Jackson case notwithstanding), was one of those who was actively sought out by clients by name, and was thus consistently one of the chambers' highest earners. Buckley intended to keep things that way, despite Kavanagh's irritating habit of occasionally allowing his high moral principles to get in the way.

The chain-smoking senior clerk and father of two could spot a spanner in the works at five hundred paces, and when he first caught sight of the congenial Paddy Spence with his shock of white hair heading for Kavanagh's door, tatty briefcase in hand, his raincoat hanging off his shoulders, his heart sank. Spence, one of Kavanagh's oldest friends from his university days in Nottingham, was a low-grade legal aid lawyer who had never lost touch with his working-class Ulster roots, but never rose much above them either. Now here he was in River Court, looking like a man with a favour to ask, and Tom Buckley knew what favours meant. After Kavanagh's door closed behind his guest, Tom hovered anxiously out in the corridor like an expectant father, lighting one cigarette from another.

James Kavanagh was genuinely pleased to see Paddy. It had been years since they had last met – and got howling drunk together – although they had stayed in touch through Christmas cards and the odd letter ever since. It didn't matter what mission had suddenly brought Paddy to his door, he would always be welcome. Kavanagh shook his hand warmly and invited him to sit down. Ten minutes and a cup of coffee later, however, he was no longer in the dark as to the purpose of the visit.

'A private prosecution – for murder?' He tried not to sound too incredulous as he sat facing the man from whom he had been virtually inseparable in his youth. They had shared a small flat together, laughed and joked together, even got laid together, and then gradually drifted apart as Kavanagh's career took him to London and greatness and Paddy stayed at the grubbier end of the market.

Paddy, thick-set and white-haired with a drinker's nose and a full mouth, smiled. 'Aye. And I want you to do it for free.' His large green eyes twinkled with the innate charm of the Irishman, and the quiff he had always sported flopped forward on to his forehead. When he was younger he had looked like Cliff Richard, now he more closely resembled Val Doonican, Kavanagh thought, as he basked in the winsome company of his companion.

Kavanagh scoffed. 'Do you, now?' He knew what Lizzie would say. Not to mention Tom Buckley. He shifted uncomfortably in his chair at the very thought.

Paddy decided it was time to lay it on thick. 'What are old friends for?' he grinned. 'Especially if they're loaded.' The Londonderry brogue was still there, even broader if

141

that were possible, but then that might just have been for effect. Paddy Spence knew only too well how to beguile someone like Kavanagh, or to prick his conscience. He was well aware how much a leading Q.C. earned, especially one as sought-after as James Kavanagh. A gentle reminder of his good fortune couldn't hurt.

It was Kavanagh's turn to grin. There had always been something about Paddy that made him go soft in the head. No matter how much he tried to resist his blasted lovableness, he never could. 'You always were a cheeky sod,' he laughed.

'Ay, but irresistible with it.' Paddy beamed and Kavanagh couldn't disagree.

'Well, Ellen certainly seemed to think so – among others. How is she, by the way?' Kavanagh remembered Paddy's common-law wife with great affection. Pretty, feisty and with infinite patience, she had put up with a good deal, not least Paddy's refusal to tie the knot. No matter who he had spent the night with or what state he was in when he got home, she was always there in the morning to give him an aspirin and cook him her famous Belfast fry.

Paddy gulped from his coffee mug. 'Parted company six years ago,' he said, his eyes noticeably duller now. The pain of their separation still stung badly, although he hated to admit it, least of all to James, who had nagged him to marry Ellen for years. Now she was some other man's wife, cooking him breakfast, and Paddy was left alone to buy a bacon roll at the local café.

Kavanagh frowned. 'Oh. Sorry to hear that.' He was genuinely sad for his friend. After his own near-miss with Lizzie, he knew how easily a relationship could fall apart.

Paddy started to explain. 'A brief indiscretion . . .' he

142

said, then, waving his hand dismissively, he added: 'Ah, what the hell, that's all history now.' Kavanagh could see him struggling inwardly and wished he knew more, but he didn't press. Ellen had endured Paddy's philandering for so many years, he wondered what had been different about the last affair. Maybe it was just the final straw for a woman who wanted nothing more than to be a wife and mother.

Paddy saw Kavanagh's mind ticking over, and interrupted him, dragging him back to the question in hand. Would he or would he not take on this case for free? That was all he wanted to know. He turned on the charm once again and leaned forward in his seat.

'So . . . how about it? I know it's been a long time and I wish I had a nice fat fee to offer you, Jim, I really do. But my client has lost his job. All of his redundancy money has gone on one of the witnesses – to pay her relocation expenses after the trial. If we get that far, that is.' He looked at his old friend and knew from the expression on his face that he had already won the battle. Kavanagh indicated that he should go on.

'Now the suspect is a nasty piece of goods – from a family of villains. But the police, they don't want to know.' Paddy had the bit between the teeth and the fire was back in his eyes. The years fell off him momentarily and he looked like the ardent young lawyer Kavanagh had first seen in a punch-up in a student bar all those years before – a fight that had apparently started over Paddy's fervent views about civil rights in Northern Ireland.

Kavanagh sighed. 'All right, Paddy. I get the picture. Why don't you start at the beginning.' He picked up a pad and pen and started taking notes. God knew how he would explain this to Tom and Lizzie.

*   *   *

The picture Paddy Spence painted was certainly a bleak one. Graham Foster, a seventeen-year-old 'likely lad', who had been in trouble with the police before, had attended an all-night rave party in an old disused factory in south London with his girlfriend Hazel Dwyer, a young woman from the same council block in the East End.

The couple were young and in love; it was generally agreed that they were the best thing that had happened to either one. Both had survived unhappy childhoods and had got into trouble in the past, but now they had big plans for their future together and hoped to put their sadness behind them. As they emerged from the factory at around 7 a.m. hand in hand, life felt good. Hazel was black and nineteen, two years older than the white Graham Foster, but the age difference had never bothered her. He was tall, handsome and looked older than his years. He had the finely chiselled features of a model, she always claimed, and together they made a great team. She wore her Afro hair closely clipped and chose her clothes carefully. Dressed that morning in tight tiger-print trousers and a black leather jacket, she flung her arms around her 'toy boy', as she jokingly liked to refer to him, and gave him a long, lingering kiss.

Seconds later, walking along a deserted pavement, the couple heard the sound of a car accelerating near by. As they turned and looked in surprise, they saw a gaudy electric-blue Ford Escort mount the pavement at speed and almost hit them. Before they could even catch their breath, the car screeched to a halt, and the driver leapt from his seat and started running towards them. It was Ian Vincent, a local villain and teenage boxing champion, someone they knew was not a man to be messed with.

'Graham!' Hazel shrieked hoarsely when she realised that Vincent was waving a handgun at them. Vincent, his flattened face contorted with rage, ignored her and shouted at Graham Foster: 'Right. Get in!' He indicated the car with the gun.

Graham, scared witless and unable to comprehend what was going on, put one of his arms in the air and tried to keep hold of Hazel with the other. If Vincent wanted money, he could take his wallet, he still had forty pounds in it. He hoped to God he didn't want to get him out of the way so he could harm Hazel in some way.

But Vincent didn't seem to respond to Graham's gesture of compliance. If anything, he looked even more angry. Running round towards them from the driver's side, he thrust the pistol into Graham's ashen face and shouted at him again: 'Get in! Get in the car now!' His expression was nothing short of murderous.

Hazel Dwyer had never been so frightened in her life. Clinging to her boyfriend and cowering, she did all she could to prevent Vincent from grabbing him and taking him from her. 'Graham! Graham!' she yelled hysterically as she struggled with the gunman.

Both hands in the air now, and frozen to the spot with terror, Graham Foster allowed himself to be dragged at gunpoint towards the car, as Hazel tried to fight Vincent off. Vincent turned the gun on the wailing young woman briefly and shouted: 'You, bitch, shut up!' Hand to her mouth, she faltered just long enough for Vincent to manhandle Graham Foster into the driver's seat and then kick him roughly across into the passenger seat with his foot.

As Vincent jumped into the driver's seat, slammed the door and gunned the powerful engine, spinning the wheels, Graham Foster, wide-eyed and looking like the frightened young teenager that he was, faced his girlfriend through the passenger window, his sweaty hands pressed against the glass, and mouthed her name. Hammering on the outer side of the window with her palms, tears and mascara running down her face, Hazel called out Graham's name once more before the car, and its occupants, sped off down the empty street, sending litter and fallen leaves flying into the air.

Three miles away and two hours later in a Docklands bombsite under a rusting steel bridge, Ian Vincent slammed his fist once more into Graham Foster's face. The teenager was on his knees, slumped forward in front of Vincent's car, his wrists tied with rope to the tow-hitch. There was no longer anything recognisable about his once-fine features; they had been beaten to a pulp. Blood matted his shoulder-length brown hair and the white linen shirt Hazel had bought him for his seventeenth birthday was stained crimson. Fragments of teeth and smashed bone filled his mouth cavity and his eyelids had long ago been squeezed shut by the grotesque swelling from his shattered nose and cheekbones.

'Don't mess me about!' Vincent shouted at him for the last time, his heavy-lidded eyes wild, a note of hysteria in his voice. 'Where's the case?' He lifted Graham's drooping head by his hair and went to hit him again but stopped himself when he looked into the battered face and realised that the teenager could no longer hear a word he was saying.

'A week later his body was fished out of the Thames,' Paddy Spence told Kavanagh. 'The autopsy showed that he'd been tortured and beaten to death. Three of his fingers were broken – bent back.' He held up his own fingers and bent them backwards, indicating how it must have been done.

Kavanagh winced. 'Do we know why?' He had been appalled by the story of this brutal murder, which appeared so far to be without motive.

'For stealing a briefcase from a car,' Paddy answered

146

with a shrug. 'It belonged to the thug with the gun – Ian Vincent.'

Kavanagh still couldn't fathom how such a simple theft could lead to such a tragic end. He was confused. 'Why aren't the CPS dealing with this?' Like most lawyers and many police officers, he was no great fan of the bean-counting civil servants who ran the Crown Prosecution Service, but it did, at least, still largely serve its purpose in that those who committed the most heinous crimes – where there was a good percentage chance of success – were pursued through the criminal courts in the public interest. The trouble was that, if a case looked in any way doubtful or fell below the estimated success rate, then it was dropped on the grounds of being too expensive to pursue.

Spence explained the CPS's decision to shelve this case. 'The girlfriend – Hazel Dwyer – was intimidated into withdrawing her witness statement. The police had to release Vincent without charge.' He waved his hands helplessly. It was an all-too-familiar scenario to him, a legal aid lawyer whose low-profile cases often fell through the CPS net, but it had still been very hard to tell Graham Foster's father that his son's murderer had been set free. When George Foster had asked what could be done next and Paddy had explained that the only possible way forward was a massively expensive private prosecution for murder with a slim chance of success, he had never for one minute expected the man to take the suggestion up.

Everything was becoming clear to Kavanagh, and the clearer it became, the less inclined he felt to take on the case. 'This Hazel was the only witness?' he asked, already suspecting the answer.

'Aye. She knew Vincent because she'd worked for his stepfather – bloke called Ron Babb. Runs this aggregates

147

company on the river but his real game is crime – protection mostly. It was his heavies that scared the wee girl off.' Paddy remembered how terrified Hazel had been when he first met her at George Foster's flat. She couldn't stop shaking as she described how Babb's henchmen had manhandled her and she wept when she told Paddy and George that she was too afraid to testify.

Kavanagh peered at his old friend over his spectacles and stopped taking notes. Whichever way he went in this one, it was not going to be easy. But before he made his final decision, he needed to know everything. 'Why did Graham steal the case?' he asked.

Spence shrugged again. 'Apparently, he'd steal anything.' He registered the look on Kavanagh's face and knew it wasn't sounding too good. The one hope they had of success was if the jury sympathised with the murdered teenager, did not think of him as a low-life toerag who deserved all he got, or who could have been killed by any one of his criminal associates. The theatrical machinations that counsel for both sides would deploy to portray their own client as the innocent victim in this case would rely heavily on the background and character of those involved.

'But to kill him, though.' Kavanagh threw his pen on the desk in exasperation and folded his hands together to form a pyramid. Graham Foster hadn't been much younger than Matt, for God's sake. And he now knew that even Matt wasn't above stepping on the wrong side of the law occasionally. What if it had been him who had stolen a briefcase and then suffered such a severe punishment? Wouldn't he and Lizzie pursue the killer through every court in the land? Time and again, Kavanagh had come across villains like Vincent who viewed life so cheaply, as a mere commodity in other people to be used and disposed of, like so much rubbish. He loathed and detested such men

– and they generally were men. He had seen the anguish their callousness caused, he had grieved with the families of the victims and raged at the legal system that sometimes let these people off scot-free.

Paddy Spence had already filled him in on Graham's father, George. Divorced with a long-standing drink problem, he had been made redundant earlier in the year, and now this – his only son brutally murdered. His first reaction had been to get blind drunk, but then on the night Vincent was released by the police, he had watched him and Babb swagger into his local pub on the Isle of Dogs and order champagne 'to toast the Old Bill'.

Staggering to his feet, George Foster had thrown a punch at the man who had killed his son, but was unceremoniously ejected from the pub and tossed into the gutter by Babb's laughing henchmen. Lying there in the rain, his heart all but broken, he vowed to fight back. The following morning, he had presented himself at Paddy Spence's office door, an envelope in his hand containing all the money he had in the world – his redundancy pay-off – demanding justice.

Spence watched his friend's face carefully. 'My guess is that there was something in the briefcase that incriminated Babb or Vincent in some way. Something that Vincent was desperate shouldn't get out.' He paused and raised his right eyebrow. 'I don't know about you, but I can't stomach seeing an arrogant sod get away with murder.'

Kavanagh rested his chin on his hands and closed his eyes against the charm offensive. Whichever way he jumped, this was going to be tough.

Tom Buckley's face twisted into a grimace and he groaned aloud. 'Oh, not another freebie, Mr Kavanagh, please!' He had been waiting in his office with a sense of foreboding ever since he had seen Paddy Spence leave with a smile

149

on his face. Now his highest-earning Q.C. had sauntered in, casual as you like, to tell him that his worst fears had come true.

Kavanagh played with his tie defensively. 'I don't do that many,' he moaned pitifully. He liked Tom but, like all barrister's clerks, the man was naturally obstreperous and Kavanagh knew how difficult he could make his life if he so chose. It wouldn't do to get on the wrong side of him, or he could end up with an 'In' tray full of family law trials at Birmingham Crown Court, or pleading personal injury cases at the High Court.

Tom pulled in frustration on the bright red braces criss-crossing his tailor-made Pinks shirt and stuck out his bottom lip. 'You're gonna bankrupt us, sir,' he said, getting up from his desk and staring angrily at the large multicoloured wall chart that told him which of the barristers at River Court were covering what cases at any one time. The listings chart filled one huge wall of the administrative clerks' office which was the nerve centre of the chambers. Next to the wooden floor-to-ceiling shelving in which each barrister had his own pigeonhole for post and new cases, the wall chart was the focus of most attention in the chambers. Looking up at it now, Tom sighed out loud. There were at least three 'Big Fives' lined up for Kavanagh – cases that earned the chambers at least a five-figure sum – and here he was telling him he was going to waste his time instead on a no-hoper. He didn't know why he bothered sometimes.

Turning round to chastise Kavanagh some more, the man who could so easily have become an East End barrow-boy like his father and grandfather before him stopped himself mid-sentence when he saw the look on the senior counsel's face. It was that of an anxious young schoolboy waiting outside the headmaster's study to be caned. Tom knew that feeling only too well from his youth, and he still hated to see it in others.

He softened and sighed heavily again. 'All right,' he conceded. 'But no junior . . . sorry. Not from River Court anyway.' Walking back to his desk, he reached for his cigarettes and lit one.

Kavanagh rolled his eyes. He knew how difficult a case could be without the support and advice of a junior counsel. He had come to rely on Charles Beaufort a great deal in the past year and had been looking forward to having his back-up on this one. It didn't have to be Charles, even. There was Helen Ames – she was infinitely capable as a junior even if her specialisation was fast becoming commercial law – not to mention several others in the chambers who would be perfectly suited to the job. He tried plea-bargaining.

'But think of the kudos,' he pointed out, 'for the chambers. There have only been four private prosecutions for murder in the past century. It's a little piece of history.' He raised his thick white eyebrows hopefully. He knew that, above all, Tom was intensely proud of River Court and its illustrious client list. A win like this would be one in the eye for the rival chambers, not to mention Buckley's fellow members of the Association of Senior Clerks among whom competition was intense.

Tom wasn't going to be swayed. 'Yeah?' he said with a sneer, exhaling a lungful of smoke. 'And how many of them were won . . . sir?' He scowled at Kavanagh, before adding, more softly: '. . . with respect.'

Kavanagh knew he would have to go this one alone. 'All right,' he acquiesced. 'Just look as it as a . . . a loss leader, then. It'll bring in work later.' He reached into his pigeonhole for his post and made to leave.

Tom, sitting back at his desk, looked up at him

151

disparagingly. 'If you say so, sir,' he said. As the door closed behind Kavanagh, the senior clerk turned to his young assistant Gary with a pained expression and threw a folder across the desk. 'God save us from silks with a social conscience,' he muttered under his breath.

In the members' bar at the Beerbohm Club, Jeremy Aldermarten, Q.C., was in his element. Impeccably dressed in a black suit and yellow tie, he was mingling ingratiatingly with the great and the good, the very men whose company he hoped soon to be joining. The bar was packed after a members' meeting and a social event, and thick cigar smoke created a layer of grey fog which hovered just above the heads of those assembled. Jeremy inhaled deeply and closed his eyes. This was so . . . so him, he thought. A last bastion of male supremacy.

Huge wall mirrors behind the bar reflected the tasteful glow of the gold-leaf lights against the dark green walls, and row upon row of single-malt bottles gleamed on the counter below. White-uniformed waiters scurried to and from their charges with silver salvers laden with cut-crystal tumblers and plates of nuts, and several of the heavy leather seats had been pulled around one end of the room where a chess tournament was being played.

Chatting to a senior government official while watching over one of the on-going games, Aldermarten chortled a little too loudly, incurring a black look from one of the players. Lowering his voice only fractionally, he chatted idly to his companion about the fate of one of the club members who had recently been ousted from a top government post. 'But, you know, with respect, Michael,' Aldermarten prattled on, 'the fact that one works at the Treasury doesn't necessarily mean that one's totally *au fait* with what's going on out there in the real world, does it?'

He snorted through his nose so stridently that he was led gently away from the players to another table. Carrying on with his conversation undaunted, he continued: 'Well, I mean, you know, take the ordinary chap on less than, say, forty thou a year . . .' Several heads looked up simultaneously, all with less than approving expressions on their faces. Impervious to all, Aldermarten took a swig of his twenty-year-old Laphroaig and carried on talking.

Peter Foxcott weaved his way towards Aldermarten with his friend and fellow committee member Sir Geoffrey Pack-Martin. 'Jeremy,' Peter said, grabbing his elbow and moving him still further away from the throng.

Sir Geoffrey, a rotund Toad-like figure in tweed three-piece and cravat, took the other elbow and smiled, showing the large gap between his front teeth. 'Sorry to have abandoned you for so long. You know committees.'

Aldermarten was positively beaming. 'Oh, no, no, not at all, Geoffrey,' he simpered, his head bobbing from side to side as he spoke. 'I admire your devotion to duty. And somebody's got to run the place.'

One of the chess players near him hissed: 'Ssshhh!'

'Sorry,' Aldermarten guffawed, as Peter Foxcott led him still further away.

'Something to show you,' said the older man, smiling. To the members near by, he enquired: 'Don't mind if we borrow him for a few minutes, do you, gentlemen?' Several members shook their heads a little too vigorously.

They led Aldermarten into the opulent surroundings of the club library, where his mouth fell open on to what little chin he had and he marvelled at the hundreds of immaculate leather-bound volumes stacked floor to ceiling on mahogany shelves. Bronze statues of great literary figures on marble columns adorned each end of the room, and the huge overhead chandelier was the finest he had ever seen, its crystal droplets forming a cascade of glass over fifteen feet high.

Led speechlessly to a highly polished walnut table in the centre of the room, Aldermarten followed his companions' gaze as they pointed triumphantly to what it was they were so keen to show the prospective new member. 'There we are,' said Sir Geoffrey. 'First on the list.' He held up a white piece of paper embossed with the club's distinctive heraldic trefoil, under which was typed 'New Members' Election List', followed by a short line of names, freshly submitted after the recent committee meeting.

Aldermarten blushed and stood, Prince Charles-style, hands held behind his back, looking down at it like a proud father. 'Ahhhh – at last,' he said. He was almost too overwhelmed to speak.

Sir Geoffrey saw the tearful expression on his face and offered some caution. 'The election's still some way off,' he reminded him, with a sideways glance at Foxcott.

But Aldermarten could not be swayed from his moment of glory. 'No, no, no . . . No matter,' he sighed, blinking hard. 'The end is in sight.' Grinning confidently at the two men who had nominated and seconded him, he basked vaingloriously in their vote of approval.

At Babb Aggregates, Ron Babb stepped purposefully out of the dirt-stained Portakabin set high between the vast conveyor belts that carried sand and gravel to the hungry concrete mixers and started walking down the wrought-iron steps to his car, a manila envelope gripped firmly in his hand, his black Armani suit hidden by a full-length camel overcoat.

He had just spent the previous five minutes combing out his lank, dark hair, slicked back with Brylcreem, so that it clung to his temples and deftly covered the small monk's ring he was developing on the top of his pate. He was proud of the grey hairs that gave his sideburns a distinguished air, and had instructed his hairdresser only that morning to cut them so that they were shown off to the best advantage.

His heavily cratered face, pocked with ancient acne marks and several other indiscernible scars, was an unpleasant sight at the best of times, but looked particularly menacing today. He had the appearance of a man with a grievance.

Scurrying down the steps after him, Ian Vincent tried in vain to get his stepfather's attention. 'I can sort it myself, Ron,' the square-faced young man with the cropped haircut insisted. With his boxer's face, scarred lip and broken nose from many a teenage fight, he looked more than capable of 'sorting' anyone. He wore a silvery grey suit, two-tone in its nap, over a black collarless shirt. He had seen John Travolta wearing a similar outfit in *Pulp Fiction* and modelled himself on his hero.

Behind him his mother Shirley followed, buxom, over-dressed and completely out of place on a works site in six-inch-high stilettos, a jungle print dress and heavy gold jewellery. 'Mutton dressed as leopard,' was how the lads at Babbs often described her behind her back. Her peroxide blond hair and bright red lipstick were the only outstanding features of an otherwise hardened face.

Babb turned on the bottom step and snarled at his stepson. 'What, like you sorted Graham Foster? Look, Tarantino, the last thing I need right now is the police round here again. So you want to get off this summons . . .' He waved the manila envelope in his face. '. . . you do exactly what I say, right?' He waited for an answer but Vincent turned away, his jaw clenched in frustration. Ron Babb slapped him hard on the side of his head to make him face him. It worked. 'Right?' Babb repeated.

Vincent, crimson, nodded. 'Right.'

Babb moved his face a few inches from his stepson's. 'Good,' he sneered. 'And for now that's nothing. Just leave it to me. Now get back in your kennel and get on with some work.' He turned on his bespoke heel and stepped down into the passenger seat of his chauffeur-driven Jaguar before speeding off.

Vincent stood watching the man he hated more than anyone else, his face still red and smarting from the slap. His mother, in a camel coat similar to her husband's, only trimmed with mink, sidled up beside him. 'He's right, you know, Ian,' she said in the Cockney twang she had never lost from her barmaid days.

'Shouldn't talk to me like that,' her son sulked. 'Dad wouldn't have.' He closed his eyes and wished for the thousandth time that his father were still alive, that his mother had never married Ron Babb and that he, not Babb, were running the family business.

Shirley Babb had heard it all before. 'Maybe so,' she said. 'But if it wasn't for Ron, all this'd be gone by now . . .' She waved her jewel-encrusted hand at the vast works around them. '. . . and you'd be on remand. Just you remember that.' She poked him in the ribs with a false red fingernail and then turned and climbed precariously back up the steps as her son stood at the bottom watching her.

By the time Ron Babb and his gorilla-faced driver Charlie had pulled up outside George Foster's council flat on a sprawling estate on the Isle of Dogs, the sun had come out and it was an unusually warm November day. Without seeming to notice the weather, the two men pulled on black leather gloves and, still in their overcoats, climbed the urine-scented stairs to the first-floor landing of the ten-storey block.

Looking around furtively as they approached the door to

flat number 22, Babb flanked his burly companion while he undid his overcoat and kicked in the front door with a size 12 shoe. The single door lock flew off its fixings and the two men quickly burst through into the shabby hallway. All was silent as they made their way stealthily into the lounge and on into the bedroom.

The flat was airless and stank of stale food and booze. The 1960s lounge suite was dirty and torn and an antiquated television rested on a pile of old magazines in a corner. In the bedroom, the bed was made up with a threadbare candlewick bedspread and there were a few insignificant personal effects around, but something wasn't right. Yanking open a door on the melamine wardrobe, Babb's face fell as his sudden action rattled the empty wire coat hangers on the rail. Pulling off each finger of his right glove with his teeth, he scowled.

At the very second that the two men were searching his flat, George Foster was trudging through Wanstead cemetery, a battered leatherette suitcase in his hand. Wiry, goggle-eyed and thin as a rake, he had his mouth clamped tightly shut as he stopped on a path and set his suitcase down. Hands in the pockets of his tan leather jacket, the unemployed print worker looked around and listened to a robin singing as the winter sunshine beat down upon his back. Half his family were buried in this cemetery – his mum and dad, his grandfather and his younger sister, Mary, who had died of leukaemia all those years ago. He had bought his own plot when he was still working and flush with cash, never expecting that it would be used for anyone else. Now here he was once again, to pay his respects to the dead.

Stepping forward slightly, he blinked back the tears as he knelt in front of a newly placed tombstone adorned with fading flowers.

Graham John Foster
Born 23rd April 1978
Died 15th October 1995

A few inches above the inscription, a photograph of Graham smiling out of an oval frame had been set into the stone. It had cost him an arm and a leg to have that done, far more than he could afford to spend, but it was worth it, he thought now, as he reached into his jacket pocket and pulled out a half-bottle of whisky.

The ground was cold and damp, despite the sunshine, and it created a seeping wet patch on each knee. As he sat back on his heels, staring at the inscription, a cloud passed in front of the sun, momentarily diminishing the glare. The grey granite tombstone was highly polished, just the way he'd asked it to be, but in the bright light, he realised for the first time that it acted like a mirror and he could see his own skeletal features reflected in it. The bottle cap unscrewed and the contents halfway to his lips, he stopped and studied his image, adjacent to that of his son's, and faltered. Swallowing hard, he lowered the bottle, replaced the cap and let it fall to the soft earth as he covered his face with his hands and sobbed.

11

Ron Babb carefully parted the folds of his £800 camel coat and made himself comfortable on the edge of Paddy Spence's worn wooden desk. He smiled down at the Irish lawyer sitting stiffly behind it, revealing two gold teeth glinting at the back of his mouth.

'I'm a businessman, Mr Spence,' he said, his south London accent whining. 'All I want is a bit of peace and quiet.' He twirled his heavily engraved white-gold wedding ring around his finger and surveyed the run-down office from which the lawyer conducted his business. The only chair other than Paddy's rickety Edwardian leather-and-wooden swivel one was orange, plastic and cracked. The desk, which was disappearing under a mound of files and papers, was propped up with old books, and a single certificate of legal practice hung at an angle on the wall, the glass cracked. A metal coatrack stood in the corner by the door, a dirty white raincoat and a broken umbrella hanging from a hook. Even the name stencilled on the glass panel of the door was in need of some attention. 'ATRICK SPENCE, LAWYE,' it read.

Ron Babb turned to Spence and appealed to his sense of decency. 'I don't need all this aggravation – a trial, the media. Who would? Not George, I'm sure ...' He paused meaningfully. 'Not if there was an alternative.' His Bermondsey drawl with its prolonged vowels and twangy sound might once have charmed the likes of Shirley Vincent when she was recently widowed and financially flush from her husband's hefty life insurance policies, but it did nothing to mask its threatening intent to Paddy Spence, born and bred in Bogside.

'What exactly are you saying?' Paddy asked, eyeing Babb carefully while keeping a watch on his visitor's 'driver', who stood cracking his knuckles by the door. Paddy tried to keep his voice level, not to sound as intimidated as he felt.

Ron Babb levered himself off the desk and walked a few paces away, before spinning round to face the lawyer. 'George should be compensated, financially,' he announced with a nod, adding, with a raised forefinger, 'Not that I think he's justified ... don't get me wrong. But as a businessman ...' He smiled again, the smile of a crocodile. '... well, let's just say, jaw-jaw is better than war-war.'

Spence, sweating in his seat in shirtsleeves and tie, stared Babb out. He already knew what George Foster's response would be. He swallowed hard and asked: 'And if he rejects your offer?'

Babb tossed his head back and laughed. 'Persuade him,' he suggested, the smile suddenly wiped off his lips. Moving closer to the desk, he raised an eyebrow and added: 'Hey, nice little commission in it for you, as well. He can even name 'is price ... within reason. Now what with that and his redundancy money, he can drown his conscience till the millennium comes, if he likes ... as long as his liver lasts.' It seemed that everyone knew about George Foster's drink problem.

Spence sat up in his revolving chair with sudden deliberation. 'I doubt if he'd be interested, Mr Babb,' he said in his Ulster brogue, as casually as he could, 'and, er, I'm certainly not – with or without commission.' He tried not to appear unduly concerned and made as if to start on some important paperwork on his desk.

Something flickered across Ron Babb's eyes and he inhaled deeply. His driver, Charlie, took two paces closer. Leaning forward over the lawyer's desk so that he was virtually head to head, Ron Babb said quietly: 'You got a family, Mr Spence?'

The lawyer looked up and met the steely gaze.

'Only if you have, you'll understand the sort of emotions that get stirred up when this sort of thing happens. On both sides.' Babb moved his head even closer, so close that Spence could feel the heat of his breath and smell the neat Scotch that Babb had downed at lunch-time. 'George has lost a son. My wife stands to lose hers. Me, a stepson. It'd be a shame to see anybody else get hurt here. Wouldn't it?'

Spence swallowed hard and nodded in agreement. 'Especially if one of them is a professional man – with friends at Scotland Yard,' he said, standing up defiantly. Babb's face fell as the lawyer walked around his desk and opened the door. 'Good day to you, Mr Babb,' he said, looking straight ahead of him as Babb and his companion left without another word.

Closing the door behind them, Spence went back round to his desk and sat down hard, exhaling, he felt, for the first time in several minutes.

James Kavanagh stopped in his tracks, his mouth falling open. 'How much?' He could hardly believe what he had just heard from Jeremy Aldermarten as the two of them walked into River Court with Peter Foxcott.

'Seven hundred pounds a year,' Aldermarten repeated, proudly, as if he had just announced the weight of his firstborn son. He flicked the tip of his umbrella up in front of him to emphasise the point. His raincoat was buttoned up to his neck.

Foxcott, close behind in a mackintosh and spotted bow tie, corrected him. 'Six hundred and ninety-six, to be exact. Plus VAT, of course,' he said, with a smile. Kavanagh was still unimpressed.

Aldermarten snorted nasally. 'Minus, praise be, *les femmes*.' He cocked his head and grinned knowingly at Peter Foxcott, who had collected a newspaper from the hall table and was following the pair absent-mindedly.

Kavanagh turned to face Aldermarten with a frown. 'You're a single man, Jeremy, and you've waited *seven* years to join a club with no women?' The more he came to know Aldermarten, the less he understood him. He was not blessed with good looks, natural charm or even professional brilliance, and yet he was probably the perfect Mr Right for someone somewhere. A wealthy, eligible bachelor barrister, newly accepted as a Q.C., with an elegant London townhouse and innate good taste in music, food and wine, and yet he seemed ruled by snobbery and a disturbingly competitive streak. Kavanagh shook his head in wonderment.

Aldermarten gave him his most patronising sneer. 'We're not all governed by our groins, James,' he said, wishing secretly that his groin had even a small part to play in his life. 'And the Beerbohm does have other attractions.'

Kavanagh, briefcase in hand, raincoat undone, stood his ground. 'Such as?' This he had to hear.

Peter caught up with them and answered for his companion happily. 'Oooh, two dining rooms, bar, reading room, television room, billiard room, card room, library. Excellent conversation.' Kavanagh thought of Peter's dowdy wife Eleanor, sitting at home with her gardening books and bridge parties, and had no doubt that the conversation at the Beerbohm would be preferable.

Aldermarten nodded enthusiastically. 'Contacts – especially in this business. Its reputation, of course.' Pulling himself up to his full six feet one inch, he added: 'Frankly, James, I'm honoured that Peter consented to put my name down.'

'All those years ago,' Peter reminded everyone, including, it seemed, himself. Not for the first time he wondered at the different opinion he had now to the one he had then of Jeremy Aldermarten. At first acquaintance a charming and able man, he seemed perfectly suited as the new junior at River Court. Latterly regarded as something of a prat, which several colleagues had openly called him, he could be insufferably overbearing, had an unfortunate manner with women and was constantly putting his foot in it. Still, Foxcott thought charitably, he didn't really mean anything by it and he did have some good qualities – he just couldn't think of one right now.

Kavanagh sighed and nodded sagely. 'Well,' he said, with some reluctance, 'I suppose these clubs have one thing going for them.'

Both Peter and Aldermarten were taken aback. Aldermarten tilted his head, waiting for the rare compliment. 'Mmm?' he said. This he was going to enjoy, coming from his arch rival and the man he envied most.

Kavanagh squared up to him and wrinkled his nose. 'Keeps a lot of old farts off the streets.' Peter Foxcott laughed aloud as Kavanagh turned on his heel and headed for his office, shaking his head in wonder at the enduring appeal of gentlemen's clubs.

Aldermarten watched him go with a rueful look. 'Sad, really,' he told Foxcott, with another tilt of his head. 'Sour

163

grapes . . . He's never been invited to join one, you see.'
Foxcott couldn't help but raise an eyebrow.

Kavanagh looked aghast as Spence sat in his office half
an hour later and recounted the unsettling details of the
visit the previous afternoon by Ron Babb. 'Did you go to
the police?' he asked, genuinely concerned for his friend's
safety. He had read through some of Spence's notes on Ron
Babb and knew he was not a man whose threats should be
taken lightly. Coupled with the report that George's flat
had been broken into but nothing stolen, the visit took on
an even more sinister meaning.

Spence shook his head as George Foster, sitting at his side,
eyed him. 'I find the old "friends at the Yard" line usually
does the trick. It seems to make criminals very nervous
about coming too close – to me or my clients.' Spence
smile reassuringly at George, who looked uncomfortably
out of place in Kavanagh's opulent office in a blue suit
and tie.

'Risky, though, I'd have thought,' Kavanagh remarked,
surprised at the relaxed way in which Spence seemed
to have taken the threat to life and limb. He wasn't
so sure he'd have been so blasé about it, especially
not with the suggestion that family members could be
affected. Kavanagh had experienced something like this
before, when both he and Lizzie had been threatened by
a villain and his thugs, and he knew how frightening it
could be. But then, he reflected, Paddy wasn't married
with kids, and most of his family back home would
give as good as they got to any Johnny-come-lately from
London.

Spence winked. 'As a matter of fact, I do have a friend
at Scotland Yard,' he added. 'Very useful he is too.' When
he gave Kavanagh that leprechaun grin of his, the barrister

relaxed. If Spence was happy, he knew there was nothing to worry about.

Kavanagh sipped from a mug of coffee and turned to his new client, a man who looked, by contrast, as if he had the weight of the world on his shoulders. 'And how are you, Mr Foster? Where are you staying?'

George was clearly nervous. He licked his lips to moisten them and stared, wide-eyed, at the man who was asking him a question. 'I've found a room across town.' He was in awe of the great James Kavanagh; he had heard of him, read about him in newspapers, and now, sitting here facing him – the famous Q.C. who had inexplicably agreed to take on his case without a fee – he found himself quite lost for words. If only he could have a quick nip, he thought, that always seemed to make him relax and loosen his tongue.

Kavanagh tried to put him at his ease. 'And Hazel?' he enquired, offering him a digestive biscuit, which he declined.

George, suspicious of everyone, replied only: 'With a friend. North London somewhere.' He had seen the look of terror in Hazel's eyes after the visit by Babb's men and he wasn't going to tell anyone where she was now, not even his counsel. He wouldn't put it past Babb to try to buy Kavanagh's co-operation. It had even crossed his mind that this might have been the real reason the Q.C. had offered to take the case on without a fee.

Kavanagh saw George's hesitation and decided to get straight to the point. 'So Babb's offer is of no interest?' It was a question that had to be asked even if he suspected he knew the answer.

George Foster's face came alive. His eyes flared and nearly bulged from their sockets. 'You think scum like that can buy me off?' He started trembling, the usual morning shakes he suffered from, and he held his hands in his lap so that no one would see. Regretting his outburst, he drew breath. Looking down, he added softly: 'Was a time maybe I would have. Not now.' Meeting Kavanagh's stare, he added: 'Changes you, something like this.'

Kavanagh nodded. He glanced down at his notes and carried on with the job in hand. 'I'll be wanting the jury to hear evidence about Graham. I take it you'd be happy to describe their relationship?' He had virtually ticked the answer off from his long list of questions when George answered.

'No.' The father of Graham Foster was quite adamant.

Kavanagh looked up in surprise. 'But it's important to build up a picture of what sort of person he was,' he started to explain. He knew only too well that without the sympathy of the jury, the case could be lost.

George's eyelids flickered. Through pursed lips, he told the Q.C.: 'The sort of person Graham was . . . was a liar – and a thief.' Remembering the last time he had seen his son alive, the day before he died, when he caught him and Hazel snorting a finely chopped line of cocaine up their noses, he added: 'He did drugs.' Pausing to compose himself and control the trembling, he said: 'I tried after my wife left, but, well . . . I'm surprised he didn't turn out worse, if you really want to know.' When his eyes met Kavanagh's again, they were full of tears. 'Not much of a character reference, am I?' His shame was almost palpable.

Kavanagh and Spence glanced at each other and looked away in pity and embarrassment. This case was not getting any easier.

Later that evening, as Lizzie took Paddy Spence's coat and hung it up on a hook in the hall of their comfortable Wimbledon home, it was clear she had been fully briefed.

'It all sounds a bit grim from what Jim tells me,' she said, and turned to face the man she had never met but had heard so much about over the years. He looked different to how she'd imagined him – shorter, fatter and far from the demigod her husband had worshipped at university.

'Aye, well, that's the underclasses for you, Lizzie,' Spence beamed. 'They just don't know how to behave themselves.' He handed her a bunch of chrysanthemums bought from a garage forecourt and admired her once again. Simply dressed in a plain black shift with pearls, she really was lovely with those deep blue saucers for eyes, high cheek-bones and that glossy chestnut hair. Those aristocratic good looks he'd only ever seen in photographs had never left her. If only she wasn't his best friend's wife, why, he might have given it a try. He could have done with a bit of upper-class skirt, he thought to himself. Might have helped his career, not to mention his seemingly insatiable libido.

Looking around the elegant Victorian hallway to take his mind off sex, he admired Kavanagh's home even more than he had from its imposing exterior. Everything was in the best possible taste, from the peachy colour-washed walls to the delicate stencilled border above framed black-and-white prints of Lincoln's Inn. An antique mahogany console table adorned with a huge vase of white lilies took centre stage. Lizzie would probably toss his cheap flowers in the bin, he thought.

He followed Lizzie through into the huge open-plan kitchen and breathed in the smell of cooking. The room was huge, and full of expensive bleached oak units with terracotta tiles on the floor. It was clearly the heart of the house and looked like something straight out of a designer homes magazine. Half recognising a pungent aroma, he glanced quizzically at Lizzie and said: 'Mmm, that smells interesting.' He was secretly wondering if they should have met at a restaurant – perhaps with Lizzie's privileged background, she just couldn't cook.

Lizzie shrugged her shoulders as if it were nothing to do with her and led him through to where James, oven glove in hand, was lifting a large earthenware casserole dish out of the oven. 'It's some speciality from the old days, apparently,' she told him. Spence raised his eyebrows and wondered what on earth she could mean.

Kavanagh, dressed casually in a blue cardigan and matching corduroy trousers, greeted his old friend by handing him a Shipstone's pale ale. 'Paddy . . . there you go,' he said, triumphantly, as his friend peered down at the old-style brown glass bottle, trying to decipher the label. 'Oh, don't say you've forgotten.' Kavanagh frowned. 'It's the only stuff we used to drink. It's a pig to find down here as well.' Raising his bottle to his lips, he added: 'Cheers.'

Paddy reciprocated before taking a swig. Distorting his face into a grimace, he nearly spat it straight out. 'Oh God, did we?' he groaned.

Kavanagh sniggered. 'Filthy, isn't it?' He took the bottle from Paddy's hand and replaced it with a wineglass. 'Rioja?'

Paddy smiled with relief. 'That's more like it.' Looking over his friend's shoulder at a steaming hot dish bubbling violently under a lid on top of the green enamel Aga, he asked, somewhat suspiciously, 'Er, what are we having? . . . This smells familiar.'

Lizzie looked similarly intrigued as she stood waiting for her glass to be replenished. 'He's being rather secretive about it,' she confided. Truth was, he'd not let her near the kitchen all evening and she was more than a little put out. She was a wonderful cook, the kitchen was very much her special domain, and she resented not being able to prepare something special for her husband's oldest friend.

Kavanagh poured them all a glass of wine and then lifted the lid of the cast-iron casserole dish with a great flourish. '*Ragout de poisson à la sauce piquante de tomate*,' he said in his best French accent, bowing slightly.

Paddy Spence could hardly believe his ears. Creasing his face up into an expression of horror, he asked: 'Pilchard stew?', peering doubtfully at the simmering tinned food concoction that was all they could ever afford to eat in Nottingham.

'Spot on.' It was Kavanagh's turn to twinkle.

Jeremy Aldermarten browsed absent-mindedly through the leather-bound signing-in book in the cool central lobby of the Beerbohm Club and privately congratulated himself on recognising so many of the celebrated names. There were judge and politicians, peers and princes – even a former prime minister. He was, as ever, impressed. Allowing his fingers to run lovingly over the ink signatures of those he most admired, he was distracted from his devotional task by the sound of footsteps on the marble floor behind him.

'Jeremy Alderman, isn't it?' a clipped voice enquired. The Q.C. turned to face a slim, middle-aged man with a mop of silver-grey hair, who was holding out a thin, bony hand.

'Um, er, Al-Aldermarten,' he stammered, grasping the proffered hand and wishing once again that his palms were not always quite so clammy.

'Oh, I do beg your pardon. Charles Lesser,' his companion announced with a smile. 'I saw you in the dining room earlier with Peter Foxcott and I thought I must say hello. I've heard a lot about you.' He gave the prospective member a curious look.

Aldermarten fiddled with the button of his overcoat and almost blushed. 'Oh, well, really?' His head rotated like a ninepin.

'Mmm, you're quite a presence these days – the talk of the club. And up for membership, too, I see.' Charles Lesser, still smiling, didn't take his eyes off the younger man for a second.

'Yes,' Aldermarten responded, with a sigh and an exasperated roll of his eyes. 'Finally.' He could still hardly believe that after seven long years of waiting he was now top of the list.

Lesser leaned forward conspiratorially. 'So what do you think, then? Fingers crossed?' He watched Aldermarten blush further and make several incomprehensible sounds in his throat. He goaded him further: 'Oh, come now. You can't be expecting any trouble, surely – with your proposer and seconder both on the committee?'

Aldermarten stopped his head mid-roll and tried his best to look serious for a moment. 'Well, that can't hurt,' he admitted, pulling his shoulders back and jutting out his chin. 'Although, you know, of course, one . . . one likes to feel one has something to offer in one's own right.'

'So I've heard,' said Charles Lesser quietly. Beaming at Aldermarten again, he pulled on his distinctive red-and-blue striped club tie and added: 'Sounds like you should start thinking about ordering one of these, then?' He tapped the tie with his long forefinger.

Aldermarten gazed lovingly at the hallowed object of his affections and started to protest. But seeing the open, friendly face above it, he leaned in towards him and whispered: 'Between you and me, it's already in the top drawer.'

Charles Lesser's face fell. 'Is it?' he said. 'Is it really?' Regaining his composure at the sight of Peter Foxcott approaching, he added: 'Well, very good to meet you, Jeremy,' and walked off briskly just as Peter approached from the gents', briefcase in hand.

'Well, well, what a charming chap,' Aldermarten remarked, smug at having made his latest well-placed acquaintance all by himself.

Peter Foxcott frowned. 'Lord Lesser?' he responded. 'Mmm, yes,' he added, unconvincingly. Aldermarten, still flushed after his good lunch and reassurances of success, didn't bat an eyelid.

Kavanagh picked up the ladle and plunged it deep into the still-steaming casserole of oily fish and tomatoes. Swallowing his own mouthful of food, he turned to Paddy Spence and asked him if he would like some more.

Dabbing at his lips hastily with his napkin, Paddy replied: 'Er, no. No, that was . . . er, quite enough, thanks.' Lizzie watched his obvious discomfort and hid behind a candle to conceal a smile.

Kavanagh helped himself to another large ladleful – the fish bones and heads slopping messily on to his empty plate, spattering the green linen tablecloth. 'I haven't had this in thirty years,' he said enthusiastically, sitting down and dipping a large hunk of bread into the vivid sauce.

Lizzie grimaced and gave up trying to swallow her forkful. 'I wonder why,' she teased, pushing her plate away from her. She had found the whole meal quite revolting.

The chirp of Paddy's mobile phone broke the uneasy silence and he reached into his pocket apologetically. 'Oh, that's me. I'm sorry,' he said. 'I . . . I'm on the duty roster. I'll . . . I'll take it outside.' He stood up and fled to the next room, the phone clamped to his ear.

Kavanagh greedily gulped down another spoonful of sauce and looked up at his wife. Her face was like stone. In fact, now he thought about it, she'd been very quiet all evening. 'What's the matter?' he asked.

Lizzie's eyes flashed angrily at her husband. 'I think he's

got a bloody nerve,' she hissed. 'I mean, he hasn't seen you for what? Thirty years or more? He's never offered you work in all that time and he just waltzes in and asks for a favour.' Lizzie had been listening to her husband's conversation with Paddy Spence all evening and was resentful of him putting upon her husband so.

Kavanagh wiped a piece of bread thoughtfully around his plate. 'It's a worthwhile case,' he said. 'Unusual. And we were best mates at Nottingham. The same year.' He remembered his time at university with such affection he found it almost impossible to be objective about his old friend.

'Big deal!' Lizzie scoffed. 'Look what he's landed you with – an alcoholic client.' She knew there were bigger principles involved, and she was secretly quite proud of her husband for taking such a case on, but she couldn't help being piqued about the manner in which it was brought to him. She was also concerned about what losing another case might do to him. She had never seen him so upset as after the Jackson trial. It was as if the verdict had been a personal slight.

Kavanagh sighed and admitted that the Foster job was going to be tough. 'Yup,' he said. 'Precious little hard evidence, and everything riding on one terrified witness.' He knew it didn't look good, but there was something about it that made him feel alive again. At least it wasn't some slippery ambassador and his cronies. These were real people with real problems and he wished Lizzie wouldn't spoil it for him.

Paddy returned to the table and sat down heavily. 'That was Hazel. She's had a bust-up with her friend, she's moving out.' Much as he was reluctant to leave such a beautiful dinner, he told them with feeling, he'd have to go and sort her out.

*　　　*　　　*

An hour later, he was still fighting chronic indigestion when he spotted Hazel Dwyer standing with a rucksack outside King's Cross station. She looked vulnerable and afraid as he grabbed her arm and greeted her. The relief on her face when she saw him made him wish he hadn't stayed for the arctic roll ice-cream dessert, another 'delicacy' from their misspent youth, apparently.

'Is this everything?' he asked, reaching down and picking up the dilapidated suitcase at her side. He felt immensely sorry for the young woman whose life had been shattered by Graham's murder, and who was now being passed from pillar to post as she fled from the villains who were hounding her.

'Yeah.' Hazel nodded, close to tears. 'Sorry about this, Mr Spence. She got scared of having me there.' She didn't elaborate but Paddy knew that the girlfriend Hazel had been staying with was a single mother and he guessed she was as frightened for her child as for herself. Ron Babb's reputation was pretty much London-wide. Paddy patted her shoulder reassuringly and told her not to worry. 'Where are we going?' she asked, anxiously.

'Ah, a friend of mine has a place down here. You can stay there for a few nights. You'll be all right.' Hazel tried to look convinced, but a voice in her head had been screaming at her for days to get out of London and away while she still could.

Kavanagh switched off the bathroom light and climbed into bed next to his wife. She was half propped up on the pillow of their king-size bed and looking up at him with her big blue eyes. Waving his finger at her, he gave her a warning. 'If you say "I told you so . . ."'

Lizzie sighed and flopped her head back on her pillow,

staring up at the ceiling. She loved this room; it was their one softly coloured haven against the world – work, the kids, everything. It was here that she felt closest to James, here that she worried about him the most as she lay awake at nights, and here that they had their most honest conversations. Tonight was no exception. 'It's just that . . . sometimes . . . I mean, I don't know, you just seem to go out of your way to find the maximum aggravation,' she said, staring across at him, her hands folded across her cream silk pyjamas.

If he lost this case too – and the odds were certainly stacked against him – what might this mean for his self-esteem, not to mention his future at River Court? She knew there were plenty of younger barristers waiting to step into the Kavanagh shoes, and none more so than Charles Beaufort. What James needed right then was a dead-cert winner, a high-profile, high-earning criminal case that put him back on the pedestal where he belonged. Not some grubby civil action with no fee and no chance of success – all for the sake of an ancient friendship.

Kavanagh, also lying back, furrowed his forehead in concentration as he tried to remember a line from his university days. ' "For evil to triumph it is sufficient only that good men do nothing," ' he quoted, adding 'Or words to that effect,' before rolling over and turning off the bedside lamp.

Damn him for always being right, Lizzie thought. And how infuriating of him to use a quote from one of her all-time heroes, Edmund Burke, the Irish-born statesman and philosopher, one of the greatest political thinkers of all time, somebody she used to spout quotes from daily in her youth. Duly chastised, she rolled over and enfolded her husband in her arms with a smile. 'And here endeth the first lesson,' she said, before burying her face in his neck.

*   *   *

Having dropped Hazel Dwyer off at an old girlfriend's house in the crummier end of Camden Town, Paddy Spence took a black cab back to his tiny bachelor flat in Rotherhithe and stepped on to the pavement just after midnight. After paying the driver off, he was three paces from his front door when a dark figure suddenly emerged from the shadows. Paddy clutched his hand to his chest and jumped backwards. 'Jesus, you put the heart across me,' he gasped, sighing with relief at the sight of Chris Sampson, an old acquaintance from Criminal Intelligence at Scotland Yard.

Sampson's lip curled. 'Sorry, Paddy. Give you a fright?' Dressed in a shabby leather jacket and jeans, his hair lank and greasy, his thin face unshaven, Sampson looked nothing like the detective chief inspector he was, but just the part for his specialisation, undercover work – deep surveillance, fraternising with the criminal underworld, getting evidence and information to send back to his investigative teams. Originally from the roughest quarter of Manchester, Sampson was one of those men who could have worked well either side of the fence. Paddy was very glad he had chosen the good side.

'I thought you boys knocked off at five?' he quipped, his heart still pounding in his chest. He had been much more disturbed by Babb's visit than he had let on to anyone, least of all Kavanagh, and one minute earlier, when he had first seen the man in the shadows, he had thought his number was up.

Sampson raised an eyebrow. 'Yeah, if only.' His workload was such that he regularly stayed up all night and rarely got a full night's sleep. The cumulative effect showed in his eyes, which were cowled and ringed with deep shadows. Handing the lawyer a large brown envelope, he announced: 'Ron Babb, and all his works.'

Spence was genuinely delighted. 'Oh, great,' he said, taking it from him and slitting open the seal with his finger. 'Any thoughts about the briefcase? What might have been inside it?'

Sampson lit a roll-up and looked indifferent. 'Well, only that you're barking up the wrong tree,' he said in his Northern drawl, the hand-rolled cigarette stuck to his bottom lip. 'Babb keeps Vincent away from all the criminal stuff . . . He's not the brightest of lads, you see.' He winked.

'Oh,' Paddy said with disappointment as he pulled a sheaf of photocopied police files from the envelope and flicked through them casually. If that were true then the motive he and Kavanagh had been working on no longer held water. It would mean a completely new approach, and in a case where they were fast running out of time and information, he couldn't imagine what that could be.

Sampson stuffed his hands into his bomber jacket pocket and looked around warily. 'Careful how you tread, Paddy,' he said. 'You've no idea what you're getting yourself into.' His eyes flashed his old mate a warning as he added: 'And Hazel Dwyer – got a two-year suspended hanging over her, for perjury. Lied for a friend in court and got found out. Word is she'll say anything for a price.' Paddy's face fell as Sampson concluded: 'If you want my advice – forget it.'

Almost as suddenly as the police officer had arrived, he was gone, leaving Paddy alone and shivering in the dark.

12

The morning of the trial dawned all too soon for Ian Vincent and his family. Civil cases take far less time to come to trial than criminal cases, and it seemed only a short while since he had first confronted Graham Foster. Four months had passed and there had been so little time to prepare, he thought, and such sparse encouragement from his mother and stepfather. He had spent the intervening period, especially Christmas, in a sort of limbo, never knowing what was going to happen next, afraid of the knock at the door, the sound of footsteps behind him. If only things had gone differently, he thought, if only his father had never dropped dead of that heart attack five years ago. None of this would ever have happened.

Arriving in a taxi with his mother and Ron Babb at the grand columned entrance of the Inner London Crown Court on a crisp, clear January morning, the young man who felt as if his life were careering out of his control wiped the sweat from his top lip with the back of his hand when he saw the pack of photographers and journalists waiting for him on the court steps. That was all he needed, the bloody press. Well, he wasn't going to let them see his fear.

His lawyer, Michael Pashley, was the first to step out into

the mêlée. Vincent, dressed in a smart double-breasted grey suit and mottled tie, followed purposefully as the flashguns popped and a dozen tape recorders were pushed into his face. 'Anything to say, Mr Vincent?' the hacks shouted. 'Look this way!' He battled his way silently through the crowd as Ron Babb and his wife followed on behind.

In a specially bought designer outfit, six-inch heels and newly coiffeured hair, Shirley Babb looked for all the world like a gangster's moll as she tottered up the steps. 'I can't believe we've come to this,' she told her husband in her nasal whine. Whatever else Ron Babb had been or done, he had always protected her from unwanted intrusions and made sure that she was well looked after. Now here she was being jostled by the media and about to watch her son stand trial for murder. She found it incredible that Ron hadn't done something sooner. The expression on her husband's haggard face, as he elbowed the 'monkeys' and their cameras out of their way and prised reporters' hands off his best suit, said that he could hardly believe it either.

A second black cab pulling up outside the court suddenly diverted the cameramen's attention away from the trio and they were left standing alone on the top step, dusting themselves down. Ian Vincent straightened his tie as he turned and watched Paddy Spence leap from the taxi to herd Hazel Dwyer through the sea of faces and high-tech news-gathering equipment. 'Hazel! Hazel!' the cameramen called, trying to get the chief prosecution witness to lift her head for a photograph. But, turning her face into Paddy's broad shoulder, she allowed him to lead her blindly through the mob. The only time she looked up, her eyes locked on to the stare of Ian Vincent, standing menacingly above her on the steps. His expression was utterly malevolent, and she shuddered under its shadow.

Inside the court, Kavanagh, gowned but with his well-worn wig in his hand, was climbing up the curved stone staircase with George Foster to Court 8 on the first floor. The latter looked even more out of place than he had in Kavanagh's office a few months ago. His beanpole frame was in the same ill-fitting suit, covered this time with a weatherproof jacket. His bulging eyes darted nervously around him. The pair stopped halfway up the stairs when they saw the main double doors swing open downstairs and Vincent and his family rush into the lobby, followed shortly afterwards by a terrified Hazel Dwyer, gripping the arm of Paddy Spence as if her life depended on it.

Ron Babb and his wife strode up to a sharp-faced woman barrister, in her mid-forties, standing waiting for them, her hand outstretched, while Vincent – hands in pockets – stood staring at Hazel Dwyer, willing her to look back at him from the shelter of Paddy's shoulder.

'Who's their brief?' George asked, indicating the barrister, who was patting Shirley Babb's arm and telling her not to worry.

'Susan Craxton, Q.C.,' Kavanagh told him, a flat tone to his voice.

'Any good?' George asked nervously. Something about the strong jaw and large nose on the counsel as she shook Ron Babb firmly by the hand made him suspect that she was.

'Very,' Kavanagh answered, without elaborating further. He didn't want to let George know how many times he had crossed swords with Ms Craxton in the past, not always emerging the victor. She had a formidable reputation in Lincoln's Inn, not least because of the type of hardened criminal she generally defended.

George saw the expression on Hazel's face and became even more worried. 'What happens about her record?

You know – the perjury?' he asked. He was getting last-minute jitters.

'Came as no surprise to the defence,' Kavanagh said, picking his way towards the courtroom door, a bundle of books and papers tucked under his arm.

George was downcast. 'Wish I'd know before I offered her the money,' he commented, ruefully. The closer he got to the court, the more he wondered if he were doing the right thing. Kavanagh knew what he was feeling and sympathised, but there was nothing anyone could do now. 'In God and truth we trust,' he thought to himself as he pushed open the heavy double doors to the court and stepped inside.

Downstairs, Hazel Dwyer had gone a pale shade of green and looked as if she might puke, Paddy thought. Stepping towards the ladies' lavatory, she told the lawyer: 'I've gotta go in here.' Concerned, he held her elbow and asked her if she was okay. 'Feel a bit sick,' she said, swallowing hard and turning the door handle.

Paddy nodded in understanding and patted her arm kindly. 'Well, I'll just be next door,' he said, indicating the witness waiting room a few doors along the corridor. He watched as she grimaced and disappeared behind the frosted glass.

Standing in front of the mirror inside, Hazel leaned over the sink and took several deep breaths. A knot of fear had tightened in her stomach and she could hardly breathe for fear. She looked up and studied her reflection. Slim, pixie-faced, with cropped black hair, large brown almond-shaped eyes and full lips, she had always been a looker, or at least Graham had always told her so. She tried to focus on him now, on what he would have wanted – expected – her to do. She tried not to think what the consequences of that action might be.

'Well, well. Hello, Hazel.' A voice behind her made her jump. Shirley Babb's bright red lips twisted into a smile. Walking towards her, she placed her patent leather handbag on the vanity unit and stared into Hazel's widening pupils. 'Don't worry, I won't bite,' she said.

Hazel grabbed her own bag and made a run for the door, but Shirley was too quick for her. Digging her long red fingernails into Hazel's flesh, she grabbed her arm and yanked her back to the sink, banging her lower back hard against the unit. 'I haven't finished yet,' she hissed. 'How much are you getting . . . "relocation expenses"?' She almost spat the words, and with her face contorted Hazel could see immediately who her son took after.

'None of your business . . .' Hazel started to say, struggling to break free, but before she could finish her sentence Shirley twisted her arm up behind her back and ground one of her six-inch stilettos hard into the toe of Hazel's soft leather shoe. She squealed in pain. 'Five thousand pounds,' she whispered, as Shirley pulled away from her and tutted out loud.

'Ten – if you do the decent thing,' she said, her tone momentarily conciliatory. 'And if you don't. . . .' She squeezed Hazel tightly round the arm again but stopped herself as the door opened and a woman walked into the lavatory. The stranger stopped and stared at the two women by the sink and Shirley Babb released her grip. Seeing her chance to get away, Hazel broke free and fled, Shirley's words still ringing in her ears.

She almost ran straight into Paddy, standing waiting for her at the door. Gasping for breath, she flashed him such a look of panic he wondered what was wrong. 'Are you okay?' he asked, reaching for her. Hazel considered telling him what had happened but she knew there was nothing he could do, so she hung her head and nodded with a sob. Paddy led her gently away as Shirley Babb emerged from the lavatory, a determined look on her face. Her husband might have lost his touch intimidating witnesses, but she certainly hadn't.

Tom Buckley lit another cigarette and carried on inputting case details into the computer records as the Head of Chambers stood by his desk checking through the week's court listings. Tom liked Peter Foxcott. Everybody did – he was an avuncular figure, kind to everyone, even if he wasn't the world's greatest barrister, or one of River Court's highest earners.

Many in the chambers had been surprised a few years earlier when Kavanagh had lost the election for the position and Peter had been nominated instead. Kavanagh was widely believed to have been the best man for the job, and there was disappointment from some quarters when he didn't get it. Tom Buckley was the only one not surprised and Kavanagh was the only one relieved. They both knew that the administrative and financial duties associated with running a leading chambers would simply have been too onerous for someone like Kavanagh. All that paperwork, committee meetings and man management. He couldn't see himself hosting genial chambers dinners or coping with the complicated budgets. Peter Foxcott was perfect for the job – a gentleman in the true, old-fashioned sense of the word, sensitive to the needs of his staff, level-headed and scrupulously fair. And his election left Kavanagh in the amiable position of being the barrister to whom all others deferred, without having any of the responsibilities.

Jeremy Aldermarten popped his head around the office door to see if there was anything in his pigeonhole. Catching sight of Peter Foxcott, he smiled wryly and sneaked up behind him. 'Morning, Peter,' he said with a grin.

Peter Foxcott carried on with his inspection of the files, but raised his head slightly to acknowledge the greeting. 'Jeremy,' he said.

Aldermarten, his raincoat still on, a jaunty red bow tie peering out from under the collar, rounded on him to get his attention and, nervously flapping a newspaper against his side, remarked: 'Big day.'

Peter looked up, his eyebrows knitted into a quizzical frown. Was it? What on earth did he mean? Oh God, it wasn't the VAT trial yet was it?

'The election,' Aldermarten prompted, giving Peter a withering look. How could he have forgotten such a momentous occasion? The election of new members at the Beerbohm Club. The most important day of his life.

Peter suddenly remembered. 'Ah, yes. Lunch-time,' he said, putting down the files and giving Tom Buckley a knowing smile. Heading for his office, he offered nothing further.

Aldermarten shifted his weight awkwardly from foot to foot before calling out Peter's name. The Head of Chambers turned and waited to see what he wanted. Stammering, and with a faint blush, Aldermarten said: 'I . . . I don't suppose you could, you know . . . call me, could you?' He tilted his head to one side hopefully.

Peter smiled kindly and fiddled with his bow tie. 'With the result? Sorry, Jeremy. Not done, I'm afraid. One simply has to wait for the thump of vellum on doormat.' Seeing the crestfallen look on his colleague's face, he added, encouragingly: 'They are sent first class.'

Aldermarten took heart and shrugged his shoulders. 'Well,' he remarked, 'what's another day?' Peter Foxcott nodded and wandered into his office, leaving Aldermarten uncomfortable under Tom Buckley's gaze. As he turned and stalked off, the senior clerk chuckled at Aldermarten's self-imposed anxiety and, shaking his head, stubbed out his cigarette.

The six men and six women on the jury were duly attentive as Kavanagh outlined the facts of the case to them. They had already had time to acclimatise to their surroundings, had examined the austere oak-panelled courtroom and passed comment on the fact that their judge was a woman, Her Honour Judge Mary Whitrow, a redoubtable adversary of Kavanagh's when she was a Q.C. and now sitting in judgment in this case. Dressed in the scarlet-and-black robes of a High Court circuit judge, she wore her hair carefully groomed into a thick grey bun, topped by her wig, completing the appearance of stern authority by wearing tiny half-moon spectacles, balanced on the edge of her long nose and attached on either side by a long gold chain.

With nothing else to distract them, the jury focused their attention instead on the man on whose shoulders it fell to prosecute the case, James Kavanagh. Several had heard of him, some had seen him on television, and most thought he looked much shorter than they had imagined, standing before them now low in the well of the court.

It was his role, he had explained, as senior prosecution counsel, to open the court proceedings with a short speech that summarised the events which led to this trial. The length and theatricality of such speeches always depended enormously on the person giving them. Some barristers – aware that every word they said was being faithfully recorded by the press to be reproduced in the morning's papers – deliberately filled their opening speeches with juicy titbits and attention-grabbing soundbites which they knew would get the jury, and the media, salivating for more.

Others, like Kavanagh, preferred to keep their openings simple and uncluttered with rhetoric. No matter if the reporters didn't like it. It was the jury he was concerned with, the men and women in whose hands the verdict lay. Let the story tell itself, Kavanagh's first-ever legal tutor used to tell him, and the facts of this sad story about Graham Foster needed little flamboyant embellishment.

'Before long,' Kavanagh told the jury halfway into his speech, 'Vincent discovered who the thief was. So then it was simply a question of finding the right time and the right place. He chose a quiet Sunday morning – on a deserted city road. He forced Graham into his car at gunpoint and drove him to an unknown location where he tortured and beat him so severely he died.' He paused to let the jury digest this information. He intended to show them the horrific photographs of Graham's mutilated body later, when they were better prepared. But for now he wanted them simply to understand what the smartly dressed young man in the dock was accused of – taking somebody's life in a most callous and sadistic way.

'To cover his tracks,' he continued, 'Vincent had to lie and intimidate witnesses, leaving a trail the prosecution will now show incriminates him beyond any reasonable doubt.' He paid special emphasis to those last four words. The judge would fully explain to the jury at a later date that they could only convict Vincent if they believed 'beyond any reasonable doubt' that he had committed the crime. It was Kavanagh's job to prove that, and to dispel all doubt. All Susan Craxton had to do was to introduce the smallest element of doubt and the jury would be instructed to acquit. It was a formidable game.

Replacing his spectacles at the end of his speech, Kavanagh glanced down at the documents in front of him. 'As my first witness,' he announced to the court, 'I call Hazel Dwyer.'

The plump West Indian court usher rose from her seat and stepped out into the corridor, her black gown flapping behind her in her haste. Pushing open the heavy oak door of the witness room a few yards down the corridor, she cast her eyes around at the dozen people sitting drinking coffee, smoking cigarettes and reading the newspapers. Ron Babb and his wife were by a dirt-stained window in one corner, chain-smoking and staring at Hazel and Paddy Spence sitting silently in an opposite corner. 'Hazel Dwyer?' the usher called out, waiting for a response.

Paddy bent down to pick up his tatty leather briefcase and made as if to get up. Next to him, her head hung low over a polystyrene cup of water, his witness did not make a move. 'Hazel?' he prompted, his briefcase on his lap. The usher called the name out loud again. 'Yes, yes, she's just . . .' He nodded to the usher and indicated that the young woman she wanted was sitting with him and would be coming shortly.

'I can't,' Hazel said into the cup, so softly he almost didn't hear her.

'What?' Paddy's disbelief flashed across his face.

Hazel looked up at him and then beyond, to where Shirley Babb was standing, cigarette in hand, staring at her, the corners of her mouth twisted. Sitting in a black leatherette armchair next to her, Ron Babb glowered menacingly over his copy of the *Sun* newspaper. Hazel gulped and looked at Paddy pleadingly. 'I've got to . . . to think,' she said, gasping for breath in the smoke-filled room, and started rocking herself gently backwards and forwards in her seat.

Paddy spun round and glared accusingly at the Babbs. He looked back at his terrified witness and wondered what on earth he should do. There was nothing for it; he'd just have to give her some more time.

In Court 8, Judge Whitrow was getting impatient. Tapping her pen on her desk, she was just about to say something to Kavanagh when the usher rushed back in and handed him a note. Reading it reluctantly, he rose to his feet to address the court.

'M'lady, er, Miss Dwyer appears to be temporarily indisposed,' he said, trying to disguise the panic he was feeling. 'So, with your permission, I should like to call Dr Ravi Mirchandani.' George Foster's neck almost snapped with the speed with which he suddenly looked up. Sitting a few feet behind Kavanagh, he could hardly believe his ears.

The judge removed her spectacles and allowed them to dangle round her neck on the chain. She arched a perfectly plucked eyebrow before asking: 'What is the nature of Miss Dwyer's indisposition, Mr Kavanagh?'

Kavanagh swallowed hard. 'A certain, er, queasiness, I believe. Possibly nerves,' he answered with a half-smile, hoping to appeal to the judge's feminine sensibilities – not that he was sure Mary Whitrow had many. She didn't look happy but nonetheless nodded her assent. Behind Kavanagh, George Foster jumped up and almost ran from the court as Susan Craxton, Q.C., looked on. Tongue in her cheek, she looked across at Kavanagh with an expression that told him she already had him on the ropes. Kavanagh sighed heavily and wondered why on earth he had ever taken on such a hopeless case.

In the witness room, the door opened and the usher entered, calling out the name of Dr Ravi Mirchandani. Suddenly, at her shoulder, George Foster appeared, his eyes on stalks, and he called insistently to his son's girlfriend, still sitting with Paddy Spence. 'Hazel! . . . Hazel!' he yelled. He wanted her to turn and face him so that he could convey all that he was feeling, but she kept her head well down.

The usher, keen to preserve the sanctity of the witness room where members of the public are strictly forbidden in case they interfere with witnesses, barred George's way with her arm. 'Sir, please!' she scolded as an Asian doctor approached her in answer to his name, and she ushered him and George Foster from the room.

Paddy Spence, powerless in the face of Hazel's indecision, witnessed the scene with great sadness. Sitting staring at the young woman opposite him, willing her to make the right decision, he hoped to God for George's sake that she would.

Dr Ravi Mirchandani, senior Home Office pathologist, talked the jury through the grisly photographs they were now studying of Graham Foster's body. There had been a short delay when the police photographs were first produced; one of the woman jurors had told the judge she felt faint and needed to be taken for some fresh air. Other jurors had looked similarly appalled by the sight of a dead young man with hardly any face, and the judge had allowed them all a ten-minute coffee break.

Back in their seats, the jurors were sullen as they listened to the pathologist explaining the exact cause of death – multiple injuries to the head and brain – and made notes as he was taken through the finer points by Kavanagh.

'And the marks on Graham's face – do you have any opinion as to what might have caused them?' the Q.C. asked, relieved to see the horror return to the jurors' faces as he directed them once again to the relevant photos. If he had their horror, he had their sympathy, and that was really all he needed. It was no mistake that he referred to the victim only as 'Graham' throughout – it was a deliberate ploy to humanise him to the jury, to make them feel as if they almost knew him.

Dr Mirchandani, a slim, bespectacled man who spoke English beautifully, the way only foreigners can, was quite definite in his response. 'They are consistent with the pattern left by a punch from a fist wearing a ring or rings,' he said, refreshing his memory from his notes.

Kavanagh was keen to emphasise the point, so he repeated it slowly, looking at the jury as he did so. 'A fist wearing a ring or rings?' The doctor nodded emphatically. 'Thank you, Dr Mirchandani, please stay there.' Kavanagh resumed his seat, thus allowing Miss Craxton to cross-examine his witness.

The lady barrister stood up with a businesslike air. 'Dr Mirchandani,' she said, a doubting tone already in her voice, 'you say the body was recovered from the Thames on the nineteenth?'

'Yes, that's right,' the pathologist answered.

'So how can you be so sure death occurred *four* days earlier, on Sunday the fifteenth?' she asked, her expression so triumphant then the jury all looked expectantly to the doctor for an answer. Kavanagh sighed. This was going to be a long trial.

Hours later, or so it seemed, the good doctor was released as a witness at the same time as Kavanagh was handed a second note from the usher. Opening it hesitantly, he read Paddy's scrawl: 'I need more time,' was all the note said. Behind those four words, he knew, were anguished emotions as the man who had landed his old friend in this mess in the first place did all he could to retrieve the best of a bad situation. Kavanagh could only begin to imagine what inner turmoil Hazel Dwyer was going through, or what steps Paddy was taking to try to make her see sense.

Rolling his eyes nonetheless, he stood up and faced the judge. 'The prosecution calls Dr Helen Kibbler,' he said, as Judge Whitrow raised another eyebrow and scribbled down the witness's name.

Dr Kibbler, lean, boyish and dark-haired in a navy blue collarless jacket and matching skirt, described to the court how Ian Vincent had arrived breathless and agitated at the casualty department of the London Hospital, Whitechapel complaining of a serious hand injury on the afternoon Graham Foster had died. She had been duty registrar that Sunday and had diagnosed several broken bones in his hand less than an hour after he had first arrived.

'He was in a lot of pain,' she recalled. 'His right hand had swollen so badly that two of his fingers were almost black because his rings were stopping the circulation of the blood. A nurse had to cut them off – the rings, that is.' Several members of the jury smiled at her clarification.

Kavanagh attempted to bring their minds back into focus. 'And did you ask how he'd come to break his hand?' he asked, leaning back against the bench.

'Yes. He said a paving stone had been dropped on it,' the young doctor answered, before adding: 'But it looked to me like he'd been in a fight. His knuckles were bruised and grazed on both hands.' Kavanagh thanked her for the observation and sat down.

Under hostile cross-examination by Ms Craxton, Dr Kibbler was asked again and again about the marks on Ian Vincent's hands. 'So you don't know if the bruises and grazing are actually related to the fractures at all, do you?' she asked, squarely facing the doctor, a sardonic expression on her face.

The doctor stood her ground. 'The injuries are consistent with each other,' she answered stiffly. She didn't like her opinion being questioned.

'Consistent but not dependent,' Ms Craxton remarked. 'It is possible that Mr Vincent could have broken his hand in exactly the way he said, isn't it?' Her face was serious now. She knew she badly needed to win this point.

The doctor looked helplessly at Kavanagh and the judge and shrugged her shoulders. Worded the way it was, the question was untenable. 'I . . . I suppose it's possible, but . . .' she stammered.

The point won, Ms Craxton interrupted her quickly to stop her from spoiling the victory. 'Thank you,' she said firmly. 'Nothing further.' She sat down with a smile.

When Dr Kibbler stepped down from the witness box, Judge Whitrow asked the usher to take the jury to their room for a few minutes while she discussed an important matter with counsel. Kavanagh knew what was coming and could not help but show his dejection. Once the door to the jury's deliberating room had been closed behind them, the judge turned to Kavanagh with a stern expression. 'The court has been very patient, Mr Kavanagh,' said the mistress of irony, unable to disguise her impatience. 'But this does seem rather like Hamlet without the prince. Do we see Miss Dwyer or shall I stop the case?' She peered at him over her tiny spectacles.

Kavanagh rose to his feet wearily. 'I, er, take Your Ladyship's point,' he responded with a sigh. He asked for more time and was given until later that afternoon. It was all up to Hazel now, he thought, as he sat back down with a thud.

*　　*　　*

In the witness room, Hazel stood alone at a window, watching the steam curling up from her cup of coffee, and wondered for the thousandth time what she should do. Looking out across the streets of London, she thought once more about getting away, starting anew somewhere. Ten thousand pounds could buy her a lot of freedom. It would easily pay for a one-way ticket to her grandmother's home in Jamaica. She had never been but had dreamt about taking Graham there one day to meet her. Graham, oh, Graham. If only you were here now, then none of this would have happened, she thought. She closed her eyes to stop the tears and leaned against the window.

Seeing that Hazel was alone and unprotected, Ron Babb rose from his seat in one swift, silent movement and started walking towards her, expressionless, his lips wet. Just as he got near, the door opened and Paddy Spence rushed in. As Babb retreated, the Irish lawyer took Hazel's arm and led her insistently to one side, his eyes on fire.

'I've just been talking to Mr Kavanagh, Hazel,' he said, pressing her elbow tightly. 'Unless you give evidence immediately after lunch, the judge is going to call it quits.' As Hazel squeezed her eyes shut, too late to stop the tears, Paddy put his arm around her shoulder comfortingly. Quietly, he added: 'You've been through so much for this. You owe it to yourself to finish it.'

13

The cigar smoke clung to the ceiling like thin gossamer as the besuited men beneath it downed the last dregs from their brandy balloons and sauntered through from the club library to the inner sanctum of the committee room and its highly polished round table, covered today in a red baize cloth. The chatter was amiable – luncheon had been exceptionally good and everyone was feeling flushed of face and full of stomach.

The chairman of the Beerbohm Club raised his voice above the general hubbub. 'Er, if we can come to order, gentlemen. Quickly as you can.' The pace quickened slightly as, one by one, the twelve committee members took their places around the great table. Peter Foxcott's forehead was furrowed into a frown as he stood to one side talking to Charles Lesser.

Lord Lesser, severe in black suit and club tie, held his hands behind his back as he said: 'Then he told me he'd already got it in his top drawer – ready and waiting.' Seeing the look of shock on Peter's face, he added: 'You hadn't heard?'

Peter shook his head. 'No,' he said, and sat down with a worried expression as Geoffrey Pack-Martin, in his trademark tweeds, joined the table.

'Sorry to keep you waiting,' he said, pulling out the chair next to Peter's with a smile. He sat down and turned to face the elderly chairman, who was holding up a piece of paper in front of him to indicate his readiness to proceed.

'So, the election of new members,' the chairman said, announcing the first item on the agenda. Putting on his spectacles and reading from his piece of paper, he added: 'Now, first, Jeremy Aldermarten, Q.C. Proposer, Mr Peter Foxcott, and seconded by Sir Geoffrey Pack-Martin.' The two men bowed their heads slightly as their names were mentioned.

The chairman looked around the table and saw with satisfaction that each of the twelve men had one small white ball and one black ball placed in front of them, as tradition dictated. 'Reveal your balls please, gentlemen,' he said, in time-honoured fashion, as each man lifted a ball in each forefinger and thumb and displayed that he had one of each.

'Thank you,' the chairman said as he checked each man. 'And now, as ever, white for yes, black for no. And we require all white for acceptance.' Peter Foxcott stared down at the two balls balanced in his fingers with a look of great angst on his face, as the heavy wooden ballot box was passed from man to man around the table.

In the administrative office of River Court at that very moment, Jeremy Aldermarten found himself marking time by reading the *Daily Mirror*. Tom Buckley watched with some amusement. Aldermarten was most definitely a *Times* man. Everyone else had gone to lunch, but the prospective new member of the Beerbohm wasn't hungry. In fact, he felt quite sick to the stomach, he thought, as he studied his horoscope. 'Aquarius: A day of indecision due to the adverse influence of Uranus . . .'

he started to read, then threw the paper on to the table in frustration.

Tom Buckley swivelled gently in his chair and watched him out of the corner of his eye. 'Funny sort of time for an election, Mr Aldermarten,' he said, with a mischievous twinkle.

'Yes. Yes. Well, you know, Tom, these traditions, you know, they just sort of grow up, especially in clubs. Nobody quite knows how.' Aldermarten sat on the edge of Tom's desk, tapping a Biro on a book and pondering the mysteries of club life.

Tom nodded. 'All lost in the mists of time, I suppose,' he suggested.

Aldermarten smiled. 'Yes, yes, quite.'

Tom's young assistant, Gary – an earring dangling from his left earlobe – sat watching the two men with a knowing look. Only rarely did he understand the conversations that took place in River Court, but this time he really felt that he had got the gist. 'It's like at Spurs,' he offered buoyantly, as the others stared at him in wonder. 'Yes, we always go to the Park Lane end, for some reason.' Seeing Aldermarten's look of sheer incomprehension, he added: 'Spurs fans.' Aldermarten nodded and picked up his horoscope once again. Anything to take his mind off things.

The precision-tooled ballot box with its large hole carved at the top had almost gone full circle round the committee room table as each man, his hand shaped into a fist so that no other member could see what was in it, dropped in through the top a single ball, which then fell with a satisfactory 'plunk' into a secret drawer at the bottom.

Peter Foxcott watched warily as the box was returned to the chairman. Using the key which only he was allowed to keep, the octogenarian carefully unlocked the drawer and pulled it open in order to count the balls.

'Good Lord,' he said, his bottom jaw falling open as he peered down into the hallowed velvet-lined box. 'I've never seen this before.' Reaching into pick up the single white ball, he held it up between his thumb and forefinger and announced: 'The "ayes".' Peter Foxcott hung his head.

Half an hour later, leaving the committee room with Sir Geoffrey Pack-Martin, Peter looked as if he had suffered a personal loss. 'Jeremy jumped the gun,' he told his fellow committee member. 'He'd already bought the tie.'

Sir Geoffrey's portly figure stopped mid-stride. 'What?'

Foxcott stopped too and nodded, his head hung low. 'Advertised the fact to Charles Lesser. Its gone round like wildfire. Not his first *faux pas* either.' The two men walked slowly down the grand central staircase.

Sir Geoffrey, as Toad-like as ever in his appearance, suddenly understood. 'So that's why you . . . ?' He gave Foxcott the thumbs-down sign.

Foxcott, hand in his trouser pocket, his face still pained at his decision, nodded. 'Yes. A seven-year wait to become a laughing-stock. It just wouldn't be . . . humane.' He carried on down the staircase grim-faced.

Hazel Dwyer followed the usher into Court 8 at the Inner London Crown Court a few steps in front of Paddy Spence. Her head spinning, her eyes wide, she shied away from a staring Ian Vincent as she walked past the dock. Gingerly stepping up into the witness box, she tried hard to concentrate on what the court clerk was telling her as he handed her the Holy Bible. Her insides had turned to jelly, she felt sick and afraid, and she still had no idea what she was going to say once she had taken the oath.

'Take the book in your right hand and read from the card, please,' the usher was saying, as her head swam. She took the card and blinked hard to focus on the words in front of her.

'I swear by Almighty God . . .' she began, as Spence sat down behind Kavanagh with a frown. Leaning forward, he whispered a word of warning.

'She's all over the place. God knows if she'll deliver.' He sat back with a sigh. Kavanagh frowned and watched cautiously as Hazel struggled with the wording of the oath.

'. . . that the evidence I shall give shall be the truth, the whole truth and nothing but the truth, so help me God.' She handed the Bible back and stood, head bowed, clutching her stomach.

Kavanagh rose to his feet and put on his spectacles. In a gentle voice designed to put her at her ease, he asked: 'Are you feeling better now, Miss Dwyer?' He willed her to look at him and only him, to maintain the eye contact that he needed to get her through the next few minutes.

Hazel swallowed hard and raised her head a little. Glancing up at him, she whispered 'Yes,' but her head dropped down again.

Judge Whitrow leaned forward over her bench and addressed the witness. 'Please speak up, Miss Dwyer. We all want to hear you,' she said with a sympathetic smile. Hazel nodded almost imperceptibly and studied her hands once again.

As Chris Sampson, Spence's police contact, slipped into the back of the court, dressed in a suit and tie, his lank hair washed and brushed, Kavanagh began his questioning gently. 'Miss Dwyer, would you tell the court where you were in the early morning of Sunday, October the fifteenth last year?' Sampson and Vincent exchanged glances.

At the sound of his voice, Hazel allowed herself to look

up at Kavanagh's friendly face. But just beyond him, a few feet away, sat Ian Vincent, and her eyes were drawn into his deadly stare. She swallowed hard as he leaned forward in his seat and slowly closed his grip around one of the iron rails at the front of the dock. Unable to look any more, she dropped her head and found herself unable to speak.

Kavanagh tried to help. 'Were you with anyone?' he prompted. Hands clamped behind her back, her chin on her chest, Hazel squeezed her eyes shut against the voices in her head screaming at her to run. A frisson swept the court at the awkward silence, and the judge peered at Kavanagh over her spectacles with a look that said she expected him to do something and soon.

Kavanagh removed his spectacles and placed his hands on the bench in front of him, leaning in towards Hazel, a few feet away in the witness box. 'Hazel?' he asked with a kindly smile. 'Did you know Graham Foster?'

The sound of Graham's name acted like an electric shock to Hazel. The voices in her head were silenced and an image of Graham's face flickered before her eyes. 'Yes,' she answered softly, close to tears. As she looked up, her eyes locked on to Kavanagh's and stayed there.

'How did you know him?' he asked quietly, in a manner more like a one-to-one chat than a courtroom examination-in-chief.

Hazel's large brown eyes moist, she told the court: 'He was my boyfriend.'

'How long had you been together?' Kavanagh asked, standing straight, but maintaining eye contact.

'About a year.' Hazel relaxed slightly and took a deep breath.

'A year,' Kavanagh repeated, pleased that she was finally responding. 'So you started going out with him when he was just sixteen?' Hazel nodded. 'And how old were you?'

'Eighteen,' she replied.

'You were older than him?' Kavanagh asked, as the judge started to take notes.

'Didn't matter,' Hazel said, thinking now of the young man she had teased mercilessly about being her 'toy boy'.

'No?' Kavanagh invited her to explain.

'No. He . . . he was special, you know.' She looked down again, fighting to control her emotions, to stop the tears that welled up in her eyes every time she thought of Graham and how much she missed him.

Kavanagh saw her soften and was relieved. 'Special? In what way?' he asked, building up the trust between them.

Hazel clenched her jaw. 'He didn't try to make me do what I didn't want to – like most people.' There was bitterness in her final remark, bitterness that dated a long way back to her miserable childhood, her interfering stepfather and her abuse at the hands of the children's home staff.

'He respected you?' Kavanagh suggested.

'Yeah.' Hazel nodded her agreement, as if this were the first time she had realised. That was exactly what Graham did, he showed her respect – respect she had never had from anyone else in her life, before or since.

'He let you be yourself?' Kavanagh knew he was tapping into a rich seam of emotion here, emotion that, he hoped, would lead Hazel down the right path.

'Yeah,' she responded. 'And with me he was himself, an' all.'

'And how was that?' Kavanagh prompted.

Hazel looked up at him, her eyes glistening. 'Kind . . . Funny . . . Made me laugh.' A hundred images of happy moments spent with him flashed across her eyes. George Foster, a few seats behind Kavanagh, looked up at her in astonishment, as if she were describing someone he had never known.

Kavanagh knew it was time to be a little tougher. 'Some people would say he was just a petty criminal, a thief,' he said, hoping that his question wouldn't have the wrong effect and set Hazel back.

Hazel flashed him a look of anger. 'Doesn't make him a bad person,' she snapped. 'Anyway, that was just 'cos of his dad.' She glared at George Foster, who shifted uncomfortably in his seat.

Kavanagh coaxed her on. 'How d'you mean?'

Hazel picked at the edge of the witness box with her nails as she answered, crossly: 'Never had any time for him, except to shout at him. When he wasn't pissed, that is.' She stared accusingly at George. Seeing the look on the judge's face after her outburst, she added: 'Sorry, drunk.'

Kavanagh needed more. This was good, sympathy-provoking stuff; he could see the jury taking a close interest. 'You mean he committed these crimes just to get attention from his father?'

Hazel nodded. 'I think so,' she said.

'But you did have time for him?' he suggested.

'I . . .' Hazel started to speak, but the lump in her throat stopped her.

Kavanagh finished her sentence. 'Loved him?'

Hazel nodded and started to cry, the tears coursing down her cheeks.

'What happened must have been very hard for you, then? His death and . . . the way his body was found?'

Her chest heaving up and down, Hazel could no longer control herself. Holding her hand to her eyes, she sobbed heart-rendingly. The judge leaned forward and asked: 'Are you all right to continue, Miss Dwyer?' Hazel, her head in her hands, shook her head, wiped away the tears and apologised. 'Would you like a short break?' Judge Whitrow asked, glancing at Kavanagh.

Hazel sniffed loudly and raised her head, the tears rolling down her face. 'I'm okay,' she said, wiping her nose with the back of her hand.

Judge Whitrow looked again at the prosecution counsel. 'Mr Kavanagh, might we go to the day in question, please?' she asked, anxious at about the time already lost.

Kavanagh nodded and, willing Hazel to keep herself together long enough to answer his questions, he asked: 'Hazel, were you with Graham in the early morning of Sunday, October the fifteenth last year?' Seeing her look up fearfully at Ian Vincent, who put his hand to his neck and drew a finger slowly across his throat, Kavanagh added insistently: 'Look at me, Hazel. There's nothing to be scared of.'

Hazel was almost gasping now, as she fought for breath. Sobbing, she cried: 'Yes . . . Yes.'

'You were with Graham that morning?' Kavanagh's tone was firm, insistent. Come on, Hazel, you can do it, he was willing her on.

'Yes.'

'What happened?' he asked. She looked again at Vincent and hung her head. 'Hazel, what happened on that Sunday morning . . . ?' he urged, his voice raised, '. . . to Graham Foster? The young man you *say* you loved.'

Stung by the rebuke, Hazel snapped: 'I did love him.'

'Then tell us what happened.' Kavanagh was clearly getting impatient.

Hazel's head jerked up. Breathlessly, she suddenly let it all out in a torrent of words – words that she had kept locked inside for so long. 'He took him away.' She pointed at Ian Vincent, almost screaming. 'He jumped out with this gun and I . . . I couldn't believe it. It was like a film,

201

you know. I mean, we was just walking down the road. I thought he was gonna shoot us but he made Graham get in the car. And I never saw him again.' Overcome by emotion, and the release of tension now that she had finally spoken out against Vincent, Hazel Dwyer collapsed in the dock, her head in her hands, sobbing. The vision of Graham's face through the car window had haunted her for months and would stay with her for ever. Giving up all attempts to control her grief, she cried till she thought her heart would break.

George Foster allowed the tears to spill down his own face as he watched his son's girlfriend recount Graham's final moments. Although he had seen the photographs and read the police reports, he had never heard the sequence of events from Hazel's own lips before. Now that he had, he felt even more shocked and saddened by the manner of his son's death.

From the dock, Ian Vincent stared at the witness in disbelief, his misery apparent. He couldn't believe it, after all he had been promised. She had actually stood up in the box and spilled the beans. He was gutted. What now? What the hell was going to happen now to his little schemes?

Detective Chief Inspector Chris Sampson, sitting at the back of the court, eyed the defendant warily. Running his hands through his hair he sighed heavily and left the courtroom, reaching for his rolling tobacco.

After a lunch-time break to give Hazel time to compose herself, it was Susan Craxton's turn to cross-examine her. Kavanagh and Spence had already congratulated Hazel on her testimony; now all they had to do was try to prepare her for the ferocious questioning ahead. It was Ms Craxton's job, they explained, to try to make her out in the worst possible light to the jury, to put an end to any sympathy they were feeling for her, and to portray her as either a wholly unreliable or a vindictive witness.

She had spent much of the adjournment in the ladies' lavatory, being sick, while Spence stood guard outside. Declining the offer of anything to eat, she felt empty and afraid as she retook the witness stand and faced Ms Craxton, whose manner and expression were of ice. Kavanagh wondered if she were really ready to face such a grilling over what he knew would be a cruel few hours.

Susan Craxton, Q.C., rose to her feet and her full five feet ten inches. She turned to the witness, a fixed smile on her face, and spoke through clenched teeth. 'Until last September, you worked at the same company as Ian Vincent, didn't you, Miss Dwyer? Babb Aggregates Ltd, as an office junior?'

Hazel, her hands clamped behind her back to stop herself shaking, nodded. 'Yes,' she said quietly. Kavanagh had warned her what might be coming.

'And isn't it true, Miss Dwyer, that you hold a grudge against him because it was his complaint about your aggressive attitude that led to your dismissal from that job?' She laid special emphasis on the word 'aggressive'.

Hazel shook her head in indignation. 'I was sacked 'cos I didn't go out with him,' she said, her nose wrinkled in disgust at the thought of having any physical contact with a man she had always regarded as pretty low down the food chain.

'You were sacked,' Susan Craxton repeated, with great deliberation. 'And now you want to get your own back by making up this elaborate story about Graham Foster's abduction at gunpoint?' She arched her eyebrow as if to express the preposterousness of it all.

Hazel, feisty now, came back at her quickly. 'It's not a story.'

'Isn't it?' Again, the arched eyebrow.

'No. It's true.'

'I see.' Ms Craxton smiled at her, the smile of someone who didn't believe her. Hazel had seen that smile before – on the face of her mother when she complained about her stepfather's nightly visits to her bedroom; on the face of the superintendent at the children's home when she told him of the beatings staff doled out; and now here, in this courtroom, when she had finally done the decent thing and told the truth about Graham's death.

Susan Craxton wasn't finished. 'And is it also true that, having retracted your statement to the police, you only agreed to testify today after the promise of five thousand pounds if you did so?' She looked across at the jury to let her words sink in.

Hazel started to speak. 'Yeah, but . . .' she began. She was going to tell the court that she had also spurned the offer of ten thousand pounds for not speaking, but before she could say anything, an incensed Kavanagh was on his feet in a flash and addressing the judge.

'The money to assist the witness was fully disclosed to the defence,' he complained. 'And I am more than happy to say *why* it was offered – if my learned friend so wishes.' He knew the last thing Susan Craxton wanted the jury to hear was that the money was for Hazel's protection, in the face of vicious death threats from Vincent's family.

Susan Craxton quickly conceded the point. 'The witness need not answer, m'lady,' she said, as Kavanagh sat down, groaning inwardly, his top lip curled in anger. By introducing the evidence about the money, he knew Craxton had achieved what she wanted, even if the point had been retracted later. Now the jury probably thought of Hazel as a money-grabbing liar whose grief over Graham's death was a sham. He would have to try to recover the lost ground.

*   *   *

Two hours later, her ordeal finally over, an emotionally drained Hazel Dwyer was escorted from the courtroom by Paddy Spence and whisked downstairs to a back door where she would be taken to a secret, safe location. Kavanagh, looking daggers at Susan Craxton, pulled off his wig and walked into the lobby with George Foster hangdog behind him.

The two men watched as Ian Vincent, freshly released from the dock, met up with his parents and had a heated exchange with them. Ron Babb raised the palm of his hand at his stepson in a placatory gesture, but Ian Vincent, furious that his stepfather had ever allowed the case to go this far, waved a finger at him threateningly and stalked off.

George Foster, his eyes red-rimmed, shook his head. 'And he gets to go home every night,' he said, still unable to accept that, under the civil system, a man on trial for murder isn't automatically locked up.

Kavanagh clarified the position for his client. 'He's not in custody,' he pointed out.

'Yet,' George Foster responded under his breath. Then, as the Babbs left the building, he added: 'Do you think Hazel's done enough?' His expression was one of quiet concern.

Kavanagh started down the court steps before he answered. He didn't want to get George's hopes up – as Tom Buckley had pointed out, a successful civil case for murder was extremely rare and there was still a very long way to go. He chose his words with caution. 'I could have done without that stunt by his counsel,' he said. 'And there's her record, of course.' Turning briefly and seeing the look of disappointment in George's eyes, he added: 'But, yes, enough for me to have a crack at his alibi.'

George rallied a little and followed Kavanagh down the

steps. 'It . . . it really sounded like Hazel felt something for Graham,' he said, an element of surprise in his voice.

'I think she did, Mr Foster,' Kavanagh remarked as he saw his client's hand go to his chin in thought. He wondered again at how little George Foster seemed to know his son, and whether his determination to bring Vincent to justice was born out of guilt rather than revenge.

At the back door of the court, Hazel Dwyer took her place in the back of a white Leyland Sherpa van provided by a mate of Paddy Spence's, as Paddy went to close the door behind her. She had stopped crying now, but the tears had stained her face, and she looked pale with sadness. Paddy gave her an encouraging smile and patted her knee. 'I'll be with you in, er, half an hour, tops.' Hazel's eyes widened in fear. 'Don't look so worried,' Paddy reassured her with a twinkle. 'It'll be fine.' He shut the door and patted the side of the van, indicating to the driver that he could set off.

Pulling out of the rear gates to the court, the van lurched forward and found a path between the hordes of waiting photographers and reporters. Hazel averted her head as cameras, held up to the back window, flashed and popped their lights at her sitting inside.

Waiting by the gates, Chris Sampson sat in a dark saloon car, its engine running. A plainclothes officer emerged from the gates and nodded at him as the van pulled away. Sampson put his car into first gear, let his foot off the clutch and followed.

Later that night in his room in a cheap hotel in Paddington, George Foster lifted his battered suitcase on to his bed and pulled out a dog-eared photograph album he had retrieved from his council flat before he fled.

Sitting on the edge of the bed, he flicked open the album's

plastic-covered sheets and looked down at the photographs of much happier times – Graham as a baby with his mother, June, the only woman George Foster had ever loved, whom he had driven away with his depression and his drinking. There was Graham at the zoo, pretending to be a caged animal behind bars; Graham on a tricycle, beaming up at the camera for his daddy. And later ones, of Graham, the teenage tearaway, his hair long, his hands stuffed in his jeans pockets, the same impish grin on his face.

George allowed his fingers to caress the photograph lovingly as wave after wave of emotion swept over him. Hazel was right – he had neglected his only son. Maybe Graham was trying to get his attention by thieving; only he'd been too drunk and too stupid to see it. Now it was too late, Graham was gone, and he could never tell him how much he loved him. He closed his eyes to shut out the pictures but they remained – just as vividly – in his head. Leaning over the album, his bitter tears splashed on to the clear plastic covers and trickled down the pages holding the only mementos he had left of his son.

On the other side of London, James Kavanagh poured out two brandies from a cut-crystal decanter and handed one to his wife, Lizzie, sitting on a comfy sofa in their living room. She took the glass and smiled up at him, shoes off, her feet tucked under her.

'So, she came up with the goods, then? Despite what your man in Criminal Intelligence said?' She was genuinely pleased for her husband; she knew enough about the case to realise that if Hazel Dwyer had failed to testify then he would almost certainly have lost. When she had first heard the goods news on *PM* on the car radio on the way home, she could hardly believe it, not after all the doubts surrounding the trial. She felt guilty for criticising him and decided to help him celebrate his day by cooking him his favourite dinner. But getting home, she was surprised to find her husband pensive, and not nearly as elated as she expected him to be.

He stood before her now, digesting the delicious pasta supper she had made him, and studying his reflection in the large overmantel. 'Mmm,' he responded, deep in thought, as an image of DCI Chris Sampson, the man he had met for the first time earlier that week, flickered before his eyes. 'And he's not "my" man at Criminal Intelligence. He's Paddy's,' he said. Lizzie frowned up at him and wondered at the distinction.

In a crummy hotel bedroom near King's Cross station, Hazel Dwyer sat on the end of her bed eating crisps and listening to the weather forecast on the television after watching the ten o'clock news. She had been surprised to find herself the subject of one of the news items, but was relieved to see that none of the cameramen had got a clear view of her face.

Paddy Spence sat dozing in an armchair next to the bed, but the sound of the advertisements coming on made him jump and wake up. Blinking and looking at his watch, he made as if to stand up. Hazel dropped her bag of crisps and spun round to face him. 'Don't go,' she pleaded, her eyes wide.

Paddy hesitated. 'I . . . I can't stay here all night, Hazel,' he said, straightening his tie and thinking wryly how unprecedented it was for him to be saying that to a beautiful young woman.

Hazel looked down at the stained carpet with its cigarette burns and sighed. 'I'm scared, Mr Spence,' she said, admitting openly for the first time what Paddy had never doubted all along.

Paddy stood up. 'I know, but there's no need to be,' he said, sitting on the edge of the bed next to her. 'There's just the Babbs' alibi evidence, and then it's all over.'

Hazel wondered if it would ever really be over for her. Looking up at Paddy with her big brown eyes, she begged: 'Please don't go.'

Always a sucker for a pretty girl, Paddy relented. 'Okay,' he said, patting her leg and reassuring himself that he was only doing his job. Hazel smiled with relief as he stood up and drew the bedroom curtains.

Sitting in the driver's seat of a dark saloon car parked in the street below, Chris Sampson lit a cigarette and watched the curtains being drawn. Exhaling a mouthful of smoke, he blew out the match burning between his thumb and forefinger and tossed it into the ashtray. It looked like it was going to be another long night.

14

After seven long years, the Big Day had finally arrived. Jeremy Aldermarten could scarcely believe it. He had hardly slept a wink all night for anticipation and now, standing at the huge front window of his Georgian townhouse in a trendy Islington square, he stopped midway through a piece of toast as he saw the postman approaching with his Royal Mail trolley.

In shirt and braces, his hands pressed against the window to get a better view, Aldermarten held his breath as the postman pulled out a bundle of letters and walked up the steep steps to his front door. Chewing frantically to finish his toast, he ran from the dining room and into the airy hallway just in time to see the white vellum envelope, with its distinctive embossed crest, drop satisfyingly on to his Harrods doormat.

Stuffing the final piece of his toast into his mouth, he rubbed his hands together gleefully and lifted the envelope delicately from the mat, a satisfied smile on his face. Turning it over and over in his hand, he wandered back into the dining room to the ten-foot mahogany dining table, where his housekeeper, Mrs Baker, had laid out his usual breakfast things along with a huge vase of freshly cut flowers.

On the table in front of him a pot of coffee steamed gently next to a glass of orange juice, an open jar of marmalade and a bowl of fresh fruit salad. Aldermarten sat down, discarded the other post and held the envelope before him, studying the handwritten address label with admiration. Raising it to his lips, he ran it under his nose, inhaling its distinctive aroma, before carefully placing it down on the table, resting against his glass. Stretching his arms out in front of him to pull up his shirt cuffs, he reached for the pot of coffee, pouring himself a cup as he gazed down at the envelope before him.

It was his clear intention to finish his breakfast before opening it, but – unable to wait a moment longer – he suddenly grabbed the envelope from its resting place, and using his toast knife to slit it open at the top, he pulled the folded contents from their sanctuary.

Shaking the letter open and holding it slightly away from him so that he could focus on the handwritten words, Jeremy Aldermarten allowed himself a small smile in this, his moment of triumph. Scanning the lines quickly, his face fell as he tried to take in what he was reading. Nostrils flaring, his jaw clenched, he read and reread the words in front of him in utter astonishment and indignation. This was nothing short of an outrage.

In Court 8 at the Inner London Crown Court, Judge Mary Whitrow was addressing counsel on the opening day of the defence evidence as Ian Vincent looked on from the dock. Kavanagh had closed the prosecution case the previous afternoon; all his witnesses had been called and it was now up to the defence to call theirs. Kavanagh's work was far from over; in many ways it was just beginning. Cross-examination of the opposite side's witnesses was his forte, although – under the rule of law which sometimes seemed to offer every protection to the defendant and none to the prosecution – he would not know who those witnesses were until the moment they were called.

'Miss Craxton,' the judge asked, looking down at the defence with some seriousness, 'have you advised your client that the stage has now been reached at which he may give evidence? And if he chooses not to do so, or, having been sworn, without good cause refuses to answer any questions, that the jury may draw such inferences as appear proper from his failure to do so?'

All eyes were on Miss Craxton as she stood to give her answer. 'He has been so advised, m'lady, and he will not be called as a witness in his own defence,' she said, without even flinching. The jurors looked very surprised and glanced over at Vincent in the dock. Kavanagh grimaced at the lost opportunity to cross-examine the nasty piece of work – the very reason why Vincent's counsel had decided against putting him on the stand. Miss Craxton ignored the murmuring in court and continued: 'I would like to call Ronald James Babb.'

In Room 7 at the Carlisle Hotel, King's Cross, Paddy Spence pulled back the curtains and peered out. 'There's no one there now,' he called, and stepped back into the room.

Hazel, still on the edge of the bed, was feeling very twitchy. 'I'm telling you, he was there, watching,' she said, as Paddy stood in front of the mirror, putting on his tie. 'Oh look,' she added, 'just give me my money and I'm off.' She couldn't wait to get away, away from this horrible room and from everything that reminded her of Graham.

Paddy looked aghast and turned to face her. 'I . . . I can't,' he said. 'Not until the trial's over.' His instructions were quite clear.

Hazel was tired of all the waiting. 'But I've done my bit,' she said, looking up at him. All she wanted was the cash and then she could run away and get her head sorted out.

'Aye, I know,' Paddy admitted, putting on his jacket. 'But we might need you again. You never know in this game.'

'Game?' Hazel responded with a gasp. It wasn't a bloody game to her, losing Graham like that, being frightened out of her wits, facing a life on the run away from the likes of Ian Vincent and his family.

Paddy knew he had chosen the wrong word and he was sorry. Moving towards her, he tried to reassure her. 'It'll be a couple more days, three at the most, and then you're away free.'

Hazel rolled her eyes. 'Three days?' She'd go mad in three hours stuck in this place, she thought.

Paddy glanced at his watch. 'Oh, look, I've gotta go. You just lock the door behind me and don't answer it to anyone.' Hazel sat dejectedly on the edge of the bed. 'Do you understand me now?' he asked her. Feeling sorry for leaving her like this, he added: 'I'll come back when the court is over for the day and, er, we'll sort something out.'

Hazel turned and stared at him. 'What?' she asked, her eyes blazing.

Paddy reddened. 'Look, you just lock the door.' And with that he was gone.

At River Court, Jeremy Aldermarten, minus his overcoat, marched down the carpeted corridor and past several colleagues, none of whom he acknowledged. Striding into the administrative offices commanded by Tom Buckley, and interrupting the senior clerk's conversation with his assistant Gary, Aldermarten, his voice cracking with emotion, asked: 'Is Mr Foxcott in?'

Tom Buckley had never seen him so upset. 'No, sir, not

yet,' he answered, and shot Gary a sideways glance. This could only mean one thing.

Jeremy Aldermarten, red in the face and close to tears, turned on his heel and scuttled to his own office, his briefcase crashing against the door frame as he left.

Ron Babb's examination-in-chief by Susan Craxton had been nothing short of a farce, Kavanagh thought. The defence counsel had done her best to portray this arch-criminal as a concerned stepfather and a respectable businessman, shocked at the thought that his beloved stepson could have been charged with such a heinous offence.

Now, as he rose to his feet, it was his turn to cross-examine Babb, and he had no intention of letting the jury go home that night with the same impression.

'Mr Babb, you've told this court that Ian Vincent was with you from Saturday evening, October the fourteenth, until half past six the next day, Sunday. The day of the murder.'

Ron Babb, scarred of face, his long black hair greased back, stood in the witness box in a smart blue pin-stripe suit and smiled. 'That's right,' he said, with the air of a man who was only too willing to assist the court.

'He came to supper, stayed the night and then helped you with the patio you were building?' Kavanagh continued, reciting almost exactly from Babb's earlier statement.

'At the time, yes.' Babb, hands behind his back, nodded.

Kavanagh placed his own hands in his trouser pockets and leaned back. 'And just after Sunday lunch you accidentally dropped a paving slab on his hand, breaking it.'

Babb knew how to play to the gallery. He's actually enjoying this, Kavanagh thought, as he watched the witness

215

smile. 'They're very heavy and I'm not as young as I used to be,' he said, just stopping himself from winking at the jury.

Kavanagh was floundering in the face of such a professional. 'Mmm,' was all he could manage to respond. 'And then you took him to the hospital.'

Babb nodded. 'Because he couldn't drive himself, on account of his hand,' he reminded the court. He knew his lines only too well.

'And at around six o'clock, once he'd been treated and his hand put in a cast, you drove him back to his flat?'

Babb smiled. 'Yes,' he answered, giving the jury his most winning smile.

'So what happened to his car?' Kavanagh asked, watching closely as Babb's eyes flickered momentarily. 'Because it was still at your house, wasn't it?'

Babb's mind was working overtime, but his face retained a fixed smile. Pausing to compose his thoughts, he added: 'I drove it round the next day.'

But Kavanagh wasn't finished. 'He gave you the keys, then?'

Babb shrugged. 'Obviously.'

'When?' The pace was quickening.

Babb swallowed. 'Well, I don't remember exactly. Er, when I dropped him off, I suppose.' The 'er' told Kavanagh all he needed to know – he had Babb on the run.

'But how did you get back from the flat – if you'd gone there in his car.'

Babb, as motionless as a statue, blinked. There was a four-second pause before he answered. 'My wife . . . she came around in our car and I drove us back.'

Kavanagh, having got what he wanted, moved on. 'I see,' he said, glancing down at his notes through spectacles held to his nose. 'Now, you're Ian Vincent's stepfather, aren't you, Mr Babb?' he asked, looking up.

216

Relieved that the hard part was over, Babb answered this one quickly. 'Yes,' he said, nodding.

'How would you describe your relationship?' Kavanagh asked.

Babb bristled. 'In what way?'

Kavanagh smiled and looked around the court. 'Well, children and step-parents, there's often friction, isn't there?'

Babb was on his guard. 'Yes, but I don't see what that's got to do with anything,' he replied. At that moment, Paddy Spence entered the courtroom and took his place next to George Foster. Checking on his clothing, he did up the buttons on his cuffs.

Kavanagh explained. 'I'm trying to establish the sort of relationship you had with your stepson, Mr Babb.'

Babb glanced at Ian Vincent in the dock. 'Normal, I suppose,' he said.

'And what's that exactly?' Kavanagh asked with some impatience.

'Normal, you know.' Babb raised an eyebrow. 'Up and down – like most relationships.'

The judge interjected. 'Is this leading us anywhere, Mr Kavanagh,' she asked wearily, glancing at her watch. It was fast approaching lunch and she had a date with her granddaughter in addition to her concern that the case was already over schedule.

The prosecution counsel resented the intrusion and his face showed it. Addressing the judge, he said: 'To a clearer understanding of the family background of the accused, m'lady.'

Judge Whitrow consented. 'Very well,' she said, peering at Kavanagh over her spectacles, 'as long as the light shines sooner rather than later.'

'M'lady.' Kavanagh nodded.

*　　*　　*

Peter Foxcott sat rooted to his seat behind his vast leather-topped walnut desk and watched Jeremy Aldermarten pace the green carpet in front of him. If he carried on much longer, he'd wear a hole in the Persian rug, Peter thought.

Aldermarten was flapping a piece of paper about in his hand. 'No reason!' he shouted. 'Nothing! Not a single, solitary word of explanation – after seven years!' His face was purple with rage and indignation.

Peter, looking genuinely contrite sitting under an eighteenth-century oil painting of Judge Jeffries, tried to calm him down. 'I'm so sorry,' he said for the seventh time.

Aldermarten was still pacing. Holding up the piece of paper as if his whole future depended upon it, he read aloud: ' "Your application for membership has been unsuccessful this time." ' Turning to Foxcott with a gawping stare, he threw his head back in exasperation. 'This time? What does that mean? That I'm supposed to put my name down again? In the hope that in seven years' time, the black-balling swine that shafted me will have snuffed it?' His eyes were on fire and he had an expression of such hurt on his face that Peter Foxcott found it hard to look at him.

'Jeremy,' he said, as gently as he could, 'I know it's very upsetting, but it's really not the end of the world,' he reminded him. 'Really. There are other clubs.'

Jeremy Aldermarten obviously didn't think so. Ignoring his friend's words, he pursued the point. 'Why?' he asked, moving towards him, a pleading expression on his face. 'You're on the committee, Peter, you must know.'

Peter stiffened. 'It's a secret ballot,' he said, trying to fend off any further prying. The last thing he wanted was to have to tell Jeremy the whole story.

Aldermarten wasn't going to be fobbed off. 'But, I

218

mean, you must have heard something, some whisper, surely?'

Put on the spot, Peter Foxcott looked pained. Peering up at Aldermarten over spectacles balanced precariously on his nose, he said: 'Well . . .' and looked away.

Aldermarten blushed visibly. He hadn't really expected Peter to answer him, let alone come up with something he was sure he didn't want to hear. His eyes wide with surprise, he prompted: 'What?'

Foxcott swallowed and gave his companion a direct answer. 'Some business about trying to pass yourself off as a member . . .' He was unable to hide his contempt. 'With a club tie you bought.'

He looked down with a sigh, hoping that this would now be the end of it. The whole affair had upset him much more than he cared to admit and he wished to God now that he had never put Aldermarten's name forward in the first place.

Aldermarten studied his Head of Chambers in stunned silence, unable to take in what he was being told at first. Suddenly, his brow knotted and his bottom lip clamped his mouth shut in realisation. 'My God,' he said.

His response was not what Peter Foxcott had quite expected and he looked up at him quizzically. 'What?' he asked.

Aldermarten was incandescent with rage. 'Peter!' he shouted. 'I've been slandered!' and with that he fled the room, leaving Peter Foxcott utterly speechless at his desk.

Ron Babb was not an easy witness. Every time Kavanagh tried to get him to slip up, or give something away, the experienced villain outfoxed him. It was deeply frustrating, and he wasn't even denting his armour.

'So you gave Mr Vincent a job in his father's old business? With some responsibility?' Kavanagh, hands on either side of his gown, tried a different tack.

Babb nodded. 'Deputy general manager,' he replied, tired of all the questions.

'Deputy general manager,' Kavanagh repeated, looking around the court. 'Which means what, exactly?' He frowned.

Babb thought the answer obvious. 'He deputises for the general manager,' he said, slowly, as if having to explain something to a child.

'You?' Kavanagh asked.

'From time to time.' Babb was still holding his ground.

'And what does he do when he's not deputising for you?'

Susan Craxton looked across at her learned friend and wondered where this was leading. She flashed a warning look at Ron Babb.

'All sorts,' the witness answered.

'Such as?' It was like getting blood out of a stone.

'Bit of everything.'

Kavanagh decided to give the witness a multiple-choice question. 'Negotiating contracts?' he asked, looking down at a file in his hand.

Babb looked wary. 'A bit.'

'Dealing with clients?'

'Sometimes.'

'Delivering documents?' He looked up and studied Babb carefully.

Babb stared straight back. 'We use the Post Office for that, or the fax,' he said, a smile tugging at the corner of his mouth.

Kavanagh smiled back. 'But overall, he had a good general idea of the business?'

220

'Yes.'

'And you'd be sorry to lose him?'

'I would.' Babb nodded enthusiastically.

Kavanagh's tone changed. 'So sorry, in fact, that you would do anything to keep him out of prison, wouldn't you, Mr Babb? Like tell this court a pack of lies?' He glared at the witness in anger and frustration.

Babb's pockmarked scalp shifted back an inch as he feigned surprise at the outburst. 'I don't have to lie,' he said with a wide smile, 'because he's innocent.'

Kavanagh nodded in clear admiration of Babb's responses under pressure and smiled back. No matter, he'd only lost a battle, not the war.

Hazel Dwyer lay across the bed in her hotel room in a T-shirt and jeans, flicking through a woman's magazine Spence had bought her, the television still on in the background. She wasn't really reading the magazine, she'd flicked through it like this a dozen times already, but she was bored and needed something to take her mind off things. The lunch-time news was on and the newscaster was discussing a new landfill tax for industrial waste. Hazel turned back to her magazine in irritation and tried to concentrate.

The telephone in her room suddenly rang and she jumped. Sitting up on the bed, she stared at it for a moment and wondered if she should answer. Spence had told her not to open the door; he hadn't said anything about the phone. Maybe it was him calling with some good news. Gingerly, she reached for the telephone and picked up the receiver.

'Hello,' she said softly.

'Hazel Dwyer?' said a man's voice. It wasn't Paddy.

Hazel waited a moment and then answered cautiously: 'Yes.'

'I've been taking a look at your record . . . doesn't look very good, does it?' the voice began.

Hazel looked panic-stricken and shouted into the phone: 'Who is this?' but the voice didn't tell her. It just kept talking.

The expression on Shirley Babb's face as she stood in the witness box was one of deep discomfort. She still couldn't quite believe she was here, in this court, having to give evidence on behalf of her son. As if that wasn't bad enough, she had been kept apart from her husband ever since he'd given his evidence, for fear of something the usher called 'witness contamination'. So she'd had to sit alone in that smelly witness room all morning and then through lunch-time, waiting her turn. It really was too bad of Ron to let it get this far, she was thinking, as Susan Craxton led her through her evidence.

'And they left for the hospital at what time, Mrs Babb?' Ms Craxton asked her final question, her expression encouraging and helpful.

Her voice tremulous, Mrs Babb answered: 'Oh, must have been three fifteen, three thirty, somewhere around there.'

Ms Craxton smiled. 'Thank you,' she said, then, looking across at the prosecution counsel, she told the witness: 'Er, stay there, please,' before sitting down.

Kavanagh was quickly on his feet as Shirley Babb looked nervously up at her husband in the public gallery. Dressed in a plain black suit and white blouse, her trademark gold jewellery adorning her neck, earlobes and fingers, she tried to look as demure as her son's barrister had asked her to look. She had even toned down her lipstick, from cosmic red to cherry shimmer, in an attempt to look less like the barmaid she had been for most of her early life.

Kavanagh sipped from a glass of water before he began.

He watched as Shirley Babb squirmed in the silence. She gave him a little smile that was almost endearing. It said 'Be gentle with me', when they both knew he had no intention of doing any such thing. Finally, without a trace of sympathy on his face, he spoke. 'Your testimony is remarkably similar to your husband's, Mrs Babb. Word for word, almost.'

Her face hardened. 'Is it?' she asked, her nasal twang even more evident than it had been before.

'Mmmm,' Kavanagh responded. 'You didn't rehearse it together, did you, by any chance?' He smiled an inquisitive smile.

Shirley Babb feigned a look of indignation. 'No,' she said. 'If it's the same, it's 'cos we had the same experience.' She remembered her lines perfectly.

'Ah – until your husband took Mr Vincent to the hospital,' Kavanagh reminded her. 'You didn't go with them?'

'No,' she frowned, wondering where this was leading.

'Despite the fact that you're his mother?'

'Well, I had things to do,' she said.

'They went in whose car?' Kavanagh leaned over his bench, resting his elbows on it and waving his spectacles in the air.

'My husband's,' she answered, flatly.

'So Mr Vincent's car was left where, exactly?' Kavanagh asked the question as if it were just another in a long list, but his eyes narrowed as he waited for her answer.

Shirley Babb floundered. Her bottom lip moved up and down but nothing came out. Finally, she spluttered: 'His car?'

'Mmm,' Kavanagh confirmed, smiling at her. 'The one he'd arrived in.' Looking down at his notes, he held his spectacles to his eyes and read from the statement: ' "A whale-tailed Ford Escort Cosworth in pearlescent midnight blue."' He looked up from the statement and straight into the staring eyes of Shirley Babb.

Her mouth flapping as she tried to think and speak at the same time, Shirley Babb finally answered: 'It was parked outside, I suppose.'

'In your drive?' Kavanagh asked.

Shirley nodded. 'Um, yeah.'

Kavanagh challenged her. 'You don't sound very sure, Mrs Babb.'

Her thought processes had finally kicked in. 'Well, it wasn't the most important thing on my mind at that moment,' she countered.

'It wasn't in the way, blocking access or anything?' Kavanagh asked.

She smiled, relieved at having got through that one. 'No,' she said.

'So you did see it, then, at some point?' the Q.C. asked, pushing the issue.

She blinked and nodded. 'Yeah.'

Kananagh moved in for the kill. 'So what happened to it?' he asked, a strange expression on his face.

Shirley Babb blinked hard. 'His car?' she asked, fighting to think.

'His car,' Kavanagh repeated.

'When?' she asked.

'When it was in your drive,' he said, a more insistent tone in his voice now.

Shirley Babb blushed and looked up at her husband, his face murderous. 'I . . . I don't understand,' she stuttered.

'All right, I'll put it another way,' Kavanagh said, sounding angry now. 'How long was Mr Vincent's car left in your drive after he'd broken his hand?' He spoke the words slowly, to allow them time to sink in.

Shirley Babb frowned and shook her head. 'I can't

'remember,' she said, deciding that ignorance was her best defence. It had always worked in the past.

'Well, was it just overnight or longer?' Kavanagh was losing patience.

'A couple of nights, I think,' Shirley said, hoping that would be the end of it.

But Kavanagh was far from finished. 'A couple of nights?' he repeated with some surprise.

Shirley faltered. 'Yeah . . . I think so.'

Kavanagh nodded. 'Mr Vincent reported his car stolen the next day, and it was later found burnt out, off the M1, near Bedford,' he reminded her.

Shirley Babb shrugged her heavily padded shoulders. 'Well, it must have just been overnight then.'

'But it wasn't stolen from outside your house,' he reminded her once more.

'No.' Shirley Babb decided to try to keep her answers down to the minimum from now on. Her husband was staring daggers at her and she didn't know what she'd done wrong.

'So it must have been moved from your house to wherever it was stolen from,' Kavanagh suggested.

'Yes,' she answered, happy to be getting away with monosyllabic answers.

But then Kavanagh went and spoiled it all. 'Who did that?' he asked.

She blushed again. 'What?'

Kavanagh rolled his eyes to the heavens. 'Who moved Mr Vincent's car from outside your house?'

Shirley Babb started shaking. 'Why is it so important?' she asked, as much to her husband upstairs as to James Kavanagh. She gave Ron Babb a baleful look.

'Just answer the question, please,' Kavanagh urged.

'Look, I don't know,' she answered, her voice raised. Ignorance again, her best option, she hoped.

But she was disappointed to see Kavanagh looking as if she had just confessed to stealing the crown jewels. 'You don't know?' he asked, his thick white eyebrows forming a perfect arch.

'No. I wasn't there when it happened,' she responded.

Kavanagh's next expression worried her even more. 'Really?' he asked.

'No. I was out, down the shops,' Shirley stammered, quickening her pace in the hope that it would all be over sooner. Something deep inside her told her that her husband wasn't very pleased with her performance, especially after all the practising he'd made her do.

Kavanagh turned and looked around the court for greater emphasis. Inhaling deeply, he informed her: 'This morning your husband told this court that *he* drove the car to Mr Vincent's flat and *you* went round in your car to pick him up . . . Which is the correct version of events?'

Shirley Babb felt as if there must be steam coming from her ears as she fought to concentrate on what she was being told and tried to figure out its implications. Hesitating only for a moment, she suddenly blurted: 'My husband's.' She knew better than to contradict Ron Babb. Looking up at the sneer on his scarred face, she almost started to cry. 'I was confused . . . . I . . . I couldn't remember properly,' she faltered, her eyes pleading with Kavanagh to spare her from further embarrassment.

But James Kavanagh couldn't care less about Shirley Babb and what her husband did to her after this. His only concern was for Graham Foster, a young lad whose life was brutally snuffed out by her son. Rounding on her, through thin lips, he came to a climax. 'Isn't the truth, Mrs Babb, that despite everything else being identical, you and your husband have given wildly differing accounts of what happened to Ian Vincent's car because it was never

226

outside your house at all?' Shirley Babb shook her head so vigorously her dangling gold earrings were in danger of falling off. 'Because Ian Vincent was never at your house that Sunday, was he?'

'He was.' Shirley Babb was close to tears, as Susan Craxton averted her gaze, unable to watch the spectacle of one of her chief defence witnesses crumbling.

'You got together, with Vincent and your husband, and you have simply made the whole thing up, haven't you?' Kavanagh was almost shouting at her now.

Shirley Babb looked wildly around the court for support but found none. Glancing up at the lady judge whom she hoped would intervene, she found her just sitting on the edge of her chair and peering at her, her eyebrows raised. 'No,' she replied, tearfully, cowering under the judge's stare.

'Because when you say he was with you,' Kavanagh concluded, a vein in his neck throbbing, 'your son was actually torturing and murdering Graham Foster, wasn't he?'

Shirley Babb could hardly bear to listen to the suggestion. Her face contorted with emotion, her heavily made-up eyes filled with tears, she cried out: 'No, no . . . he was with us.' But few in the court believed she was telling the truth.

Paddy Spence missed Kavanagh's great moment in court. He had more pressing problems to deal with. Just after Shirley Babb had taken the oath, he had been handed a note from the usher which read: 'I'm outside, I need to talk. Hazel.' Rising quickly and slipping out the back, he found Hazel Dwyer in a denim jacket and jeans, pacing up and down in the lobby, her fingernails bitten to the quick.

It was soon apparent what she wanted. 'Look, I'm not gonna argue with you,' she told Spence, wagging her finger at him. 'I just wanna know how to do it, that's all. Who I've got to talk to and that.' Her eyes were those of a frightened animal.

Spence laid on the Irish charm. 'Look, let's sit down for a moment,' he said, a glint in his eye, taking her arm and gesturing to a chair.

Hazel shook her head. 'What for? You're only gonna try and make me change my mind, and I'm not going to.' Her face was flushed red with fear and frustration.

Spence had done with reasoning, now he was on the offensive. Moving his face close to Hazel's, he spoke bluntly. 'If you retract your evidence, this case will collapse. Vincent walks free,' he spat.

Hazel shook her head and turned away. 'Not my problem.' She hadn't liked seeing the nice Mr Spence looking at her with such contempt.

Spence was hard on her heels. 'Yeah, well, what about Graham?'

It was Hazel's turn to be angry. Her fist clenched in front of her face, she snapped: 'Don't come that again. I loved Graham and I wish he wasn't dead but you don't know what it's like, what I'm going through.' As she said those last words, her face crumpled in pain.

Spence wasn't going to give in that easily. 'Whatever's happened, the best thing you can do is tell me about it,' he said firmly. 'Don't keep it to yourself.' He tried to sound paternal.

Hazel had heard it all before and turned away. 'Why? What are you gonna do? Stay every night?' She leaned up against a wall and glared at him.

'Ssshhh!' Paddy waved his hands to quieten her. He didn't want it bandied around that he had spent the night with the chief prosecution witness. Moving closer to her and softening his voice, he asked: 'Look, what's happened? If it's serious, the police will . . .'

Hazel interrupted him with a laugh. 'The police?' she scoffed. 'It *is* the police!' Spence frowned. 'I've just had a phone call, from a copper.'

'At the hotel?' he asked, incredulous.

'Yes.' Hazel's hand was on her chin and she looked frightened.

'And he told you to retract?' Spence looked really worried now.

Hazel nodded. 'Or they'd fit me up.' She stared at the man she had spent the previous night with and wondered how the hell he was going to get her out of this one.

15

Jeremy Aldermarten had never been so enraged as when he strode into Cutler's wine bar off Pall Mall, with a look of determination on his face. The outrage of it, the humiliation! He could hardly believe what Peter Foxcott had told him and now, seeking out Charles Lesser to confront him directly with the accusation, he was purple with anger.

He spotted Lesser alone at the large wood-panelled bar, quietly sipping a glass of wine while reading the *Financial Times*. His right fist firmly shoved deep into his pocket to prevent himself from punching his adversary, Aldermarten approached him almost at a run.

'I'd like you to repeat to my face what you've been saying about me behind my back,' he said by way of introduction, in as level a voice as he could muster.

Charles Lesser looked up in open-mouthed astonishment. 'I beg your pardon?' he said, his glass midway between the bar and his lips.

Aldermarten pulled his right hand from his pocket and placed it, palm down, on the well-polished bar to recite the sentence he had practised several times over on the way to the wine bar. This time, his voice was verging on the hysterical. 'I said I'd like you to repeat to my face what you've been saying about me behind my back. At the Beerbohm. This tie business.' His face, by now, resembled a glossy aubergine.

Charles Lesser was unimpressed. 'Oh, that.' He nodded and carried on with his wine as if there were nothing more to be said on the matter.

Aldermarten's head bobbed around on his shoulders with fury. 'Oh, you're not denying that you repeated our conversation, then?' He straightened his shoulders to emphasise the challenge.

Lord Lesser looked nonplussed. 'No,' he answered with a frown.

'With a little embellishment here and there?' Jeremy suggested. His left hand flapped frantically as he added: 'I had no intention of wearing that tie until after I was elected, as well you know.'

Lesser put his glass down on the bar and looked at Aldermarten in exasperation. Shaking out his broadsheet to better read it, he remarked casually: 'Well, I may have mentioned it to one or two others, but if things then got twisted . . .' He pretended to read.

Aldermarten pulled himself up to his full height. 'Sorry, but that's not good enough,' he said. Something about his tone made his companion look up. 'And being something of an expert in the law of slander, I should warn you that I'm not going to let this pass. Unless you have the good grace to put the matter straight immediately.'

Lord Lesser's forehead furrowed as he tried to take in what Aldermarten was saying. 'Are you threatening to sue me, Jeremy?' he asked, with an incredulous smile.

'Thanks to you, somebody black-balled me.' Aldermarten's voice rose to a near-shout as other drinkers in the bar looked round. He ignored them all. The very thought of his rejection from the Beerbohm still almost reduced him to tears; he didn't care who knew about it.

Lord Lesser's face took on a peculiar expression. 'Somebody?' he laughed, his tongue in his cheek. Then, seeing the look in Aldermarten's eyes, he added: 'Well, be my guest, old man. But you'll only make yourself look more of an arse than you do already.' Aldermarten pursed his lips and stuck his chin out in indignation, but Lord Lesser wasn't finished. 'You see, what people really don't like, Jeremy,' he added acidly, 'is people who make assumptions.' His face changed and he smiled once more as he folded his newspaper in half and prepared to leave the bar. 'Shame in a way,' he added. 'It really would have been *most* entertaining to have had you in the club. Good luck.' With that, he walked out, leaving Aldermarten speechless and utterly perplexed.

Kavanagh stood huddled in a corner of the courthouse lobby with Paddy Spence. After such a successful day he was disappointed to emerge from the courtroom and find his old friend waiting for him with a sombre look on his face. When Paddy told him what had happened and what Hazel was now proposing, he dragged his barrister's wig off and held it in his hands, a picture of dejection. What next? This case was already one of the hardest he had ever dealt with. First the chief prosecution witness nearly didn't give evidence at all, then – when he had finally managed to get her to open up in the witness box – she had decided to retract her evidence because of some anonymous telephone threat.

'How did she know it was a policeman?' he asked Spence, who stood, hands in his pockets, leaning against the wall. He knew he had landed Kavanagh in it with this one and he wished to God it hadn't turned out this way, but Hazel was adamant.

'He recited her record over the phone,' Spence whispered, his face pained. 'Places, dates, court appearances back to when she was thirteen. If it wasn't the police, it was somebody in there giving them access. It wouldn't take much to put her away, either, with that suspended sentence she's got.' He sighed and looked at Kavanagh's crestfallen expression, before adding: 'You'll have to disclose it.'

Kavanagh's eyes widened. 'To the defence? I've just spent the day wrecking Vincent's alibi.' He hated the thought of letting Vincent get away with this – that was the reason he'd taken the case on in the first place.

The complicated legal rules governing what prosecution counsel should disclose to the defence before, during and sometimes after a trial were well known to Kavanagh. Designed to help prevent miscarriages of justice, the regulations stipulated that if the prosecution counsel became possessed of information so pertinent to the other side that it could have a material effect on the outcome of the trial, they were honour-bound to disclose it, even if that information could be detrimental to their own side.

It was his respect for the very same rules, and the principles of the Bar that demanded that the jury be told the truth, which had led Kavanagh to disclose the familial relationship between Lise Auerbach and Natasha Jackson, even though that information had probably contributed to his client's ultimate conviction. Now he had to consider whether or not to tell the court that Hazel Dwyer had changed her mind yet again, and wished to retract her testimony.

Paddy knew what his friend was thinking as he stood, stony-faced, at his side. But he had spent the past two hours with a distraught Hazel and he had no choice but to tell Kavanagh how she felt.

'She's falling apart, Jimmy,' he said, using the abbreviated version of his name that nobody but he had ever used. The use of it was not lost on Kavanagh; it conveyed Spence's own anguish over the situation, and he softened slightly.

'All right,' he conceded. 'What if I tell Craxton that our key witness is thinking about retracting and then Hazel suddenly decides that she won't, after all?' It was a moot point and very possible, the way things were going. He watched as the lawyer nodded his acceptance of the possibility and wondered what to do next.

'She can't stay in that hotel,' Spence remarked, knowing that if some bent copper working for Vincent knew she was there then it might not be long before Babb's men paid a visit. Kavanagh agreed with a nod of resignation. 'I'm running out of favours,' Spence added. 'I . . . I suppose I'll have to put her up.' Kavanagh's head jerked up and he glared at his friend accusingly. Spence looked defensive. 'Well, what does that mean?' he asked. 'You don't think I'd sleep with her, do you? For God's sake, man, I'm old enough to be her father . . . her grandfather, more like.'

Kavanagh's eyes narrowed. 'Hmmm. Conscience never stopped you in the past,' he pointed out as Spence blushed.

Before he could answer, George Foster rounded the corner in the lobby and called out anxiously, 'Mr Kavanagh, I've been looking for you.' He approached the two men with a smile, happy with the way the day had gone. But, seeing the look on their faces, his own face fell. 'Something wrong?' he asked.

Kavanagh shot Spence a glance and said: 'You could say . . . I'll tell you more tomorrow.'

Three hours later, in a seedy pie-and-mash café near Spitalfields, east London, James Kavanagh sat at a table looking very out of place in his dark suit and tie. He would much rather have been at home having dinner with Lizzie, but there was something he had to do, someone he had to see, and he had telephoned and arranged the meeting soon after Spence had left him at the court.

Sitting staring into a steaming mug of tea, he thought long and hard about Hazel Dwyer, Ian Vincent and the threatening phone call. He wondered what he should do, whether he should go strictly by the book, or try to keep the lid on the case until the verdict.

The café was dank and depressing, with steamed-up windows and the smell of years of overboiled cabbage. It was almost empty. A filthy old tramp sat in a corner at one of the fake marble-topped tables, eating a meat pie with the traditional green liquor gravy and mushy peas. An ageing hooker sat at another table, chain-smoking, leaning against the white-tiled walls, and lost in her own thoughts, before she took to the streets and started work. This was not a place Kavanagh knew, or hoped to see again, but it had been suggested as a good rendezvous by the person he was meeting, a man who walked in at that moment and took a seat opposite him.

'Mr Kavanagh?' The younger man with the shoulder-length hair held out a hand and the barrister shook it.

'DCI Sampson?' Kavanagh half stood in greeting and the two sat back down on the hard wooden benches. 'It was good of you to come out at such short notice.'

Chris Sampson unbuttoned the jacket of his crumpled taupe-coloured suit and rested an arm on the table. 'Sounded important,' he said, waiting to be told why he had been summoned.

Kavanagh, fingers intertwined on the table in front of him, looked into the heavily lidded eyes of the man whose job it was to protect the likes of Hazel Dwyer. 'Er, Paddy tells me that you have been watching Ron Babb for a long time,' he said.

Sampson nodded, his lank hair greased back but still touching his collar. 'From a distance, yeah,' he said, wondering where this was leading.

'And he's never been in prison, has he?' Kavanagh asked, not taking his eyes off his companion.

Sampson, feeling somehow uneasy, answered: 'No.'

Kavanagh nodded slowly and chose his words with caution. 'Do you think that might be because he has friends – in the force?' he asked.

Sampson studied his fingernails briefly before answering. 'It's a possibility, but we've found no evidence of it to date.' His deep Mancunian accent rumbled like thunder.

'So you have been looking?' Kavanagh asked.

Sampson chose his words carefully. 'We keep an open mind,' he said, staring his inquisitor out.

Kavanagh looked down, nodding. 'Well, I thought I ought to report that a police officer, or someone with information from a police officer, phoned Hazel Dwyer today. Threatened to pin something on her if she didn't withdraw her evidence.'

Sampson looked puzzled. 'How did he find her?' Kavanagh shrugged his shoulders. Sampson added: 'If it was a "he"?'

'Oh, yeah,' Kavanagh confirmed.

'Did she say anything about him? What he sounded like?' Sampson asked, his fingers twirling a vinegar bottle round and round on the table.

'Only that he didn't have a London accent,' Kavanagh responded, with a smile.

Sampson smiled back. 'Well, that narrows it down a bit,' he said. Looking up, he asked: 'What's she gonna do?'

Kavanagh looked non-committal. 'Well, she's considering her options but my guess is she'll stand by what she said.'

Sampson studied the ceiling briefly before asking his next question. 'And how do you rate Vincent's chances if she doesn't retract?'

Kavanagh didn't honestly know the answer, but he wasn't going to let the detective know that. 'Slim, I'd say,' he replied.

Sampson thought for a moment before raising an eyebrow. 'So they might have another go at her?'

Kavanagh shrugged again. 'Maybe.'

Sampson looked concerned. 'Well, where is she?'

Kavanagh paused. 'Safe.'

Sampson studied his nails again. 'Good,' he said, biting his bottom lip. Then his face broke into a grin. 'Well, thanks for telling me,' he added. 'I'm not sure what I can do about it, though. Not a lot to go on, is there?'

Kavanagh spoke with slow deliberation. 'I just thought you should know,' he said.

Sampson got to his feet and said: 'Thanks.' He looked as if he were ready to say goodbye, but Kavanagh wasn't quite finished.

'Oh, there's one more thing,' he said, looking up at Sampson with a puzzled expression. 'Er, you told Paddy that Babb kept Vincent away from all his criminal activities, didn't you?'

Sampson stood at the table and nodded. 'Yeah.'

Kavanagh still looked confused. 'Only, in the witness box,' he recounted, 'Babb described him as deputy general manager.'

Sampson stuffed his hands in his pockets and nodded again. 'Of the aggregates, yeah.'

Kavanagh was perplexed. 'Yeah, but that's just run as

a cover for his criminal side, isn't it?' He remembered reading Spence's file on Babb and all the dodgy deals he was supposed to be doing – protection rackets, arms, money-laundering, you name it.

Chris Sampson shrugged his broad shoulders. 'It's just a title, to give him some status. It doesn't mean anything.'

Kavanagh blinked several times. 'So you still think the idea that Vincent had something in his briefcase incriminating him and Babb is off course?'

Sampson rolled his eyes to the ceiling and then back down to Kavanagh. 'I do,' he said, firmly.

Kavanagh frowned. 'Then why would he kill to get it back?' His eyes were locked on to Sampson's now, waiting for an answer.

Sampson shifted on his feet and paused for a moment. 'If that was the motive,' he said, staring back at the barrister. 'Criminal mind, Mr Kavanagh. You don't need me to tell you how hard it is to work out sometimes.'

Kavanagh chuckled. 'No,' he responded, as Sampson turned on his heels and left the café without another word. The Q.C. made no attempt to follow. He just sat stock still in his seat staring after the detective, his mind in turmoil.

In a puddle-filled side street in south London, Ian Vincent was pacing up and down, his ear to a mobile phone, his expression one of disbelief. His top lip was curled and a fine layer of sweat had formed on his forehead. The fire exit to the pub he had just been drinking in with a few mates was flapping open in the wind as he had left it when his mobile rang and he had run out the back for some privacy.

Kicking a stone down the street in anger as he paced and listened, listened and paced, the square-faced young man swapped the phone from one ear to the other, hardly able to take in what he was being told. This had all gone terribly wrong, from the minute Graham Foster had come on to the scene, and now it was getting even worse.

'Oh yeah? Well, cheers,' he said into the mouthpiece, a note of bitterness in his voice. 'Well I'm gonna 'ave to, ain't I . . . 'cos I've got no bloody choice!' He snapped the two halves of the telephone shut and stood, gasping for breath, looking around him, his chest heaving with sighs. Hand to his head, he thought desperately, hoping that a solution to all his problems would suddenly materialise. But it didn't, and as he prepared to go back into the pub, he had never felt so afraid in all his life.

Jeremy Aldermarten, his black overcoat buttoned up to the neck, walked down from Pall Mall and along Waterloo Place towards the Mall with Sir Geoffrey Pack-Martin, wearing a similar overcoat but topped with a flamboyant spotted bow tie and a large black hat. Both men had their hands in their pockets, both were well protected against the crisp winter's day, and both had dour expressions on their faces.

'If you want my advice, Jeremy, you should drop it,' Sir Geoffrey told Aldermarten, and not for the first time.

But Aldermarten didn't seem to have heard him. Deep in thought, he continued in the same vein as he had throughout lunch, his indignation evident in his voice. 'One man decides to . . . to misinterpret something I say during a perfectly innocent conversation,' he told his companion, removing his hands from his pockets and waving them around frantically, 'and the next thing you know, I'm not just black-balled but . . . labelled as some sort of grubby parvenu for the rest of my life. I'm sorry, but no, I won't. At the very least I'm going to

240

write to the committee.' He was determined not to let the matter rest.

Sir Geoffrey knew that the time had come to say something. Stopping halfway down the York stone steps to the Mall, he called out Aldermarten's name in a firm but insistent tone as his companion carried on. 'Jeremy!' he repeated, with even more emphasis.

Aldermarten, a few steps ahead of him and still mid-flow, stopped and turned. 'What?' The look on Sir Geoffrey's face worried him.

His hands stuffed even deeper into his pockets, Sir Geoffrey's reptilian features looked pained. 'I don't know how to say this gently,' he said. Aldermarten turned to face his companion head on. Sir Geoffrey took a deep breath and blurted his information out as best he could. 'It wasn't one man,' was all he said.

Aldermarten's head jerked like a chicken as he peered up into Sir Geoffrey's face to try to ascertain if he meant what he thought – no, feared – he meant. 'Sorry?' he said softly.

Sir Geoffrey knew there was no turning back now. As sympathetically as he could, he spelled it out for Aldermarten. 'It wasn't just one member who voted against you . . . on the committee,' he said, as he watched the younger man's mouth drop open. 'It was all of them. Except one . . . me. Sorry.' Unable to watch Aldermarten's suffering further, he shrugged and carried on down the steps, patting his shoulder as he passed.

Jeremy Aldermarten, his expression that of a wounded animal, stood alone on the steps, his eyes moist. Great clouds of steam emerged from his lips and into the frozen air as he fought for breath. Searching his memory banks as he rewound and replayed the last scene in his mind, he suddenly realised the full implication of what his friend

241

had told him. 'Peter?' he said, to no one in particular, his face ashen with shock.

James Kavanagh sat pensively, hand on his chin, in Court 8 as Susan Craxton rose to her feet to address the judge. Should he or shouldn't he disclose Hazel Dwyer's change of heart to the court, he agonised again and again, as he had done all night, after his meeting with Chris Sampson.

Paddy Spence had arrived in court that morning looking drained and with no real news – Hazel was still very upset and was still insisting that she wanted to retract. Kavanagh had a little time, he didn't have to make a decision just yet – the defence still had to work through their list of witnesses: forensic examiners, a nurse at the casualty department of the hospital, various others whose evidence Ms Craxton hoped would cast doubt on that brought by the prosecution. The next witness on her list was that of a second pathologist, who would claim that Graham Foster's facial injuries were not caused by a ring-wearing hand.

Susan Craxton's grating voice filled the court. 'As my next witness I call Ian Vincent,' she announced. Kavanagh thought he hadn't heard her correctly at first, but when he looked across and saw her contrite expression, he realised that she was serious and jumped to his feet.

'My Lady!' he cried in indignation. This was highly irregular, springing the defendant on him when he had least expected it, not allowing him time to prepare for his cross-examination. And after such a sleepless night, he was hardly ready for sharp-witted exchanges.

The judge was as angry as he. Turning to Miss Craxton, she told her sharply: 'You specifically told the court that the defendant would not be testifying.' She didn't like counsel who took it upon themselves to disrupt the routines and rituals of her court and her expression showed her feelings.

Miss Craxton's demeanour was one of obsequiousness. 'That is correct, my Lady,' she said, softly, bowing her head. 'But, er, he's now most anxious to clarify certain points in the evidence which has been given on his behalf.'

Kavanagh, sitting bolt upright, commented in a stage whisper: 'Yes. Now he's heard it,' but Miss Craxton ignored him.

Judge Whitrow put on her spectacles and leaned forward to address the prosecution counsel. 'Do you have an objection to the defendant testifying, Mr Kavanagh?' she asked. She knew he wouldn't have – no prosecution silk worth his salt would miss the chance to destroy a defendant in the witness box – but she shared his views on the unhappy timing of the decision.

Kavanagh rose to his feet, his hands hooked into his gown's lapels. 'Far be it from me to stand in the way of a man speaking in his own defence, m'lady,' he said with a wry smile. 'Even at this late stage.'

Judge Whitrow took his point and nodded at the defence. Shuffling the papers on her desk to make way for the notes she needed to take on the new witness, she said, with some frostiness: 'Very well, Miss Craxton,' and waited for the defendant to take the oath.

Peter Foxcott was in the highest of spirits when he arrived at River Court that morning. Humming an extract from *La Traviata*, the Verdi opera he had seen the previous night at the Coliseum, before an excellent supper with some of his favourite clients, he was sporting a jaunty tie and was all smiles.

Walking along the corridor to his office with a bounce in his step, he saw Tom Buckley emerge from the administrative office. 'Morning, Tom, lovely day,' he said, grinning. Not only had the evening been a rip-roaring success in its own right, but at the end of it he had been invited to sit on a new government commission on employment law reform – a lucrative and prestigious post. Even Eleanor was suitably impressed. Nothing could take away his *joie de vivre* – or at least that is what he had thought, until he saw a stony-faced Jeremy Aldermarten leaning against the architrave to his office.

'*Et tu*, Peter?' Jeremy called down the corridor, a catch in his voice, as the smile fell from Peter Foxcott's lips. The Head of Chambers tilted his head in an expression of mock incomprehension, so Aldermarten clarified the position for him. 'I've been talking to Geoffrey – about the election,' he said, his arms folded high across his chest, his chin jutting out. Peter blushed and his step faltered.

'Ah.' The penny dropped. 'Um ... my room?' he suggested, as he brushed past Aldermarten and into his office, gently closing the door behind them. So much for it being a lovely day.

Susan Craxton was nothing if not painstaking as she took Ian Vincent slowly through his evidence. For over two hours he stood in the witness box in his pale grey suit, his hands gripping the sides, giving carefully worded answers to all her questions about his movements on the day of the murder. As Ron and Shirley Babb looked down from the public gallery, the former boxer gave an astonishingly calm and deliberate performance. Kavanagh could only sit by helplessly and watch the jurors' faces change from open hostility to acceptance and finally even sympathy for this charming young man who some of them obviously thought had been wrongly accused of such a wicked crime.

'And where did you park your car?' Miss Craxton was asking.

'In the drive,' Vincent responded, leaning in slightly

towards the microphone that amplified his answers around the courtroom and recorded them on to tape.

'It was there overnight?' Miss Craxton asked.

'Two nights,' Vincent answered slowly, eliminating all previous doubts raised by his mother's evidence. 'The Saturday night when I stayed over, and then the Sunday night when I couldn't drive it on account of my hand.' Shirley Babb nodded her perfectly coiffeured head in time to the well-rehearsed rhythm of her son's answer.

'And then how did it get back to your flat?' his counsel asked, smiling, a fountain pen poised in her hand.

'My stepfather drove it round the next day – the Monday,' Vincent answered, maintaining eye contact with the jury.

'And then how did he get back to his house?' Miss Craxton asked.

'My mother picked him up,' Vincent responded, glancing down at Kavanagh, whose head was resting in the palm of his hand as he witnessed all the good he had done being undone.

Miss Craxton shot her learned friend a look before clarifying the point. 'You're sure about that?' she asked.

'Positive.' Vincent nodded, adding, for good measure: 'She gets a bit forgetful when she's wound up, you know. Like we all do, I suppose. But she definitely brought their car along and he drove them both home.'

Kavanagh, his head shaking in exasperation at the systematic destruction of all his earlier efforts, put his spectacles on and wondered what his next move should be.

Jeremy Aldermarten had chosen a jet-black suit that morning, to match his sombre mood. Standing in it now in Peter Foxcott's elegant Wedgwood-blue office, in front of his huge walnut desk, he stood tall and erect and fought to control the pitch of his voice as he told Foxcott what he had come to say.

'Do you know the most galling aspect of this whole episode?' he said. 'That even if everyone else in the committee had voted "yes", you, Peter – my proposer – your black ball would have kept me out.' His left hand flapping in the air, he tried to find words to express what that meant as he added: 'I . . . I f-find that . . . very . . .' He blinked back the tears and looked to the ceiling for inspiration, but Peter, standing behind his desk, interrupted him.

'Jeremy, this tie business. Frankly, I was appalled,' he said, the smile long gone and replaced with a dour expression and a gruff tone.

Aldermarten, red of face, protested his innocence. 'I never intended to wear it until . . . unless I was elected.' He flinched at his *faux pas* and hoped it wasn't noticed. His look of indignation was matched by that of his companion.

'Appalled not by *you*, Jeremy,' Foxcott countered, his eyes blazing, 'but by . . . what it brought up. Is this the company, I thought, into which I want to bring one of my most valued friends?' Aldermarten, his bottom jaw opening and shutting in silent astonishment, could not speak, so Foxcott carried on. 'And what's more, sting him seven hundred pounds a year for the privilege? No, I decided, it was not.'

Aldermarten's power of speech returned. He rocked back on his heels and waved his arm in the air like a frenetic conductor, laughing hollowly. 'Oh, I see,' he shouted as if in sudden realisation, 'you were doing me a favour?' He then glared at Foxcott with a withering look that said he could not possibly expect to get away with such a pathetic explanation.

Foxcott, like Sir Geoffrey before him, knew now that he would have to be frank. Stepping cautiously round

246

from behind his desk, he tried to explain as unto a child. 'Jeremy,' he said softly, 'one's . . . reputation. Such a . . . fragile thing, isn't it?' He sat on the front edge of his desk. Aldermarten, head bowed, bottom lip out, looked up as he continued. 'Too precious, I feel, to be put in the hands of people who'd simply make one a . . . well, the butt of their so-called wit.'

Aldermarten frowned in concentration and then straightened his neck above his burgundy silk tie. 'You . . . you mean they were, er, making jokes about me?' His tone was unbelieving, tearful almost, as he peered into Peter's face, hoping beyond hope that he had got it all wrong.

But Foxcott nodded, his jaw set. As Aldermarten struggled to contain his emotions, the Head of Chambers rolled his eyeballs and said: 'Oh, James was right. We really are a bunch of old farts, Jeremy, even the young ones.' Looking at his friend with a sympathetic smile, he added: 'For what it's worth, I've resigned from the committee.' Hoping to see less resentment and more acceptance on Aldermarten's face, Foxcott concluded: 'You're better off out of it . . . altogether.' But Jeremy Aldermarten could only stand, voiceless, choked with feeling and misty-eyed before him.

16

The prosecution counsel's voice was so soft at first that Ian Vincent almost couldn't hear him. Leaning forward slightly to catch what he was saying, the young man listened closely as Kavanagh began his cross-examination. The experienced barrister had been given little or no time to prepare and yet, as he had listened carefully to Ms Craxton take the defendant through his evidence, he had been able to get the measure of the man, to appreciate just how devious he really was. He was surprised to realise that Vincent wasn't just the mean-faced killer he had first thought he was, but a young man capable of real cunning and someone who had to be handled with extreme caution.

'Quite a week, wasn't it, Mr Vincent?' he said. 'First your stepfather drops a paving slab on your hand. Then your nice new car is stolen. And then you're arrested in a murder investigation.' The volume of Kavanagh's voice increased with the mention of each new disaster to befall the hapless defendant.

'Yes.' Vincent was succinct.

Kavanagh smiled. 'But I'm forgetting . . . breaking your hand wasn't your first piece of bad luck that week, was it? You had your briefcase stolen, didn't you?'

'Yes.' Vincent nodded.

'But you didn't report it to the police?'

Vincent shook his head. 'Well, no point. They'd never have got it back.'

'For the insurance?' Kavanagh asked, as Ms Craxton, head resting on her hand to hide her anxious expression from the jury, watched closely.

'It wasn't worth that much,' Vincent answered flatly.

Kavanagh put on his spectacles and read from a statement. 'But you did want it back, didn't you? According to police enquiries, you put the word about, among your associates, that you were very keen for the case to be returned and – if possible – to know who'd taken it.' He peered up at the defendant over his glasses.

Vincent knew the answer and recited it carefully. 'Well, it was a present from my mother. I didn't want her to think I hadn't looked after it,' he said, playing the role of the dutiful son. Shirley Babb smiled down at him from the public gallery.

Kavanagh nodded as if in understanding. 'So, it was the case itself you wanted to get back? Not what was in it?'

'That's right,' said Vincent.

'What *was* in it, Mr Vincent?' Kavanagh watched the defendant closely.

Pausing a moment, Vincent stared the Q.C. out before blinking. 'My flask and sandwiches,' he said with a smile. 'Nothing important.'

Kavanagh had hardly expected more and he nodded again. 'And did you get it back?' he asked.

'No,' came the answer, and the defendant looked as if he was telling the truth.

'So it's still out there somewhere – with your flask and sandwiches?' Kavanagh suggested, looking at the jury with a smile. He was pleased to see several members return it.

'Probably on a tip somewhere – or in the river,' Vincent responded, a slight frown creasing his wide, flat forehead at the shared joke between his prosecutor and the jury.

Kavanagh, still smiling, nodded. 'Hmm . . . Your car, though, you reported the theft of that to the police.'

'Well, that was worth something.'

'Strange, then, don't you think, that the thief decided to burn it?' He looked perplexed when in reality things had never been more clear.

Vincent realised that everything he said would be twisted back on him and he needed to be more careful. It was like a game, but he – like his stepfather before him – seemed to have an answer for everything. 'Well, it was probably kids. Joy-riders, you know. They often do that,' he mused.

Kavanagh ignored his musings and added: 'Because it's a good way of getting rid of any trace of who's been in the car, isn't it, Mr Vincent?' There was a sterner tone to his voice as he made the clear suggestion that it was Vincent himself who had burned the car out to avoid police finding any trace of Graham Foster's blood on or in it.

Vincent wasn't fazed. 'It's more likely they just like burning things,' he said, his expression quite calm.

Kavanagh glanced down at his notes and decided on a different tack. 'Your stepfather,' he said. 'How do you feel about him, Mr Vincent?'

Ian Vincent blushed visibly for the first time and looked up at the public gallery. His eyes met those of Ron Babb, and the two men locked stares as the defendant considered his answer. 'He's all right,' he responded, as Ron Babb allowed a small smile to tug at the corner of his mouth. Shirley Babb exhaled when her son answered.

'How did you feel about your mother marrying him?' Kavanagh asked next.

Again, Vincent's eyes glanced upwards and he met

his mother's hard stare. 'I dunno,' he answered with a lie.

'You don't know?' Kavanagh asked as all attention focused on the defendant.

'Well, who she marries is her lookout.' Vincent looked uneasy, frightened almost. He obviously didn't like this line of questioning and it showed.

Kavanagh began circling his quarry. 'Her "lookout"?' he repeated with a sneer.

'That's right.' Vincent wished he hadn't used the expression.

'You think she has some reason to be on guard, then?' Kavanagh pursued the point, using the same sort of language the defendant had used.

Vincent closed his eyes and shook his head. 'No, I didn't say that.'

'It's what you meant, though, isn't it?' Kavanagh came back at him quick as a flash, his eyes glistening with the thrill of the chase.

'No.' Vincent looked even more uncomfortable.

'Something to do with the business perhaps? Mr Babb taking over?' Kavanagh listed Vincent's options as to why he might have thought his mother should be on guard.

Vincent refused to rise to the bait. 'No,' he said, shaking his head vehemently.

'Were you expecting to be in charge when your father died?' Kavanagh asked, scratching at old wounds as he watched Vincent squirm.

'I was only sixteen,' the defendant responded, unable to hide the pain he still felt at the memory of his father's sudden death and all that happened immediately afterwards. The look he had first seen in Ron Babb's cold eyes on the day of the funeral, as he pulled Shirley towards him and told her to 'let it all out'. The day a few months later when his mother announced she was getting married. He winced at the memory.

'But one day?' Kavanagh pursued, as Vincent shrugged his shoulders. 'By now, even? Did that cause difficulties with your stepfather?'

Vincent looked up at Ron Babb, scowling at him in the public gallery, and answered Kavanagh without lowering his gaze. 'Well, like he said – we've had our ups and downs,' he replied, as his mother shot her husband a glance.

'But it's all right now, between the two of you?' Kavanagh continued.

'Yes,' Vincent answered untruthfully, as his mother's head nodded in agreement.

'After all,' Kavanagh cogitated, 'you were helping him to build a patio, weren't you?' Vincent nodded. 'And you'd stayed for a meal the night before?'

'That's right.' Vincent bobbed his head.

'And he's given you an important job in his business? Or is that the *family* business?' Kavanagh wouldn't let it go.

Vincent swallowed hard and blinked. 'It's *his* business,' he said with a simplicity that belied his emotions.

'But an important job – deputy general manager,' Kavanagh went on.

Vincent's eyes narrowed. 'Can be,' he replied.

'Your stepfather said, er, you did a "bit of everything"?' Kavanagh consulted the notes he had made during Ron Babb's cross-examination.

'Yes.'

'Which includes negotiating deals?' Kavanagh, spectacles on, looked as if he were still reading from Ron Babb's statement.

'It can do.' Vincent looked wary.

'Talking to clients?' Kavanagh, head bowed, kept on reading.

'Sometimes, yes.'

'And delivering documents?' Kavanagh said it blandly, as if it were just another part of Ron Babb's statement.

Vincent grinned, happy that he hadn't been caught out. 'No,' he said, firmly. 'No documents.' He stared Kavanagh out.

The Q.C. raised his head and looked at the defendant in open admiration. There would be no getting past that well-rehearsed defence. Vincent wasn't going to slip up as his mother had, and Kavanagh was fast running out of tricks. It was time for something new and more than a little risky.

He smiled back at Vincent and nodded. 'No. That's right,' he said, removing his spectacles. Waving them in his right hand, he added: 'But talking to clients, sometimes?'

Vincent knew he'd won an important point and relaxed a little. 'Yes,' he replied, his eyebrows arching as if to say: 'Come on, then, give it your best shot.' Little did he know what was coming.

Kavanagh's expression changed suddenly. Staring straight ahead of him, his lips taut, he said, with some deliberation: 'Tell me, Mr Vincent, have you ever talked to a client by the name of Sampson? . . . Chris Sampson?'

Ian Vincent looked as if he had been kicked in the stomach. The colour drained from his face, his eyes widened in disbelief, and he tried to gulp down whatever it was that was forming a tight knot in his throat. DCI Sampson, sitting at the back of the court, suddenly sat up and looked at the defendant helplessly. He then glared at Kavanagh with open hostility.

'Mr Vincent?' Kavanagh was asking, his eyes on fire as he watched his well-aimed question hit its mark and send ripples of shock through the defendant's body.

Ian Vincent's bottom lip quivered visibly as he tried to

formulate an answer. Locked on to Kavanagh's gaze, he wanted the ground to open up and swallow him whole. After several seconds of embarrassing silence, all he could muster, in a tremulous voice, was: 'Wh-who?'

Kavanagh felt the blood coursing through his veins and his heart pounding in his chest as the adrenalin of the moment spurred him on. This was what being a barrister was all about, instances like these. At that precise moment, he wouldn't have traded places with anyone in the world. His face was alive and he felt like a young man again. 'Sampson,' he repeated, enjoying every minute. 'As in the Bible . . . I believe he might be a client.'

Vincent still hadn't got a grip on himself, and he stood wide-eyed in the witness box, sweat trickling down his face, his hands gripping the sides for support. His mother and stepfather frowned in perplexed consternation as they watched him, both wondering what on earth the matter was. Shirley Babb looked across at her husband as if to say 'Do something', but he didn't know what it was all about either. Vincent finally found his tongue. 'N-no,' was all he could say.

Kavanagh persisted. 'The name seems to ring a bell,' he suggested, as Vincent shuddered visibly and staggered forward in the witness box, fighting for breath. At that moment DCI Sampson stepped from the back of the court and handed a hastily scribbled note to Paddy Spence, who took it with a frown. He didn't know what the hell Kavanagh was up to either. Why on earth mention the name of his mate at Scotland Yard? And why was Vincent so affected by the name? He took the note and read it as Kavanagh tried to get a response again. 'Mr Vincent?' the Q.C. asked, this time through gritted teeth.

Paddy Spence tapped Kavanagh on the shoulder and handed him the folded piece of paper as the court waited for a response from the defendant. Unable to speak or even breathe as he looked around at the sea of faces waiting for his answer, Ian Vincent looked as if he might collapse. Judge Whitrow was concerned for his wellbeing. Removing her spectacles, she leaned forward in her seat to ask: 'Are you all right, Mr Vincent?' Unable to get a response either, she repeated his name as the defendant looked up at her and then back at Kavanagh and again at the judge in total panic.

James Kavanagh read the note that had been handed to him and sighed heavily. He knew there had been a risk of this but he had hoped it wouldn't happen. He looked up at the judge with an expression of anger and frustration on his face. The last thing he had wanted at this stage was an interruption when the defendant was so obviously on the ropes. But he had been left no choice. 'M'lady, might I suggest a short adjournment?' he asked, with some reluctance.

Judge Whitrow looked at the defendant and smiled. 'For the witness's convenience?' she suggested. The Q.C. attempted a smile. 'Very well, ten minutes, Mr Kavanagh.' Ian Vincent's head spun round to look at the judge and then back at the barrister with an expression of such imploring that James Kavanagh felt almost sorry for him.

The court adjourned and Ian Vincent slumped back down in the witness box, his head held in his hands. An usher approached with a freshly poured glass of water but he refused the offer. Studying his thick rubber-soled black suede shoes and averting his eyes from the public gallery, his mind swam as he considered his options. Bolting from the court was nigh on impossible, one floor up and with all these court officials and coppers about. It all depended on what happened next, on what Kavanagh was going to do, and the agony of not knowing the barrister's plan nearly stifled him. For the first time since his father's death, he felt like sobbing openly.

Kavanagh ignored Vincent's shattered demeanour and strode from the court, his black gown flapping, followed closely by a baffled Paddy Spence. In the deserted lobby outside, DCI Chris Sampson was waiting for them, his arms folded defensively across his chest.

Kavanagh was furious. 'Don't you think you should have let me in on the secret a little earlier?' he fumed at Sampson, his face purple. 'He's an informant, isn't he?'

Sampson nodded. 'My informant,' he clarified, as Paddy Spence stood between the two men listening in astonishment.

'Betraying his stepfather to the police.' Kavanagh suddenly saw it all.

'And if it comes out, Babb'll kill him – in or out of prison,' Sampson pointed out, looking equally angry, his hands on his hips.

Paddy Spence was livid at the deception and rounded on the copper he had known from his earliest days as a lawyer, a man he had thought of as a friend. 'Why the hell didn't you tell us?' he snapped. Kavanagh thought the Irishman might hit him.

Sampson laughed out loud as Kavanagh watched him with thinly veiled contempt. 'Oh?' the detective countered. 'And you'd have kept it to yourself, would you? Could you, legally? You'd have had to have disclosed it to your client at least, and I couldn't have risked that.'

Kavanagh interrupted the spat between the two men and spoke with considerable venom. 'So you've been trying to protect him in other ways,' he told Sampson. 'Even seeing there was no prosecution brought in the first place? That's what was in the briefcase. Something linking the two of

you. Something on Babb that Vincent shouldn't have had
. . . What?' His final word was a demand.

Sampson sneered at the Q.C. and gave his Mancunian
accent full rein. 'Look, as far as I'm concerned, that's
irrelevant. The point is . . .' he began.

But Kavanagh interrupted him and took one step closer
to the long, thin face he was coming to detest. 'And as far
as I'm concerned, it is central to this trial.'

Sampson carried on talking, regardless. His argument
was directed at Spence. 'The point is, Babb is doing a deal,
right now, to bring into this country a large quantity of
illegal arms – using his business as a front. Now Vincent
is gonna help us track them down to their delivery points
around the country. But he can't do that from inside.'

Kavanagh blinked at the detective, unable to believe that
he could so blatantly disregard the crux of the matter. 'He
committed a murder,' he said, angrily.

Sampson was unmoved. 'And how many more people
are going to get murdered if those guns get out on the
streets? Would you want their blood on your hands,
Mr Kavanagh?' The detective was pleased with the way
in which he had shifted all the responsibility on to the
barrister's shoulders.

Kavanagh hung his head with a sigh as he considered all
that he had been told. Spence, slightly calmer now, stuffed
his hands into his pockets and waited. Turning to DCI
Sampson, he asked: 'So what do you want us to do?'

Kavanagh was incensed and rounded on the lawyer.
'We're not working for him, for God's sake,' he said,
poking Sampson in the ribs in indignation. 'And he's not
telling us out of kindness.' He turned and started to walk
away, but Spence was quickly on his heels.

'Listen, Jimmy, he's got a point,' he pleaded, leading his
friend to one side of the lobby as people started to emerge

from the courtroom. 'One lad's already dead because of this. D'you wanna kill another?' The Irish charm was still trying to work its magic, but it was lost on Kavanagh now.

Beyond Spence, he could see Sampson whispering to a fellow detective about what was going on. He looked back into the sparkling eyes of Paddy Spence with some sadness. How quickly the lawyer seemed to have forgotten the vicious nature of Graham Foster's death; the post-mortem photographs of the teenager's broken body, the close-ups of his battered face, the heartbreak of his father. Now he was labelling Vincent as just another 'lad' like Graham. It wouldn't do. It was out of his hands and he told Spence so. 'I cannot keep something like this to myself, Paddy,' he said, tapping his spectacles on the lawyer's chest.

Spence looked astonished. 'You're not going to disclose this to Foster and the defence?'

Kavanagh sighed once more. 'You know the rules.'

'Not in this situation, no, and I doubt if you do either,' the lawyer said, jabbing at him with a finger. 'It'll only get back to Babb on another route.'

To Kavanagh, the position was quite clear and he spelled it out for Spence. 'Vincent killed Graham Foster. *His* father is *my* client.' He pointed across at the detective before adding, angrily: 'Not Sampson, not the Crown – George Foster.' He bobbed his head at Paddy to punctuate the point and walked away, wishing once again that he had never got involved in the first place.

Paddy Spence pulled his hands from his pockets and followed. 'Fine,' he said, his eyes blazing. 'Kill him, then.' Kavanagh pushed through the double swing doors to the court with such force that they swung back in Paddy's face.

*   *   *

259

Kavanagh arrived back in the courtroom looking like a large black crow. His face like thunder, he turned and looked up at Ron Babb, sitting high in the public gallery above, and stared at him with nothing short of contempt. Babb shifted uncomfortably in his seat and wondered what the look could mean. His wife looked to her husband for reassurance, but found none in his narrowed eyes.

Turning and resting his gaze on Ian Vincent, sitting cowering tearfully in the witness box, Kavanagh fought to control the maelstrom of emotions swirling within him. He knew that Vincent was a cold-blooded killer, a young man who had tortured and beaten poor Graham Foster to death, but could Kavanagh now sign his death warrant – play the hangman? He slumped down on his bench, his jaw set, and tried to consider his options.

'The court will rise.' The clerk stood and announced the arrival of Judge Whitrow, who resumed her seat high on the bench in front of both counsel and looked at the prosecutor expectantly.

'Mr Kavanagh,' she prompted as Ian Vincent stared at the Q.C., a pleading expression in his eyes. But the counsel remained seated and speechless, staring back at the defendant, his pulse pounding rhythmically in his head. 'Mr Kavanagh?' The judge used a more impatient tone. She didn't like being kept waiting.

Vincent exchanged glances with the judge and then looked back at Kavanagh, his mouth dry, the whites of his knuckles visible from his firm grip on the box. If Ron Babb ever suspected what he had been up to, who Chris Sampson was and what the two of them had been hatching, then he was a dead man, and the manner of his death would make Graham Foster's look as if he had died peacefully in his sleep.

James Kavanagh knew that his choices were limited.

Ignoring the looks of Spence, Vincent and Sampson all boring into him, he rose slowly to his feet and addressed the court. 'Er, m'lady, before I continue with my cross-examination,' he began slowly, 'I feel it incumbent upon me to inform the court . . .'

Ian Vincent, his eyes moist, his chest heaving, suddenly lost control. 'Wait!' he shouted, his voice near-hysterical, and he turned to the judge to plead for her intervention. Whatever else happened, he had to stop Kavanagh from saying anything more.

Judge Whitrow peered down at the defendant, who was obviously in some considerable distress, and spoke softly. 'Mr Vincent, if you wish to address this court, you must do so through your counsel.'

Vincent stared back at Kavanagh, his expression that of a frightened rabbit, and ignored the judge's warning. These were desperate times and they called for desperate measures. 'I wanna say something,' he shouted, gasping for breath.

The judge was losing patience and she took a more insistent tone. 'Well, then, Mr Vincent, I repeat . . .'

But Vincent knew the moment of judgment had come. 'I did it!' he blurted out. 'I killed him!'

There were gasps from around the courtroom, and a single heart-wrenching sob from the public gallery, as Shirley Babb fell against her husband. Susan Craxton jumped to her feet to protest on behalf of her client, but Vincent wouldn't be quietened.

'It was because of Hazel,' he continued, his eyes locked on to James Kavanagh's. 'I . . . I didn't mean to . . . I just . . . I just lost it, see.' Susan Craxton sat back down with a thump and listened, open-mouthed, to her client's outpourings. 'I couldn't stop myself hitting him. It was . . . it was the two of them together . . . I couldn't . . . I couldn't stand it . . . I'm sorry,' Vincent said, his lips wet with spittle, the droplets of sweat running into his deep, dark eyes. The courtroom was silent as he finished, the waves of shock rebounding off the walls and back again. His objective achieved, Vincent sank forward and bent double, leaning on the edge of the witness box for support as his legs gave way. It was over. Two uniformed police officers moved in to contain him as DCI Chris Sampson left the courtroom in disgust.

Shirley Babb sat in the public gallery looking around wildly, unable to take in the fact that her son had just confessed to murder. After her initial rasping cry she had been unable to make another sound. What the hell had happened? Had she missed something? Her mouth, smeared in scarlet lipstick, was twisted into a silent cry. Her tears had run her mascara all down her face and she tugged at her handkerchief rhythmically.

Ron Babb sat next to her, still and silent, on the edge of his seat, watching his stepson through steely eyes and trying to piece the last few minutes together in his mind. Even he hadn't thought the boy was that stupid, and yet here he was, giving it all away for no apparent reason. And then there had been that look from Kavanagh. He ignored the shivering wreck of a woman sitting next to him and wondered what it could all mean.

Paddy Spence and George Foster were equally shocked and sat slumped in their seats, staggered by the sudden and dramatic end to the case they had both secretly thought they never had a chance of winning. Kavanagh was a genius; he had backed Vincent so far into a corner that the young man had shot himself, saving the Q.C. the job. As they watched the defendant now, his face creased up against the consequences of what he had just done, they were unable even to get to their feet and congratulate the barrister – congratulations that would have gone unheard by Kavanagh, who stood numbed in front of them.

Less than two hours later, as Ian Vincent was led, red-eyed and handcuffed, into the back of a prison van, the words of the judge were still ringing in his ears.

'Ian Vincent,' Judge Whitrow had pronounced as the packed courtroom stayed dutifully silent, 'by your own admission you have committed a heinous, premeditated and brutal act against a young man whose only crime was to fall in love with the person you, yourself, desired but could not have.'

Several members of the jury, men and women whose duties were never required, sat stiffly in the jury box and looked cheated. The judge concluded: 'The law allows only one sentence for such an act – life imprisonment. Take him down.'

As the prison van door banged shut, blocking off the last ray of sunlight Ian Vincent would feel as a free man, he shuddered and wondered how long it would be before the bars and locks that would guard him would keep him safe from the wrath of Ron Babb.

Jeremy Aldermarten stepped into the administrative office at River Court, handed Tom Buckley's assistant Gary his post for franking, and headed back to his office to pack up his briefcase for the night.

Tom took the pile of letters with a smile and called out, as innocently as he could: 'Off to the club tonight, then, sir?'

Aldermarten spun round at the doorway to confront the senior clerk and to see if there was any trace of a smirk on his face. Finding none, he answered only: 'Hmmm?'

'Club?' Tom repeated, his face a picture of genuine concern.

Aldermarten hesitated, sensitive to any possible rebuke after Peter Foxcott's shocking revelation that he had been the butt of jokes at the Beerbohm, and answered: 'No, not this evening.'

Tom Buckley couldn't resist pursuing the matter. 'Oh?' he said, a frown creasing his forehead, as if in surprise. Gary stood behind him with a similar expression on his face.

Completely taken in, Aldermarten decided to open up to the man he had known for years but didn't really know at all. 'Actually,' he said to Tom, 'I'm having severe doubts on that front.'

Tom Buckley blinked several times and leaned back in his swivel chair, a pencil balanced in his hands. 'Oh, really, sir?' This he had to hear.

More confident now, Aldermarten nodded. 'Mmm. Food's gone right off, you know. And perhaps seven hundred pounds a year might be better spent elsewhere.'

Gary had a great idea. 'I could get you a season ticket for that, if you like, sir,' he said. Seeing Aldermarten's confusion, he added: 'Spurs?'

Aldermarten's mouth opened and shut as he tried to think of something to say that wouldn't hurt the young man's feelings. 'Thank you, Gary,' he eventually managed. 'But I was rather thinking of more . . . um . . . more feminine . . . um . . .' His hands opened and closed in front of him as Tom Buckley watched him struggling.

'Orientated activities?' he offered, helpfully, as Aldermarten nodded with relief.

'Precisely, Tom. After all, I am somewhat eligible, I believe.' His eyes shone. 'Why deny the female of the species any longer?' he added.

Tom Buckley's eyes shone back and he pointed his pencil

264

at the tall, balding barrister. 'Why indeed, sir,' he said, barely able to contain his laughter as Aldermarten disappeared down the corridor.

George Foster used his new key on the repaired front door of his council flat and opened it. Leading James Kavanagh and Paddy Spence inside and through to the spartan surroundings of his lounge, he beamed happiness.

'I don't know which button you pushed, Mr Kavanagh, but it was brilliant,' the goggle-eyed man was saying, as he pointed to a tatty plastic chair for the barrister to sit down on. Kavanagh walked in, his raincoat on, and looked around the sparsely furnished flat, his nose wrinkling at the smell of stale air.

The front door opened and Hazel Dwyer rushed in with a smile. 'Welcome home,' she told George.

Paddy Spence beamed at the young woman as he said: 'Didn't think you'd make it.' The twinkle was even more evident in his eye, but when Hazel returned it, with a look of adoration, Kavanagh flinched visibly.

'I came as soon as you called,' she told Spence softly, her hands clasped together in front of her, her demeanour suppliant.

George Foster registered the exchange too, but was past caring. 'You can give me a hand, then, girl,' he told Hazel, and left the room for the kitchen with her following closely behind.

Spence, a spring in his step, wandered over to a stony-faced Kavanagh. 'So do you think Babb bought it, about the jealousy?' he asked. But Kavanagh didn't answer, he just shrugged his shoulders and stepped to the chair to sit down as glasses rattled in the kitchen.

Spence followed and stood in front of his friend. 'So, are you gonna tell me what you were gonna say?' Kavanagh looked puzzled, so he went on: ' "I feel it incumbent upon me to inform the court . . ." ' he recited from Kavanagh's last words in court.

' ". . . that I wish to see Your Ladyship in chambers – for guidance on a matter of disclosure." ' Kavanagh finished the sentence he had never got the chance to say. Spence beamed at him in open admiration.

At that moment George Foster and Hazel returned with a bottle of champagne and four glasses. George, his tie loosened under his suit, held the bottle up triumphantly. 'I put this in the fridge ages ago, just for luck,' he said, setting it down on a small table with the glasses. 'I didn't think it'd still be there, or cold.' He sat down and stared at the yellow Veuve Cliquot label as Hazel and Paddy sat down on the sofa opposite him. 'That's what comes of having your electricity on direct debit, I suppose,' he added, his face hardening.

Looking across at Kavanagh, his eyes misted over. 'Graham's idea,' he said, his voice cracking. 'I was always forgetting to pay it, you see.' Still holding the bottle in his hand, he didn't attempt to stop the tears rolling down his cheeks. 'I gave up the booze for Graham when we started this,' he sobbed. 'I don't suppose he'd mind his old man having a little drink now, to celebrate?' Racked with sobs, he bowed his head and let the months of grief and tension pour out. Hazel hung her head in embarrassment and Paddy sat silently watching his client go to pieces.

Kavanagh couldn't bear another minute. Rising from his chair with a sigh, he walked over to George Foster and gently took the bottle from his hand, placing it on the table, next to the empty glasses. 'Let's, um, let's do this some other time, eh?' he said, as George Foster's face creased with pain. Kavanagh patted him on the shoulder and made as if to leave the room.

Hazel's hand reached across to Spence's and rubbed it. 'I'll see you later,' she said, her eyes liquid. Paddy blushed and rose awkwardly to his feet, hardly able to meet Kavanagh's accusatory stare.

'I'm sorry, Mr Kavanagh,' George Foster called out, 'I was just ...' Overcome with emotion, he could say no more.

Kavanagh turned at the doorway and watched him. 'No, no. I'm sorry, George,' he said. 'For your loss. Truly.' And with that, he was gone. Without a fee or even a glass of champagne, the man who had achieved justice for Graham Foster left the room.

Outside, walking side by side in silence down the ramp leading to the carpark, Kavanagh glared at Spence with a look of utter condemnation.

Spence turned on the charm as he buttoned up his overcoat. 'What?' he said, then, realising that the game was up, that his friend knew about him and Hazel, he added: 'Don't worry. Nothing happened – till after she'd testified.'

Kavanagh's expression remained fixed. 'Oh, that's all right, then,' he said, with great sarcasm, and continued walking down the ramp.

Sounding just like the teenage Lothario Kavanagh had first met at Nottingham University, Spence added: 'She made herself available. What did you expect me to do?'

Kavanagh rolled his eyes and pursed his lips. 'You took advantage ... like you always do.' Lizzie was right.

Spence stopped and turned to face his old friend. 'We won, Jim,' he said, the twinkle positively flashing. 'For both of them.' He smiled and added, mischievously: 'I think we ought to do it again,' pulling the collar of his coat up around his ears.

James Kavanagh looked at the man he had spent so much of his youth with and realised that Peter Foxcott had been right all those months ago. It was wrong to rekindle old fires. He saw Paddy Spence now in a new light and he didn't much like what he saw.

'Maybe we should quit while we're ahead,' he said, his face grim, as Paddy's sparkle faded.

Spence looked at the Q.C. with sadness and shrugged his shoulders. Shame, he thought they made a great team. Nodding in acceptance, however, he thrust out his hand to shake that of the great James Kavanagh.

Kavanagh looked down at the offered hand and then up into the big green eyes, smiling at him now, for old times' sake. He took his own hand out of his pocket and shook Paddy's firmly, a gesture that said, unequivocally, goodbye.

PART THREE

In God We Trust

17

A long time was to pass before James Kavanagh dared take on another 'freebie'. He had promised both Lizzie and Tom Buckley that he would bottle his social conscience for a while and get on with the job in hand. They were quite right, of course. He wasn't a charity, and the cases that filled his time in the intervening months were almost all high-profile and successful – not to mention extremely lucrative. In fact, it was the best-ever year on record for River Court, and Tom Buckley had never been happier.

Kavanagh's family were all fine, thankfully. Kate had passed her finals with flying colours, a double first, and was having a well-earned break. Matt was living – lawfully, for a change – in rented accommodation in Tooting Bec with a group of friends, doing odd jobs and still deciding what he wanted to do with his life, and Lizzie was still busily involved with the hospital trust that seemed to take up more and more of her time. As well as the odd blissful weekend on *Nicholson's Sloop*, they had even managed to take a three-week holiday in Italy – renting a villa near Castiglione del Lago in Umbria, with the kids joining them for the second week. It was a break they both needed – Lizzie looked as tired as Kavanagh sometimes felt.

Life at River Court hardly changed. Peter Foxcott was fully recovered from his broken leg – snapped in two during his first ever skiing trip to St Moritz. Inspired, Kavanagh suspected, by the renewal of his friendship with Teresa Ashburn and a mini mid-life crisis, Foxcott had packed Eleanor off on a bridge holiday in Majorca, while he went skiing with his eldest son. The trip had ended in disaster – he had fallen on the second day and had to be med-evac'd home. Hobbling into River Court a week later on crutches, he appeared shamefaced at Tom Buckley's doorway to be met with the indignant greeting 'What have you done to me, Mr Foxcott?' It took Buckley two months before he forgave his Head of Chambers for interfering with the well-oiled listings system that had to be completely reorganised to allow for the injury and subsequent operations. But, aside from that hiccough, Peter was still running a tight and happy ship – Helen Ames had proved an able and competent replacement for Kavanagh's old friend and junior Julia Piper; Charles Beaufort was coming up fast on the inside track; and Jeremy Aldermarten, whom none of them would really be without, was his same irascible self.

Kavanagh had kept in close touch with Julia Piper in the years since she left to get married and move abroad. Her first, disastrous, marriage to David, the cricket-playing Foreign Office high-flyer, who really only asked her to be his wife to further his career, had ended in less than a year. But she had stayed on in Nairobi and met a black American civil rights lawyer, Phil Robinson, whom she had moved back to his native Florida with and married. Once settled there, the couple had set up a practice on a shoestring, helping inmates on Death Row through the lengthy appeals system, and her letters spoke fulsomely of the good works she and her new husband were doing.

Sometimes she wrote for her old pupil-master's advice, sometimes she just wrote to vent her frustration at the system which she found so barbaric. Where Kavanagh could offer his advice he did – he had become a member of the Florida Bar six years earlier when he had successfully represented Errol Wyndham at a Supreme Court hearing, and in any event, one appeal hearing was much like any other, regardless of the country it was held in. Sometimes he just let her rage and raged with her in his return letters, equally shocked by the system that allowed innocent men to be executed.

Lizzie had always liked Julia; she had never viewed her as a threat, and she too wrote back to her on occasion, gossiping about the things Julia missed in London, filling in the details about River Court that Kavanagh omitted. Theirs was an easy-going relationship, born out of genuine friendship and a common love of the same man – Julia's a father-figure kind of feeling, and Lizzie's the devotion of an adoring wife.

Kavanagh sat in his office in Lincoln's Inn one bleak February afternoon, listening to the rain beating on his window, and soaked up the sunshine that seemed to pour from Julia's latest missive. She and Phil were very well and happy, she wrote. They'd bought and restored an old plantation house in a place called Coconut Grove on the outskirts of Tampa, and were in the final stages of decorating it. The tone of her letter changed only when she discussed the relentlessly depressing nature of her work – the dreadful fight against the clock to free men from the fate of the electric chair in the face of often insurmountable odds.

Fuelled by President Clinton's latest law-and-order drive, the people of Florida were entrenched in their views on capital punishment. Florida was one of thirty-eight US states to still enforce the death penalty, and the State Governor, Stamford P. Cotton, had enjoyed unprecedented support for many years in the wake of his successful campaign in 1976 to reinstate the ultimate punishment, and few were sympathetic to Julia and Phil's daring suggestion that some of the men awaiting electrocution might be innocent.

Her current, most pressing case was her desperate attempt to push through an appeal hearing for a young black man on Death Row by the name of William Dupree, a twenty-four-year-old mental retard convicted of shooting dead a respectable black couple and their eight-year-old son, and seriously injuring their four-year-old daughter, leaving her severely brain-damaged. Julia needed all the help she could get on this one and sent Kavanagh a fat envelope of newspaper clippings covering the celebrated trial four years earlier. The graphic descriptions of the case made Kavanagh's blood run cold.

Dr David Anderson, a respectable paediatrician, his wife Marsha and their two young children, Tyrone and Leanne, had been on their regular Saturday morning trip to do the supermarket shopping when they returned to their home in an up-and-coming suburb of St Petersburg, near Tampa. Spilling from their station wagon into the driveway of their large detached wood-panelled home, surrounded by palm trees and mangroves, they had nothing more on their minds than spending a quiet weekend doing chores, going to church and having a family barbecue.

Dr Anderson had done very well for himself. From a poor New Orleans family, he had pulled himself out of the slums and put himself through college, becoming the first professional in his family for over five generations. He had met Marsha at medical school, where she was training to be a nurse, and the couple had married in their late teens. Now in charge of his own clinic downtown, Dr Anderson specialised in helping children from poor families, fighting TB and other poverty-related diseases, and instituting a care-and-prevention programme which Marsha helped him administer. Their two children were their pride and joy, and now that they had all moved into their first proper house together, life seemed sweet.

But as they crossed the veranda of their house at 19 Fairvale Avenue that autumn Saturday morning and opened the screen door, they could never have foreseen the massacre that was about to take place. Each of them holding a brown paper bag full of groceries, the four members of the Anderson family filed happily into their home and straight into the line of fire of the intruder who had just rifled the house, looking for valuables. All the neighbours heard was Dr Anderson shout 'What the hell?' before the first shot was fired and he shouted no more.

There was a pause of several seconds before the next voice. It was Marsha, who had heard the gunshot and ran into the kitchen where her husband lay bleeding to death on the linoleum floor. With a scream, she called out her husband's name before the second shot was fired. Tyrone Anderson, just eight years old, heard his mother's cry and ran to her aid. 'Mamma, Mamma, what is it, Mamma?' he called desperately, before the third shot. Finally, and perhaps most poignantly, little Leanne, standing by the half-open front door, her groceries still in her hand, watched the whole episode, open-mouthed, before asking, innocently: 'Hey, mister, what you doing?' It was then, neighbours said, that the fourth shot rang out and the child fell against the front door, slamming it shut with the weight of her tiny body.

The police were quickly on the scene, and the sight that greeted them would haunt them for the rest of their lives.

The four members of the Anderson family lay dead or close to death in pools of blood. Tyrone's heart had been blown away by the point-blank blast to his chest. Leanne's life was saved by paramedics at the scene, but the loss of blood she suffered, coupled with the severe damage to her spinal cord from the bullet that passed through her head and out the other side, left her blind, paralysed and little more than a vegetable.

There was widespread public outrage at this latest in a series of violent crimes against people in their own homes. Governor Cotton made an emotional broadcast on network television vowing to catch those responsible, District Attorney James Buford promised that the police department had a good lead, and within a week an arrest was made – William Dupree, a known burglar and felon who'd moved to Florida from neighbouring Alabama, with a long criminal record dating back to his teenage years.

The trial attracted unprecedented publicity, and was transmitted live across the state. The black-and-white still photographs of the murder scene, especially one showing Leanne's blood-spattered black-faced doll lying on the floor by the front door, made several of the front pages. Kavanagh looked at the copy of this photograph which Julia had sent him and flinched. He could just imagine the baying for blood that the release of such emotive images to the American press would engender.

District Attorney Buford conducted the prosecution case in person, and the newspapers faithfully reported every word. In his opening speech, he told the all-white jury that this had been a 'terrible crime'. In the vast main courtroom of the Radley District Court building, with its whirring fans overhead and its wood-shuttered blinds across the windows, DA Buford milked the case for all it was worth. 'A decent, hard-working family murdered in their own home,' he told the jury. 'To give the Andersons justice here today, I ask you to set aside any feelings of revulsion in your heart, and judge this case on the evidence alone.' Kavanagh had to admit that, on the face of it, that evidence was overwhelming, and as he read through DA Buford's opening speech once again, his heart sank for Julia.

'You have the evidence of Eugene Styles, who saw the accused, William Dupree, come out of the house moments after shots were heard,' the lawyer told the court. 'You have the evidence of the accused's fingerprints all over the crime scene. You have the forensic evidence that the gunpowder engrained in Dupree's skin was consistent with that found in the contact wound in the body of little Tyrone Anderson. You have the evidence of the bloody footprint found in the Andersons' kitchen. You have the sneakers which left that imprint – found by Detective Valkenburgh stuffed in the back of the closet in Dupree's apartment. You have the incontrovertible forensic evidence that the blood found on Dupree's sneakers was Dr Anderson's blood.'

Raising himself to his full six feet two inches, DA Buford walked to the jury box and engaged direct eye contact with the jurors. 'Ladies and gentlemen,' he concluded, 'short of a photograph of the accused pulling the trigger, I ask you, what more do you need to convict William Dupree?'

What indeed? thought Kavanagh, as he studied a photograph of the accused, his wide, flat nose and large brown eyes peering out of a smooth, chocolate skin under his shaved head, with the frightened look of a small child. He compared it to the photograph of the smiling, white-skinned Buford, taken on the court steps after his opening speech, and imagined how believable he would have been to the jury, with his lilting Southern accent, and his neatly groomed greying hair combed back to frame a handsome, athletic face – the all-American boy grown up.

In contrast, Paul Cantrell, Dupree's state-assisted defence lawyer, was an overweight, sweaty and dishevelled man, large-featured, with a beer-drinker's gut hanging over his belt. His defence evidence lasted less than a day, and Kavanagh found his speech to the jury severely lacking in clarity, structure or conviction. Reading through it all these years later, he groaned inwardly at the system, in both Britain and America, that often gave those most in need of a good defence the worst possible advocates.

Cantrell's unconvincing and surprisingly brief address to the jury concluded with the lines: 'Mr Dupree freely admits that he burglarised the Andersons' house. But he left Nineteen Fairvale Avenue before the Andersons returned home. Simple as that. How the sneakers came to be in Mr Dupree's apartment is a matter of conjecture. Mr Dupree had put the sneakers out in the trash earlier in the week. So how they came to be in his closet, in his apartment – well, that's anyone's guess.' Kavanagh winced. 'So I ask you to bring all your experience and common sense to bear on this case, as I know you will, and bring in a verdict of not guilty to murder.'

Not surprisingly in the face of such brilliance, the jury convicted Dupree unanimously after deliberating for less than an hour, and – according to Florida state law – he was sentenced to death. Judge Henry J. Lee described Dupree as one of the most evil men ever to come before him and handed down three death sentences, one for each member of the Anderson family who died, plus an additional sentence of twenty-five years' imprisonment for the maiming of little Leanne.

Governor Cotton made a state-wide broadcast again that night and promised his commitment to protecting the people of Florida. 'When I was elected Governor,' he said, his bespectacled, well-tanned face under a silver mop of hair peering out of the voters' television sets, 'I made a pledge to the people that I would do everything in my power to reduce crime. My message to the wrongdoer is clear and simple. If you commit a crime in the state of Florida, you will pay the price.'

Dupree was sent in chains to the dingy first-floor cells of Death Row at the notorious Hope Correctional Facility on the outskirts of Tampa, and as in all death penalty cases, his sentence was sent immediately to the State Court of Appeals. Julia and Phil offered to take up his case a few months later when all other legal avenues had failed.

'It is hard to imagine,' she wrote, 'what the final hour of life is like for the men who face the electric chair. Their heads shaved bald to assist the executioners with the administration of gels and wires on their skin, they are served their favourite meal – although few have the appetite to stomach it. The metal-lined execution chamber is cleaned and scrubbed ready for its next guest, while protesters wave banners and placards noisily outside. The archaic wooden execution chair – built in 1933 – is dusted down and the brass buckles on its leather straps polished until they are gleaming. The prisoner is brought from his cell, manacled hand and foot, while the prison padre follows on, reading aloud passages from the Bible. The prisoner is strapped bodily to the chair and a metal helmet placed on his head. As a gum-chewing Governor Cotton and his cronies watch through a thickened glass screen in the observation chamber, the switch is thrown.

'The electrical charge is such, Jim,' Julia added, 'that the lights throughout the whole prison flicker and dim for the thirty seconds that it takes the prisoner to die. The other prisoners bang their cell doors in recognition of the passing of a life, and the prison guards on Death Row wander up and down the corridors smilingly telling those yet to face the chair that it means one less mouth to feed and that their day is coming "real soon". It is the most cruel and savage end imaginable and Phil and I are committed to trying to save those who face that fate unjustly.'

By the time Kavanagh had read through the case papers, the cuttings and the letter Julia sent him, he knew that she was asking for more than just postal advice on this one, and in any event, how could he begin to write down all the questions he had to ask her about the case? His workload was relatively flexible at the moment – even Tom Buckley admitted that, albeit reluctantly – and it would be a chance for a change of scene.

Sitting sipping a gin and tonic on a British Airways flight to Tampa two weeks later, he wondered whether he was doing the right thing. The last time he'd done anybody a favour like this had been with Paddy Spence, and that experience had altered their friendship for ever. He'd hate for the same thing to happen to him and Julia; he loved her like a daughter and he cherished their special bond. But something in her letter had touched him deeply. There was an urgency in her words, a sense of desperation, and he felt instinctively that she needed him by her side.

Lizzie had been brilliant, as usual. Sitting having breakfast with her the morning after he had received Julia's package, he casually mentioned that he was considering going to the States for a few days. She had been taken aback at first, and had spun round to face him with a look of genuine surprise. 'How long?' she asked, her eyes wide.

Shuffling to the breakfast table in his pyjamas and dressing gown with a mug of coffee in one hand, a newspaper in the other, he tried to sound as nonchalant as he could. 'Oh, a couple of days, a week. Ten days at most,' he said.

Lizzie sat down opposite him, the lines around her eyes and mouth catching the morning sun through the patio doors. She didn't look happy. Pouring her husband some orange juice, she said: 'But you haven't worked on a capital appeal since Errol Wyndham. Are you sure you want to go through all that again?' She remembered only too well how much the case had taken out of James. He had won the appeal only at the eleventh hour, and the frustrations of working within the complicated American legal system had taken their toll.

Kavanagh leaned back in his chair and studied the woman he'd shared his life with. 'Well, it's not as if I'd have to appear. Julia's handling the court end. She just wants her old pupil-master to cast an eye over things, help prepare the case.' He shrugged his shoulders and kept his expression deliberately non-committal. He didn't want Lizzie to see how much he wanted to go.

Lizzie frowned. 'But her husband's an appeals lawyer, isn't he?' She remembered reading all about the 'wonderful' Phil in Julia's letters. What on earth did Julia need Kavanagh for?

'He's tied up on a case in Miami. He's flying backwards and forwards,' Kavanagh explained, lifting his coffee cup to his lips and scanning the headlines in the morning paper.

Lizzie sighed and studied him for a moment. 'Well, what did you tell her?' she asked, although she suspected she knew damn well what he'd told Julia.

Kavanagh shrugged again. He didn't dare tell Lizzie he'd already booked the flight. 'I said I'd talk it through with you,' he said, opening the newspaper to hide his lying eyes.

Lizzie had heard it all before. She knew when Jim had made his mind up about something, and she also knew there was no point in holding him back, even if she had the most pressing of reasons. 'Common courtesy?' she replied, with a telling look.

'No,' Kavanagh protested, looking hurt.

'You want to go.' Lizzie stated the obvious.

Again the shrug. 'Well, it wouldn't be the end of the world if I didn't – no,' he said, his face downcast. Adopting what he hoped was his most appealing look, he added thoughtfully: 'It would've been a chance to pull one back, though. Might not get another.' Looking up at Lizzie's reluctant expression, he added: 'Still, there we are.' He'd just have to cancel the flight.

Mrs James Kavanagh watched her husband over the rim of her coffee cup and softened. Where was the harm? she thought. They'd had some good times together this summer, and it would only be for a week or so. Looking up, she smiled. 'Don't over-pack,' she said, and watched as her husband's head rose over his *Daily Telegraph* with a relieved grin.

Thinking of Lizzie now as he sat in the back seat of the taxi that had collected him from the airport and was driving him the fifteen miles to Julia's office, Kavanagh wondered if he should have come after all. Lizzie had been under a lot of pressure lately and it was beginning to show. Even the three weeks in Italy hadn't relaxed her quite as much as he had hoped it would. He knew she hated it when he went away; she never slept well in that big house alone and she really needed her sleep. Never mind, he'd make it up to her when he got home. Perhaps a dirty weekend in Paris – he had already notched up enough air miles.

Dragging his jet-lagged mind back to the job in hand, he took off his sunglasses and looked out of the window. 'Welcome to the Sunshine State,' a huge sign on the road from the airport had announced, and the sun was already

282

sizzling at nine o'clock in the morning. Peering out at the passing 'drive-thru' burger bars, vast car lots, furniture warehouses and giant hypermarkets that lined either side of the dual carriageway, Kavanagh was struck by how many British retail parks were beginning to look like American highways. Enormous billboards advertising everything from motels to fishing bait to haemorrhoid cream peppered the route. One billboard featured a smiling black man, giving the thumbs-up, with the words: 'I'm backing Cotton. He really cares.' Kavanagh shook his head and studied the sausage-like fingers of his overweight, white taxi driver on the sheepskin-covered steering wheel. Seeing a local newspaper resting on the passenger seat in front of him, he leaned forward and asked: 'Can I look at your paper?'

'Sure,' came the heavily accented reply, the slow Southern drawl with its swallowed vowels and clipped consonants still very new to Kavanagh. 'I'm just about through. Nothin' much in it. Excepting that sonofabitch killer Dupree,' the driver continued, patting a dried-out alligator head stuck to his console. 'Robber. Done killed hisself a mess of coloured folks about four or five years back. Still . . .' The driver's eyes gleamed at his passenger in the rear-view mirror. '. . . his turn now. Yes, sir, come next full moon, we're gonna fry his ass like a shrimp on a griddle.' Pulling his sweat-stained baseball cap back on his head slightly, he added, with a twist of a smile: 'You all don't get that in England, do you?'

Kavanagh shook his head. 'No, we gave up on it. Kept hanging innocent people.' His irony was lost on the driver.

'Uh-huh,' the large man answered, fingering the dried rattlesnake skin that was hanging off his rear-view mirror like a trophy. 'Well, we kinda figure it's a good idea. It bein' an eye for an eye an' all. You know?'

283

Kavanagh buttoned his lip and wondered again at the hypocrisy of the American Bible belt. These people all went to church each Sunday and readily quoted the words of 'the good Lord', but they twisted so much of the Bible's text in order to justify their own prejudices and barbaric practices. These were the same people who were the very last to recognise the American civil rights movement and, as Julia had made quite clear in her letters, racism was still 'alive and kicking' in America's southernmost state. She'd experienced a lot of it herself, being married to a black man, and she sometimes worried for Phil's safety.

Pulling up outside a converted Victorian church, with a sign reading 'Florida Resource Centre' above the open doorway, the cab driver prised himself out of his seat with some difficulty, lifted the tailgate and unloaded Kavanagh's two suitcases from the trunk on to the sidewalk. Glad to see the back of him, Kavanagh paid him off and wandered inside, where he discovered a modern, split-level, open-plan office built within the high vaulted ceiling and mullioned, stained-glass windows. Announcing himself at reception, he was approached by a tall black man in casual shirt and trousers, who held out his hand and flashed him a winning smile. 'Mr Kavanagh? Phil Robinson, the husband,' he introduced himself, and Kavanagh shook his hand firmly.

In an upstairs office ten minutes later, the two men, who had heard so much about each other, studied one another over a cup of coffee. Phil was much more attractive than Kavanagh had imagined. Slim, clean-shaven, athletic, with quite hypnotic brown eyes and a face that was open and friendly. An honest man, Kavanagh thought, and felt happy for Julia. Phil was surprised at how old and white-haired Kavanagh was – he had always been secretly jealous of the 'James' his wife had been writing to all these years, and imagined him to be a much younger, more debonair man, not someone who was old enough to be her father and, in many ways, actually resembled Old Man Piper.

'I'm intrigued,' Phil finally admitted, as he took his seat at a large oval table under a framed photograph of Martin Luther King. 'What makes a high-flying English lawyer travel three thousand miles to work on a no-win case for free?'

Kavanagh took a seat opposite him with a laugh. 'I'm surprised you have to ask,' he said, wryly.

Phil was still perplexed. 'Well, I know why I'd do it,' he said. 'This is where I live. But with the greatest respect, sir, it's hardly your fight.'

Kavanagh smiled again. 'You have a very persuasive wife,' he said.

Phil chuckled and remembered how Julia had pursued him in Nairobi and proposed to him instead of the other way round. 'Yes I do,' he admitted.

Kavanagh looked around the very basic office which was in little more than a shared municipal building and wondered how Phil and Julia managed for money. 'How long have you . . .' he started, waving at the modest surroundings.

Phil interrupted him. 'Oh, too damn long. I suppose now I should move into something that pays, huh?' His accent was smoother, softer than the taxi driver's. He gave Kavanagh a look which suggested that, despite their nice new home, he and Julia were not as flush for cash as they could be and, in truth, could never even have afforded their new house if Julia's father hadn't given them a nice fat wedding cheque.

'Well, what's stopping you?' Kavanagh asked. Social conscience was all well and good, but you still had to eat, as Tom Buckley would say.

'Oh, I don't know,' Phil said, clasping his hands self-consciously between his knees. 'These guys, I guess.' He nodded to the wall beneath the Martin Luther King picture on which hung a row of fifteen photographs, all men, black and white, in black-edged frames. These were the people he and Julia had tried to save from the electric chair, and failed.

Kavanagh nodded ruefully. Reaching for the folded copy of the *Tampa Tablet* the cab driver had given him, he added: 'I saw this on the way in.' He handed the paper to Phil and pointed to the front-page article whose headline read: 'Dupree hearing set for end of month.'

Phil took it and spread it out on the table in front of him. 'Oh, yeah. Cotton dropped it on us yesterday.'

Kavanagh knew why. 'Election time,' he said. 'I saw the campaign posters.' Politicians were the same the world over, he thought, eager to make political mileage out of even the most awful situations.

Phil topped up Kavanagh's coffee and nodded. 'Yeah, Governor Cotton got in on a strong law-and-order ticket. Dupree's just his way of reminding folks it'll be "business as usual" if they just keep the faith.' He remembered the outrage at the time of the Anderson murders and feared for Dupree's life.

Kavanagh read his thoughts. 'What are our chances if this runs the distance?' he asked, sipping his second cup of coffee in an attempt to ward off the creeping effects of jet-lag.

Phil threw his head back and laughed. 'Clemency? . . . Right. Cotton hasn't commuted a death sentence in four years. And it's not just a political thing. The man really enjoys his work. Sees himself as . . . oh, I don't know, some sort of modern-day Emperor Nero at the Circus Maximus. A day's just not the same if he doesn't send

286

someone to their death.' Phil's long eyelashes closed on his big brown eyes as he paused for breath. 'So are you looking for mercy, Mr Kavanagh?' he asked, pronouncing the barrister's name 'Cavan-R'. ''Cos I'd look somewhere other than Governor Stamford P. Cotton.' He sipped his coffee as Kavanagh rested his weary head on his hands.

Just at that moment, Julia burst through the door, calling out her husband's name. Catching sight of Kavanagh, she shrieked with glee but retreated suddenly, shouting: 'Oh my God, you're here, James. Wait! Wait!'

Kavanagh rose to his feet, laughing. 'Julia? What is it?' he chuckled to an empty doorway. Suddenly, a large bump in a purple dress appeared in profile, followed by Julia's grinning face. 'You're . . .' Kavanagh began.

'Up the duff!' Julia screamed like a naughty schoolgirl, and ran into the room to hug her old friend.

Kavanagh was genuinely pleased, if a little surprised. There had been no mention of it in her letters. Perhaps that's why she'd asked for his help. 'Oh, that's wonderful,' he said, making as if to return her hug but finding it difficult to negotiate her bulging stomach.

Julia giggled at his nervousness, a giggle he hadn't heard in years. 'Don't worry, it won't break,' she told him, looking as radiant as an expectant mother should. Gone were the carefully coiffeured long brown hair and the black designer suits so favoured at River Court. In their place was a shoulder-length tousled look which really suited her, brightly coloured, comfortable clothes, and sensible, flat sandals. Her sculpted face and emerald-green eyes were just the same, dark and beautiful, and not in need of make-up. She wore impossibly long earrings which danced on her shoulders as she jumped about excitedly.

'Congratulations,' Kavanagh said, as she pulled him

towards her and buried his head in her hair. 'When's it due?'

'Oh, about six weeks,' she beamed, holding both his hands. 'Oh, I'm sorry I wasn't at the airport,' she apologised. Kavanagh shrugged it off. Suddenly remembering why she hadn't been there she explained: 'Late scan . . . look, they took a photograph.' She reached into her enormous brown leather handbag and handed the picture to Phil, with a look of such love and devotion on her face that it almost made Kavanagh's eyes well up. All three of them stood around her while she pointed out the features of her unborn child. 'Do you see the mouth? The nose? It's sucking its thumb,' she said, a proud mum as Phil stood with his hand on her shoulder and beamed. Julia suddenly felt guilty. 'Look, it's not even born yet and already I'm a complete baby bore.' She stuffed the photograph back into her handbag, cross with herself.

'No, no you're not,' Kavanagh protested, thinking happily of the day he hoped would come when he and Lizzie stood around Kate like that, studying the first grainy images of their yet-to-be-born grandchild.

'I am, I know I am,' Julia confessed. Then, patting Kavanagh's shoulder, she invited him to sit down, saying: 'Oh, it's so good to see you. How is everyone?'

He sat down next to her and grinned. 'Oh, fine. Everyone in chambers sends their love.' With a mischievous smile, he added: 'Er, Jeremy in particular wants to be remembered.' He hoped Phil knew all about the ghastly Aldermarten and his outrageous attempts to get Julia to marry him, including even persuading her to pose as his fiancée when he was trying to be elected as an MP. He failed, naturally, on all counts, but he still whole-heartedly believed that she was wrong to turn him down, especially after her divorce and subsequent remarriage to a black man. 'I mean, James, surely she could do better than that?' he had simpered when he heard.

Julia threw her head back and giggled at the memory of Aldermarten. 'How could I forget?' she laughed. She and Kavanagh were already into the 'Do you remember when . . .' stage. Phil looked at the pair of them and knew that his presence was not required. Offering to go and make his wife a cup of camomile tea, he left the room, pleased to see Julia so happy. As soon as he'd gone, Julia reached across the table and held James's hand. 'I want all the news, all the gossip,' she beamed. 'Well, how are you, for starters?'

Kavanagh smiled back and waved his hands around meaninglessly. 'Oh, you know, same old, same old.' He laughed.

Julia shook her head in exasperation. She'd waited three years to see him – she had hoped he was going to be much more forthcoming than this. 'Well, how's Lizzie?' she tried, her head tilted to one side.

18

Washing down a mouthful of Creole shrimp with a beautifully chilled glass of Californian Chardonnay, Kavanagh was feeling much more at ease. After a couple of hours' sleep, he had showered, changed and unpacked, before driving in his hire car from his hotel to join Julia and Phil at their elegant detached home for dinner.

Phil had cooked a real Southern meal in honour of his guest – blackened tuna with red rice and beans, followed by the deliciously spicy shrimp dish. In a cream linen jacket, navy slacks and an open-neck shirt, Kavanagh was dressed just right for the occasion. Good old Lizzie, she always knew how to organise his packing. He had been mightily impressed with the sumptuousness of the Robinsons' home, with its wide veranda running round all four sides of the house, turreted towers at each corner, beautifully tended tropical gardens and large, airy rooms. He thought it looked for all the world like Tara in *Gone with the Wind*, and he had made Julia giggle when he told her so.

Sitting at the enormous hardwood table in the moss-green dining room, with its heavy chenille curtains and huge windows, Kavanagh had got to know a little about Phil over dinner. A conscientious and diligent lawyer, he had cut his teeth in Florida, before moving to South Africa to fight for the rights of wrongly imprisoned members of the African National Congress. A quiet man by nature – which was just as well with the exuberant Julia around – he was passionate about civil rights and, when apartheid had ended, he had moved to Nairobi, working there for a while, which is where he met Julia. Within a year he had brought her home to help take up the cudgel for his own people. The pair of them had never looked back.

Up to date with all the news from their respective personal lives, Julia started to lead Kavanagh through the many complexities of the William Dupree case and reminded him how the American legal system worked, with appeal after appeal sometimes taking place before final judgment was reached.

'Where are you with it?' Kavanagh asked, his mouth full of food. If Lizzie had been there, she would have shot him a disapproving look.

'Dupree's been through this whole process once already,' Julia answered, sipping a glass of iced tea. 'Now we're back at State Habeas.'

Kavanagh was impressed she'd even managed to get back to that point with the evidence against the defendant. 'You got it remanded for an evidentiary hearing on what?' he asked, incredulous.

'It was a mixed bag,' Julia answered. 'Evidence of mental retardation which the jury should have heard at the penalty phase; IAC – ineffective assistance of counsel; and possible professional misconduct.' She put her fork down and studied her old friend with a serious look.

Kavanagh, his eyes smarting from the piece of red chilli he had just bitten into, took a draught of water. He was confused. 'Nobody saw fit to mention any of this on the first appeal?' he asked.

Julia rolled her eyes. 'Huh. It was limped through Direct Review by some local ambulance-chaser who slept in his car and spent most of the fighting fund on whisky.' It still made her furious to think of it.

Phil took up the story. 'So, when his liver gave up the ghost, it was handed down to a kid fresh out of law school who filed for inappropriate applications for, I don't know what, a year or so.' Phil got up to open a second bottle of wine.

'Then to us,' Julia finished. Kavanagh liked the way they ended each other's sentences. It was something he and Lizzie had done for years. It showed a couple who were comfortable with each other, he had always thought.

'What about his original trial lawyer? Cantrell?' Kavanagh asked, recalling the man's name from the case files.

'He jumped ship a couple of weeks after the sentence was handed down. Landed himself a job at the Attorney-General's office,' Julia explained with a raised eyebrow.

Kavanagh scowled. 'Public defender to state prosecutor? Just like that?' Although he occasionally took on cases as a prosecution counsel, he knew only too well that they were two very separate disciplines, and it was unusual for someone to shift so completely and so suddenly. The vagaries of the American legal system never failed to astound him, but that should surely have caused some concern.

Phil returned with a bottle of claret and poured Kavanagh a glass. 'Hey, Cantrell's an up-and-coming man. Campaign worker for the Cotton camp,' he said, a note of sarcasm in his voice.

Kavanagh was still amazed, having read through all the defence notes. 'He must have sharpened up his act. To my mind, the grounds for ineffective assistance of counsel are inarguable. I mean, what were you saying about Dupree – in and out of children's homes?'

Julia looked at the fan whirring on the ceiling to stir the still, hot air and closed her eyes while she scanned her memory banks. 'Violent, abusive father. Taken into care. Foster homes. Juvenile detention. Worked his way up to the "big house" by the age of twenty-one.' She had already explained that the 'big house' was the local felons' nickname for the Hope Correctional Facility, where Dupree was now incarcerated.

'And what was he doing at the time of his arrest?' Kavanagh asked, nodding his approval of the new wine to Phil. He made a mental note to take some of this stuff home to Lizzie. She loved a good claret.

'On parole, working as a groundsman at one of the university frat houses.' Kavanagh knew all about the fraternity houses of the American university system. Each college was divided into houses, as in an English public school, with fraternity houses for the boys and sorority houses for the women. Each had a house father and its own special name, insignia and motto – usually adopting the letters of the Greek alphabet, such as Alpha, Beta, Gamma and so on.

Largely occupied by the children of the rich and almost predominantly white community, the young men who made up their numbers – known originally as WASPs (White Anglo-Saxon Protestants) – often indulged in bizarre initiation ceremonies and legendary drinking parties, and got themselves into all sorts of trouble. Hollywood movies had been made about them. One – *Animal House* – was Matt's all-time favourite film, and Kavanagh had been forced to sit through it with him a dozen times, drinking beer and pretending to be amused by the childish antics of the drunken students. Somebody like William Dupree, black, mentally subnormal and with a history of youth offending, could have been severely put upon by those whose grounds he was tending.

'And what about new evidence?' Kavanagh asked, hopeful that Julia had more to go on than the incompetence of someone like Paul Cantrell, who was now so obviously well thought of by the very type of person they hoped to appeal to.

Julia nodded and leaned back in her chair, rubbing her hands across her overextended stomach. 'Well, there is one bright spark,' she said. 'Detective Valkenburgh, the officer who found the sneakers at Dupree's apartment? She was suspended last month pending an Internal Affairs investigation into allegations of racism.'

Kavanagh raised his eyebrows. That was good news. It would certainly help with their suggestion that Dupree's bloodstained sneakers could have been planted by the police. 'Who made the allegations?' he asked, making a mental note to follow up on that.

'Valkenburgh's partner – Detective Fuller,' she replied, as Kavanagh raised his glass thoughtfully to his lips.

After dinner, Phil ordered his wife and guest out of the kitchen while he cleared up and did the dishes. Wandering out on to the white-painted veranda to enjoy the last rays of the evening sun and inhale the scent of the orange blossom plants she was growing in tubs, Julia and Kavanagh sat contentedly in two enormous wicker chairs.

'He's a good man,' Kavanagh told Julia. He meant it.

Julia exuded happiness. 'Yes, he is. He really cares. He wants to change things,' she said, arching back in her seat to stretch her spine.

'So, you've no regrets about coming out here?' Kavanagh asked, crossing his legs and patting his own full stomach. It certainly was a beautiful place and a long way away from River Court.

'No,' she answered without hesitation. Then, suddenly remembering, she added: 'Oh, well, Mum and Dad, of course. Especially now with the baby. Apart from that, no.' She looked entirely convinced. Aldermarten would be disappointed.

Kavanagh was delighted for her. 'Good,' he said.

Julia raised her glass of ice tea. 'Thanks for coming, James.' She looked as if she could burst with health, vitality and gratitude. She hadn't mentioned it to him, and probably didn't need to, but the stresses of being pregnant for the first time, coupled with such a particularly difficult appeals case, had led her to ask him to come.

Kavanagh was glad he had taken up the offer. He raised his glass of red wine and smiled broadly. 'Here's to you . . . Mrs Robinson,' he said, and they laughed together companionably.

Later that night, full and contented, in his hotel room, Kavanagh kicked off his shoes and sat on the edge of the king-size bed, reflecting on a delightful evening. With two or three more glasses of wine in him than he should have had, he felt more than happy with the world. There was only one thing missing now, of course – his beloved Lizzie. Looking at the clock, he tried to work out the time difference. It was past one o'clock in the morning here; that would make it about 7 a.m. in London. It would be nice to give her an early morning wake-up call.

Flicking on the television with the remote control, he dialled the number and listened as the telephone rang. The image on the screen flickered into focus and he watched an all-black gospel choir singing 'Hallelujah' for all they were worth. Bloody Bible belt, he thought, and flicked the television off again. Still the telephone remained unanswered, ringing out again and again in his ear. His forehead creased into a frown. Where could she be? he wondered.

*   *   *

Three thousand miles away, in the avocado-green *en suite* bathroom of their home in Wimbledon, Lizzie Kavanagh gripped the sides of the sink and cried out in agony. Retching for the sixth time, she heard the telephone ringing in the bedroom, but was unable to move for pain. Still in her pink pyjamas, her shoulder-length chestnut hair plastered to her head with sweat, she tried to call out her husband's name, but another wave of pain shuddered through her body and nothing emerged from her lips but a scream.

The heavy iron gates to the Hope Correctional Facility jerked into life and slid slowly open, as Kavanagh gradually increased the pressure on the accelerator of his gleaming, air-conditioned Chevrolet and inched forward. He and Julia had driven the twenty miles to the prison and had already passed through what seemed like acre upon acre of high barbed-wire fences interspersed with ominous-looking smoked-glass watchtowers. Now they were in the inner sanctum, he was surprised at how intimidated he felt.

Inside, having been searched carefully and their briefcases meticulously checked, they were allowed to pass through several high-tensile steel interlocking doors before they found themselves being escorted down a long corridor and into an internal recreation area, crowded with inmates. As they passed through yet another airlock system, they came upon a narrow walkway, to the left of which was an open-mesh wall sealing off an area filled with tables and chairs, each table with half a dozen prisoners seated around it. As soon as the door slid open on to the corridor, the fifty or so men – mainly black and all dressed in regulation grey T-shirts and sweatpants – abandoned their games of cards or chess and rushed noisily to the fence, hooking their fingers through the holes and clambering up it to get a better view of whoever was visiting their prison.

A cacophony of lewd insults and jeers followed as Julia and Kavanagh – who was closest to the fence – passed slowly by, escorted by four burly armed guards. 'Hey, baby, pucker up,' shouted one inmate, his packet of cigarettes folded up inside the capped sleeve of his T-shirt. 'Hey, beautiful, hey, sugar. You've sure got a pretty mouth,' another yelled, making kissing noises. Kavanagh, in his best Ede & Ravenscroft navy suit and tie, felt his face flush crimson for Julia's sake. She, heavily pregnant in a blue pinafore dress and crisp white cotton blouse, was waddling along beside him without even batting an eyelid. He supposed she was used to it.

It was only when one of the inmates offended his senses by shouting out 'Yo, baby. Yo, come over here. I wanna ride that sweet pink ass of yours to hell and back' that Kavanagh felt honour-bound to say something.

'Don't take any notice,' he said, in his most reassuring tone, trying to protect her from the onslaught. He wondered how she could be so calm.

Julia looked across at Kavanagh with a wicked smile. 'What on earth makes you think they're talking to me?' she said. As Kavanagh looked from her to the men on his left and realised that the kisses were being blown at him, not Julia, the hairs on the back of his neck bristled and he quickened his pace.

Up on the first-floor landing of N block, the men who were on Death Row lived, one to a small cell, in the bright orange T-shirts and sweatpants that differentiated them from the other inmates. Almost all of these men were black, Kavanagh noticed, and each one looked cheerlessly out at the two Brits, strolling past them, briefcases in hand, *en route* to cell number 17 – the home of William Dupree.

If Kavanagh had expected to see gratitude on the face of the man they were trying to help, he was quickly disappointed. As the electronically operated barred door slid open, Dupree sat motionless on his bunk, his knees up to his chest, staring up at his visitors with complete indifference.

'Mr Dupree, this is Mr Kavanagh,' Julia introduced her friend as the door slid shut behind them with a terrible clang. Dupree said nothing, but his eyes flickered across to the white-haired man and he stared him out.

'How do you do,' Kavanagh said with a slight nod of his head.

Julia, still smiling into the face of a man who had shown no response whatsoever to their arrival, continued: 'Mr Kavanagh has flown over from England to help you with your appeal.'

Dupree's wide nostrils flared and he snorted through them. Finally, he parted his thick pink lips to reveal two gold front teeth among a row of white tombstones and laughed, a deep and throaty rumble. 'No kiddin',' he said, his voice even deeper than his laugh. 'I've been hearing that for four long years, and I'm still here. So if I don't jump up and down, you'll have to excuse me.' His Alabama accent was thick and guttural, like half-melted chocolate. The only part of him that moved was his huge brown eyes, and as he shot them across to address Julia, the whites flashed at Kavanagh. 'Did you bring me the candy I asked for?'

Julia nodded and reached into her voluminous handbag, pulling out a giant bar of almond-flavoured chocolate. Seeing it spurred Dupree into getting up at last, and he rose from the long low bunk in one effortless, fluid movement, pulling himself up to his full six feet four inches without a sound. He took the chocolate bar and held it lovingly in his hands, stepping the two paces it took for him to reach the other side of his eight-by-six cell. Looking across at Kavanagh, still rooted to the spot by the door, Dupree said, in a low rumble: 'I ain't scared. And I don't want you to be thinking I'm scared, 'cos I ain't.'

Kavanagh shrugged his shoulders as if to say he hadn't given it much thought.

Dupree continued: 'I may be walking through the valley of the shadow of death an' all, but when it comes to my time to walk the wing I'll hold my head up high like an ancient king.' He flashed Julia a gilt-edged smile, as she sat down heavily on the end of the bunk opposite the only other piece of furniture in the room, a small metal washbasin.

Kavanagh decided to get straight down to business. 'Mr Dupree, it's our view that your original trial was badly mishandled by your attorney,' he told his new client.

Dupree's expression changed to one of fury. 'Damn right it was!' he said, pushing himself away from one of the heavily riveted walls. More quietly then, he added: 'I've done some bad things in my time but I didn't never kill those folks.'

Kavanagh, still standing, sighed. 'I'm afraid it'll take more than a point-blank denial from you to convince them,' he said. He thought again of the weight of overwhelming forensic and other evidence against the defendant.

Dupree turned and leaned back against the metal wall, shaking his head. 'By the time they were shot, man, I was on the other side of town having myself a beer.' He hung his shaved head to reveal a fine sheen of sweat.

'That was never offered in evidence,' Kavanagh pointed out.

Dupree nodded. 'I know. I told Cantrell but he never

300

brought it up in court.' He frowned and flashed Julia a look of frustration. 'I told him if he'd have sent someone down there he'd have found someone as coulda said they seen me. And I wouldn't be where I am right now.'

Julia and Kavanagh exchanged glances. 'Well, what was the name of the bar?' Kavanagh asked, his hands still in his pockets.

Dupree hung his head and sighed. 'I can't rightly remember right now. Flamingo, maybe. I dunno. I've been to a lot of bars.' Looking over at Julia in appreciation of her blossoming figure, he added, with a gold-toothed smile: 'A lot of bars . . . a lot of girls.'

Julia blushed and reached into her handbag to hide her embarrassment. 'Well, obviously we're gonna go through the whole aspect of the case, starting from the original 911 call through to the forensic and witness statements. But it would help if you could take us through exactly what happened at the Andersons'.' She pulled out a file and a pen and sat poised to take notes.

Kavanagh interjected. 'Perhaps you could start by telling us how you got down there.' He pulled off his jacket and folded it across his arm. An armed guard strolled slowly past outside, peering in through the bars to make sure the visitors weren't coming to any harm.

Dupree stood in front of the washbasin so that he was exactly between the two counsel. 'Bus,' he said. 'I took the bus. I just went there to rob the place, you know, that's all.' He shrugged his shoulders and held out his huge black hands in a gesture of innocence.

Kavanagh nodded. 'You didn't wear gloves,' he said, a frown creasing his forehead.

Dupree looked down, as if he were trying to remember. 'I thought I wiped everywhere I touched.' Looking up at

Kavanagh with a rueful expression, he added: 'Kinda sloppy, I guess.'

'And you left the house how?' Kavanagh was still frowning.

'Same way I came in – through the back door.'

Remembering the evidence of the eye-witness Eugene Styles, who said he saw Dupree leave by the front door, Kavanagh asked: 'You're sure about that?'

Dupree rushed at Kavanagh, his face inches from his, his jaw clenched. 'That's what I said, didn't I?' There was desperation in his voice. The guard outside gripped one of the bars of the cell door with his hand and reached for his baton. Dupree backed off a little, a disappointed look on his face. 'That Styles, man. That Eugene Styles said he see'd me come out the front door. He's a born liar.' Dupree hissed the last four words.

Kavanagh dragged his eyes away from the defendant and looked down in a non-threatening gesture designed to get him to back off completely. 'And after that you went to the bar, the Flamingo?' he asked, trying to change the subject. There was something in Dupree's eyes that bothered him.

The inmate, still inches from Kavanagh, turned slightly towards Julia and nodded. 'Yeah, I think that's what it's called.' He looked down. 'I . . . I don't read too well,' he explained, ashamed. 'But there was a damn big pink bird outside.'

Julia, reading through her notes, brought up another topic. 'Cantrell never dealt in court with the gunpowder found engrained under your skin,' she said. It had been a point that had worried her from the start.

Dupree turned his anger on her. 'I told you, I never shot no one!' he rumbled, moving towards her. Julia stared him out and didn't flinch. Kavanagh was impressed. 'I was out

302

in the glades with a friend a few days before. His gun. I never owned a gun,' Dupree explained, twisting his head round to glare at Kavanagh again.

Kavanagh leaned back against the wall, tired of standing and tired of all the excuses. 'Why wasn't your friend called to give evidence?' His pained expression indicated his doubts.

'He was on the run himself,' Dupree explained. 'Mr Cantrell tried to find him but once that Weasel go to ground, man, ain't nobody can find him.'

Julia held up her pen. 'What was his name?'

'Marlon . . . Marlon Jarrett.' Dupree watched as she wrote it down.

Kavanagh decided to raise a delicate issue and hoped Dupree wouldn't take it too badly. 'We'd like you to meet a psychiatrist,' he said, speaking slowly for his words to sink in. 'We need to prove that your attorney failed to offer proper mitigation. A report from the psychiatrist as to the effect of an abused and deprived childhood.'

Dupree interrupted him with a frown. 'So, if the court agrees that Cantrell should have got me a shrink,' he said, just as slowly, 'they'll put me back for resentencing?' He looked as if the penny had only just dropped.

Kavanagh nodded. 'More or less.'

Dupree, impressed by the thought, turned and sat down on the bunk next to Julia. Smiling up at Kavanagh, he added: 'If you want me to see him, man, I'll see him.' Pausing as he took in all that he was being told, he had a faraway look in his eyes. 'I ain't always walked in the ways of the righteous,' he said. 'It's like Father O'Brien says, like Daniel, you know.'

His reference to the prison padre worried Kavanagh, who didn't know his biblical texts. 'Daniel?' he asked.

Dupree's huge mouth opened into a golden grin and he

quoted from the text. 'My God has sent an angel, and has shut the lions' mouths. They have not hurt me.' His voice was almost a whisper again. Looking across at Julia and up at Kavanagh, he added, forcefully: 'You all gonna be my angels now.'

As they made their way back through the prison, Kavanagh was relieved to find the recreation room empty, and the inmates all gone for their lunch. Now he could concentrate on the job in hand without pretending not to be embarrassed. 'If he's telling the truth,' he told Julia, 'we've got to accept that after Dupree left, someone else broke in to rob the Andersons and shot them.' Such a coincidence was certainly hard to swallow.

Julia nodded in agreement and asked the question she still wasn't sure she knew the answer to herself. 'Do you buy it?'

Kavanagh didn't want to commit himself at this stage, or admit that he might have flown three thousand miles on a wild-goose chase. 'I've heard more plausible stories,' he said, knowing that the crux of the question wasn't whether Dupree was innocent or guilty, it was whether or not he had received a fair trial and a fair sentence in the light of that trial. No man deserved to be sentenced to death on the basis of an inadequate defence. He reflected on how Dupree was facing up to the idea of the electric chair, if it went against him. 'He didn't seem overly worried by what they've got planned for him,' he pointed out.

Julia had seen and heard all that before. She took considerable solace in the fact that so many of the men she had met on Death Row had come to a sort of uneasy acceptance of their fate, largely through their religious faith. Not a believer herself, she nonetheless recognised that for those who listened to the good counsel of Father O'Brien some comfort was found and some sense made. 'So, how do you rate our chances?' she asked Kavanagh. Now that he had met Dupree face to face, it was the time to ask.

Kavanagh remained non-committal and tried to concentrate on the work they yet needed to do. 'It'll be uphill,' he said, honestly. 'You'd best go and see if Valkenburgh's partner's willing to talk to us. First person we've got to get hold of is Cantrell. Set up a meeting with him.'

The next three days were to be full of pitfalls and frustrations for Kavanagh and his former pupil. Cantrell was forever busy or in a meeting, according to his secretary, who took all his calls and deftly deflected the British lawyers in a nasal, whining voice. After the seventh attempt to talk to him, it was clear he had no intention of speaking to them and they would have to try and confront him one to one.

Sifting through the mass of documents and photographs, maps, forensic reports and police statements also proved to be a thankless and depressing task. Kavanagh had already had a taste of how distressing the murder scene had been, but looking at all the official police photographs now, seeing Mr and Mrs Anderson and their two young children lying where they were so callously shot, and later on the post-mortem slabs, did nothing to improve Kavanagh's mood. If Dupree were guilty of this terrible crime, then who was he to stand in the way of this country's system of justice? The inner turmoil he felt was not helped by the jet-lag he didn't seem able to shake off, and the relentless heat that left him permanently sodden. How Julia stood it in her condition, he didn't know. But then each time he looked across the large desk they shared, and saw her deep in thought on the telephone or writing notes, never once flinching from the task she had set herself or giving in to the urge to quit, he felt spurred on again.

Trying Cantrell's office for the eighth time, he got the same response from the secretary whose voice he was beginning to hate, and decided it was time for some fresh air. 'Let's go and have a drink,' he suggested to Julia, and they set off in his car, to the only Flamingo bar he had found listed in the Tampa telephone directory.

The building was not what they'd expected. Close to the railway station, it was built into the ground floor of a shabby brick-built hotel that was obviously home to several hookers and frequented by truck drivers, judging by the number of huge articulated trucks parked outside. Stepping in through the swinging double doors, they were met by a sea of faces, all white, and many of them wearing cowboy hats. A huge confederate flag hung behind the bar, country and western music was playing on the juke-box, and the smoke-filled room with its illuminated Budweiser and Coors signs looked like something straight out of a low-budget Hollywood movie.

Kavanagh and Julia braced themselves and started at opposite ends of the room. Picking their way between the drinkers, repeating 'Howdy' to whoever would speak to them, they showed as many people as they could the copy of a large black-and-white photograph of William Dupree, and asked if they remembered seeing him. The responses they received were all negative and generally abrupt. Quite soon people stopped being so nice to them.

Reaching the middle of the room at about the same time as Julia, Kavanagh approached a motley group of men, all wearing brightly coloured shirts and baseball caps, and asked for their help. 'He used to drink in here about four years ago. I wonder if you might remember him?' Kavanagh asked, loosening his tie at the collar as the heat and the cigarette smoke started to get to him.

The huge man he handed the photograph to peered at it from under his cap and cleared his throat to speak. 'Does this look like a nigger joint to you, mister?' he asked with a sneer. Grinning a gap-toothed smile at the friends he was sitting with, he added: ''Cos it sure as hell don't look like a nigger joint to me.' Before Kavanagh could say another word or snatch the photograph back, the drinker was waving his arms expansively to his friends. 'Does this look like a nigger joint to you, Dwayne?' he asked.

The man called Dwayne, who was sporting a Hawaiian-style shirt and a red baseball cap with the letters USA embroidered on it, sniggered. 'No, sir,' he said, as all of the men chuckled to themselves.

Kavanagh tried to intervene. 'If you'd just look at the picture,' he said, a note of impatience in his voice. Julia came up and stood behind him with a look of real fear on her face. She squeezed his arm to let him know she was there.

The fat-faced cowboy swigged from his beer and looked down at the photograph, flicking his forefinger at it. 'It's Dupree,' he said. 'He's on Death Row for killing a nigger doctor or something.' Tipping back the brim of his cap, he looked up into Kavanagh's face and asked: 'What you fussing yourself over trash like that for, huh?'

Kavanagh winced in the face of such blatant racism and sneered back at his inquisitor. 'You're a people person, aren't you?' he said, with a sarcastic smile.

The fat cowboy's eyes flickered as he tried to figure out whether he had just been insulted or not. Deciding that he had, he stood up, pushed back his bar stool and towered menacingly over the British barrister, who was still dressed in his best suit. 'Say what?' he said, as the bar fell suddenly silent all around them.

Julia squeezed Kavanagh's arm again and stared up into

the glowering eyes of the cowboy. 'Let's leave it, Jim,' she said, as Kavanagh stood, seething, his expression that of a man with a foul smell under his nose.

The cowboy spat his next sentence out. 'If I were you, mister, I would listen to the little lady and go running back to my nigger friends.' Kavanagh blinked and swallowed hard as the man added: 'Go on – get!'

Realising that there was little point in being pulverised by a brute of a man whose brain was probably the size of a shrunken pea, Kavanagh did as he was told. Looking at the group with an expression of open contempt, he turned and left the bar with Julia on his arm, the sniggers of the drinkers still ringing in his ears.

Back in the sanctuary of his hotel room, he threw his jacket on the bed, tossed his room key on the table and headed straight for the telephone. He needed Lizzie; he needed to speak to her, and to have her make some sense of what he was doing in such a god-forsaken place. Dialling the international code and then his home number, he pulled off his tie and listened to the telephone ringing out. He let it ring and ring, but there was no answer. Damn it. Glancing at his watch, he couldn't understand it, it was seven o'clock at night. Where the hell was she when he needed her?

On the other side of the world, in a private room of a London hospital, Lizzie was sitting up on the edge of the bed in a flimsy cotton hospital gown, a look of sheer terror on her face. The doctor who was taking her blood pressure said nothing as he listened through his stethoscope to her heart beating as he released the pressure in her armband. All the colour had drained from Lizzie's face and the lines around her eyes, which Kavanagh had noticed weeks earlier, were even more pronounced. Staring straight ahead of her, she tried desperately to focus on a spot on the wall, to distract her mind from what was happening to her, and to think of Jim, her beloved Jim, somewhere far away and oblivious to her pain.

19

After a quick shower and a club sandwich from room service, Kavanagh went down to the hotel lobby to meet Julia. She had arranged a rendezvous with Detective Eddie Fuller in the underground carpark of Kavanagh's hotel at three o'clock. Fuller, the former partner of Detective Valkenburgh – the woman officer who had found the bloodstained sneakers at William Dupree's apartment – didn't want to meet them anywhere public; it had been all Julia could do to persuade him to meet them at all. His evidence could be vital to their case.

Detective Fuller was a man in his early forties with a moon face and collar-length grey-brown hair. Standing in the light afforded by the full beam of his car headlights, he wore a lemon-yellow sports top and blue jeans with the ubiquitous baseball cap as he faced the two counsel, hands stuffed in his jeans pockets.

'So you didn't find the sneakers?' Julia asked him.

Fuller's accent was deep and rich. 'No. I mean, I looked in that closet myself,' he said, his big round eyes open and wide.

A frown creased Kavanagh's forehead. 'Are you saying that there weren't any sneakers in that closet?' He found the consequences of what Detective Fuller was saying hard to take in.

Fuller shrugged. 'Not that I saw.'

Julia, hands on her hips, her huge stomach pushed out, was puzzled. 'Well, are you saying that Valkenburgh put them there?' She, like Kavanagh, found the idea hard to swallow, bearing in mind what was found on the sneakers.

Fuller stood his ground. 'They weren't there when I looked,' he said, firmly.

Kavanagh was incredulous. 'In that case, she must have stained them somehow with Dr Anderson's blood.'

Fuller studied the white-haired barrister. 'Like maybe she had a rag soaked in blood that she removed from the scene of the crime?' Kavanagh nodded. 'Uh, I wouldn't like to speculate on that.' Seeing the look on his inquisitors' faces, he straightened his back and added: 'Now I just wanna do the right thing. I mean, if we're gonna move forward, people like Valkenburgh, bigots and suchlike . . .' A sneer creased his face. '. . . they don't belong on the force.' Kavanagh and Julia looked askance at each other and wondered at his words.

The meeting was short and not very enlightening, and as Kavanagh watched Detective Fuller drive away he felt somehow cheated. It had not been a good day. Still, every cloud had a silver lining and he had done his homework during the lunch break in his room. Unable to get hold of Lizzie, and waiting for his sandwich, he had flicked through the equivalent of the Tampa Yellow Pages under 'Bars' and come across the name of one that might just fit the bill.

Driving Julia there now, he pulled up alongside a long, low building with green awnings. Stepping from his car, Kavanagh looked up at an enormous illuminated flamingo

312

on the wall and grinned at Julia. ' "I don't read too well but there was a damn big pink bird outside," ' he quoted Dupree, and tossed his car keys up into the air to catch them with his other hand. At last. They were getting somewhere at last.

Two hours later, back in Julia's office, jackets off, Kavanagh and his young colleague hit the telephones. They had a lot of calls to make, a lot of people to speak to, and they needed a break. Kavanagh, his shirtsleeves held together by his favourite gold cuff links, the ones Lizzie had bought him for his fiftieth birthday, was getting very cross with someone on the other end of the line.

'We've requested details of the original 911 call several times now. What you're saying is that you've lost it?' He looked across at Julia and raised his eyes to the heavens. This was all they needed. Then, into the phone, he added: 'Yeah. Yes. I would appreciate that.'

Julia took a statement from a bundle and wandered round the other side of the desk. Her face lit up as Phil walked in, wearing a dark grey suit and tie, briefcase in hand. 'Oh, I thought you'd gone,' she said, beaming at him.

'Well, the flight's not till four. Just thought I'd pop in and see how my baby was doing.' He reached over and patted Julia's bulging stomach fondly.

She held her hand over his and then led him to her desk where she sat down. 'Well, we've found Marlon Jarrett, aka the Weasel,' she said.

Phil was delighted. 'Great,' he said. Maybe this Jarrett guy could help with the gunpowder on Dupree's skin.

But Julia didn't look so happy, and Kavanagh, off the telephone now, explained why. 'Killed by another inmate in Louisiana State Penitentiary last July.'

Phil leaned over Julia's desk and sighed. 'Not so great,' he said, with a shrug. Realising there was little more to add, he said: 'Well, if you need me you can reach me at the Miami office, okay?'

Julia reached up and pulled Phil's head down to her face, giving him a kiss on the mouth. 'All right. 'Bye, darling,' she said. Kavanagh, dialling another number, waved from across the desk.

''Bye,' said Phil, as he picked up his briefcase.

'Take care,' Julia told him, and he started to leave the room.

Kavanagh put on his most businesslike tone and spoke into the receiver. 'Paul Cantrell, please,' he said, and waited to be connected to the dreaded secretary.

Phil turned at the door and listened. 'Are you still after Cantrell?' he asked Kavanagh. 'Well, Governor Cotton's got a campaign rally at Braddock University tonight. Cantrell's part of his team, so he ought to be there.' He smiled at Julia and blew her a kiss. ''Bye.' Julia blew a kiss back and then spun round to face her co-worker with a grin.

To prepare themselves for what they suspected would be a confrontational meeting, the pair of them had supper at a great crawfish joint Julia knew down near the wharf, and then headed for Braddock University sports hall to catch the tail-end of Governor Cotton's rally. Neither of them felt they could stomach the whole event, and when they pushed through the double doors with the distinctive 'Kappa Pi Gamma' insignia etched on the glass, heard the thumping brass band and saw the giant posters of Governor Cotton bedecked with stars-and-stripes banners, they were glad they'd missed it.

Governor Cotton, in a white dinner jacket and bow tie, was in his element on the stage among all the red, white and blue balloons – kissing pretty girls, slapping campaign workers on the back, throwing streamers up into the air. The clearing-up had already begun after a rallying evening for the party faithful, but many of the most devoted followers had stayed on, hoping to shake hands with the closest thing they had to their very own President.

Paul Cantrell, in a black dinner jacket and tie with a frilly white shirt, stood uncomfortably in the centre of the sports hall floor as Kavanagh and Julia grilled him about his defence of William Dupree.

'You offered very little in the way of mitigation,' Kavanagh pointed out to the big man who towered over him in both height and bulk.

'His Honour Judge Limburger's not partial to special pleading,' Cantrell argued, one hand in his trouser pocket, the other waving dismissively in the air. 'Little I could have said would have influenced his decision, and I resent the implication.' His expression was one of boredom with the subject, and he watched Governor Cotton on the stage out of the corner of his eye.

Julia, dressed in a roomy black trouser suit, decided to try again. 'Well, you never mentioned the fact that he suffered at the hands of an abusive and alcoholic father,' she said.

Cantrell squinted as Governor Cotton stepped down from the stage and approached the trio. 'So have many people, ma'am,' Cantrell countered with a half-hearted smile. 'It doesn't make them all turn out to be cold-hearted killers.'

Governor Cotton, unsurpassed at identifying a possible new voter in his midst, stepped forward and broke into his well-practised routine. 'Well now, well now, well now. Who've we all got here?' he asked, peering at Kavanagh and Julia through his large square-framed spectacles, a huge red carnation in his buttonhole.

315

'Governor,' Cantrell acknowledged, shifting from foot to foot and pulling up his sagging trousers at the waist.

The state Governor chuckled and held out his hand. 'Any friend of Paul Cantrell is a friend of mine. Governor Stamford Cotton at your service.' Kavanagh reluctantly withdrew his hand from his trouser pocket and shook the proffered one. Julia did likewise. The Governor hardly paused for breath and turned to a cropped-haired young man at his side. 'This is my grandson Skip.' Skip, his face still scarred from the acne that had plagued him in his youth, nodded his head. His eyes darting from side to side nervously, he was clearly embarrassed by his grandfather and looked as if he would have been much happier drinking beer with his frat-house friends, but he attempted a smile.

The Governor turned to introduce another man in a white dinner jacket, a suspicious-looking moustachioed heavyweight who looked as if he could open beer bottles with his teeth. 'Mr Chadway, who does a lot of fine work for the party.' Chadway nodded a hello while the Governor prattled on. 'You folks having yourselves a good time tonight?'

Before Kavanagh could think of an answer, Cantrell interrupted. 'Oh, er, Mr Kavanagh and Mrs Piper-Robinson are working out at the Resource Centre on the Dupree appeal. You know, the Anderson murderer,' he explained. Kavanagh thought he detected a warning note in his voice.

But if there was one, the Governor never showed it; the smile never left his face. 'Is that a fact?' he said, in his Southern drawl, his eyes locked on to Kavanagh's. Looking up suddenly at the vast space around him, he asked his visitors: 'What do you think of my little hall?' Before they could answer, he boasted: 'The Stamford P. Cotton Sports

Arena. Eight million dollars and some change.' Cantrell, Skip and Chadway all nodded ingratiatingly at his side.

Kavanagh's eyes narrowed at the silver-haired, silver-tongued Governor. 'Unusual choice of a venue for a political rally,' he said. Julia shot him a look.

Governor Cotton moved his face close to Kavanagh's and, his mouth still fixed in a smile, he wagged a forefinger at him. ' "Train a child the way he should go and when he is old he'll not depart from it," ' he quoted from Proverbs 22. 'You see, myself and Skip here, we're both Braddock men, you understand?' His eyes wide, his hands held open in front of him, he beamed at Kavanagh and Julia with pride. 'Not but one male Cotton in the last hundred years has not graduated from these hallowed halls, *magna cum laude*.' Reaching forward and grabbing each of their forearms with great force, he squeezed hard and added: 'Awful nice meeting you folks. Hope you have a fine time in this country of ours. Goodnight, all.' He shook Kavanagh's hand warmly again and patted Cantrell on the shoulder. 'See you in the car, Paul,' he said, before walking off, still smiling, his two stooges at his side.

Cantrell waved an arm. 'Yeah, with you in a minute.'

Kavanagh watched them go and then started in again. 'Mr Cantrell, we'll need to talk further,' he said. What did he have to do to make this man understand his duty? he wondered.

But Cantrell, who was following the Governor's progress through the hall, spun round to face the barrister, his eyes blazing, his face shiny with sweat. 'Look, I know what you're trying to do here,' he said through gritted teeth. 'You're looking to go to IAC with this thing, I know that.' Moving closer, he spat: 'You think you can just come waltzing on over here and show us old colonials how it's done. Well, you go ahead. You put me on the stand. Take your shot.' Prodding a large, fat finger in Kavanagh's chest, he concluded: 'You come after me and I promise you, you're gonna be the sorriest limey son of a bitch that ever drew breath.' He laid his sweaty palm heavily on Kavanagh's shoulder and walked away, leaving the two British visitors shaking their heads.

The struggle went on. Back in Julia's office, the endless round of telephone calls continued, the statements were processed, and so progressed the gradual chipping away at the evidence against Dupree. It was hot, laborious work. They lived on oversized plastic beakers of cool, cloudy lemonade and great long sandwiches the locals called 'subs'. Phil phoned when he got to Miami and gave what encouragement he could, and Kavanagh tried without success to reach Lizzie. She wasn't even at work and nobody seemed to know where she was. He just couldn't understand it.

Julia had reserves of energy that astounded him. Despite her condition and the heat, she continued to flit around the office, taking statements from secretaries and tirelessly offering cheer to all those who felt snowed under by their work. There were several other cases in the pipeline. Dupree may have been the one she was giving most attention to right now, but after him there was a long queue of others on Death Row seeking her help. Kavanagh watched her work with a mixture of amazement and admiration.

It was during one of her regular morale-boosting trips around the office that she was approached by an elderly black man, clean-shaven, with a pale blue cotton suit and a large straw hat. Taking his hat off and holding it in his hands out of respect, the white-haired man stood before her and coughed. 'Good afternoon, ma'am,' he said.

'Good afternoon,' Julia responded, and looked up into

318

the friendly open face of the stranger with the kind smile.

'I believe you're looking for anyone from the El Flamenco Bar and Grill as knew Willie Dupree?' Julia's eyes opened wide. She and Kavanagh had, indeed, found the right bar two days ago, but could find nobody amongst the all-black clientele who could remember being there on the day of the murder. Ever hopeful, they had left his photograph with the barman and persuaded him to ask around for them. The friendly, grateful responses they had received from all they met there had been in stark contrast to their reception at the previous bar.

Julia now led the man who introduced himself as Sam Cook over to where Kavanagh was sitting, and invited him to take a seat. Accepting both the seat and a glass of iced tea, Mr Cook confirmed that he was happy to make a statement on Dupree's behalf. Julia started to take notes.

'So you saw Dupree at the El Flamenco on the afternoon of the twentieth?' she asked, her pen poised hopefully above a notepad.

Cook nodded. 'That's right, ma'am,' he said respectfully.

Kavanagh, sitting to her right beneath a huge stained-glass window, clasped his hands together in front of him and asked the witness: 'Why didn't you come forward at the time of the trial?'

Cook smiled. 'I didn't know he was in trouble.' He shrugged.

Kavanagh frowned. 'Are you sure it was him?'

'Yes, sir,' Cook confirmed. 'Willie was a regular at the bar. We had talked often.' He seemed entirely believable.

It was Julia's turn to frown. 'Are you sure it was the twentieth?' she asked, her expression one of disbelief. In all the time she had been doing this kind of work, she had never had such a witness fall into her lap and she couldn't quite credit it.

Cook grinned. 'Yes, ma'am. We had a bet on the game. Dolphins and Bills. A hundred bucks.' He looked knowingly at Kavanagh. 'And Willie arrived just as the first quarter got under way.'

If it was true, it was wonderful news. A cast-iron alibi for Willie Dupree. As Kavanagh sat listening to Mr Cook, he wondered if perhaps he had misjudged Dupree. Maybe he really was an innocent victim in all this, caught up in something much bigger.

As he and Julia made their way through the dark underground carpark to her car that evening, they mulled over the possibilities of what Cook had told them. He had to be checked out, of course, but sauntering along, side by side, briefcases in hand, they were genuinely excited by the prospect of him being for real.

'I'd say you were in good order,' Kavanagh was saying, after Julia had explained how she had spent the rest of the afternoon getting the statements prepared. 'Any joy with Cook?'

Julia grinned. 'Yes. I checked his story with a football almanac and the Dolphins met the Bills on the twentieth. He's also come through with a "clean sheet" from Radley County PD.' She knew it was good news. The Police Department had assured her that Sam Cook had no previous convictions as far as they knew, and the almanac confirmed the timing of his story.

Kavanagh agreed. 'Oh, good,' he said, taking her car keys from her hand so that he could drive her home.

Still chatting, and stepping between her car and the one parked next to it, Kavanagh suddenly came face to face with a sweaty, heavy-set white youth who leapt up from a crouching position, his baseball cap on back to front, a gun in his hand. 'Give me your money!' the mugger shouted, grabbing the lapel of Kavanagh's suit with his left hand. Pushing Kavanagh backwards and seeing him falter, he clenched his teeth and shouted: 'Do it, man. I'll kill you. I swear I'll kill you,' as he jabbed the gun in Kavanagh's chest.

Julia stood stock still, frozen to the spot, and watched helplessly as the mugger waved the gun at her. 'You too. Give me your money unless you want me to hurt him.'

'No, no . . .' she whimpered as Kavanagh reached into his breast pocket and pulled out his wallet, the much-loved soft black leather one Lizzie had given him ten years earlier. The mugger snatched it eagerly as Julia fumbled around in her huge handbag for her purse. Kavanagh, his eyes locked on to those of the desperate young man who was threatening to kill him, felt his life flashing before him. He'd read so many stories of British tourists shot dead in Florida, and now he'd walked himself and the heavily pregnant Julia straight into a dangerous situation without even being streetwise enough to expect it. What an idiot.

Suddenly, to his left, he heard Julia say something he thought he must have misheard. 'See you and raise you,' she said, coolly. Turning to look at her at the same time as the gunman, he was as astonished as the mugger to see her standing, Starsky and Hutch-style despite her condition, legs apart, arms raised and held out in front of her, hands clasped around a gleaming silver handgun pointed straight at his attacker.

'Shit!' the mugger said, and Kavanagh's thoughts echoed his words. The barrister stood trembling, open-mouthed, and watched in amazement as Julia smiled at the gunman.

'Look, if you don't give that back to my friend I'm afraid I'm going to have to shoot you,' she said, as composed as if she were ordering lunch.

The mugger's eyes were like saucers as he pleaded: 'Don't shoot.' Beads of sweat trickled down his unshaven face and he stared alternately at the barrel of Julia's weapon and then at her deadpan expression. He still had his gun pointed at Kavanagh, but it was clear from his demeanour that all his intent had gone.

'So, drop your gun . . .' Julia told him. The pistol duly dropped from his hands and fell to the concrete floor with a clatter.

'Give my friend back his wallet . . .' The wallet was quickly handed back as if it were hot to the touch.

'And get lost. There's a good chap,' Julia concluded.

Hands held quiveringly in the air, the young mugger ducked round between them and sped off up the carpark ramp, as fast as his little legs could carry him.

Kavanagh, his wallet still held in his outstretched hand, watched him go, and then spun back to face Julia. ' "There's a good chap?" ' he repeated breathlessly, as Julia stood before him, her hand still extended, the gun now shaking visibly in it. 'Since when have you carried a gun in your handbag?' He grabbed her wrist and tried to prise the weapon from her trembling fingers.

Julia stammered. 'S-since I got held up in my car,' she said, her face ashen, as she helped Kavanagh unlock her own grip.

'Would you have used it?' the barrister asked, still in shock and clasping both her hands in his. She looked like she'd just seen a ghost.

Julia's breath came in short gasps. 'Well, that would have been tricky. It's not loaded,' she said, and started to laugh. But suddenly, she bent double and cried out in pain. 'Aaargh!' she groaned, and her fingernails dug deep into his flesh.

Kavanagh moved forward and held her. 'Julia? What's

the matter?' he asked, helping her to lean back on the bonnet of the car.

Julia, still shaking and panting now, looked down on the ground. 'Oh my God. James. My waters have broken,' she said, her eyes filling with tears. She knew this was far too premature. Looking up at her friend, she pleaded: 'Get me to the hospital now. Now.'

Kavanagh, still recovering from one shock, now faced another. Helping her round to the passenger door, he eased her inside and ran round to his side. Hospital, hospital, where the hell was the hospital?

Phil Robinson flew in from Miami as soon as he possibly could, and sped to the Radley County Hospital in a taxi from the airport. Breathless and afraid, he burst through the double doors to the intensive care unit, and ran to a waiting nurse. 'Hi, I'm the father. Where is she?' he asked, as the young nurse pointed to a special side room.

'She's through there,' the nurse said, her expression grim.

Phil slid open a clear glass door and stepped into a small glass-panelled room reverberating to the sounds of electronic bleeps and monitors. Julia, in a gingham dressing gown, her eyes red from crying, her hair plastered to her head, got to her feet and fell into her husband's arms, sobbing uncontrollably. 'Oh God, oh my God,' she kept saying as Phil enfolded her in his arms and tried to comfort her.

Kavanagh, waiting on the other side of the glass screen, watched sadly as the two of them hugged tearfully before wandering over to a small glass incubator, in which their gravely ill baby daughter lay motionless and hooked up to a dozen wires and drips, her tiny eyes squeezed shut against the world.

*   *   *

Back in his hotel room later, lying on his bed, his shoes kicked off, Kavanagh dialled Lizzie's number and finally got through. She'd been busy, she said rather abruptly in answer to his questions, nothing more, and he interrupted her to tell her the sad news about Julia's baby.

'The doctor had a few words with me before Phil arrived,' he explained. 'It's not brilliant. She could . . . well, the baby, you know . . .' He couldn't bring himself even to say it.

Lizzie, lying propped up on pillows on her bed at home three thousand miles away, her eyes red-rimmed, twisted the telephone cord round and round her finger. 'Poor Julia. How's he taking it?' she asked, wondering whether Phil was offering any support.

'Bearing up,' Kavanagh replied. 'He's a good man. I like him.'

Lizzie sighed and studied the ceiling of her bedroom while she blinked back her tears. 'I suppose you'll be staying on?' she asked, afraid of the answer.

Kavanagh, also playing with the telephone cord, shrugged. 'Well, Julia's not going to be in any state to handle the appeal.' He didn't want to stay any longer than he had to, but he couldn't abandon Julia now.

Lizzie, dressed in baggy black sweatshirt and trousers, released the telephone cord and started instead to twist her chestnut hair round and round her finger. 'No, no, of course not,' she said.

Kavanagh thought he heard something in her voice but couldn't place it. Pressing his mouth close to the receiver, he said: 'Come out.'

Lizzie sighed and almost laughed. 'You don't want me under your feet.'

Kavanagh was disappointed. 'I do . . . I miss you,' he said. Pausing to try to assess her reaction, he asked: 'You don't want to come?' He was hurt now; he thought she'd jump at the chance of a holiday in Florida – all that sun, sea and shopping.

Lizzie faltered, her head deep in her pillow. 'I . . . I can't. I . . . I just can't down tools,' she said, twisting her hair into such a tight rope that it began pulling on her scalp.

'Why not?'

She heard her husband's pleading voice down the phone and wanted to cry. Testily, she snapped: 'I can't.' She closed her eyes against the thought and remained silent, afraid of what she might say.

Kavanagh, frowning now, began: 'I just thought . . .' Stopping himself, he asked, 'Are you all right?' There was something in her voice. What was it?

Lizzie sighed heavily. 'Yes,' she said. There was a long pause. 'I . . . I'm resting. I, um . . . I didn't sleep very well, that's all.'

Kavanagh smiled, relieved. Poor old Lizzie; she never slept well when he was away, he knew that. 'Best let you get your head down, then,' he said, pleased that nothing serious was wrong.

There was silence. Then Lizzie said softly: 'It's good to hear your voice.'

Kavanagh paused. 'You too,' he said. 'I'll ring you later . . . 'Bye.'

''Bye,' Lizzie whispered, and listened as her husband replaced the receiver at his end. Putting down the phone, she looked at it longingly and caressed it. If only he were coming home, she thought. If only.

The following morning, Kavanagh drove to the hospital and walked into Julia's room, carrying an enormous bunch of flowers. Julia, still a physical and emotional mess, pulled herself up in bed and took them from him.

325

'They're lovely. Thank you,' she said, before bursting into tears yet again.

Kavanagh leaned over and patted her shoulder. 'Hey . . . Hey. Come on,' he said. He was never any good with this beside-manner stuff. Julia, who could only make strange little noises through her open mouth, pulled him towards her and fell sobbing into his arms. He smiled and kept patting her shoulder.

'I'm sorry – I'm so sorry,' Julia wept. 'I've tried to contact my mum and dad and I can't get hold of them . . . and the baby, James, she's so tiny.'

Kavanagh took her by the arm and shook her gently. 'You've got to trust the doctors,' he said. 'They know what they're doing. She's going to be fine.' Reaching for a box of tissues on Julia's bedside table, he handed it to her and she pulled one out.

'The case, what about the case?' Julia looked up at him guiltily, the tears coursing down her cheeks. She was obviously in no fit state even to think about it.

'Look, forget the case,' Kavanagh told her firmly, resting his hands on the bed. 'I'll take care of that. I may be a bit ring-rusty but as a fully paid up member of the Florida Bar, I'm still entitled to appear.'

Julia sniffed and managed a smile. 'Oh, I'm sorry, James,' she said, smoothing down his tear-stained lapel.

'Just relax. It's all going to be okay,' Kavanagh told her, as she buried her face once more in his shoulder.

The baby was still in intensive care and Kavanagh wandered upstairs to see her, his cream linen jacket folded over his arm. Phil was there, leaning across the incubator, his head resting on his arms, staring straight down at the tiny matchstick creature that was his daughter.

'You slept?' Kavanagh asked, coming up behind him.

Phil, in a casual T-shirt and trousers, shook his head and hurriedly wiped away his tears. 'Not really, no.'

The two men looked down at the wide-eyed infant staring back up at them with incomprehension and sighed. Kavanagh patted Phil's arm. 'Come on, let me get you a coffee.' The sleep-deprived lawyer nodded and followed like a puppy, dabbing his eyes as he walked.

Sauntering along a corridor from the canteen a few minutes later, each with a plastic beaker of coffee in his hand, Phil sighed and shook his head. 'Of all the damn days to be outa town, huh?'

'You weren't to know,' Kavanagh protested.

Taking a seat in a waiting area, Phil rambled with the incoherence of an exhausted man. 'Things you think about . . . I've been reading a lot of books, you know. Baby books. Trying to prepare. I thought I'd be more prepared.'

Kavanagh tried to offer reason. 'Well, you can't prepare for something like this,' he said, sitting opposite his new friend.

Phil hung his head and stared down into his cup. 'I just feel so goddamn useless,' he said, his eyes misting over again.

Kavanagh sipped from his cup and told him: 'You're doing all anyone can do.'

Phil shook his head. 'Yeah, but it's not enough.' Pausing, he looked up at his companion and asked suddenly: 'Are you a churchgoer?'

Kavanagh paused before answering, thinking of the times Lizzie had asked him to go to church with her on the odd occasion that she felt the need. 'No,' he said, rather guiltily.

'No, me neither,' said Phil, looking as if he wished he were. Like Julia, he had seen religion make sense of things to some of the inmates on Death Row as they tried to come to terms with what lay ahead. Facing death now, or the awful possibility of it for his child, Phil wondered at the power of faith and whether or not he should try it. He'd been up to the hospital chapel on the top floor, he'd even peered around the door and seen people on their knees praying, but had stopped himself from going any further. In the face of such a desperate situation, though, he somehow felt the need, and thought he might go back later that afternoon.

Kavanagh read his thoughts and wondered how he would cope in such a situation. He had never been very good with illness; Lizzie used to banish him from the house when she or the kids were poorly. And when his father, Alf, had suffered a stroke a year back, he had stood around the hospital bed like a spare part, not knowing what to do or say. His brother and sister-in-law had packed him back off to London and told him they'd call when things were better. They did, and Alf recovered, thank God, but none of it was down to James Kavanagh, Q.C. Still, he thought, dragging his mind back to the present, right now he had other things on his mind.

20

'Your Honour, we believe that there is an immediate case for resentencing on the grounds of Ineffective Assistance of Counsel, insofar as Mr Cantrell failed to bring to the jury's attention details of Mr Dupree's family background.'

Kavanagh was standing at a rostrum in the middle of the large airy courtroom, the light from the huge floor-to-ceiling windows shining down on him through thin wooden blinds. The county judge, Henry J. Moffat, sat imperiously above him on a raised oak dais between two huge pennants – one the stars and stripes, the other the predominantly red-and-white flag of the state of Florida.

The wooden pews that lined the courtroom behind him were packed – the Dupree case had always attracted a great deal of interest and the media were there in force. Other interested parties were also in attendance; friends and relatives of the murdered Anderson family, associates of Dr Anderson and people from the American Bar Association, fascinated by the appearance of a British barrister in one of their courts.

District Attorney James Buford, appearing for the prosecution as he had done during Dupree's trial, sat to Kavanagh's left, as impossibly handsome as he had looked in those first newspaper photographs Julia had sent to London. He was ably supported by two junior counsel who had no doubt researched every minute aspect of the case, and they were surrounded by case notes and files.

William Dupree, his lips shut tight against his gold teeth, sat alone and heavily manacled in his bright orange prison uniform on the bench behind Kavanagh. There were no friends or family supporters in the court for him – and no junior counsel to help Kavanagh. He had been forced to muddle through the final days' preparations on his own.

Judge Moffat, a short, square-faced man with pale blue eyes and thin grey hair pasted across his scalp, looked at Kavanagh with something approaching a sneer. 'Court's familiar with the appeal brief, Mr Kavanagh,' he said in response to Kavanagh's opening line, his mouth snapping shut like a turtle. 'Given that time is money, I'd appreciate it if you'd, er, cut to the chase.' Kavanagh allowed himself a small smile – it seemed that courts around the world were all up against the same financial constraints.

Pulling himself up to his full height in his dark blue suit, and wearing the grey-and-white spotted tie that Lizzie favoured, Kavanagh continued: 'We also have Brady material which undermines the greater portion of the state's case, and strong evidence of prosecution misconduct with regard to the sneakers.' He used American legal jargon and tried to make it all sound so much more substantial than it really was.

Judge Moffat nodded. 'Uh-huh,' he said, his arms folded across his voluminous black gown. 'Okay. Who's first to bat?' Kavanagh frowned slightly, unaccustomed to the casual way in which American judges ran their courts, but he tried to overcome his distaste.

'I had hoped to call Deputy Attorney-General Cantrell,'

he said, 'but I am informed he will not be available until after lunch.' He did not disguise his pique.

Judge Moffat stared Kavanagh out. 'I'm sure Mr Cantrell's a very busy man,' he said, with a knowing look.

Kavanagh was beginning to wish he'd never come to Florida in the first place. Eyeing the judge with mistrust, he said: 'Call Eugene Styles,' speaking into the microphone on his rostrum.

Styles was a young man in his late thirties, with thin, black hair, receding well into his scalp, and dark, bushy eyebrows. In a grey suit and red tie, he took the stand and sat looking askance at Kavanagh with suspicious, shifting eyes.

'Mr Styles, you said at trial that you saw William Dupree come out of the front of the house,' the counsel reminded the witness.

'Yes, sir,' Styles answered flatly.

'When you say the front of the house, do you mean the front door?'

'Yes, sir,' came the reply.

Kavanagh picked up a photograph from the rostrum and walked across to where the witness sat, half slouched in his seat. 'I would like to ask you to look at this photograph, if you will,' he said, handing Styles the black-and-white picture Kavanagh had first seen back in London, of little Leanne Anderson's blood-spattered doll lying up against the door, next to a pile of unopened mail on the doormat. 'That is the inside of the Andersons' front door,' Kavanagh explained to the witness.

'Okay,' said Styles, handing the photo back to the counsel, and still not getting the point.

Kavanagh, standing a few feet from the witness now, said: 'If I was to tell you that when the emergency services arrived they found Leanne Anderson lying jammed up against the front door on the floor of the hallway, and that forensic evidence confirms she hadn't moved from where she fell when she was shot, would you still maintain that Dupree came out of the front door?' Styles shifted in his seat, suddenly uncomfortable, and stared at Kavanagh.

The counsel continued: 'You see what I'm getting at? How did he open the front door?' Styles sat stock still, staring at Kavanagh and trying to think of an answer. 'How did William Dupree get out of the front door if there was an injured child lying up against it?' Kavanagh repeated. The courtroom was silent, waiting for an answer. A thin-faced elderly black woman sitting directly behind District Attorney Buford looked over at Styles with a frown and blinked.

Styles hardly opened his mouth when he spoke. 'I saw what I saw,' he said, his eyes half closed. 'He come out of the front door.' He looked at Kavanagh with a scowl.

Kavanagh screwed his face up in an expression of open incredulity. 'A door against which an injured child was lying?' he asked again. With no answer forthcoming from Styles, he added: 'No further questions,' and returned to his rostrum, happy that an important point had been won.

The next witness, Detective Frances Valkenburgh, was a woman of confidence, who took the stand and the oath with ease and sat looking around the courtroom, a slight smile on her face. Short-haired, dark and with finely plucked eyebrows that formed perfect arches over her large brown eyes, she was petite of frame but not of sarcasm, as Kavanagh was soon to find out.

'Detective Valkenburgh, what made you so sure that William Dupree was your man?' he asked from his rostrum.

The detective flicked a non-existent speck of dust from

332

the shoulder of her pale blue designer trouser suit and looked across at Kavanagh as if she had only just noticed the strange little gentleman from London, England. She chuckled, her face sparkling with glee at such a question.

'Well, apart from his fingerprints being all over the crime scene?' she said, her singsong Georgia accent stronger than any Kavanagh had heard. 'I guess it was just on account of he is a low-life criminal, Your Honour,' she added, addressing the judge, but staring at Kavanagh with considerable amusement.

Kavanagh persisted. 'That he was black didn't influence your opinion?'

Valkenburgh's face broke into an attractive grin. 'I don't like criminals, Your Honour, I don't care what their colour is,' she said, studying Kavanagh through twinkling eyes.

Kavanagh tried to bring her back into line. Putting on his spectacles to read from his notes, he said: 'You're currently being investigated by the Radley County PD Internal Affairs Department. Is that right?'

'That is correct, Your Honour,' came the answer. Still the smile, not even a flinch. This woman was a real pro, thought Kavanagh.

Taking off his spectacles, he leaned on the rostrum and asked: 'What is the nature of the allegations against you?' He smiled now.

Frances Valkenburgh snorted through her nose and stared Kavanagh out. 'They're allegations of racism, Your Honour.'

'Who made these charges?' he asked, increasing the pace.

'My former partner, Detective Eddie Fuller,' Valkenburgh said, without batting a perfectly made-up eyelid.

Kavanagh struggled on in the face of such armour. 'Detective Fuller accompanied you when you went to arrest Mr Dupree?' he asked.

She nodded. 'That is correct, Your Honour.'

'Did Detective Fuller assist you in the search outside Mr Dupree's apartment?'

Valkenburgh threw her head back and laughed. 'If I remember right, Detective Fuller had himself a siesta in the back of the car until Dupree showed up,' she said.

Kavanagh left the rostrum and walked over to Valkenburgh, standing a few feet in front of her when he asked his next question. 'When Mr Dupree returned home, did Detective Fuller search Mr Dupree's apartment?' He leaned his arm on the witness box and frowned at Valkenburgh.

She looked slightly less amused. 'He did, Your Honour,' she said, turning to face the judge as she spoke this time.

'Did Detective Fuller find anything of importance when he searched the apartment?' Kavanagh asked her, his jaw set.

'No, Your Honour.' The officer again turned to the judge, but then turned back to Kavanagh with a half-smile to goad him on.

'You then searched the apartment while Detective Fuller remained with Mr Dupree?' The questions came slightly faster.

'I did.'

'And you found what?'

Valkenburgh looked at the judge and smiled. 'Pair of bloodstained sneakers in Dupree's hall closet,' she said, a note of triumph in her voice.

Kavanagh, still leaning on the witness box, looked puzzled. 'How was it that you found the sneakers when Detective Fuller had not?' he asked.

Valkenburgh sighed, looked down as if she were thinking, and then looked up at the judge. 'Well,' she said, in her Southern twang. 'Seems to me there is two choices, Your Honour. Either Eddie's just not a very good searcher, or

334

else he put those sneakers in the closet for me to find.'
Judge Moffat eyed her with a smile.

Kavanagh rubbed his chin. 'Another possibility,' he said, as if thinking aloud, 'is that you found the sneakers amongst Mr Dupree's trash and put them is the closet yourself.'

Valkenburgh was obviously enjoying this. Swaying her head from side to side as she spoke, she almost laughed as she said: 'And Detective Fuller's so dumb he didn't notice me carrying a pair of sneakers around the place, yeah? That's right . . . that's what I must have done.' Stealing a sideways glance at the judge, who was toying with his gavel and shaking his head slowly from side to side, she added: 'Pretty damn smart of me to pick out a pair soaked in Dr Anderson's blood, though, wasn't it?' Her sparkling eyes shot back to Kavanagh.

The barrister lifted his arm off the witness stand and stood back a little to make his next accusation. 'You have heard of cross-contamination of evidence, Detective Valkenburgh?' He tried to look more convincing and less angry that the examination-in-chief was not under his complete control.

Detective Valkenburgh shifted in her seat and squared up to him. 'You sure I just didn't take out my little old phial of Dr Anderson's blood, which I'd been carrying around should just such an opportunity arise, and sprinkle it on the sneakers?' She glared at him angrily.

The judge interjected. 'All right, Officer,' he told her.

Valkenburgh faltered. 'I'm sorry, Your Honour, but I mean . . . Jesus.' Her face hardened for the first time and she glowered at Kavanagh. 'None of you people went in the Andersons' house and saw them folks and kids. I went after the man that committed the crime and I went after him right.'

*　　*　　*

335

Kavanagh knew when he was beaten and he let the witness go. His next witness was Valkenburgh's former partner and he hoped for better success with him.

'Detective Fuller, had Detective Valkenburgh used racial epithets in your hearing?' he asked, standing back at the rostrum.

Eddie Fuller, dressed in a black suit and tie, his shoulder-length grey-brown hair still moulded in the shape of the baseball cap he had been wearing all morning, nodded. 'Er, yes, sir. With Frankie it was always "n ..." this and "n ..." that.'

Kavanagh was surprised that political correctness in America should have developed so far as to prevent a police officer from saying the word 'nigger' in a court of law, while the rednecks in the bar across town used it freely. He nodded in understanding and asked: 'She didn't like black people?'

'No, sir.'

'How did she feel about William Dupree?'

Fuller looked across at Dupree with sympathy. 'She didn't like him. She said she was gonna get that N-word real good.' Dupree sat expressionless and quiet.

'Were you with Detective Valkenburgh when the sneakers were found?' Kavanagh asked, his Mont Blanc fountain pen tapping his hand.

'No, sir.'

'Had you searched that closet yourself?'

'Yes, sir.'

'Thoroughly?'

'Yes, sir.' Fuller gave his answer even greater emphasis.

'But you didn't find any sneakers in there?'

'No, sir.'

Kavanagh raised his voice so that the entire court-room could hear. 'Yet they were in there when Detective Valkenburgh searched the closet?'

Fuller looked as perplexed as anyone by the conundrum. 'They were,' he said, shaking his head. Kavanagh, several points clawed back, sat down with a smile to let DA Buford cross-examine his witness.

Buford was out of his seat like a greyhound from a trap. Pencil in hand, a serious expression on his finely chiselled features, he marched right up to Detective Fuller and asked: 'Are you married, Detective Fuller?'

Kavanagh wondered what on earth this had to do win anything and was about to say so when Fuller answered uneasily. 'Er, yes, sir.'

Buford nodded, already knowing the answer. 'You live with your wife?'

From the look on Fuller's face, Kavanagh knew what the answer would be and started to feel suddenly uneasy about the line of questioning. 'No, sir,' Fuller answered, blushing and studying his fingernails.

Up at the witness box now, both hands resting on it and leaning in towards the detective, Buford went for the jugular. 'No,' he repeated. 'Where does she live, Detective Fuller?' There was a pause as Fuller, his face crimson, said nothing. 'Does she live with Detective Valkenburgh? The officer against whom you made allegations of racism?' Buford asked, a sneer on his face.

Fuller hung his head, closed his eyes and gave a muffled answer. 'Yes, sir.'

Buford nodded again. 'When did she move in with Detective Valkenburgh?'

Fuller swallowed. 'About six months ago.'

'And when did you make these allegations?'

Fuller avoided eye contact with his inquisitor. 'Couple of months back,' he answered, as Kavanagh held his head in his hands.

Buford finished Fuller off completely. 'What is the nature of their relationship?' he asked, his question ringing out around the courtroom. Fuller swallowed even harder and blinked several times. He didn't answer. 'Detective Fuller?' Buford prompted, moving round behind him.

'Friends, I guess,' was all Fuller could muster.

Coming round to the other side of him, so that those in the court had an uninterrupted view of his face, Buford smiled slightly and said: 'It's more than that, Detective . . . isn't it?'

Fuller glared at Buford and finally snapped. Forgetting what he had come to the court to do, he barked at the counsel: 'How the hell do I know what the sick bitches get up to?'

Buford's eyes opened, as if in surprise, and there were gasps from around the room. 'Sick bitches?' he repeated. 'Now who's prejudiced, Detective Fuller?' Almost skipping back to his seat, the counsel added lightly: 'No further questions.' Kavanagh sat, his jaw clenched, and watched as his case fell apart.

Sam Cook, the old man who said he saw Dupree in the El Flamenco Bar and Grill on the day of the murder, was the next witness. Kavanagh led him through his testimony and hoped to God Buford had no more tricks up his sleeve as he rose to start his cross-examination.

Buford stood at the rostrum to ask his questions. 'Mr Cook, you told counsel that you knew it was the afternoon of the twentieth you saw William Dupree at the El Flamenco because you watched a Dolphins/Bills game.'

Cook, heavy-lidded but respectable-looking, nodded. 'That's correct, sir.'

Buford came round in front of the rostrum, his pencil in hand. 'Not the first time they met that season, though,

338

was it? I mean, they'd also played each other a few months earlier, hadn't they?' He spoke like one fan to another.

Cook nodded. 'Yeah, yeah, I guess so.'

Leaning on the front of the rostrum, Buford suddenly changed tack. 'Mr Cook, would it be fair to say that you have an alcohol abuse problem?' Kavanagh felt as if he had been poked by an electric cattle prod.

'No, sir.' Cook stared Buford out. 'Drink hasn't passed my lips in two years, three months and eight days.'

'You are a recovering alcoholic?' Buford suggested.

Cook nodded. 'Yeah, I guess you could call it that.'

'Did you have an alcohol abuse problem in the fall of 1993?'

'Yeah, yeah,' Cook chuckled, and looked down at the straw hat he was turning in his hands, 'I believe I did.'

'Do you remember being arrested for drunken behaviour by law enforcement officers of the Radley County PD on the evening of the twelfth of September 1993?' Buford was up and running now and Kavanagh could see what was coming.

Cook shook his head emphatically. 'No, sir,' he said.

'Or that you were sentenced to ten days in the county jail subsequent to that arrest?' Kavanagh wanted the ground to open up and swallow him whole.

Cook looked embarrassed and studied his hat. 'Yeah, I did spend some time in jail around that time. That's correct, sir,' he admitted.

Buford put both him and Kavanagh out of their misery. 'So, if you were in the county jail from the fourteenth to the twenty-sixth of September,' he said, doing a slow circuit of the rostrum so that he could study Kavanagh's face as he spoke, 'you couldn't have seen Dupree at the El Flamenco on the afternoon of the twentieth – could you?'

339

Mr Cook smiled and looked apologetically at Dupree. 'Well, er, maybe not that day, no, sir, no.'

Buford turned and addressed the judge. 'Your Honour. I do not believe Mr Cook has come here today to wilfully mislead the court. He has a long history of alcohol abuse. And what is at fault here today is his memory. I would commend him for the steps he is taking to regain control of his own life.' It was a slick move. Cook nodded a smile at Buford, who returned it before resuming his seat.

Judge Moffat was not in such a magnanimous mood. 'I agree that a charge of perjury would be inappropriate in the circumstances,' he growled. Glaring at Kavanagh, he added: 'However, counsel should take note that it might be wise to test the reliability of a witness before wasting the court's valuable time.' It was more than a warning shot across the bows and Kavanagh knew it.

In the dank cells beneath the courtroom an hour later, Kavanagh sat dejectedly at a table in his shirtsleeves and braces and looked across at his client with a mixture of exasperation and anger. His briefcase was open on the table and he sat in the only pool of daylight, which poured through the small window high up in the thick brick wall.

William Dupree stood in the shadows against the wall on the other side of the cell, a cell that was twice the size of the one he had lived in at the Hope Correctional Facility for the past four years, and listened to his counsel's words.

'You should have told me about Cook,' Kavanagh said impatiently, aware now that he had been the victim of a set-up by Dupree and wishing once again that he had been allowed more time, and more help, to prepare his case.

Dupree's rumbling chocolate voice whispered from the shadows. 'I didn't remember him. If he remembers seeing me, well, that's just fine. How the hell am I supposed to know the damn nigger's a drunk?'

Kavanagh told his client: 'We ran a check on him – he came back clean.'

Dupree, still manacled hand and foot, emerged from the shadows and into the pool of light with a murderous expression on his face. 'You screwed up, man,' he said, a thick rope of veins in his neck throbbing. 'You didn't do your job! So why are you sitting there blaming me?'

Kavanagh was no longer intimidated by the big black man he had flown all this way to help. He was tired and frustrated and fed up with having to do all of this on his own. Waving a finger at Dupree, he said: 'Listen, right now I'm the only friend you've got.'

Dupree's face twisted into a contemptuous leer and he bent over the table where Kavanagh was sitting, his eyes on fire. 'So what do you want me to do? Bow down and kiss your white ass? Thank ya, Jesus?' Moving inches from Kavanagh and locking on to his eyes, he added, with venom: 'You ain't here for me, man. You're here for you, so don't go trying to tell me different.'

Kavanagh looked away and down at the table, so Dupree bent closer and forced him to look up into his eyes. 'You here for when you go back home,' he told him. 'All your rich, white liberal friends can pat you on the back and say: "That Kavanagh, he's so fine for trying to help those poor dumb niggers."'

Kavanagh met Dupree's accusing stare and wondered if he were right. Maybe he did only come here to impress the Foxcotts and the Aldermartens of this world. He certainly took on more no-fee cases than anyone else at River Court, but he had always led himself to believe it was because of his sense of wanting to give something back to society. This trip had certainly been no picnic and there were plenty of things he could have been getting on with at home which could have made more valuable use of his time, but was he really in it for himself or the poor man he was trying to save? With a heavy sigh, he told Dupree: 'You want to instruct fresh counsel, Mr Dupree, you just say the word.' The thought of catching the next flight home to Lizzie and putting all this behind him suddenly held tremendous appeal.

Dupree was close to tears. Turning his back to Kavanagh, he gripped the bars of the cell and looked up at an imaginary sky. 'Listen, man, I don't need you!' he shouted, a desperate catch in his voice. Then, much quieter, he added: 'They ain't gonna fry me. No way, no how.'

Kavanagh shook his head and wished he shared his client's optimism. 'Just tell me, before we go back in, have you got anything else like Cook up your sleeve?' He looked exhausted.

Dupree remained where he was, looking upwards. 'The only thing I got up my sleeve, man, is aces,' he said. Breaking down suddenly, the tears streaming down his face, his wide nostrils flaring, he sobbed and quoted the Florida state motto: 'In God we trust, Mr Kavanagh ... in God we trust.'

Kavanagh was not looking forward to the afternoon's session. After such a disastrous morning, he wouldn't have thought much else could go wrong, but something about the swagger of Paul Cantrell as he sauntered up to the witness stand with a broad grin on his fat face placed a chill across his heart.

As the court usher approached him with the Bible to take the oath, the Deputy Attorney-General smiled and took the book from her hands. 'Oh, it's okay, Sonya, I've been here before,' he said, before reciting the oath from memory: 'I swear that the evidence I give shall be the truth, the whole truth and nothing but the truth so help me God. Paul Cantrell, Deputy Attorney-General, for the record,' he concluded, patting Sonya on the buttocks and winking at the young woman shorthand writer, whom he obviously also knew.

Judge Moffat looked positively grateful for his arrival. 'The court thanks you for taking time out of your busy schedule to join us here today, Mr Cantrell,' he said, beaming at his distinguished guest.

Cantrell undid the button of his tightly fitting double-breasted dark suit, and sat down in the witness box, leaning towards the microphone. 'Pleasure's all mine, Your Honour.' Kavanagh almost thought he might wink at the judge, so sickening was this act.

The judge glared at Kavanagh in a way that was intended as a warning and said stiffly: 'Proceed.'

Kavanagh, spectacles on, pen in hand, standing at the rostrum, drew breath. 'Mr Cantrell, you defended William Dupree at his original trial.'

'I did,' responded Cantrell, sitting well back in his seat and staring at the British barrister with utter contempt. It was clear he was not enjoying this.

'Prior to Mr Dupree's case, how many murder trials had you appeared in?' Kavanagh asked, his Lancashire accent distinctively different to those listening in the court.

Cantrell smiled slightly and raised his head as he spoke. 'Er, Mr Dupree's case was my first,' he said, settling his head back down on to his thick double chin.

'Did you feel you were well equipped to handle such an important case?' Kavanagh asked, peering at Cantrell over his spectacles.

Cantrell's responses were well rehearsed. 'I defended him

343

to the best of my ability,' he said, his mouth snapping shut after each line.

'In the matter of mitigation at sentence, do you feel you adequately represented his best interests?'

'I do,' Cantrell answered, without even flinching. Dupree stared daggers at the man in the witness box.

'What mitigation did you offer on his behalf?' Kavanagh asked with a frown.

'None.' Again the double chin wobbled as it settled back on the grubby collar of Cantrell's white cotton shirt.

'None,' Kavanagh repeated, removing his spectacles with a flourish and allowing the word to register with the court. 'Given that Mr Dupree had suffered an abusive and deprived childhood, you didn't feel it was appropriate for a psychiatrist to examine him to ascertain his mental health?' There was a clear note of hostility in his voice.

Cantrell, still slouching in his seat, folded and unfolded his hands. 'Er, I saw no reason to go wasting the court's time with a whole heap of mind-bending psychobabble,' he said. 'You pay a shrink enough money, he's gonna swear black's white.' Judge Moffat's mouth tried unsuccessfully to resist a smile.

'But if you had presented evidence of the defendant's mental retardation to the jury, it could have affected his sentence,' Kavanagh pointed out angrily.

Cantrell tilted his head to one side and frowned. 'It might,' he conceded.

'So why didn't you do your job?' Kavanagh asked, shouting now.

Cantrell smiled at the barrister, a smile that said there was something he didn't know, something that was going to save the Deputy Attorney-General from further questioning. An eyebrow raised, he asked Kavanagh: 'You wanna know why I didn't offer mitigation?'

Kavanagh swallowed hard and found himself unable to answer.

Cantrell continued anyway. 'I didn't offer mitigation because William Dupree told me he shot the Andersons,' he said, his trump card produced, as gasps and murmurs ricocheted around the court.

Kavanagh was speechless. His teeth clenched, he looked at the smirking Cantrell with undisguised loathing and knew he had been well and truly outmanoeuvred.

Judge Moffat broke the silence. 'If you're of a mind to take fresh instruction, counsel, you just say so,' he told Kavanagh with a meaningful smile.

21

The heavy metal door to the prison cell slammed shut behind Kavanagh as he stood looking down at Dupree lying on his bunk. He was back in the inappropriately named Hope prison where he was fast running out of hope.

'The Supreme Court has turned us down,' he told Dupree flatly, as he stood facing him with his hands in his pockets. There was no briefcase this time. No reason to bring one – there was little more that could be done.

'How's that?' the Death Row prisoner in the orange uniform asked, still unsure of the way in which the appeals system worked.

'Cantrell saying you confessed didn't help,' Kavanagh pointed out.

Dupree shook his head. 'I . . . I told you, I never confessed. Cantrell just threw that in to make hisself look good.' He waved his hand at Kavanagh dismissively.

'All I know is, I walked into that court with a pretty good case and in less than three hours the prosecution demolished it.' Kavanagh looked as dejected as he felt.

'So all we got left is the pardon, parole and the Governor, huh?' Dupree looked up hopefully from his bunk.

'We're awaiting a date from Pardons and Parole,' Kavanagh told him.

Dupree's face broke into a grin that flashed his large gold teeth. 'I'll get clemency,' he said, as if it were a fact, not a wild, impossible dream. Kavanagh shrugged. Dupree asked: 'How's Mrs Piper-Robinson's baby doing?'

'Improving,' Kavanagh answered, pleased that he had some good news at last.

'That's good.' Dupree smiled. Resting his hands behind his head, he stared up at the ceiling with a faraway look. 'I like kids. I'm planning on having me a big family when I get out of this place.' Kavanagh nodded at his client and smiled, but his hands remained firmly in his pockets.

In less than two days Kavanagh found himself once again appealing on his client's behalf, this time in the opulent surroundings of the first-floor Pardons Board hearing room at the County Courthouse. The four men and one woman on the board sat stony-faced behind a long mahogany table as they listened to Kavanagh's plea. Behind them, heavy red velvet drapes blocked out almost all the light in the oak-panelled room and Kavanagh stood on a deep-pile green carpet behind a low desk, rather than at a rostrum as before. Dupree was not present – the rules did not allow it – and Kavanagh was alone on his side, while Buford and his team took up the other side.

'You heard earlier from Dr Gartenbaum who gave evidence as to William Dupree's mental retardation,' Kavanagh reminded the board in the first part of his summing-up speech. His fists resting on the desk in front of him, he continued: 'It was his professional opinion that William Dupree has the emotional maturity of a thirteen-year-old boy. Before you begin your deliberation, I would ask you to try to imagine a thirteen-year-old boy sitting in the death house. A boy deserted by his mother, abused by his father. A boy the system should have protected but singularly – shamefully – failed.'

District Attorney James Buford addressed the court with his customary pencil in his hand. Standing behind his desk, as Kavanagh had done, he spoke softly and quietly, his lilting Southern accent in sharp contrast to that of the British barrister. 'The truth of the matter,' he said, 'is that far from being railroaded, Mr Dupree's had every opportunity to present evidence of his innocence in the four years since his original trial. He's had appeals at state and federal levels. The courts never expressed any doubt that Dupree killed the Andersons or that he was fully cognisant of his actions at the time.'

On his feet for the last time to address the panel, Kavanagh maintained eye contact with each of the board members in turn as he told them: 'When murder has been committed, we do not end the tragedy by putting another human being to death – we compound it, and help perpetuate the endless cycle of violence.' Leaning forward over his desk to emphasise his final words, he added: 'You have a chance today to break that cycle. William Dupree has never asked a soul for anything. Experience taught him it would not be given. But he is asking you now – for his life.'

Kavanagh was saddened to see that little Leanne Anderson had been brought into the hearing room, in her wheelchair, for Buford's closing speech. Her head slumped to one side, her eyes lifeless, she presented an emotive image to the board as they were about to make their life-or-death decision. He saw several panel members watching her and the old black lady sitting at her side, as Buford started to speak. His speech, Kavanagh thought, encapsulated the difference between the British and American people on the issue of capital punishment. Its coldness chilled him, its lack of compassion frightened him.

'The death penalty,' Buford told the board, 'is a message sent to a certain number of our society who choose not to follow the rules. It's only for one crime – the crime of capital murder. It is for those who choose to violate the sacredness and sanctity of human life. These were terrible, brutal murders – and the time has come for justice to be done.' The old woman sitting with Leanne, a large gold crucifix hanging round her neck, nodded her head in silent agreement.

Kavanagh used the call-box in the grand marble lobby of the courthouse to phone Julia and Phil at the hospital once the board had retired to make their decision. They'd already been out an hour when he called, and he told Julia that the longer they were out, the better their chances. Julia apologised again for not being there, but said the baby had a new infection on her chest and she didn't want to leave her. Kavanagh understood and wished her all the best, before replacing the receiver with a sigh.

Putting his change in his pocket and turning to head back to the hearing room, he almost tripped over Leanne Anderson in her wheelchair, which her grandmother had pushed right up against him, blocking his path.

'How can you do what you're doing in there?' the old woman asked, her eyelids swollen from four years of crying. In a smart blue jacket, black dress and white straw hat, she looked like a nice, respectable woman, Kavanagh thought. 'This is my granddaughter, Leanne,' she said tearfully, pointing a white-gloved hand at the blind eight-year-old child slumped in her wheelchair. 'She's this way 'cos she was shot in the head by the man who killed her mamma, her daddy and her little brother – the man you're working to free.'

Kavanagh held his hands down in front of him and nodded his head in respect. 'Mrs Johnson, I am truly sorry for your loss, believe me,' he said. He knew her name off by heart – he'd read all the case notes a dozen times; pored over the medical reports on Leanne's brain damage in the hope that she might recover and identify her attacker as someone other than William Dupree; he knew that Mrs Johnson was not in the best of health, that she had been left to look after Leanne alone, and that her claim for criminal injuries compensation to pay for Leanne's future care had been stalled by Dupree's appeal.

'Then how can you do what you're doing in there?' Mrs Johnson asked, her voice breaking. 'You look at Leanne and tell me.'

Kavanagh looked down at the severely handicapped child and watched the saliva dribbling from her open mouth, saw her hands twitching with involuntary movements. What had happened to her was tragic and avoidable, he knew that.

Sighing, he asked her: 'What if Dupree didn't do it?'

Mrs Johnson wouldn't even countenance the idea. 'He's been tried. Tried and found guilty,' she almost spat.

'So have many men new evidence has proved innocent,' Kavanagh pointed out, but seeing the tears welling in the old woman's eyes he stopped himself from going on.

'I lost my baby girl,' she said, her face a picture of abject misery. 'My husband died of the shock of it, of a broken heart. My grandson Tyrone . . .' She sobbed and held her hand to her mouth. 'Leanne is all I've got left. Who's gonna take care of her when I'm gone, huh? You tell me.' She clicked off the handbrake on her granddaughter's wheelchair and turned quickly away, wheeling the child off down the corridor, still sobbing. Kavanagh clenched his fists and stood, motionless, wishing he'd never received Julia's last letter.

It came as no great surprise to Kavanagh that the Pardons and Parole Board denied William Dupree his appeal. The chairman of the board told those who had reassembled in the hearing room two hours later that clemency would be denied. 'Execution will be carried out, as scheduled, thirty-six hours hence, at six a.m.,' the chairman concluded, and both Kavanagh and Mrs Johnson, sitting a few feet behind him, closed their eyes and nodded in acceptance of the verdict.

Kavanagh drove slowly to the Radley County Hospital to break the news to Julia. She took it well; she had grown much stronger emotionally in the last few terrible days and she had always known that Dupree was unlikely to win. Looking down at her child, she listened and nodded and offered what comfort she could.

'They've placed him on Death Watch. He asked me to be his spiritual adviser,' Kavanagh told her, sadly. Him, with his poor knowledge of the Bible and even less interest.

'What did you say?' Julia asked, twisting a lock of tousled hair round and round her finger while half watching her child.

'I agreed. What else could I do? It's the only way I can get unrestricted access to him.' Kavanagh shrugged his shoulders and realised how little he relished the next thirty-six hours.

The door to the intensive care unit slid open and Phil walked in. He'd run off to answer his pager a few minutes before. 'Anything?' Julia asked.

'Just Jackie. Paperwork on the 911 came through. Guy called Zandalee. Neighbour.' Phil looked at Kavanagh's face and sincerely hoped it would help.

Kavanagh nodded. 'Better late than never.'

'So, what you gonna do?' Phil asked, slipping his arm around Julia's shoulder.

'Keep trying,' Kavanagh said. 'Keep trying.'

After a long, hot soak and a shave in his hotel bedroom, Kavanagh slipped on his red paisley dressing gown and started to sift through the mountain of paperwork, photographs and notes from the original Dupree trial. There had to be something here, something that could help him now, at the eleventh hour. He wiped his face with a towel, switched on the taped transcript, and recognised the dulcet tones of James Buford leading the witness Eugene Styles through his evidence.

'*Mr Styles, how did you know it was the Anderson's house?*' Kavanagh could imagine Buford, pencil in hand, at the witness box.

'*I didn't at the time. It was only when I read about it in the paper that I realised that was the same house I'd seen him come out of.*'

'*You couldn't be mistaken?*'

'*No, sir. I saw the number of the house as I went by. Number nineteen.*'

Kavanagh frowned suddenly and held the towel to his face as he pondered something. Rushing over to a table piled high with papers and documents, he reached into the middle of the pile and pulled out a black-and-white photograph of the Andersons' front door, the checked plastic tape with the words 'Police Line: Do Not Cross' taped all over it. The numbers 1 and 6 could be seen clearly, the 6 slightly down and to the right of the 1. Kavanagh carried on listening to the tape while his thought processes worked overtime.

'*All right. You saw him come out of the Andersons'. Did you see anything else?*' Buford coaxed Styles.

'I saw him run off down the road.'
'Which direction?'

Kavanagh clicked the machine off and reached for his trousers.

He pulled up outside 19 Fairvale Avenue thirty minutes later and walked up to the front door. Just as he was about to ring the doorbell, he stopped and studied the numbers in front of him, a 1 and a 9 side by side. Placing his finger on the 9, he unfastened it from the small, loose screw holding it in place at the top and watched as it dropped from its place, swinging upside down on its final screw, making the number 6 down and to the right of the 1, exactly as he had seen in the police photograph taken on the day of the murder. Closing his eyes in sudden realisation, he turned on the veranda and looked across the street to the neighbouring buildings.

Almost running to the large detached house opposite, his jacket draped over his left arm, he climbed the rickety veranda steps and looked up at the number 16. Next to it was a huge hand-painted sign pinned to the railing. 'No trespassing. This property is not for sale,' the sign read. He guessed that was one way of getting rid of pushy estate agents.

Before he could ring the bell, a sour-faced middle-aged man in a red baseball cap appeared on the other side of the screen door and asked what he wanted. A half-empty bottle of beer in his hand, he stood in a sweat-stained vest and peered at Kavanagh through the holes in the screen.

'Were you living here when the Andersons were shot?' Kavanagh asked, as the flies buzzed all around him.

The old man shook his head. 'No, sir. That would have been Aguilla. Ramon Aguilla. Colombian fella, lived here before us.' He took a swig from his beer.

'Would you have an address for him?' Kavanagh asked, hopefully.

The old man held the bottle to his lips and chuckled. 'He's dead,' he said, with a smile. 'Got hisself shot by the Drugs Enforcement Administration down along the keys. Running drugs.' He sneered at Kavanagh to show his distaste for the late Mr Aguilla.

'I see.' Kavanagh nodded. He paused before adding, almost as an afterthought: 'I'm also trying to trace a Mr Zandalee, a neighbour of the Andersons.'

The old man smiled. 'Old Thad? Thad moved out couple of years back.'

Thad Zandalee had, it seemed, fallen on hard times since he had been a resident of the up-and-coming Fairvale Avenue, so sought after by estate agents. Shortly after the Anderson murder, his wife left him, taking the kids with her, and he resorted to drink. He lost his job soon after and now worked the boats, living in little more than an old tin shack down by the wharf.

Kavanagh found him late that evening, sitting in his shack in semi-darkness, on a heap of old fishing nets, nursing a bottle of Jack Daniels. The evening sunlight shone through the cracks in the shack wall on to his unshaven face and lit up his drinker's nose. It took a few minutes before he could get him to open up, but when he did Zandalee seemed to have good long-term recall.

'Yep, I made the 911 call that day,' he confirmed.

Kavanagh, standing before him in the open doorway, asked: 'Did you see anyone come out of the house, Mr Zandalee?'

The part-time fisherman stood up, revealing a filthy grey vest under an unbuttoned red checked shirt. He was wearing an oil-stained baseball cap and his eyes were red-rimmed from years of drinking. 'No, sir,' he said. 'I took it he must've got in his car and gone – while I was on the phone.' He poured some whisky into a chipped tin mug and tried to forget the terrible sounds of gunfire and screams he had heard from the Andersons' house that day.

Kavanagh frowned. 'What made you think he had a car?' Dupree had always maintained that he had arrived at the house by bus.

'I saw it,' Zandalee said, looking up from his mug. 'It was parked right across the street from Dr Anderson's house. When I come back from the phone it weren't there no more.' He held out a half-full mug for Kavanagh, but the counsel waved his hand in a gesture of refusal.

'Did you get the licence plate?' Kavanagh asked, pulling a small notepad out of his pocket and clicking on his pen.

'No, sir,' Zandalee answered. 'I did describe the car to the officers that came by, but I never heard nothing more about it.' He sipped from the mug he'd offered his visitor, his own still in his hand.

'What was it like?' Kavanagh asked, taking notes.

'Red sportster. Fresh out of the showroom.' Zandalee seemed quite clear about that. 'Had one of them little sticker things in the back window.'

Kavanagh's eyebrows furrowed. 'What sort of a sticker?'

Zandalee shrugged his shoulders. 'Radio station, like as not. "K" something.' He looked at the ceiling and squinted as he searched his frazzled memory banks. 'Ended with a "T" maybe. Funny little letters. Russian or something. Well, foreign anyhow.' He'd seen enough foreign trawlers coming into port to know that some country's letters just weren't the same as the rest.

Kavanagh's eyes darted from right to left as he tried to remember where he, too, had seen what Mr Zandalee seemed to be describing. As it came to him in a flash, he hastily scribbled something on his notepad and held it out for the old man to see. 'Anything like that?' he said, showing him the Greek letters denoting the Kappa Pi Gamma fraternity house of Braddock University.

Zandalee's eyes opened wider than they had been in years. 'Yeah,' he said, nodding. 'I'd say that's about right.'

From the insalubrious surroundings of Thad Zandalee's rusting tin shack, Kavanagh found himself an hour later sitting in the comfortable main office at the Father's House of Braddock University, staring at a huge embroidered sampler on the wall. 'Faith Honour Love Fraternity,' the words encircling the distinctive insignia read.

George Bellamy, House Father, took a seat under the embroidery which had pride of place in his office and invited Kavanagh to sit down opposite him, but the barrister remained standing while he listened.

'I hadn't been House Father at Kappa Pi Gamma very long when it happened,' said the balding, middle-aged man with a bushy grey moustache. 'I remember Dupree, of course. He was only with us a couple of months.'

'What was he like as a worker?' Kavanagh asked, standing by the window.

'Unreliable. I don't think he was on time once.' Mr Bellamy leaned back in his big leather chair and rubbed his chin as he spoke.

'How did he get on with the students?' Kavanagh's questions were clipped.

'He had little to do with them,' Bellamy answered, thinking privately how little this British lawyer knew about the inbred prejudices of the WASPs who attended his house.

'Did he drive?'

Bellamy frowned as he tried to remember. 'No. No, I don't believe he had a car,' came the response. He loosened his tweed jacket and leaned forward, folding his hands together on his desk and wondering what all this was about.

Kavanagh saved his most important question for last. 'Any of your students here at that time drive a red sportster?' he asked, holding his breath as he awaited the answer.

Eugene Styles ticked off some items on his clipboard and watched the forklift truck drivers manoeuvring in and out of the huge retail warehouse, shifting boxes. Stepping round from the back of one of the forklifts into the middle of an aisle, James Kavanagh, Q.C., in an open-necked blue shirt and grey trousers, called out his name. 'Mr Styles?' he asked, above the noise of machinery.

Styles put his hands up in the air in a backing-off gesture and told Kavanagh: 'I have nothing to say to you.' He walked quickly away from the man who had given him such a hard time in the witness box and went towards the small makeshift office where he worked as deputy warehouse manager.

Kavanagh followed. 'How did you know the Andersons lived at number nineteen, Mr Styles?' he asked. There was that same accusatory tone to his voice.

Styles turned and frowned. 'You shouldn't be here. I'm asking you to leave now before I have to call security.' He walked into his office and made as if to reach for the telephone. Kavanagh made no move to go and simply repeated his question. Styles sighed and said: 'I saw the number on the house when I went by.' He thought the answer obvious.

There was a strange expression on Kavanagh's face. Styles looked at it and suddenly realised it was anger.

'Never mind he came out of the front or the back or what the time was,' Kavanagh spat. 'You weren't even there, were you?' Styles pretended to be studying some paperwork, so Kavanagh spelled it out for him. 'The number nine had slipped. The number read sixteen, not nineteen that day.'

Styles spun round and faced him. 'You're out of your mind.'

'Who put you up to it, Mr Styles?' Kavanagh asked, his eyes narrowing to slits.

Styles faltered, glanced over his shoulder and then looked around him, as if he were afraid that someone might be listening. Slumping back down on the edge of his desk, he looked into the far distance and spoke softly. 'You're getting yourself into something you don't wanna get into,' he said. Looking up at Kavanagh, he added: 'You want your family to see their daddy again? The best thing you can do is to go home.' His big blue eyes were wide open and he stared at his visitor with fear.

'Is that a threat?' Kavanagh asked.

Styles was indignant. 'No, man. I'm trying to look out for you. Just leave things be.' He paused and looked around him again. 'Now go on, or I'll have to call security on you.' He looked like a frightened man, not a man making threats, Kavanagh concluded, as he turned and walked away.

The familiar clank of the prison doors and buzzers as electric locking systems opened and closed greeted Kavanagh at the Hope Correctional Facility. He'd come straight from seeing Styles to tell Dupree what he had discovered, and he couldn't wait to give him the news. Signing in at the front desk, his eye suddenly caught the signature of the previous visitor to William Dupree. Kavanagh's hand stopped in midair in shock.

Pulling up a chair in Dupree's cell with a loud bang, he

sat down and faced the man he had so obviously misjudged. 'What did Cantrell want?' Dupree's eyes flickered a frown, as if he were going to deny it, so Kavanagh interjected: 'I saw his name in the register. "P. Cantrell visiting Dupree." What did he want?'

Dupree, sitting, as ever, on the edge of his bunk, studied his hands. 'He came to say he was sorry things hadn't worked out.' He knew, as he said the words, how unbelievable they sounded to someone as astute as Kavanagh.

Kavanagh decided it was time to inform him of what he knew. 'He came to make sure you were going to go through with the deal,' he suggested. Dupree snorted through his nose and hung his head. Kavanagh continued: 'What did they promise you if you kept your mouth shut? Last minute the phone would ring? Cotton would commute your sentence to life?' He spoke the words in an incredulous tone.

Dupree looked up, angry. 'You don't know shit,' he said, leaning his elbow on the edge of his washbasin and rubbing his hand across his closely shaved head.

'I know why you weren't worried about the gloves when you went to the Andersons'. You thought you were committing a crime that would never be reported. You went there to rip off a dealer you'd heard about at number sixteen. Ramon Aguilla?' As he said the name out loud, Dupree, his head still in his hand, bit his bottom lip. Kavanagh went on: 'But you got the wrong house – you and the man who drove the car.' Dupree stared Kavanagh out as the barrister leaned in towards him. 'Do you think they're going to let you live, knowing what you know?' he asked.

Dupree's deep voice growled at Kavanagh. 'Anything happens to me, man, Cantrell goes public.' He almost smiled, he was so confident of success.

Kavanagh leaned back in his chair and held his hands

between his knees. His bottom lip was taut. 'How do you think a fourth-rate idiot like Cantrell got a post in the Attorney-General's office in the first place?' he asked, spelling it out for the man with a mental age of thirteen. Dupree frowned, his limited intelligence struggling with what he was being told. 'Horse-trading,' Kavanagh continued. 'Think about it . . . Cotton's got an election to win. How would he go down with the voters if he granted you clemency now?'

Dupree's huge barrel chest heaved up and down with emotion as he started to understand what Kavanagh was saying. 'But . . . we had a deal. They promised,' he pleaded, his eyes wide open in fear. Kavanagh now understood why he'd never seen that fear before. All that talk about aces up his sleeve. The poor deluded fool.

He shrugged. 'Well, it's your call,' he said. 'But it's gonna be a bit late to change your mind once they've strapped you in that chair.'

Dupree looked suddenly terrified. 'You really think they're gonna go through with it?' Kavanagh hung his head. Dupree looked up at him with moist eyes. 'I don't want to die, Mr Kavanagh,' he begged.

'Then tell me what happened,' said Kavanagh, leaning forward again, a new urgency in his tone.

Dupree got to his feet and walked to the small reinforced glass window that afforded him the only view of the outside world. His arms folded across his chest in a hugging gesture, his expression pained, he said: 'He was meant to be keeping lookout. I mean – we were both pretty stoned at the time.' His eyes filling with tears, he added: 'If he'd have done his job and kept a lookout like he was supposed to . . .' Looking up at Kavanagh, he added softly: 'It weren't my fault.'

'Go on,' Kavanagh said, not sure that he wanted to hear the rest.

'I . . . I just heard the door. I thought it was Aguilla, the dealer, come home. I heard his footsteps along the hall. I . . . I just fired through the kitchen doorway. I . . . I didn't mean to hit him – just scare him off.'

Kavanagh found it difficult to believe that the man he had flown all this way to save had just confessed to the murder of Dr Anderson. Blinking, he asked: 'And the rest? . . . Mrs Anderson?'

Dupree's voice dropped to little more than a whisper. 'No, sir. I didn't kill her – or the kids,' he said, shaking his head slowly from side to side. 'He took the gun off of me and finished it.' He almost spat the last words, appalled by the memory of what his companion had done.

Kavanagh closed his eyes and hung his head. It was over.

The middle-aged prison officer responsible for the general maintenance of the most controversial chair in Florida's history dipped his cloth into the cleaning fluid and rubbed it on to the thick brass buckles holding the leather straps together. He might have been given all the dead-end shifts and the sex offenders' wing to work after twenty-three years in the prison service, but he took real pride in this aspect of his work. If Governor Cotton was going to be sitting on the other side of that reinforced glass panel in less than an hour's time, he wanted him to see those buckles gleaming and to know that the man standing to attention next to the electric chair had done his job.

A few doors down the hall, in a special room set aside for the prison padre and special visitors, James Kavanagh sat in the small pool of light beaming from an angle-poise lamp and dialled a telephone number. The call was picked up after two rings by an answerphone. 'Thank you for calling the Governor's office. Our hours of business are Monday to Friday . . .' His face ashen, he replaced the receiver and looked into the far distance.

22

The door to William Dupree's cell slid open and he shuffled out in his stockinged feet, the long steel chain dangling between his legs binding the manacles on his ankles to those around his wrists. Flanked by prison guards and Father O'Brien, and wearing the white cotton shirt and jeans he had last worn four years before – the day he arrived at the prison – he peered out over the landing to the cells in the block below as the inmates called up to him.

'Hey! Hey! Dupree, you just hold it down there!' one shouted. 'Don't let 'em grind you down, Willie,' another yelled. 'Keep your head high, man,' called another. He'd heard the calls of encouragement before, as other prisoners left Death Row for the chair, but he never thought the day would come when he'd hear them called out to him. It was the one and only time the inmates of the Hope Correctional Facility were nice to each other, or showed any kindness. The common bond between them was that there but for the grace of God went they. Dupree heard their calls and wanted to weep.

Kavanagh was still trying to dial another number for the Governor when he heard the prison doors slide open to allow someone into the corridor and up towards the death chamber. Looking up, he saw Governor Cotton, his grandson Skip, the man called Chadway and several others all enter the corridor *en route* to their date with Dupree. Slamming down the telephone, he rushed to the gated door between him and the distinguished party and stood stock still, staring Governor Cotton out. 'I know who killed the Andersons,' he said, his face flushed red.

Cotton, in a black suit and silvery tie, nodded. 'So do I, sir,' he said. 'That's why we're here.' He gave Kavanagh a smug smile.

Kavanagh gritted his teeth. 'I know who drove the car and I have the evidence to prove it.' The door between them slid open with a buzzing sound and a clank and Cotton, his jaw set, led Kavanagh and Skip into the side room he had just been dialling from. The others carried on.

Shutting the door behind them and turning to face the counsel, Skip nervously standing at his side, the Governor was flustered. 'What's this all about, Kavanagh?' he asked.

Kavanagh stared at Skip and told the Governor: 'Your grandson drove Willie Dupree to Fairvale Avenue . . . to rip off a drug dealer who lived at number sixteen.'

Skip Cotton shifted from one foot to the other and his acne-scarred face flushed scarlet. 'Bullshit!' the frightened young man called out from behind his grandfather's shoulder.

'I've tracked down a witness who saw your car parked across from the Andersons' house,' Kavanagh informed him.

Skip, a film of sweat on his top lip, looked petrified.

The Governor interjected. 'He never did nothing but drive the sonofabitch over there,' he snapped. As he spoke, the sliding door in the corridor outside opened and Willie Dupree, shuffling awkwardly along between his guards, peered into the room at the three men, a look of such panic on his face that Kavanagh could hardly bear to see it. Father O'Brien walked along beside him, reading from the Bible. 'May goodness and mercy,' he recited, '. . . all the days of our life. I shall dwell in the house of the Lord . . .'

Kavanagh jerked his head back to face Cotton. 'That's not the way Dupree tells it,' he snapped. 'And it's not the way he told it to Paul Cantrell, either.' Seeing the Governor's unflinching stare as the death chamber party shuffled by, he decided to lay all his cards on the table. 'Cantrell came to you,' he said quickly, 'offered to help take care of Dupree in exchange for a post with the AG's office. Chadway, your friend who "does a lot of good work for the party", put Styles up as a witness.' He spoke low and fast, aware that with every word another second ticked by on the clock.

In the observation room to the Hope prison death chamber, Leanne Anderson's grandmother, Mrs Violet Johnson, gripped her handbag and watched silently with several other witnesses as the door opened on the other side of the glass partition wall and Willie Dupree was ushered in in chains.

As he was manhandled into the seat of the gruesome electric chair, the prisoner's white cotton socks were carefully slipped off, and the chain that bound his manacles together fed slowly through its fastenings with a rattle. His trembling hands were strapped down by their wrists to the wide wooden arms of the contraption, and two wide leather belts buckled round his waist and chest as he sat staring at the people on the other side of the glass, his bottom lip quivering.

Trembling uncontrollably from head to toe, he listened to the words of Father O'Brien and tried very hard to concentrate on them. 'Though I may travel through the shadow of the valley of death, I shall not . . .' A soft leather strap suddenly appeared from behind him, manipulated by unseen hands, and was tied tightly across his mouth. He was wimpering now, and as his nostrils fought to inhale his final draughts of air, a large metal helmet was lowered on to his naked skull and buckled tightly under his chin. The last glimpse he had of anyone or anything was of Mrs Johnson sitting watching him through the glass, her face full of horror at the sight before her. A second soft leather strap was placed across his eyes and tied tightly to the back of the headrest holding his head still as he made the mumbling sounds of someone trying to speak.

In the darkness that was now his world, he felt hands moving deftly around his head, administering cold gel to his scalp through special holes in the helmet and clipping each of the moistened electrodes on to the special terminals on the metal skullcap. He could hear Father O'Brien saying his last words of prayer, ending with: 'Spiritus Sancti . . . Amen.' There was silence, a few shuffling footsteps, and then he heard the word 'Clear', which, he knew, was the signal for everyone to leave the death chamber, to leave him to his fate.

Kavanagh glanced up at the clock on the wall and saw that there was less than a minute to go before 6 a.m. A bead of sweat trickled down the back of his neck. Governor Cotton was seated in front of him now, his hand to his head, considering his options. Looking up at the barrister with a smile, he finally spoke. 'So how much do you want?'

Skip, his face bright crimson, stood beside his grandfather, chewing his way through what was left of his fingernails.

Kavanagh stepped forward briskly and leaned over the desk, a menacing expression in his eyes. 'If you don't stop this execution, the signed affidavits I have from Zandalee and Dupree will be turned over to officers of Radley County first thing.' He looked like he meant it.

Cotton, rocking back in his chair, chuckled and leaned forward, so that his face was a few inches from Kavanagh's. 'Oh, let's hang on to this thing a minute, huh?' he said, smiling as if to one of his voters. 'I'm sure we can come to some arrangement.'

Kavanagh hung his head and then snapped it back up again. 'You don't have time to trade,' he shouted, the veins in his neck pulsating. Picking up the telephone and holding it up for Cotton, he barked: 'You ring through right now and grant clemency!' It was an order, not a request.

The Governor, his face downcast, looked up at Kavanagh and then down at the telephone receiver held out to him. Taking it in his left hand, he held it to his ear and placed his right forefinger on the first button of the three-digit number he had to dial.

As he did so, there was a sudden flickering and dimming of the lights throughout the entire prison. The electrical current passing through William Dupree's body at two thousand volts a second momentarily drained all the power from the prison's giant generators. Kavanagh, aghast, looked up at the clock on the wall and watched as the second hand reached six o'clock.

In the observation room opposite the death chamber, Leanne Anderson's grandmother leapt from her seat at exactly the same time as the switch was thrown to end William Dupree's life. As if she could feel the electrical current searing through her own body, she shuddered in time to the rhythmic jerks and twitches of Dupree's sizzling body, as his blood coagulated in his veins and his brain reached temperatures in excess of 120 degrees. Opening her mouth, she let out a heart-rending scream, before collapsing, semiconscious, into the arms of those around her.

A few doors down, James Kavanagh stepped quietly from the room where he had conducted the most important legal appeal of his life, his eyes glazed. Walking purposefully towards the sliding exit gate, he heard a door behind him open and the sound of a woman gasping for breath. Turning slowly, he saw Mrs Johnson being led from the observation room and propped up against a wall by a young woman relative, who was fanning her and trying to calm her down. The old woman's eyes were pressed shut against the terrible image of what she had just seen, and her face was wet with perspiration. The deeply religious woman who had lost almost everyone who was dear to her had now lost something else – her peace of mind. Kavanagh turned again and walked away, his briefcase banging against his leg.

The warm, welcoming kitchen of Julia and Phil's lovely home was a much-needed contrast to the early morning scene at Hope Correctional Facility. Kavanagh had called ahead and told them the news from his hotel, and the next call he'd made was to book his flight home. He was determined to get back to Lizzie on the next available plane.

Standing with them in their kitchen now, drinking coffee and wondering what it had all really meant, Kavanagh looked as if he had the weight of the world on his shoulders.

'You took it to the wire, Jim,' Phil told him. 'No one could have done more for him.' He was sitting up on the large pine, green-painted table, his wife – still in her long white cotton nightdress – sitting at his side. Both of them knew exactly how he felt; they'd been in the same situation a dozen times themselves.

Kavanagh, in casual jacket and trousers, leaned over the table and said softly: 'I didn't do it for him. He was right.'

'Yeah, well, why you did it is immaterial,' Phil reassured him. 'You did it, that's the thing. Don't beat yourself up. Look, the day we stop trying . . .' His words of comfort were interrupted by the sound of a car horn outside.

'Oh, that's a cab,' Julia said, as Kavanagh sighed and pulled himself up.

Phil stepped down from the table and held out his hand. 'Look, thanks,' he said. 'You know, with the baby and everything. I'm gonna really miss having you around. You ever get a hankering for a sunnier climate, well, I could use a good lawyer.'

Kavanagh took Phil's hand in his and shook it weakly. 'Oh no, no, no. That's me done,' he said, with feeling. He never wanted to see Florida again.

The telephone rang just as he and Julia stepped out into the morning sunshine and Phil answered the call with a wave goodbye. As the taxi driver led the way, carrying Kavanagh's bags, he and Julia strolled arm in arm in the sunshine down the steps from the veranda towards the car.

'Are you gonna be all right?' he asked her.

'I'll be fine – once we get the baby home,' she said, smiling, her hand on his shoulder. The latest bulletin from the hospital had certainly been encouraging. Jemima – as she had now been christened – was getting stronger by the day and would probably be allowed home in a fortnight. Julia had called her Jemima because it was the closest female name to James.

'Well,' was all Kavanagh could manage as he gave Julia a fond farewell hug.

371

'You too,' Julia said, returning the hug with relish. There were tears in her eyes.

Kavanagh pulled away first and stepped into the back of the car.

'Where to, sir?' the baseball-cap-wearing taxi driver asked, closing the rear passenger door behind him.

'Home,' Kavanagh said, with a smile.

As the car set off and headed for the airport, Kavanagh sat pensively in the back, watching the passing scenery. The driver, realising that his passenger was not in the mood to talk, switched on the radio, and Kavanagh grimaced as he listened to the news announcement.

'In a surprise statement a spokesperson for Governor Cotton announced that he would not be running for a second term in office. Sources close to the Cotton camp have angrily denied that the Governor's withdrawal from the election is related in any way to the reinvestigation into the Anderson family murder for which William Dupree was recently executed at Hope Correctional Facility.'

He knew, because Phil had told him through an inside police source, that at that very moment Detective Frances Valkenburgh and six uniformed officers would be bursting into Governor Cotton's palatial, state-funded office and arresting him and his grandson on suspicion of murder and interfering with the course of justice. Even that news had failed to lift his spirits. There was only one person who could do that for him, and she was waiting at home.

Putting the key in the lock of his own front door had never given Kavanagh as much satisfaction as it did the following morning. Heaving his suitcases in through the open door with one hand, his other hand laden with bags of duty-free goods for his wife, Kavanagh breathed in the wonderful smell of home-brewed coffee and called out: 'Hello?'

Closing the door behind him, he wandered through to the kitchen and met Lizzie coming up the steps to greet him. She looked a little pale and tired, he thought, but it didn't matter. It was great to see her and he pulled her into his arms and gave her a big hug, inhaling her special scent. It was wonderful to be home.

Later that night, after a delicious home-cooked supper of his favourite pasta and one of the bottles of fine Californian claret, the two of them lay curled up together on the sofa in front of a log fire, Lizzie's head on her husband's lap. Overwhelmed by jet-lag, he was almost nodding off while Lizzie watched the flames flickering in the grate.

'Jim?' Her soft voice penetrated the fog in his head.

'Mmm?' His eyes flickered open and he rubbed her back.

'When are you think of laying up the boat?' she asked.

'Oh, next couple of weeks, I should think.' He patted her shoulder.

'Let's go down this weekend,' she said, smiling to herself at the thought.

'Yeah,' Kavanagh agreed after a moment's reflection. 'Yeah, all right,' he said, gently stroking her hair. He knew that once afloat on *Nicholson's Sloop* and with Lizzie at his side, all would be right with the world.

Two days later, after a gloriously crisp winter's morning sailing, the wind in their hair, the waves slapping on the side of the boat, they had pulled back into the estuary for a break. Kavanagh loved this old boat. He and Lizzie had had some of their happiest times here, and being here now was the perfect tonic after such a miserable few weeks.

Standing side by side in the fading sun, watching the seagulls dipping in and out of the water, they sipped on steaming mugs of Oxo and leaned against each other contentedly.

'It was a good idea,' Kavanagh said, nursing his warming drink, his face flushed with the cold and clear of the stress lines that had pinched his eyes for the first few days he was home.

'Hmm.' Lizzie smiled. 'I'm full of them.' She looked pink in the cheeks, her eyes still smarting from the wind, her hair piled up on the back of her head with a large clip. The fleecy sweater he had bought at the airport had hardly been off her since he gave it to her mid-week.

'I know,' Kavanagh grinned. 'That's why I married you.' He rubbed her arm fondly and reached over to give her a kiss on the lips.

Lizzie, her eyes like dark blue pools of water, moved away and leaned back on the edge of the boat as she tried to find the words she needed. 'Look, Jim, there's something I have to tell you,' she started, exactly as she had done on all the occasions she had practised this before he came home. 'It's not good news, I'm afraid,' she added, rubbing the tips of her fingers up and down the outside of her mug.

Kavanagh's forehead creased into a concerned frown. He'd never seen her look so serious before, especially not here. 'What is it?' he asked, a catch in his voice.

Lizzie faltered and then spoke. 'While you were away, I was sick,' she began. 'I, um, I went to see the doctor and he referred me to a specialist and . . .' Suddenly she broke off and blinked back the tears. Looking away, she turned and looked back up into the eyes of the only man she had ever loved. 'Damn it! There's no easy way to put this.' Her bottom lip was quivering.

When Kavanagh spoke, fear had pushed his voice up an octave. 'Lizzie? Just tell me,' he said. 'Whatever it is, we'll deal with it.' He clutched her arm and willed her to speak, to end this dreadful misery.

Lizzie sighed and blinked even harder. 'I've got pancreatic cancer,' she said, as her husband stood a few inches from her, willing his brain to have misheard her. But to compound his pain, she added quietly: 'It's inoperable.'

'No. No, that's, that's . . .' Kavanagh began, shaking his head vigorously and looking around him in desperation.

Lizzie wiped away her tears and carried on. 'The hospital says six months – nine at the most.' Even though the words were coming from her own mouth, from her own mind, it still seemed so unreal.

Kavanagh's eyes flickered as a wave of rage and indignation overcame him. 'We'll get a second opinion,' he insisted. Lizzie shook her head and tried to interject. 'We'll see Bruce,' Kavanagh said, thinking of his cousin who was a cancer specialist.

Lizzie could no longer stop her tears. 'I've seen him,' she said, with a firm nod of her head, the drops splashing from her eyelashes. 'I've done the rounds . . . That's it.' She made a slicing gesture with her hand to cut her husband off. Peering up into Kavanagh's shocked and pale face, she wondered if she had looked so taken aback when she had first heard the news herself just four short weeks earlier.

Kavanagh bent over and sat down slowly, as if he had been punched hard in the stomach. He had just aged ten years. The implications of what she was saying were too terrible to deal with. 'While I was away?' he spluttered. 'Well, why didn't you tell me?' There was a hurt expression in his eyes. All that time he'd been comforting Julia, counselling Dupree, worried about the baby, his own wife had been at home going through all of this on her own. He could hardly believe it.

Lizzie, still wiping tears, tried to laugh. 'Well, it's not the sort of thing you talk about on the phone.'

Kavanagh looked up at her in astonishment. 'But you didn't have to. You could have just said something was wrong, anything, and told me when . . .' He was rambling and he knew it, but he didn't seem to be able to stop himself.

Lizzie stopped him instead. 'Well, I didn't,' she said, the tears still spilling from her eyes. She wished he'd just shut up and hold her, tell her that everything was going to be all right. But he was still angry.

'I know you bloody didn't! . . . I'd have come back!' Kavanagh suddenly found himself shouting at her, shouting at the woman he loved, the woman who had just told him she was dying, and his unreasonable response only made him feel more angry.

Lizzie, who'd had a few more weeks to think about this than her husband, took control. Setting down her mug, she told him, as firmly as she could: 'Look, Jim, I . . . I don't want to argue. This is not something you can plea. I'm just trying to be practical. We've got to sort out some ground rules.' Folding her arms high across her chest, she carried on speaking through her tears, trying to explain to him what would happen, how the next few months would be. 'They tell me they can control the pain quite well . . . well, until quite late, at least.'

Kavanagh sat shaking his head, his hand to his mouth, his face ashen. 'Oh, don't say it . . . No, I can't bear it!' he begged. His eyes were filling with tears.

Lizzie finally lost her temper. 'Look, damn you!' she shouted, putting down her mug. 'This is happening to me. This is my thing. Do you understand? . . . my thing.' She tapped her chest with her forefinger. Her face wet now, her voice cracking with emotion, she added: 'I'm dying,

Jim . . . I'm dying and I'm bloody terrified but if I can stand it . . .'

Kavanagh leapt to his feet and grabbed her, holding her as tightly as he could without breaking her in two. 'I'm sorry,' he said, his own face wet.

'We just have to be strong for each other,' she sighed, her face buried in his neck, her breath coming in gasps.

'I know, it's just . . . it's the shock. I'm sorry.' He gripped her even harder.

Lizzie smiled and sighed. 'No,' she said, closing her eyes. 'That's the first rule. No more sorrys, no more regrets.' Sniffing between sobs, she added: 'We've wasted so much time missing each other. I want to make the most of what's left. There's so much we haven't done . . . So much I want us to do.' Her whole body trembling, she remained locked in his arms.

James Kavanagh, the tears dripping from his chin on to his wife's shoulder, sobbed openly. 'I don't know what to do,' he said, his heart breaking.

Lizzie knew the answer to that one. Pulling her face away from his shoulder so that her eyes were locked on to his, she said falteringly: 'All you have to do . . . is love me.'

Kavanagh nodded. 'Always,' he said, and hugged her tight again. 'Always.'